D0412330

Sarah Morgan is the bestselling author of *Sleigh Bells in the Snow*. As a child Sarah dreamed of being a writer, and although she took a few interesting detours on the way she is now living that dream. With her writing career she has successfully combined business with pleasure, and she firmly believes that reading romance is one of the most satisfying and fat-free escapist pleasures available. Her stories are unashamedly optimistic, and she is always pleased when she receives letters from readers saying that her books have helped them through hard times.

Sarah lives near London with her husband and two children, who innocently provide an endless supply of authentic dialogue. When she isn't writing or reading Sarah enjoys music, movies, and any activity that takes her outdoors.

Readers can find out more about Sarah and her books from her website: www.sarahmorgan.com. She can also be found on Facebook and Twitter.

Sleepless in Manhattan

SARAH MORGAN

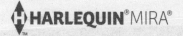
HARLEQUIN® MIRA®

Harlequin MIRA is a registered trademark of Harlequin Enterprises Limited, used under licence.

First Published in Great Britain 2016
By Harlequin Mira, an imprint of HarperCollins*Publishers*
1 London Bridge Street, London, SE1 9GF

Sleepless in Manhattan © 2016 Sarah Morgan

ISBN 978-1-848-45455-2

58-0316

Our policy is to use papers that are natural, renewable and recyclable products and made from wood grown in sustainable forests. The logging and manufacturing processes conform to the legal environmental regulations of the country of origin.

Printed and bound by
CPI Group (UK) Ltd, Croydon, CR0 4YY

Dear Reader,

I can never decide if I'm a country girl or a city girl. If you've read any of my books before, you'll know how much I love mountains (especially snowy ones) and also the beach. I love breathing in fresh outdoor air and being close to nature, and if you follow me on Instagram you will have seen plenty of my beach and mountain photos. But the truth is I also love cities. I love the energy, the buzz and the pace of life.

When my editor (her name is Flo and she is brilliant in every way) suggested I set my next series in a city, I wasn't convinced. 'I don't know if I can write about a city,' I said, to which she replied, 'But you're not writing about a city. You're writing about love, friendship and community, which is what you always write about. And besides, you love New York.'

She's right. I do. I've been lucky enough to visit New York several times, and each time has been more exciting than the last. Because New York features in so many of my favourite movies (*When Harry Met Sally* and *Hitch*, to name just a couple), I always feel as if I'm walking onto a film set. I have to stop myself from gaping with my mouth open and pointing (and in case you're wondering, my favourite New York landmark is the Chrysler building. It's magical, and yes it appears in this book.)

The idea for the characters came easily, and New York worked so well as a setting it felt like another character. It added a touch of urban sparkle to each story, and when my publisher proposed the titles, I was really excited. *Sleepless in Manhattan* is Paige's story and begins at a point in her life where everything is about to fall apart.

I hope you fall in love with these characters and enjoy following their adventures as they negotiate love and life in the Big Apple. If you want help visualizing the setting, take a look at my Pinterest boards! They're packed full of photos I used as inspiration while I was writing this series.

Welcome to From Manhattan with Love!

Love, Sarah
xx

This book is dedicated to Nicola Cornick,
who is a wonderful author
and everything a friend should be.

There is something in the New York air that makes sleep useless.

—Simone de Beauvoir

One

When you're climbing the ladder, always assume someone
is looking up your skirt.

—Paige

"*Promotion*. I think it might be my favorite word. You have
no idea how long I've been waiting for this." Swept along by
the tide of commuters, Paige Walker followed her two friends
Eva and Frankie up the steps from the subway and emerged
to blue skies and sunshine. Far above her the skyscrapers of
Manhattan reached up to fluffy clouds, a forest of steel and
glass winking in the bright morning sunlight, each compet-
ing to be taller than the next. The Empire State Building. The
Rockefeller Center. Higher, bigger, better. *Look at me.*

Paige looked, and smiled. Today was the day. Even the
weather was celebrating.

New York had to be the most exciting city in the world. She
loved the vibrancy, the promise, the pace.

She'd landed a job at Star Events straight out of college and
had been unable to believe her luck, especially when her two

best friends got jobs there, too. Working for a big company headquartered in Manhattan was her dream. The sheer energy of the city seeped through her skin and into her veins, like a shot of adrenaline. Here, she could be whoever she wanted to be. She could live her life without being asked how she was feeling twenty-five times a day. In the breathless bustle that was New York City, people were too busy thinking about themselves to have time to think about other people. Interaction skimmed the surface and never went deep. She blended into the crowd and that suited her just fine.

Paige didn't want to stand out. She didn't want to be different, precious or special. She didn't want to be anyone's poster girl for brave.

She wanted to be anonymous. Normal, whatever that was. And here in New York, finally it had happened.

Urban chaos offered its own type of privacy. Everything moved faster.

Everything, that was, except her friend Eva, who was not a morning person.

"*Promotion* isn't my favorite word. *Love* is probably my favorite word." Eva yawned sleepily. "Or maybe *sex*, which is the next best thing. I think. I can't honestly remember because I haven't had it in so long. I'm worried I've forgotten all the moves. If I ever get naked with a guy again, I might have to buy a 'how to' book. Why is no one in Manhattan interested in a relationship? I don't want a hookup. I want to mate for life. Ducks can do it—why can't we?" She stopped to adjust her shoe and soft waves of blond hair bounced forward along with her breasts, as generously curved as the plumpest cupcake. The man walking toward her stopped abruptly, mouth open, and four other men slammed into him.

Attempting to avert a human pileup, Paige grabbed Eva's arm and pulled her to one side. "You're a walking hazard."

"Is it my fault my laces untie themselves?"

"Your laces aren't the problem. The problem is that you just announced to the whole of Manhattan that you haven't had sex in ages."

"The problem," Frankie said, closing in to form a blockade, "is that a dozen investment bankers are now getting in line to manage your assets. And I'm not talking about your finances. Stand up, Sleeping Beauty. I'll tie your shoe."

"I don't have any finances to manage, but at least that means I don't lie awake at night worrying about yield and interest rates. That's a bonus, although not quite the bonus those bankers are probably used to." Eva stood up and rubbed her eyes. Before ten in the morning, she had trouble focusing. "You don't have to tie my shoe. I am not six years old."

"You weren't this lethal when you were six years old. It's safer if I do it. I don't have cleavage that should come with a health warning or a brain incapable of filtering what comes out of my mouth. And move to the side. This is New York City. It's virtually a criminal offense to block the flow of commuters." There was a hint of irritation in Frankie's voice, enough to make Eva frown as she stuck her foot out.

"You can't be prosecuted for being in someone's way. What's wrong with you this morning?"

"Nothing."

Paige exchanged glances with Eva. They both knew "nothing" meant "something," and both knew better than to push for answers. Frankie spoke when she was ready, which was usually only after she'd bottled it up for a while. "Blocking the flow of commuters could be deemed provocation." Paige said. "And she was this lethal. You've forgotten her eighth birthday party when Freddie Major threatened to beat up Paul Matthews if she didn't agree to marry him."

"Freddie Major." The memory drew a ghost of a smile from Frankie. "I put a frog down his shirt."

Eva shuddered. "You were an evil child."

"What can I say? I'm not good with men. Of any age." Frankie thrust her can of drink into Eva's hand. "Hold that, and if you throw it in the trash our friendship is over."

"Our friendship has survived more than twenty years. I like to think it would survive me throwing your junk food in the trash."

"It wouldn't." Athletic and supple, Frankie dropped into a crouch. "Everyone is allowed a vice. Unhealthy eating is mine."

"Diet cola is not breakfast! Your eating habits are life threatening. Why won't you let me make you a delicious kale and spinach smoothie?" Eva pleaded.

"Because I like to keep my breakfast down once I've eaten it, and my eating habits are no more life threatening than your dress habits. Anyway, I wasn't in a breakfast mood today." Frankie tied the laces of Eva's bright green Converse as a river of commuters flowed past them, all intent on reaching their destination as fast as possible. She winced as someone knocked into her. "Why don't you ever do a double knot, Ev?"

"Because I dressed in my sleep."

Frankie stood up and plucked her diet cola from Eva's hand, her hair tumbling in fiery flames past her shoulders. "Ouch! Excuse *me*." She adjusted her glasses and turned her head to glare at the retreating figure of a man in a suit. "It's good manners to anesthetize someone before you remove their kidneys with your briefcase." Mumbling threats under her breath, she rubbed her ribs with her hand. "There are days when I want to go back to living in a small town."

"You're kidding. You'd move back to Puffin Island?" Paige shifted her bag onto the other shoulder. "I don't ever feel that way, not even when I'm on the subway and I'm so squashed it feels as if I'm being hugged by a boa constrictor. Not that the island isn't pretty, because it is, but—it's an island. Enough said." She'd felt marooned from civilization by the choppy waters of Penobscot Bay, smothered by a thick blanket of parental anxiety. "I like living in a place where people don't know every detail of my life."

At times it had felt like collective parenting. *Paige, why aren't you wearing a sweater? Paige, I saw the helicopter taking you to hospital again, you poor thing.* She'd felt trapped and constrained, as if someone had grasped her in a tight fist, determined to keep her from escaping.

Life had been all about keeping her well, keeping her safe, keeping her protected, until she'd wanted to scream out the question that had burned inside her for most of her childhood—

What was the point in being alive if you weren't allowed to live?

Moving to New York City was the best, most exciting thing that had ever happened to her and it was different from Puffin Island in every possible way. Some would have said worse.

Not Paige.

Frankie was frowning. "We all know I can't set foot on Puffin Island again. I'd be lynched. There are a few things I miss, but one thing I *don't* miss is everyone staring at me angrily because my mother has had yet another affair with a husband who doesn't belong to her." She shoved her hair out of her eyes and finished her drink. Anger, frustration and misery radiated from her and when she scrunched the empty can in her fist her knuckles were white. "At least in Manhattan there are a couple of men my mother hasn't had sex with. Although there is officially one fewer than yesterday."

"Again?" Finally Paige understood the reason her friend was so brittle. "She texted you?"

"Only when I didn't answer her fourteen calls." Frankie shrugged. "You were asking why I wasn't in the mood for breakfast, Ev—apparently he was twenty-eight and banged like a barn door in a gale force wind. The level of detail kind of put me off my food." Her flippant tone did nothing to disguise how upset she was, and Paige slid her arm through Frankie's.

"It won't last."

"Of course it won't last. My mother's relationships never last. But in the time she's with him she'll manage to strip him of a significant quantity of his assets. Don't feel sorry for him. I blame him as much as her. Why can't men keep it zipped? Why don't they ever say no?"

"Plenty of guys say no." Paige thought about her own parents and their long happy marriage.

"Not the ones my mother hooks. My biggest dread is that one day I'm going to meet one of them at an event. Can you imagine that? Maybe I should change my name."

"You're never going to bump into them. New York City is a crowded place."

Eva took Frankie's other arm. "One day she is going to fall in love, and all this will stop."

"Oh please! Even you can't romanticize this situation. Love has nothing to do with it," Frankie said. "Men are my mother's job. Her income. She is the CEO of the BMD corporation, otherwise known as Bleed Men Dry."

Eva sighed. "She's very troubled."

"Troubled?" Frankie stopped dead. "Ev, my mother left troubled behind five stops ago. Can we talk about something else?

I should never have mentioned it. It's a guaranteed way to ruin my day and it isn't as if it hasn't happened before. Living in New York has many advantages, but being able to avoid my mother most of the time is the biggest one."

Paige thought for the millionth time how lucky she was with her parents. True, they worried and fussed a bit too much, which drove her insane, but compared to Frankie's mother they were wonderfully normal. "Living in New York is the best thing that ever happened to any of us. How did we survive without Bloomingdale's and the Magnolia Bakery?"

"Or feeding the ducks in Central Park," Eva said wistfully. "That's my favorite thing. I used to do it with my grandmother every weekend."

Frankie's gaze softened. "You miss her horribly, don't you?"

"I'm doing okay." Eva's smile dimmed a little. "Good days and bad days. It's not as bad as it was a year ago. She was ninety-three so I can hardly complain, can I? It's just that it feels weird not having her around. She was the one constant in my life and now she's gone. And I have no one. I'm not connected to anyone."

"You're connected to us," Paige said. "We're your family. We should go out this weekend. Shopping? We could hit the makeup counter at Saks Fifth Avenue and then go dancing."

"Dancing? I *love* dancing." Eva wiggled her hips provocatively and almost caused another pileup.

Frankie urged her forward. "There aren't enough gel inserts in the world to cope with shopping and dancing in the same trip. And Saturday night is movie night. I vote for a horror fest."

Eva recoiled. "No way. I'd be awake all night."

"It wouldn't get my vote, either." Paige pulled a face.

"Maybe Matt would let us have chick flick night to celebrate my promotion."

"No chance." Frankie straightened her glasses. "Your brother would jump off his own roof before he agreed to chick flick night. Thank goodness."

Eva shrugged. "How about going out tonight instead of Saturday? I'm never going to meet someone if I don't go out."

"People don't come to New York to meet someone. They come for the culture, the experience, the money—the list is long, but meeting the man you're going to marry isn't on it."

"So why did you come here?"

"Because I needed to live somewhere big and anonymous and my best friends were here. And I love certain parts of it," Frankie conceded. "I love The High Line, the Botanical Gardens and our secret little corner of Brooklyn. I love our brownstone and I will be forever grateful to your brother for letting us rent the place from him."

"Did you hear that?" Eva nudged Paige. "Frankie said something positive about a man."

"Matt is one of the few decent men on the planet. He's a friend, that's all. I happen to enjoy being single. What's wrong with that?" Frankie's tone was cool. "I am self-sufficient and proud of it. I make my own money and I answer to no one. Being single is a choice, not a disease."

"And my choice would be to not be single. That's not wrong either, so don't lecture me. I can't help feeling a little despondent that the condom in my purse has passed its expiry date." Eva tucked a wayward blond curl behind her ear and skillfully steered the conversation away from relationships. "I *love* summer. Sundresses, flip-flops, Shakespeare in the Park, sailing on the Hudson, long evenings up on our roof terrace. I still can't believe your brother built that. He's so damn smart."

Paige didn't disagree.

Older by eight years, her brother had left their island home long before she had. He'd chosen to start his landscape architecture business right here in New York City and now that business was thriving.

"The roof garden is heaven." Frankie increased her pace. "What happened to that big piece of business in Midtown? Did that come off for him?"

"Still waiting to hear, but his company is doing well."

And now it was her turn.

Her promotion was the next step in her life plan. It would also hopefully be another step to curing her family's tendency to be overprotective.

Born with a heart defect, Paige's childhood had been a raft of hospital visits, doctors and loving parents who had struggled to hide their anxiety. Growing up, she'd felt disempowered. The day she'd left hospital after what everyone hoped was her last operation, she'd vowed to change that. Fortunately, apart from the occasional routine health check, she was free from constant medical intervention and was fine now. She knew she was one of the lucky ones and she was determined to make the most of every day. The only way to do that had been to move away from Puffin Island and so that was what she'd done.

She had a whole new life and things were going well.

"We need to hurry. We can't be late." Eva interrupted Paige's thoughts.

"She cannot give us the 'part-time' speech when we were all working until the early hours last night."

Paige didn't need to ask who *she* was. *She* was Cynthia, Director of Events, and the only thing Paige didn't love about her job. Cynthia had joined Star Events a year after Paige, and the atmosphere in the company had immediately changed. It was as if someone had emptied toxic waste into a clear mountain stream and poisoned everyone who drank from it.

"I still can't believe she fired poor Matilda. Have either of you heard from her?"

"I've been calling and calling," Eva said. "She isn't answering. I'm worried. She needed the job badly. I don't have her address or I'd visit in person."

"Keep calling. And I'm going to try and persuade Cynthia to change her mind."

"What is her problem? She's so angry all the time. If she hates the job so much, why doesn't she leave? Every time I see her I want to apologize even though I haven't done anything wrong. I feel as if she's the Great White Shark at the top of the food chain and I'm a little seal she's going to eat in one mouthful."

Paige shook her head. "She is never going to leave. Which is another reason I want this promotion. I'll have less contact with her, more responsibility and my own accounts." She'd gain more experience and one day, hopefully not too far away, she was going to start her own business and be her own boss. She'd be the one in control.

It was her dream, but she wasn't prepared to stop at dreaming.

She had a plan.

"You'll be a brilliant boss," Eva said generously. "From the day you organized my eighth birthday party, I knew you were going places. Of course it wouldn't be hard to be a better boss than Cynthia. I heard someone say the other day that she isn't happy until she's made everyone cry at least once." Eva did an emergency stop beside another store window, seals and sharks forgotten in the face of retail nirvana. "Do you think that top would fit me?"

"Maybe, but there's no way it's fitting in your closet." Paige dragged her away. "You need to throw something out before you buy anything new."

"Is it my fault that I get emotionally attached to things?"

Frankie walked to the other side of Eva to stop her window gazing. "How can anyone be emotionally attached to clothes?"

"Easy. If something good happens to me while I'm wearing something, I wear it again when I need to feel positive. For example today I'm wearing my lucky shirt to make extra sure that Paige's promotion comes with a massive pay raise."

"How can a shirt be lucky?"

"Good things have happened to me while I've been wearing this shirt."

Frankie shook her head. "I don't want to know."

"Good, because I'm not telling you. You don't know everything about me. I have a mystical side." Eva craned her neck to try and look in windows. "Could I——"

"No." Paige gave her a tug. "You're not mystical, Ev. You're an open book."

"Better that than cruel and inhuman. And we all have our own, individual addictions. Frankie's is flowers, yours is red lipstick——" Eva glanced at her. "That's a nice shade. New?"

"Yes. It's called Summer Success."

"Very apt. We should celebrate tonight. Or do you think Cynthia will want to take you out?"

"Cynthia doesn't socialize." Paige had spent countless hours trying to understand her boss but still had no insight. "I've never heard her talk about anyone or anything except work."

"Do you think she has a sex life?"

"None of us has a sex life. This is Manhattan. Everyone is too busy to have sex."

"Apart from my mother," Frankie muttered.

"And Jake," Eva intervened quickly. "He was at the Adams event the other night. Sexiest guy in the room. Smart, too. He gets laid regularly, but I guess being scorching hot and having that killer body helps. I can see why you had a crazy teenage crush on him, Paige."

Paige felt as if someone had thrust a fist into her stomach. "That was a long time ago."

The thought of Jake having sex shouldn't bother her; it really shouldn't.

"First love is very powerful," Eva said. "The feeling never quite goes away."

"So is first disappointment. That feeling never goes away, either. My crush on Jake ended a long time ago, so you can stop looking at me like that."

But the relationship wasn't easy.

There were days when she wished Jake wasn't her brother's closest friend.

If he'd been some random guy from her teenage years she could have moved on, laughed and forgotten about it, instead of which she was destined to carry the embarrassing memory around like a ball and chain. It was always there, clanking behind her.

Even now, so many years later, she cringed when she thought about the things she'd said to him. Worse, the things she'd done.

She'd been naked—

The memory made her want to slide through a hole in the floor.

Did he ever think about it? Because she thought about it a lot.

Eva was still talking. "I'm willing to bet he's on a million women's bucket lists."

Frankie shook her head in disbelief. "When people are compiling a bucket list they usually choose skydiving or a trip to Machu Picchu, all amazing life experiences, Ev."

"I'm pretty sure being kissed by Jake Romano would be an amazing life experience. Much better than skydiving, but then I'm scared of heights."

Paige kept walking.

She was never going to find out.

Even when she'd thrown herself at him, Jake had never come close to kissing her.

She'd dreamed of him being overcome by lust. Instead he'd gently disentangled himself from her clinging limbs, as if he'd suddenly found himself covered in laundry blown by the wind.

His patient kindness had been the most humiliating blow of all. He hadn't been fighting lust; he had been fighting *her*, fending her off.

It was the first and only time she'd ever said "I love you" to a man. She'd been so *sure* he had feelings for her and the fact that she'd got it so wrong had governed all her interactions with men since. She no longer trusted her instincts.

These days she was very, very careful with her heart. She exercised, she ate her five portions of fruit and vegetables and she focused on her work, which always proved more exciting than any of the few relationships she'd had.

Paige paused outside the offices of Star Events and breathed deeply. She didn't need to be thinking about Jake right before the most important meeting of her life. He had a tendency to turn her brain and her knees to jelly. She needed to focus. "This is it. No more laughing. Fun is not allowed inside these walls."

Cynthia was waiting for them by the reception desk.

Paige felt a flash of irritation.

Surely she could manage *one* small smile on a day like today?

Fortunately even Cynthia couldn't spoil the job for Paige. She loved it. Managing every detail and making each event a memorable occasion was fun. The most important thing for her was a happy client. As a child she'd loved organizing parties for her friends. Now it was her job, and her job was about to get a whole lot bigger.

Anticipating the new level of responsibility lifted her spirits and she walked across the foyer with a smile on her face.

Senior Event Manager.

Already she had plans. Her team was going to work hard because they wanted to, not because they were afraid of repercussions. And the first thing she was going to do was find a way to hire back poor Matilda.

"Good morning, Cynthia."

"As far as I recall, your contract says nothing about working part-time."

If anyone could kill the excitement of the moment, it was Cynthia.

"The Capital Insurance event didn't finish until past midnight last night and the trains were packed this morning. We were—"

"Taking advantage." Cynthia glanced pointedly at the clock on the wall even though she knew perfectly well what time it was. "I need to see you in my office right away. Let's get this done."

This was a meeting about her promotion and she wanted to "get this done"?

Her friends melted away, and Paige heard Eva softly humming the theme from *Jaws*.

It lifted her mood.

Working with her friends was one of the best things about this job.

As she followed Cynthia toward her office they passed Alice, one of the junior account managers.

Catching a glimpse of reddened eyes Paige stopped walking. "Alice? Is everything—"

But Alice passed her quickly and Paige made a mental note to seek her out later and find out what was wrong.

Boyfriend problems?

Work issues?

She knew several of the staff had been horrified that Matilda had been fired after her unfortunate accident with a tray of champagne. It had created a general atmosphere of unease. Everyone was secretly wondering who would be next.

Following her boss into her office, Paige closed the door.

Soon she'd be in a position to make her own decisions about staffing. In the meantime, this was her moment. She'd worked hard for it and she was going to enjoy it.

Please let the pay raise be good.

Eva was right, they should celebrate later. A few glasses of something cold and sparkling. And then maybe dancing. They hadn't been dancing in ages.

Cynthia reached for a file. "As you know we've been looking at ways to streamline Star Events and reduce costs. I don't need to tell you that we're operating in a challenging market."

"I know, and I have some ideas I'd love to share with you." Paige reached for her bag but Cynthia shook her head and held up her hand.

"We're letting you go, Paige."

"Go? Go where?" It hadn't occurred to her that promotion might mean transferring to another office. And there was only one other office. Los Angeles. The other side of the country.

This, she hadn't expected. She loved New York City. She loved living and working with her friends. "I assumed I'd be staying here. Moving to Los Angeles is a big step." Although if she wanted promotion she should probably be prepared to accept that it might involve relocation. Maybe she should ask for a little time to think about it. That was acceptable, wasn't it?

Cynthia opened the file. "Why would you think we were relocating you to Los Angeles?"

"You said you were letting me go."

"We're letting you go from Star Events."

Paige stared at her stupidly. "Excuse me?"

"We're making cuts." Cynthia leafed through the file and didn't meet her eyes. "Putting it bluntly, business has fallen off a cliff. Everyone in the hospitality industry is laying off employees and reducing hours."

Letting her go.

Not promoting her or moving her to Los Angeles.

Letting her go.

There was a buzzing in her ears. "But—I've brought in nine major new clients in the past six months. Almost all the new business growth has been down to me and—"

"We lost Adams Construction as a client."

Shock flashed through her. "What?"

Chase Adams, the owner of the most successful construction company in Manhattan, had been one of their biggest clients. It was after an event for his company that Matilda had been fired.

Karma, Paige thought. First Cynthia had fired Matilda and now Chase Adams had fired them.

And she was a casualty.

"I wasn't in a position to argue." Cynthia continued. "That stupid girl Matilda ruined their event."

"That's why he fired us? Because of an accident?"

"Spilling one glass of champagne might be termed an accident, but dropping an entire tray is closer to a catastrophe. Adams insisted that I get rid of her. I tried to persuade him to rethink, but he wouldn't. The man owns half of Manhattan. He's one of the most powerful players in this city."

"Then he didn't need to crush poor Matilda." Paige could think of a few choice words to describe Chase Adams, none of them flattering. She certainly didn't blame Matilda.

"It's history. Naturally we'll give you excellent references for your next job."

Next job?

She wanted this job. The job she loved. *The job she'd earned.*

Her mouth was so dry it was hard to speak. Her heart pounded, a brutal reminder of how fragile life was. This morning she'd felt as if she owned the world and now control had been wrenched from her hands.

Other people were deciding her future. Closed doors and conversations. People expecting her to wear a brave face.

And she was an expert at that. She did it without thinking whenever life got tough, like a computer going into sleep mode.

She knew how to bury her feelings and she buried them now.

Stay professional, Paige.

"You told me that if I met my performance objectives I would be promoted. I exceeded them."

"The situation has changed and as a commercial operation we need to be fluid and react to the needs of the market."

"How many people? Is that why Alice was crying? She's been laid off? Who else?" Was it the same for Frankie and Eva?

Eva had no family to turn to and Paige knew Frankie would stop eating rather than ask her mother for a single cent.

"I'm not in a position to discuss other employees with you."

Paige sat still, battered by emotion. She felt a dizzying loss of control.

She'd trusted her employers. They'd made big promises. She'd delivered time and time again, worked hideous hours and put her future in their hands. And this was what they did with that trust? They'd given her no warning. No hint.

"This company has grown because of me. I can show you numbers that prove it."

"We've worked as a team." Cynthia was cool. "You are good at your job. You have a tendency to be a little too friendly toward the people who work for you, and you should say no to the client more often—that episode when you had that man's suit express dry-cleaned in the middle of a party was beyond ridiculous—but apart from that I have no complaints. This isn't about your work."

"I dry-cleaned his suit because he'd spilled his drink and he was trying to impress his boss. He gave us a huge piece of business after that. And I'm friendly because I like working in a happy team and a positive environment."

Something Cynthia knew nothing about.

Looking at her boss was like looking at a locked door. Nothing she said was ever going to open it. She was wasting her time.

Instead of a promotion and a pay raise, she was out of a job.

She'd have to turn to her family for help. Once again she'd be causing her parents and her brother anxiety. And their instinct would be to protect her.

Paige felt her heart pound and instinctively lifted her palm to her chest. Through the fabric of her shirt she felt the solid shape of the little silver heart she sometimes wore hidden under her clothes.

For a moment she was back in the hospital bed, seventeen years old, surrounded by get-well cards and balloons, waiting for her operation and scared out of her mind. Her brain had been conjuring awful scenarios when the door had opened and a doctor had strolled into the room wearing a white coat and carrying a clipboard.

She'd braced herself for more tests, more pain, more bad news, and then recognized Jake.

"They wouldn't let me in because it's not visiting hours, so I'm flexing the rules. Call me Dr. Romano." He'd winked at her and closed the door. "Time for your medicine, Miss Walker. No squealing or I'll remove your brain and donate it to medical science."

He'd always made her laugh. His presence did other things to her, too. Things that made her wish she were wearing something slinky and sexy instead of an oversize T-shirt with a cartoon on the front. "Are you doing the operation?"

"I faint at the sight of blood and I don't know a brain from a butt, so no, I'm not. Here. I bought you something." He'd dug his hand into the back pocket of his jeans and pulled out a small box. "Better open it quickly, before I'm arrested."

For a crazy moment she'd thought he was giving her an engagement ring and her heart, her misbehaving heart, had missed a beat.

"What is it?" Hands shaking, she'd opened the box and there, nestled on a bed of midnight-blue silk, was a beautiful silver heart on a delicate chain. "Oh, Jake—"

Engraved on the back were three words.

A strong heart.

"I thought yours could do with a little help. Wear it, honey, and think of it as reinforcements anytime your own is in trouble."

Maybe it wasn't a ring, but he'd called her *honey* and he'd given her a necklace.

That had to mean something, surely?

She'd stopped worrying about the operation and thought of nothing but Jake.

By the time they came to collect her to take her for her operation, she'd had a whole future mapped out with him. She'd named their children.

They'd had to drag the necklace from her clenched fist in the operating room, and the moment she was able she put it on again.

A strong heart.

She always wore it when she needed courage and she was wearing it today.

She stood up, her movements automatic. She had to start looking for jobs. She couldn't waste a moment and she wouldn't waste time fighting the inevitable.

"You should clear your desk today," Cynthia said. "We'll give you a severance package of course."

Severance.

If *promotion* was her favorite word, *sever* was her least favorite. It sounded brutal. She felt as if she was having major surgery all over again, only this time they'd taken a scalpel to her hopes and dreams. So much for climbing the ladder. So much for her plans to eventually start her own business.

Walking out of Cynthia's office, she closed the door between them.

Reality seeped in. If she'd known what was going to happen, she wouldn't have bought that coffee on the way in to work. She wouldn't have treated herself to another lipstick when she already had plenty. She stood, frozen, regretting every cent she'd spent over the past few years. In the darkest part of her life she'd promised herself that she'd live every moment, but she hadn't anticipated this.

She walked down an empty corridor into the nearest restroom, the only sound the echo of her heels.

Less than an hour ago she'd been excited about the future. Optimistic.

Now she was unemployed.

Unemployed.

Alone in the soulless room, finally she let the mask slip.

In his glass-fronted office in Downtown Manhattan, Jake Romano sat with his feet on his desk only half listening to the man at the other end of the phone.

Across from him a young, blonde reporter fidgeted and tried to check the time without him noticing. Jake rarely gave interviews but somehow this woman had managed to maneuver her way past his assistant. Because he had a certain admiration for tenacity and creativity, he hadn't thrown her out.

It was an impulse he was regretting. He was willing to bet she was, too. So far they'd been interrupted three times and each time she grew a little more frustrated.

Given that her questions so far had bordered on the intrusive, he decided to make her wait a little longer and focused on the call. "You don't need a content strategist for a lightweight application redesign. What you need is a smart copywriter."

The reporter bent her head and checked over her notes. Jake wondered how many more interruptions she'd tolerate before she blew.

He swung his legs off the desk and decided to end the call. "I know you're a busy man so I'm going to stop you there. I understand you want a beautiful design, but a beautiful design isn't worth shit if your content is bad. And theory is great but what matters is solving real problems for real people. Talking of problems, I'm going to think about yours and get back to you. If I decide we're the right people for the job, then I'll talk to the team and we'll have a face-to-face. Leave it with me." He broke the connection. "Sorry about that," he said, turning his attention to the reporter.

Her smile was as false as his apology. "No problem. You're a difficult man to get hold of. I know that. I've been trying to set up this interview for over a year."

"And now you've succeeded. So are we done here?"

"I have a couple more questions." She paused, as if regrouping. "We've talked about your business, your philanthropic goals and your company ideology. I'd like to tell our readers a little about Jake, the man. You were born in the roughest part of Brooklyn and you were adopted when you were six years old."

Jake kept his expression blank.

The reporter looked at him expectantly. "I didn't hear your answer—?"

"I didn't hear a question."

She flushed. "Do you see your mother?"

"All the time. She runs the best Italian restaurant in New York. You should check it out."

"You're talking about your adoptive mother—" she checked the name "—Maria Romano. I was talking about your real mother."

"Maria is my real mother." Those who knew him would have recognized the tone and taken cover but the reporter sat oblivious, like a gazelle unaware she was being stalked by an animal right at the top of the food chain. "So you're not in touch with your birth mother? I wonder how she feels now that you're running a multimillion-dollar global business."

"Feel free to ask her." Jake stood up. "We're out of time."

"You don't like talking about your past?"

"The past is history," Jake said in a cool tone, "and I was always better at Math. Now if you'll excuse me I have clients waiting for my attention. Paying clients."

"Of course." The woman slid her recording device into her bag. "You're an example of the American dream, Jake. An inspiration to millions of Americans who had it tough growing up. Despite your past, you've created a highly successful company."

Not despite, Jake thought. *Because of.*

He'd created a highly successful company because of his past.

He closed the door on the reporter and paced across to the window that wrapped itself around two sides of his corner office. Sun glinted through the floor-to-ceiling glass and he surveyed the high-rises of Downtown Manhattan spread beneath his feet as if he were Midas studying his pile of gold.

His eyes felt gritty from lack of sleep, but he kept them open, drinking in the view, gaining satisfaction from the knowledge that he'd earned every dazzling piece of that view.

Not bad for a boy from the wrong part of Brooklyn who'd been told he'd never make anything of himself.

Had he chosen to, he could have given the reporter a story that would have made the front page and probably won her a Pulitzer.

He'd grown up looking at the shiny promise of Manhattan from the other side of the water. He'd blocked out the incessant barking of dogs, the sounds of shouting in the street, the honking of car horns and had stared enviously at a different life. Looking across the fast-flowing tidal stretch that was the East River, he'd seen buildings reaching up to the sky and wanted to live across the water, where skyscrapers stood tall, where glass reflected light and ambition.

It had seemed as faraway and remote as Alaska. But he'd had plenty of time to stare. He'd never known his father and even as a young child he'd spent most of his time alone while his teenage mother worked three jobs.

I love you, Jake. It's you and me against the world.

Jake stared blankly at the crisscross of streets far beneath him.

It had been a long time since anyone had mentioned her. And a long time since that night when he'd sat alone on the steps to their apartment, waiting for her to come home.

What would have happened to him if Maria hadn't taken him in?

Jake knew he had more than a loving home to thank her for.

He shifted his gaze from the view to the computer on his desk.

It was Maria who had given him his first computer, an ancient machine that had belonged to one of her cousins. Jake had been fourteen years old when he'd hacked into his first website, fifteen when he'd realized he had abilities other people didn't. When he'd turned sixteen he picked a company with the largest glass office, turned up at the door and told them how vulnerable they were to cyber attack. They'd laughed, until he'd shown them how easily he could break through their security defenses. Then they'd stopped laughing and listened.

He'd become a legend in cyber security, the teenager with charisma, confidence and a brain so sharp he'd held conversations with men twice his age who knew half as much.

He'd shown them how little they knew, exposed the weaknesses, then taught them how to fix it. At school he skipped every English class, but never Math. Numbers, he understood.

He'd come from nowhere, but he'd been determined that soon he was going somewhere and he was going there so fast he left everyone behind.

It was exploiting those gifts that had put him through college and, much later, bought his mother—because that was how he thought of Maria even before she'd officially adopted him—a restaurant so that she could share her cooking skills with the good folks of Brooklyn without having them packed into her kitchen as tightly as olives in a jar.

With the help of his closest friend, Matt, he'd set up his own company and developed a piece of encryption software, which was bought by a major defense company for a sum that ensured he would never have money worries again.

Then, bored by the overcrowded cyber security market he'd turned his attention to the growing field of digital marketing.

Now his company offered everything from creative content to user experience design although he still accepted the occasional private request to consult on cyber security issues. It had been one of those requests that had kept him up until the early hours the previous night.

His office door opened again and Dani, one of his junior staff, entered carrying coffee.

"I thought you'd need this. That girl was harder to shake off than a mosquito on a blood bag." She was wearing striped socks and no shoes, a dress code followed by at least half the people working for him. Jake had no interest in what people wore to work. Nor was he interested in where a person went to college. He cared about two things. Passion and potential.

Dani had both.

She put the coffee on his desk. The aroma rose, strong and pungent, slicing through the clouds in his brain that reminded him he'd been working until three in the morning.

"She asked you questions?"

"A few thousand. Mostly about your personal life. She wanted to know whether the reason you rarely date the same woman twice is because of your messed-up childhood."

He peeled the cap off the coffee. "Did you tell her to mind her own business?"

"No. I told her that the reason you don't date the same woman twice is because at last count there were around seventy thousand single women in Manhattan, and if you start seeing them more than once you're never going to get through them all." Her expression cheerful, she handed him a stack of messages. "Your friend Matt called four times. The guy sounded stressed."

"Matt is never stressed." Jake took a sip of coffee, savoring the aroma and the much-needed pump of caffeine. "He is Mr. Calm."

"Well, he sounded like Mr. Stressed a moment ago." Dani picked up the four empty coffee cups from his desk and stacked them together. "You know, I don't mind feeding your coffee habit but once in a while you could eat a meal or sleep at night. It's what normal people do, in case you were wondering."

"I wasn't wondering." What he was wondering was why his friend was calling in the middle of the working day. And why leave four messages with his assistant rather than calling him directly? Picking up his phone he saw six missed calls. Concern tugged at him. "Did Matt say what it was about?"

"No, but he wanted you to call back as soon as possible. That reporter was impressed that you turned down business from Brad Hetherington. Is that true?" She made a grab for a cup that almost toppled off the stack. "He's one of the richest guys in New York City. I read that piece in Forbes last week."

"He's also an egotistical dickhead and I try really hard not to do business with egotistical dickheads. It puts me in a bad mood. Word of advice, Dani—don't ever be intimidated by money. Follow your gut."

"So we're not going to work with him?"

"I'm thinking about it. Thanks for the coffee. You didn't have to do that." He'd told her the same thing every day since she'd first started working for his company. She still brought him coffee every day.

"Think of me as the gift that keeps on giving." He'd given her a chance when others had closed the door in her face. She was never going to forget it. "You worked late last night and started early this morning so I thought you could do with something to wake you up." The look in her eyes told him she would happily have found other ways to wake him up.

Jake ignored the look.

He happily broke rules made by other people, but never the ones he made himself and right at the top of that list was *don't bring your private life to work.*

He'd never do anything that might threaten his business. It was too important to him. And anyway, he might be a genius with computers but he'd be the first to admit that his skills didn't extend to relationships.

As soon as Dani had left the room, he called Matt. "What's the emergency? Did you run out of beer?"

"I assume you haven't seen the business news."

"I've been in meetings since the sun rose. What have I missed? Someone hacked your website and you need an expert?" Suppressing a yawn, he tapped a key on his computer to wake it up, wishing he could do the same thing to himself. "Another corporate takeover?"

"Star Events has laid off half their staff."

Jake woke instantly. "Paige didn't get her promotion?"

"I don't know. She's not answering her phone."

"You think she's lost her job?"

"I think it's possible." Matt sounded tense. "Probable. She's cut herself off, and that's what she does when she's in Brave Mode."

Jake didn't have to ask what he meant. He'd seen Paige in Brave Mode often enough, and he hated it. He hated thinking of her scared, struggling and hiding it. "Well, hell——"

"She worked so damn hard for that promotion. It's all she's talked about all year. She's going to be devastated."

"Yeah." And he would have done anything to stop Paige being hurt. He considered how long it would take him to cross town and beat someone to a pulp. "Eva? Frankie?"

"They're not answering, either. I'm hoping they're together. I don't want her to be on her own, shutting everyone out."

Neither did he.

Jake stood up and paced to the window, mentally listing the options. "I'll make some calls. Find out what's going on."

"Why isn't she answering her phone?" It was a growl. "I'm worried about her."

"You're always worried about her."

"She's my sister——"

"Yeah, and you wrap her in cotton wool. You need to let her live her life. She's tougher than you think. And she's strong and healthy."

But she hadn't always been that way.

He had a clear recollection of Paige as a teenager, pale and thin in the hospital bed, waiting for major heart surgery. And he remembered his friend, white-faced and more stressed than Jake had ever seen him, hollow eyed after nights without sleep, nights spent sitting by his sister's bed.

"What are you doing tonight?" Matt asked, sounding tired.

"I have a hot date." Although whether he could wake up enough to perform he wasn't sure. His friend wasn't the only one who was tired. At this rate he might be the first man on earth to have sex while in a coma.

"With Gina?"

"Gina was last month."

"Do you ever see a woman for more than a month?"

"Not unless I lose track of time." He moved on. It suited him that way.

"So it's not true love?" Matt laughed. "Sorry. I forgot you don't believe in love."

Love?

Jake stared out of the window at a city washed with sunshine.

"Are you still there?" Matt's voice cut through the memories.

"Yeah." His voice was rusty. "Still here."

"If it's not true love, cancel and come over. If the three of them have lost their jobs I don't want to handle it on my own. My sister is hard work when she's stressed, mostly because she insists on pretending she's fine. Trying to get her to admit she's struggling is like drilling through steel. I don't mind her doing that with mom, but it pisses me off when she does it with me."

"You're asking me to turn down a night of sex with a Swedish blonde to help persuade your sister and her friends to be honest about their emotions? Call me boring, but I don't find that a tempting offer."

"She's Swedish? What's her name? Where does she work?"

"Her first name is Annika. I haven't asked her second name and I don't care where she works as long as it's not for my company." Jake walked back to his desk and when he sat down the woman on his mind wasn't Annika. Where was Paige now? He imagined her, pacing the streets somewhere, upset.

Alone. Hiding everything she felt. *Shit*. He picked up a pencil and doodled on a pad on the desk. "I'm no good with tears."

"Have you ever seen Paige cry?"

Jake's fingers tightened on the pencil.

Yeah, he'd seen her cry.

He'd been the one to make her cry.

But Matt didn't know anything about that.

"I've seen Eva cry."

"Eva cries at sad movies and pretty sunsets," Matt drawled, "but she didn't miss a single day at work after her grandmother died. She dragged herself out of bed every day, put on her makeup and went to work even though she was devastated. That girl is tough." There was a pause. "Look, if there is crying, I'll deal with it."

Jake thought about his date for the night. Then he thought about Paige. Paige, who he tried really hard only ever to think of as his best friend's little sister.

Little sister. Little. Little.

If he repeated that word often enough, hopefully his brain might eventually believe it.

He could refuse, but then he wouldn't be able to help her and he had every intention of helping. The situation was complicated by the fact that he knew Paige wouldn't want to be helped. She hated being protected or smothered. She didn't want to be the focus of other people's anxieties.

He understood that. He understood *her*.

Which was why he was determined to structure his help in a way that was acceptable to her.

And the first thing he had to do was move her past the shock stage, into the action stage.

"I'll be there."

His Friday night of mindless physical entertainment evaporated into the ether.

Instead of spending the night with a stunning blonde he'd be behaving in a brotherly fashion toward a woman he made a point of avoiding whenever he could. Why did he avoid her?

Because Paige Walker wasn't little. She was all grown-up.

And his feelings toward her were far from brotherly.

"Thanks." Matt sounded relieved. "And Jake—?"

"What?"

"Be nice."

"I'm always nice."

"Not to Paige. I know you two don't really get along that well anymore." Matt sounded tired again. "Normally that doesn't worry me because—well, you know why. There was a time when I thought she might be in love with you."

She'd been crazily in love with him.

She'd told him as much, in a breathless hopeful voice, her eyes full of happy endings.

And she'd been naked at the time.

There was a sharp crack, and Jake glanced down and saw that he'd broken the pencil in half.

"You don't have anything to worry about. Paige definitely isn't in love with me now."

He might not have been able to fix her heart, but he'd fixed that.

He'd been careful to kill any soft feelings she might have had for him a long time ago. Now the only emotion she ever felt in his presence was extreme irritation. It was an art form, winding her up. There were days when he even pretended he enjoyed it.

He kept her annoyed.

Kept her irritated.

Kept her safe.

"That's good to know because you are the kind of trouble my sister doesn't need in her life. You promised not to lay a finger on her. Remember?"

"Yeah. I remember." That promise had handcuffed him for a decade. That, and the knowledge that Paige wouldn't be able to handle the realities of a relationship with him.

"Hey, you're my closest friend. You're like a brother to me, but we both know you'd be bad news for my sister. Not that you'd be interested. We both know she isn't your type."

"That's right." Jake kept his voice monotone. "Not my type."

"Do me a favor? Tonight I need you to find your sensitive side. Don't poke at her or take bites out of her. Be kind. Can you do that?"

Kind.

He yanked open the drawer on his desk and took out a new pencil. "Sure I can do that."

He'd be kind for five minutes.

Then he'd make up for it by driving her crazy.

He'd do that for Paige because he cared about her and he'd do it for Matt, because he was the closest thing Jake had to a brother.

And he'd do it for himself because love, in his opinion, was the biggest lottery on earth and the only risk he wasn't prepared to take.

Two

When life closes a door, you can always break in through a window.

—Eva

"You need to burn your lucky shirt." Paige stood on the roof terrace of their Brooklyn brownstone, staring blindly through softly waving grasses toward the glittering high-rises of Downtown Manhattan. The shady garden provided a lush, fragrant oasis in a city dominated by steel and glass.

Her brother, a landscape designer, had seen the potential others hadn't and purchased the run-down brownstone for a fraction of its market value. He'd proceeded to turn it into three apartments, each with its own charm. But the jewel in the crown was the roof. Matt had magically transformed the weathered, unused space into a calming haven. Tall conifers surrounded the bluestone deck, sheltering custom-built wooden planters overstuffed with juniper, crepe myrtle and roses. It was invisible from the streets below and unimaginable to any one of the thousands of tourists trying to breathe in the crush of Times Square. It wasn't until she'd moved to the city that Paige had discovered New York's secret rooftop world, a myriad of elevated gardens topping the towering buildings like the decoration on a wedding cake.

In the summer they all met up here after work, sprawled on the loungers and deep cushions and drank and talked. Saturday was movie night and they invited friends over and watched on an improvised screen while the world passed by far beneath them.

It was Paige's favorite place.

Candles flickered in mason jars and the air was scented with lavender and jasmine. It was a peaceful summer scene that felt a million miles from the urban madness of Manhattan. Being up here almost always soothed her.

Not today.

Unemployed.

The word filled her head, leaving no room for anything else.

In front of them, the table was loaded with delicious-looking dishes. Chickpeas roasted in spices, raw vegetables dressed in good olive oil and herbs. When she was stressed, Eva cooked, and she'd been cooking all afternoon. The fridge was full of food.

No one was eating.

"I threw the shirt away." Eva's voice was thickened. "I probably shouldn't have because heaven knows when I'll be able to afford to buy a new one. I don't know why I feel so miserable. I didn't even *like* the job that much, not like you. I only did it for the money, and because you were both there and I love working with you. It wasn't my dream or anything. My dream is to turn my cookery blog into something big that people actually read. But this was your dream and you must be *so* upset."

Paige stared across the rooftops, trying to sort her feelings into order and label them. Everything felt out of control. "I'm fine." She accessed the smile with the ease of someone who had faked it a thousand times before. "You don't have to worry about me."

Frankie was on her knees tending the planters. She watered, snipped, deadheaded, trimmed and said nothing.

Paige knew what that meant.

When Frankie was upset or angry, she raged.

When she was scared, she was quiet.

Tonight she was quiet.

Because of her upbringing, the ability to support herself was everything to Frankie.

Paige felt the same way, but for different reasons.

Claws, her brother's rescue cat, sprang from nowhere, and Eva spilled her drink.

"Why does she always do that? The animal is deranged." She stood up and Paige passed her a napkin.

"I know. That cat is the reason most of my clothes are covered in marks." She reached for the cat but Claws stalked off with a flick of her tail, disdaining physical affection. "Why didn't my brother rescue a cute puppy?"

"Because cute puppies need attention and Claws is the 'The Cat that Walked by Himself.'" Frankie quoted Kipling and Claws rewarded her by taking a detour and rubbing briefly against her leg. "I'm in favor."

"If she stopped scratching and jumping on people she wouldn't be the cat who walked by itself. She'd have friends." Eva mopped at her dress. "I thought animals were supposed to be able to sense when someone is traumatized and offer comfort." Her voice wobbled. "Tonight was all about celebrating Paige's promotion and now none of us have jobs. I don't feel so good. How can you both be so calm?"

Paige watched Claws stretch out on the terrace next to Frankie. "I'm a little angry." And a lot scared, but she wasn't admitting that to anyone. "I'm angry with Cynthia because she made huge promises and, it turns out, told a few lies. And I'm angry with myself because I was stupid enough to trust that they meant what they said. If I'd sensed something, maybe we wouldn't be in this position."

Eva reached for another napkin. "It isn't stupid to trust your employer."

"It's stupid to trust anyone." Frankie reached out to stroke Claws and the cat gave a warning hiss.

Paige shook her head. "Sorry. My brother is the only one she trusts, despite the fact I feed her when he's out. There's no justice."

Eva poured dressing onto a salad she'd made. "I don't know why I'm cooking when none of us are eating. It's my stress reliever. Fuck Cynthia. Fuck all of them."

Frankie raised her eyebrows. "I've never heard you swear before."

"I've never lost my job before. It's a first, although this experience definitely wasn't on my bucket list." Eva tossed the salad violently, losing a few leaves in the process. They gleamed under the soft light of the terrace, glossy with oil. "At least I won't have to tell Grams. You know the worst thing? Not working with you two anymore." Tears glistened in her eyes and Paige was by her side in seconds.

The job was important to her, but her friends, these friends she'd known almost all her life, were more important.

"It's going to be okay." She said it fiercely, as if by injecting the words with enough passion they might come true. "We'll find something."

"We looked." Eva's voice was muffled against her shoulder. "There's nothing."

Frankie stood up and walked across to them both. "So we'll keep looking." She rubbed Eva's shoulder and Eva sniffed.

"Is this a group hug? I know things are bad when Frankie hugs me."

"It was more of a pat than a hug," Frankie muttered. "And don't get used to it. Brief lapse on my part. You know I'm about as tactile as Claws. But I feel the same way you do. I don't care about Star Events. I do care that we won't be working together anymore."

Paige felt a rush of anger and helplessness and mingled in there was guilt.

She was the team leader. She should have known. Was there something she'd missed?

She kept going over and over it in her head. "It doesn't make sense to me that Chase Adams pulled his business because Matilda dropped a tray of champagne."

"Do you think Matilda knows she was responsible?" Eva sounded worried. "Do you think that's why she's not answering her phone? I hope she isn't feeling guilty."

"We'll keep calling. That's all we can do, Ev. And if we find another job, we'll try and get her hired. When," Paige corrected herself quickly. "I mean when we get another job." Being positive had never felt so exhausting.

She'd been keeping up the fake smile all afternoon as she'd tried to boost their spirits. People lost their jobs all the time, and companies hired all the time. They had skills. They needed to persevere. She'd parroted the words and tried to believe them. And as for her ambitions to run her own company one day, maybe it would be good to get experience elsewhere for a while. The dream was on hold. It wasn't dead.

She reasoned, rationalized and tried to come to terms with it but an afternoon trawling job websites with Eva and Frankie had slowly drained away her brief moment of optimism, until finally they'd given up and retreated to the roof garden.

Now she felt a rush of frustration. Sitting up here was getting her nowhere.

Eva sat down on one of the chairs, but Paige stayed standing up, staring blindly at the planters spilling over with spring color. She should call some of the businesses they'd run events for. See if they were hiring.

The sound of male voices and the clinking of glass disturbed her thoughts and Paige turned her head and saw her brother appear at the top of the steps.

She immediately conjured up her "I'm perfectly fine" smile. Her smile lasted as long as it took her to spot the glossy dark hair and powerful shoulders of the man behind him.

No, no, no.

She was feeling weak and exposed, and the last person she wanted to be around in that vulnerable state was Jake Romano.

In a world where men were encouraged to get in touch with their feminine side, Jake was unapologetically male. Today, unusually, he was wearing a suit but his shirt was open at the neck and there was no sign of a tie. Even the perfectly tailored cloth did nothing to disguise the width of those shoulders or the raw, restrained power of his body. He was the sort of man you wouldn't want to meet in a dark alley on a dark night. Unless you were a woman.

Paige looked away, grateful for the moonlight and flickering candles that created concealing shadows amongst patches of pooled light. Jake knew her better than anyone. Too well.

He'd been the object of all her teenage fantasies and the source of her disillusionment. There was nothing so raw as rejection when you were a teenager, and Jake had been responsible for what would surely have classified as the cruelest rejection ever.

If it had been left to her, she would have made sure she never crossed his path again, but unfortunately that wasn't an option.

Like it or not, Jake was entwined in their lives.

"There is no celebration. We've been laid off. Not only is there no promotion, I'm now officially unemployed." There was a knot of panic in her stomach. She could hide her emotions, but she couldn't hide the facts. At some point she'd have to tell her parents, and her mother would worry.

She'd already caused her mother more than enough worry.

Despite the fact she'd been healthy for years, her family still treated Paige like fine china and because of their tendency to worry she did everything she could to make sure she gave them nothing to worry about. They protected her and she protected them right back.

"I saw it on the business news." Matt put the champagne on the table and pulled her in for a hug. "You should have answered your phone."

The strength and familiarity of his hug was comforting and she stood in his arms, tense as a bow. "I'm fine."

"Yeah, right." His laugh was lacking in humor. "Don't do that."

"Do what?"

"Tell me that you're fine when you're not." He closed his hands over her shoulders and eased her away from him so that he could look at her. "Why didn't you call?"

"I was busy looking for another job. I wanted to have good news, not bad."

He'd always been there for her. One of her earliest memories was of Matt picking her up when she'd fallen on her face in the sand. He'd brushed off the sand, scooped her up and carried her to the sea to make her laugh.

The only reason her parents had agreed to let her go to college in New York was because they'd trusted Matt to watch over her. At first he'd taken that responsibility a little too seriously and they'd had a few fights.

Gradually they'd learned to compromise, but he still had a tendency to ride to her rescue.

Some men were born protectors and Matt was one of those.

His fingers were firm on her shoulder. "I'm here to cushion the bad news. That's what big brothers are for. Do you want me to go and punch your boss?"

"No, but if I met Chase Adams I'd punch him myself." She was horrified by how close she was to tears.

"What does Chase Adams have to do with this?" Jake shrugged off his jacket and sprawled on the nearest chair. He reminded her of a lion or a tiger, always able to make himself comfortable regardless of his surroundings.

"He's the reason Matilda was fired and why we've all been laid off. With no warning." Paige pulled away from Matt and gave them the briefest of details. "Who does that? Who fires a kind, good person for one mistake?"

"Are you sure of your facts?" Jake picked up a plate. "Because that doesn't sound like Chase." His eyes were gray and they made her think of mountain mists and wood smoke.

"You know him?"

"We both know him." Matt sat down and Claws immediately leaped onto his lap. "I did some work on one of his properties and I agree with Jake. That doesn't sound like him."

Jake examined a bowl of chopped raw vegetables and pulled a face. "Don't you guys have anything unhealthy to eat? Greasy burger? Fries?"

"I could rustle you up an arsenic dip," Eva said sweetly, and Paige scowled at Jake.

"We've lost our jobs and you're thinking of your stomach?"

"I'm a man." Jake ignored the raw vegetables and added some olives and garlic bread to his plate. "There are two body parts that dominate my mind for most of the day, my stomach and my—"

"You're not funny."

"And you're uptight. You need to loosen up."

His words stung. "Well, forgive me for caring that I lost my job." She rubbed her hands over her arms. "I trusted that company with my future and they betrayed that trust. I worked hard, I exceeded all my targets and yet they do this. I thought I had some control over my future and it turns out I had none."

After Cynthia had delivered the news, she'd gone in search of Frankie and Eva and found them in the same position as her.

In their brownstone, Frankie rented the garden apartment, Paige and Eva shared the first floor, and Matt had the top two floors. It was the perfect arrangement, except she knew from the stiff set of Frankie's shoulders she was worried about how long she'd be able to afford the rent, even at the friendly rate Matt charged. They were all well aware that it was her brother's generosity that allowed them to live in this part of Brooklyn. Other people her age were living in the equivalent of a shoe box. But living somewhere else would have meant more parental anxiety so she'd accepted his generosity and vowed to pay him back.

At this rate, that moment was going to be a long way off.

She flopped down on a cushion opposite Jake.

Claws purred and stretched out on Matt's lap.

"The chosen one," Frankie murmured. "That cat has serious issues."

"That's what makes her interesting." Matt's fingers brushed lightly over the cat's fur. "I know you're all feeling bruised right now, but you'll find other jobs." His shirt was rolled back to his elbows and Paige noticed the scratches on his skin.

"Did Claws do that?"

"A bad-tempered holly bush. It wasn't supposed to be my job but one of my staff was sick."

And Matt would have done the work himself rather than let a client down. That was the sort of person he was and the reason his company was growing fast. He was in demand for his creative vision, but he'd never lost the ability to do the work.

"There's nothing out there, Matt."

Claws was purring, eyes closed, lost in the gentle slide and stroke of Matt's fingers.

"You can't expect to find a job in a few hours. You have to give it time."

"We don't have time. Eva and Frankie were given a measly severance package." And she knew that even if she could swallow her pride for long enough to accept financial support from her brother or her parents, that wasn't going to help her friends. Misery descended, chilling her skin. "And Eva is right. Even if we do find another job, we won't be together. We made such a great team. I don't know what to do." A solid lump blocked her throat. She hated herself for being so pathetic. She'd been through far worse than this. What the hell had happened to her backbone?

Jake's gaze locked on hers and she had a nasty suspicion he knew exactly how close she was to breaking down.

She hated that she couldn't hide her feelings from him as easily as she did with other people.

"I'll tell you what you should do." He reached for the champagne, his shirt molding to strong shoulders. He had the body of a fighter, powerful and thickly muscled. "You should celebrate. And two minutes after you've drunk that bottle of champagne, you should start your own company. You want control over what your boss does? Make yourself the boss."

Three

If at first you don't succeed, change the plan.

—Paige

Make herself the boss?

"What sort of insensitive joke is that?"

Matt gestured to the glasses. "Pour the drink and shut up, Jake. Only serious suggestions are welcome."

"That was a serious suggestion. Paige was doing all the work in that damn company anyway, why not do it for herself?"

Matt's hand stilled and Claws nudged him. "Because starting your own business isn't something you do on a whim. It's a risk."

"Life is a risk." Jake added salad to his plate. "Paige has lost her job, so it's not as if playing it safe has turned out so great. She's always talked about starting her own company one day. Maybe this is the day. That way she can choose her own staff and carry on working with Eva and Frankie. Problem solved."

Paige felt her heart kick against her ribs. It was a crazy idea. Stupid.

Or was it?

Matt winced as Claws sprang off his lap. "What you're suggesting is a really big step. Now isn't the time to make a decision like that."

"It's the perfect time." Jake dug his fork into his food and turned to Paige. "Unless you'd rather wallow for a while, in which case go right ahead. Celebration or pity party—I'm in. Pour the bubbles and let's get started."

The one point in Jake's favor, Paige mused, was that he didn't protect her. He never had.

Of course that didn't mean he didn't drive her insane. "I don't want pity." She used to love the fact that he knew her so well. Now she wished he didn't. It was hard to hide from someone who knew all your secrets. It felt like an invasion of privacy, as if she'd given him a key that he'd refused to return. "It's true that I want to have my own company one day, but I need experience. I need to learn as much as I can and plan carefully. I'm not ready."

"You mean you're scared." With a deft movement of his wrist, Jake opened the champagne and Claws jumped as the cork shot across the terrace.

"I'm not scared." Paige wondered how he always knew how she was feeling. "That isn't the reason."

"Are you good at your job or not?"

"I'm great at my job. That's why I thought I'd get this promotion, and—"

"Do you need a lot of guidance and support from above?"

Paige thought about the amount of time Cynthia spent hidden in her office. "No."

"Do you need someone else to bring you the business or are you confident going out there and fronting it? Can you win business?"

"I do that all the time! I've brought in nine new clients in the last six months and increased revenue by—"

"We don't need to talk numbers—we need to talk principles. We've established you're great at your job and that you don't need support, so the only reason holding you back is the fact that you're scared of the unknown. It's easier to play it safe and do what you've always done, but you worked for the bitch from hell, Paige, who took all the credit for your hard work. Why would you want to carry on like that?"

"The next person I work for might be different."

"The only way you'll be sure of that is if that person is you. Think about it. Cynthia was a sociopath. You don't have to work with her again. Seems like an opportunity from where I'm sitting." His voice was rough and sexy, as if he'd had a long night of kissing and hot sex.

Which, knowing Jake, he probably had.

The thought bothered her more than it should have done, as did the hot, restless feeling she got whenever she looked at him. Eva would have said that made her human because Jake Romano was just about the sexiest man on the planet, but she would have preferred to be immune.

There was something humiliating about being attracted to someone who'd made it clear he wasn't attracted to you. She wanted her body to have more sense.

"You're accusing me of being a coward."

"Being scared doesn't make you a coward. It makes you human." Calm, Jake put the champagne down. "Pick up a glass. It's time for plan B, honey."

"I don't have a plan B. And don't call me honey."

"Why not?"

"Because I'm not your honey." But she'd wanted to be. Once, she'd desperately wanted to be.

"I meant," he said slowly, "why don't you have a plan B?"

"Oh." Embarrassment burned through her like acid on metal. Being around him made her feel like a gawky, clumsy teenager, all hormones and no finesse. "I've told you. I didn't think I needed one. I was focused on promotion. Do you have a plan B?"

"Always." Their eyes locked. "You need to relax. You're too controlling. You plan every step of your life, but sometimes you have to let life happen. Change is always unsettling, sometimes scary, but you have to let go. Take a risk. Risk can be fun."

His careless dismissal of her anxiety irritated her as much as his pity would have annoyed her.

"That's easy for you to say with millions in the bank, more work than you can handle and an apartment to die for. Some of us still have rent to pay." It was a crass, stupid thing to say and she instantly regretted it, especially since she knew her response was driven by frustration about her feelings for him as much as anything else.

"How do you think those millions got there, Paige?" He didn't bother masking his irritation. "You think I woke up one morning and found myself wealthy? You think I logged on and discovered someone had transferred several million into my bank account? I built my company through hard work, graft and determination. And I pay my own rent. I always have."

There was a loud noise as Frankie dropped a pot on the terrace. It shattered, sending pieces flying.

Matt nudged Claws off his lap and stood up. "Those pieces are sharp. Don't cut yourself, Frankie."

"I'm fine." Frankie kept her head down and scooped up the pieces while Matt watched her steadily.

"Is this about the rent?" Matt asked. "Because you don't

have to worry about that. You can pay me when you're back on your feet."

A flush spread across Frankie's cheeks, clashing with her vivid hair. "I can pay my rent." Her voice was fierce. "I don't *ever* need a man to pay my rent."

Paige knew she was thinking of her mother and presumably so did Matt because he paused for a moment, and then spoke carefully.

"I'm not offering to pay your rent. I just wanted you to know that there is no hurry for payment. Anytime is fine. Wait until you have a job again. It's a loan."

"I don't need a loan. I can pay my way." Frankie scooped the shards of pottery into a bag, and then must have realized how ungrateful she sounded because her shoulders sagged. "Look—"

"You don't have to explain." Matt spoke quietly. "I understand."

Paige saw the brief flash of misery on Frankie's face and realized that it was precisely because her brother understood that Frankie was so mortified.

Everyone who had known Frankie growing up knew the lurid details about her mother.

Every new episode had killed Frankie and it still did, even though she was no longer living on a small island where her mother's bedroom activities were a source of local legend.

Frankie breathed deeply. "That was rude of me and I apologize."

"Don't apologize. I said the wrong thing."

Eva's eyes filled and she sprang from the chair and hugged Matt. "You didn't say the wrong thing. I love you, Matt. You're the best. Why aren't there more men like you in Manhattan? Ow." She pulled back as Claws swiped at her leg with a threatening hiss. "The only thing wrong with you is your cat. Why didn't you adopt a friendly, loving cat?"

"Because that cat didn't need a home. This one did." Matt lifted Claws away from Eva. "You need to give her time, that's all. She'll do okay once she learns she can trust us."

Eva looked doubtfully at Claws. "Matt, that cat is never going to trust anyone. She's psychotic."

"We all have reasons for being the way we are. If we're patient, she'll come around." He was stroking the cat but Paige noticed that his eyes were on Frankie.

Jake handed Eva a glass of champagne. "That cat has saved Matt a million times from predatory women poised to take advantage and bleed him dry. She's better than a bodyguard." He scanned the table of food. "Don't you have chips, Ev? Something greasy that's going to clog my arteries?"

Frankie pushed her glasses up her nose, leaving soil on her cheek. "Not all women are predatory."

Jake's hand stilled over the bowl. "It was a generic comment. What the hell is wrong with you? I know you've had a tough day, but that's no reason to turn into Cactus Woman."

Paige was about to say something soothing but her brother gave a brief shake of his head and walked over to Frankie. He dropped to his haunches next to her and said something.

Paige couldn't hear the words but whatever he said earned a quick smile.

Frankie murmured something back to him and Paige relaxed.

Whatever her brother had said seemed to have calmed things down.

He had a knack for saying the right thing.

Jake reached for a beer. "To playing it safe."

Paige ground her teeth.

Jake, on the other hand, had a habit of saying what he thought, regardless of time or place.

She felt like emptying her champagne over his sleek, dark head. As usual he seemed to be deliberately trying to goad her.

"Your bedside manner needs serious attention, Jake."

"I've never had complaints." Dark lashes shielded the glitter of amusement in his eyes and the spasm of sexual awareness shocked her. She should have been used to it by now. Kissing Jake had featured large in her fantasies for almost a decade, even when she'd tried hard to switch the fantasy to something less dangerous. She imagined him using all that raw power and muscle to pull in a woman, all that charisma and hot sexuality to make sure she never wanted to step away. Although she'd long since stopped hoping anything would happen between them, she'd discovered that sexual attraction wasn't something you could easily switch off. There were days when she wished he would kiss her just so that she could stop fantasizing. Everyone knew reality never came close to fantasy and she would have given a lot to have her illusions crushed.

The breeze lifted her hair and sounds of laughter drifted up from the streets below as people walked home after a night out. Lights glowed in windows, dogs barked, a siren shrieked and a car door slammed. Life went on.

She thought wistfully back to this time yesterday. She'd been planning what to wear for her interview, excited about her promotion, planning the future.

And now she was unemployed.

What was she supposed to do tomorrow? Get up, get out of bed and do what? Spend the day job hunting? Even if she found another job, it wouldn't be with her friends.

She tried to imagine how it would feel to not be working with Frankie and Eva.

"How much money would I need to set up a business?" She blurted out the words, her heart racing.

"You'd have some up-front costs," Jake said. "Mostly legal. I'm willing to pay for that. I believe in you."

Matt rose to his feet and sent Jake an incinerating glare. "Get him a bowl of chips, Ev. Enough to fill his mouth so he can't speak."

"I want him to speak." Paige knew that if she wanted a straight answer, she had to talk to Jake. He didn't protect her the way her brother did. "You really think I could do it?"

"If you adjust your attitude." Jake took a swig of beer. "You're too risk-averse. You cling to control like a climber on a rock face. You want guarantees and you won't find them running your own business. You want safe, and there is no safe. There's risk, a ton of hard work, sometimes for nothing. Businesses fold every day. It's not for the fainthearted."

If she'd been Claws, she would have scratched him. "I'm not afraid to take a risk if it's for something I want badly enough. And there's nothing wrong with my heart. It's as strong as yours." And it was beating hard in her chest, as if to back her up.

Why not?

Why not?

An idea was taking shape in her head and with it came an unexpected rush of excitement. Some of the heaviness that had been there since the meeting with Cynthia lifted. "We should do it. Frankie? Eva?"

Frankie glanced up from her plants. "Do what?"

"Start our own business."

"Are you serious? I assumed you and Jake were having one of your fights."

"I'm serious. We have skills. We're good at what we do."

"Cynthia didn't think so." Eva slumped on the cushion and Paige felt a rush of anger.

"Don't let her do that to you. We're not going to let her knock our confidence."

"All right, but I don't think I can run a business, Paige." Eva looked doubtful. "I can ice the perfect wedding cake and make good pastry. I'm a decent writer and people seem to like my blog, but strategy doesn't interest me and spreadsheets make my head ache."

"I'll do that part. Your natural ability to create delicious food is your special gift. You invent new dishes every day of the week and you're wonderful with people. Customers love you. No one soothes a tense situation better than you do."

Frankie rocked back on her heels and wiped the soil from her fingers. "None of us has any experience running a business."

"I'll learn that part." Her mind was racing. She had contacts; she was capable. She did her job well for other people; why not for herself? "We'd have control. We'd get to decide who we work for. It would be fun."

"It would be risky." Matt's expression was serious. "One of the main reasons companies fail is because they don't think about their customer or their competition. The city is full of event planners."

"So we need to be different. Better. Clients like the personal touch. If you're super wealthy, you expect good service. Star Events operated within rigid lines, but what if we don't? What if, as well as organizing your event, we're happy to handle all the little things that are clogging up your day? Cynthia moaned, but customers loved the fact that we always went that extra mile. We don't only organize their event, we're there for everything, from dry-cleaning your silk tie to cat sitting."

Eva eyed Claws. "I don't have a talent for cat sitting. And how are we going to offer all that when there are only three of us?"

"We can outsource. Have preferred vendors. We're not trying to fund a huge bloated company with staff like Cynthia, who take a salary but do nothing to bring in business. We'll keep it lean. We're not the only ones who lost our jobs. There are plenty of people who would be happy to freelance for us." Her mind was racing, leaping over hurdles and looking for possibilities and solutions. "Look at this another way. What do we have? What are we good at? We're organized and we have great contacts. We know every hot venue in town—clubs, bars, restaurants. We know how to get the best tickets for the best events. We know how to manage things when everything goes wrong. We're brilliant at multitasking and we're friendly and hardworking. What is the one thing most people in Manhattan don't have?"

Eva reached for her sweater. "You mean apart from a sex life?"

Jake smiled. "Speak for yourself."

Paige ignored him. "Time. They don't have time. People have too much to do and no time to do it in and the stress of it stops them from enjoying every part of their life. Everyone wants forty-eight-hour days because twenty-four isn't enough. That's what we're going to fix. We are going to be the people who give them hours back in their day."

Frankie adjusted her glasses. "I can't see corporations employing us. We'd be too small."

"Small can be good. Small makes us nimble and responsive. Doesn't mean we can't be as professional as a large company with offices in Los Angeles."

"It might work." Frankie stood up, for once forgetting the

plants. "How would we build a client base? Advertising would cost a fortune."

"We do what we already do. We go out and find them. Pitch. And then we do a brilliant job with their event, we turn their stressed, manic lives into peaceful order and they tell their friends."

"And if we're successful, our peaceful lives will become stressed and manic." Eva's blue eyes shone, but this time with excitement rather than tears. "I'm in."

"Me, too." Frankie nodded. "I'm sick of working for a bullying boss and having no control. Where do we start? How long until we can bring in some money?"

The question made it all scarily real and doused the excitement like water on flame.

Paige swallowed.

Her insides quailed. The theory was one thing, the practice was another.

What if she couldn't make it work? This time she'd be the one letting her friends down, not Star Events.

"If you're really going to do this," Matt said, "you could start by asking for advice."

Paige shook her head. "Thanks, but I want to do this on my own."

Jake locked his hands behind his head, watching her from under his lashes. "Paige the pigheaded. Do you want to know how many start-ups I've seen fail in the last few years?"

"No. And you were the one who told me to start my own business."

"I didn't tell you to go off like a child in a toy shop with no sense of direction. You need to think about what you're doing. Ask for advice."

"I have a clear sense of direction." How could you find

someone attractive and want to hit them at the same time? "I'll ask the advice of people who understand the business, like Eva and Frankie."

"Yeah, that's smart. Ask your friends. Because they're sure to tell you the truth." Jake drained his beer. "When you're thinking of setting up a business you don't want the opinion of your friends. You want people who are going to tell you what's wrong with your idea so you can fix it. It's going to be a tough grind and you need to be prepared for that. You need to be challenged. If you can defend yourself, then maybe, maybe, your ideas are robust."

Paige felt a rush of frustration. Needing space, she turned and walked to the edge of the terrace, away from them all.

Damn, damn.

Why did she always get emotional around him?

And what if she was being too ambitious thinking that she could start up her own business?

What if she failed?

She heard soft prowling footsteps behind her.

"I'm sorry." Jake's voice was low. He was standing close enough that she could feel the warmth of his breath against her cheek.

Desire shot through her. For a moment she thought he was going to put his arms around her and she closed her eyes, holding her breath.

He was *not* going to touch her.

He never touched her. Not anymore.

It was agonizing to find someone so attractive physically when they didn't feel the same way.

It was rare that they found themselves alone together. Not that they were exactly alone, but for some reason it felt that way as they stood, sheltered by the soft sway of the trees, while conversation drifted on the breeze from the far side of the terrace.

He didn't touch her. Instead, he stood next to her, staring across the water toward Manhattan.

Paige let her breath out slowly. "Tell me what's wrong with my idea. I want to know."

He turned his head to look at her, and the atmosphere on the terrace suddenly felt tight and intimate.

"You need to think hard about your market, your customers and exactly what it is you're offering. Matt's right. Your customers are the most important thing. More important than how you structure the company, than what your website looks like, whether you have a video of flying pigs on your splash page. Ask yourself what your customers need, and then ask yourself why they're going to come to you. If you make your offering too broad, people won't automatically think of you. Too niche and you could find yourself without business. What value are you going to place on your service?"

She found it hard to focus on business while the velvet stroke of his voice was teasing her senses.

"We can't afford to narrow what we offer. We'll take whatever business we can get."

"Don't undersell yourself. You'll be brilliant, Paige." His words drove the breath from her lungs.

"From insults to compliments. You're giving me whiplash."

"It's the truth. You're a born organizer. Your attention to detail borders on the aggravating."

She almost smiled. "Maybe you should be quiet now, before you spoil it."

His soft laugh broke the simmering silence. "Paige, you have a checklist for movie night so that we don't forget anything, even though forgetting something simply means walking down a couple of flights of stairs. You remember everyone's birthdays and have a record of every gift you've sent every person you know since time immemorial. You probably have notes on what you cooked someone for dinner two years ago."

"I do." She frowned. "What's wrong with that? Some people have food allergies. I like to make a note."

"That's my point. You take notes on everything. You miss nothing. You will be so good at this job your competition will give up and cry. I almost feel sorry for them."

"You do?"

"Yeah, but that doesn't mean I'm not going to enjoy watching you kick their butts."

"There's a lot that could go wrong."

"And plenty that can go right."

Because her knees were unsteady, she gripped the railing in front of her, fixing her gaze on the shimmering lights of Manhattan. From here it looked glamorous and tempting, a world of opportunity. "I don't know if I'm brave enough to do it." The confession spilled from her and she felt Jake's fingers slide over hers, the pressure of his hand sure and strong.

"You're the bravest person I have ever met."

His touch was so surprising that she almost snatched her hand away. Instead, she stood, her hand trapped by his just as her heart had been trapped all those years before.

"I'm not brave." She turned to look at him. He was standing closer to her than she'd thought, his face right there, angled toward hers with attentive concern.

The urge to lift herself on her toes and press her mouth to the sensual curve of his was almost overwhelming, but she stayed still, her willpower sufficiently robust to stop her moving forward but not robust enough to make her step back.

Laughter drifted across from the far end of the terrace but neither of them turned.

Slowly, he disentangled his fingers from hers, but instead of putting distance between them he lifted his hand and brushed her cheek.

She stayed still, her gaze trapped by the molten shimmer in his. She couldn't have looked away if her life had depended on it.

Usually he teased her, goaded her, drove her insane.

It was as if he'd tried to give her a thousand reasons to fall out of love with him.

This tenderness was something she hadn't seen in him since she was a teenager, and seeing it now caused a sharp pang of pain.

She'd missed this. She'd missed this easy relationship, his wisdom and his kindness.

She swallowed. "When you have no choice, it isn't brave."

"Of course it is." His mouth tilted in a half smile and she felt a twinge of envy for all the women he'd kissed.

Unfortunately she wasn't one of them.

And she never would be.

Unsettled, frustrated with herself for spinning fantasies when reality was right in her face, she turned away. "Thanks for the advice."

"I'll give you one more piece." He didn't try and touch her again, but his voice held her captive. "Weigh up the pros and cons, but don't overthink this. If you focus on the risks, you'd never do anything."

"I feel as if I've lost my security."

"Your security wasn't the job, Paige. Jobs come and go. You give yourself security, with your skills and your talent. You can take those elsewhere. What you did for Star Events, you can do for another company, including your own company."

His words gave her a burst of much-needed confidence.

And they made sense to her.

She felt like a wilting plant that had suddenly been given a large drink of water.

"Thank you." Her voice was croaky and he gave a smile.

"When you find yourself working eighteen-hour days for seven days a week you might not want to thank me." Jake strolled off to rejoin the others but Paige stayed where she was for a moment, thinking about what he'd said.

You give yourself security.

Eva and Frankie were laughing at something Matt had said and it was so good to hear them laughing that her own spirits lifted.

She walked back to them. "What's funny?"

"We've been thinking up company names."

"And?" She could still feel Jake's touch on her hand, and she wondered how the casual brush of his fingers was enough to send a thousand electrical currents soaring through her body.

"We're trying to sound bigger and better than Star Events." Eva grinned. "Global Events. Planet Events. Universe Events."

"We're not only an events company." Paige settled herself on the arm of Eva's chair, careful not to look at Jake. "We're more personal. And we need to differentiate ourselves from the competition."

"We're going to be a happy company. That makes us different," Eva said.

"It's lifestyle as well as events. While you're busy working we can choose the perfect gift for your wife, or arrange flowers for your mother-in-law."

"Or we could poison your mother-in-law," Eva said happily. "Belladonna muffins."

Frankie ignored her. "It sounds as if we're offering a concierge service."

Paige thought about it. "That's it. That's what we are. An event concierge service. We don't just organize your event, we do all the extras. If you're our client, we take care of all the little things you never have time to do."

Eva snuggled back against the cushions. "So all we need now is the name and an office."

"We need clients more than we need an office. We can work from the kitchen table to begin with. We'll be out and about most of the day anyway. Or on the phone."

Frankie frowned. "Where do we start? I'm a floral designer. A gardener. I can arrange flowers for your birthday party or your wedding, and I can do a design for your roof garden, but don't ask me to cold-call clients. I can't sell myself."

"But I can." Paige reached for her bag and pulled out her phone. Jake was right. Organization was what she did best. The excitement was back, and this time so was the confidence. "That's the point of our company. I can't do the flowers for your engagement party, but I know someone who can. That's you by the way." She glanced at Frankie. "And cooking isn't my thing, but when Eva and her team cater your work party it will be something people talk about for months."

Eva looked mystified. "I have a team?"

"You will have."

"Outsourced," Matt advised. "Don't inflate your payroll."

Frankie gave a crooked smile. "And don't make anyone kale and spinach smoothies."

"She does that?" Jake winced. "If a woman ever made me that, our relationship would be over."

"It's breakfast," Eva said cheerfully. "Your relationships never last until breakfast, so you're safe."

"Breakfast is the most serious meal of the day and the word *serious* doesn't appear in my vocabulary."

A statement Paige knew to be untrue. She knew that Jake advised on cyber security at the highest level. Her brother had once told her Jake was the smartest guy he'd ever met. It was only in his relationships that the word *serious* didn't appear.

And she knew why.

He'd talked to her about it, before she'd created a rift between them.

"This is exciting." Eva gave Frankie a light punch on the shoulder. "I'm going into business with my two best friends. Maybe you could give me a fancy title. That would make my day. How does Vice President sound?"

Paige felt a flicker of tension. Being responsible for herself was one thing, but being responsible for both her friends was something else entirely. Jake, she knew, employed hundreds of people in several cities across the globe.

How did he sleep at night?

How did Matt sleep at night?

Paige glanced at her brother and he gave a faint smile of understanding.

"Ready to ask me for help yet? You might find I know a thing or two if you ask me. And Jake deals with start-ups all the time. He gives advice and he invests. We both have contacts. We can talk to a few companies—get you introductions."

Paige didn't want to ask Jake for help.

Even that brief conversation had left her feeling unsettled. Asking for help would mean getting close to him, spending more time with him. There was no way she was up to that.

"You've helped me enough. I want to do this on my own. I can do this, Matt. You've been bailing me out of trouble since I was four years old. It's time I did something on my own."

"You do plenty on your own." He sighed. "At least let me help with the legal side. Company setup, tax, insurance—as Jake said, there's a lot to think about."

It made sense. "All right. Thank you."

Matt stood up. "I'll call my lawyers in the morning. You need a business plan—"

"I'll work on it tonight and tomorrow."

"Talk it through with me. And we need to talk about funding."

"Matt, you're smothering me."

Her brother gave her a long look. "I'm offering you business advice and financial backing, and before you turn it down you should probably check with your business partners."

"I want you to help and advise," Eva said immediately, "especially if you're not going to charge. I'll cook for you in return. In fact I'll do anything except look after your psychotic cat."

"I'll look after the cat," Frankie muttered. "She's suspicious of humans and I get that. If you'll help, I'll care for the roof garden all summer."

"You already do that for me. And you do a great job. I'd employ you in a heartbeat."

Paige glanced up from the list she was typing on her phone. "You're poaching my team before we're even officially a business?"

"All the more reason to use me in an advisory capacity. I'm less likely to steal your staff."

"Fine! You win. You can advise. But no hovering over me. I want to do this myself. If this is a success I want it to be because of me."

"But if we fail, then we could blame him." Eva's cheeks

dimpled. "I'd be happy to bask in success but losing my job twice in one week would dent my confidence horribly."

Paige heard the uncertainty in Eva's voice and a blaze of determination shot through her. She'd do this right. Whatever it took, she'd do it.

"We still need a company name, and we need it to say what we do."

"We do a bit of everything from the sounds of it," Eva said. "Whatever you want—your wish is our command." She said it with a dramatic flourish and Paige put her phone down.

"That's it."

"What is?"

"It's brilliant. *Your wish is our command.* That's our tagline. Or our mission statement or whatever it's called."

"You'll have people phoning you for sex," Jake drawled, reaching for another beer.

The flickering candles sent a golden glow across his lean dark features. Watching him woke up parts of her she would have rather stayed asleep.

She was almost relieved that he'd returned to being annoying. "Do you have anything helpful to contribute?"

"Unless you want men phoning you with indecent requests, that observation was helpful."

"Not everyone thinks about sex all the time. We need a company name that goes with that. Genie Incorporated? Genie Girls?" She pulled a face and shook her head. "No."

"Clever Genie." Frankie deadheaded a rose.

Matt stirred. "City Genie?"

"Urban Genie." It was Jake who spoke, his voice low and sexy in the darkness. "And anytime you three want to rub my lamp, go right ahead."

Paige turned toward him, a sharp rejection on her lips, and then she stopped.

Urban Genie.

It was perfect.

"I love it."

"I love it, too." Frankie nodded and so did Eva.

"Paige Walker, CEO of Urban Genie. You're in the driving seat, heading down the freeway to fortune. I'm happy to be your passenger." Eva raised her glass and frowned. "My glass is half-full."

Frankie grinned. "I would have said the glass was half-empty. I guess that says a lot about the difference between us."

"We each bring our different strengths to the business and there are no passengers." Paige reached for the champagne bottle and topped up Eva's glass. "You're driving, too."

"Hey, I can change a wheel but I'm not driving the car." Frankie brushed soil from her sweatpants. "That's your job."

Their faith in her was as scary as it was heartwarming.

"Three women drivers," Jake drawled, glancing at Matt. "Better start taking the subway."

Paige knew he was winding her up but this time she didn't care.

Anticipation and excitement rushed through her. She was starting her own business. Right now. And with her closest friends.

What could be better?

"Urban Genie. We're in business." She raised her glass. "Eva, go and rescue your lucky shirt. We're going to need it."

Four

There's no such thing as a free lunch, unless your best friend is a cook.

—Frankie

"Wake up." Paige put a cup of coffee down by Eva's bed but her friend didn't stir. "I'm going for a run, and when I get back you need to be awake and ready to go."

There was a sound from under the covers. "Gowhere?"

"To work. Today is our first day as Urban Genie. We're going to make it a good one."

Paige's head throbbed. She'd been up half the night making lists and notes. And trying not to second-guess her decision.

What had she done?

Would they all be better off looking for jobs?

"What time is it?"

"Six-thirty."

The lump in the bed moved and Eva emerged, hair wild, eyes sleepy. "Seriously? This is what time our day starts at Urban Genie? I resign."

Sun shone through the windows, illuminating the high ceilings and hardwood floors. Eva's clothes were strewn around the room, in rainbow colors and assorted textures. A pair of gold flats peeped from under the bed and three bottles of jewel-bright nail polish sat on the bedside table next to a book on how to look fabulous on a budget.

Despite her state of anxiety, Paige smiled. Eva always looked fabulous.

When she'd first arrived in New York, she'd been the only one living with Matt. Eva had been sharing an apartment with her grandmother until she'd moved into sheltered living and the apartment had been sold to fund her care. Eva had been homeless and Paige had asked Matt if she could have a roommate. He hadn't hesitated. Frankie had joined them a month later.

They were three small-town girls, living in the big city, and soon they were as close as they'd been growing up.

Living with her friends had proved surprisingly easy given their differences, one of the biggest of which was the hours they kept.

Eva was a sloth in the mornings.

"Get up." Paige gave her friend a nudge. "I want you to design a personalized menu for Baxter and Baxter. I'm calling them later."

"The ad agency? Star Events pitched for that account."

"And lost because they weren't original enough. This is a young, dynamic agency. We need to be equally dynamic. And original."

"I don't feel dynamic." Eva pulled the pillow over her head. "And I can't be original at six-thirty in the morning. Go away."

"You have until seven-thirty to shower and be ready in the kitchen with menus." Paige pulled her hair into a ponytail and glanced at her reflection in the mirror on Eva's wall.

That brief glance told her that all the panic she felt was safely concealed inside.

Her hair was smooth and straight. Even New York humidity couldn't put a kink in it.

Eva gave a grunt. "You're a tyrant. It wouldn't kill you to have a day off exercise. You're already in great shape."

"I won't be in great shape for long if I don't run. It's my stress reliever." And physical fitness was important to her. Her body had let her down once through no fault of her own. She did what she could to make sure it didn't let her down again. "Could you fix breakfast? We can eat while we work."

"I'm reporting you to human resources." Eva yawned, emerging from under the pillow. "We do have a human resources department, right?"

"I'm it, and your complaint is duly noted. Anything you want me to pick up? I could call in at Petit Pain. Walnut bread? Sourdough loaf? Bagel?" Petit Pain was one of their favorite local bakeries, run by a man who had started baking when his wife had died. He'd discovered a new passion and his business had grown, supported by the local community.

Eva sat up and rubbed her eyes. "We can't afford it. I'll make breakfast from scratch. Frankie needs to eat something that isn't full of additives. She barely ate at all yesterday. It was that text from her mother that started it."

"Yeah, well, knowing your parents have sex is weird for anyone, but when your mother is sleeping with men the same age as you and bragging about it, it's so far away from weird there is no word for it. It's no wonder poor Frankie is damaged." Paige watched as Eva scooped her mass of sunny hair away from her face. "How come you look so good when you've just emerged from under the pillows?"

"My hair looks like a bird's nest."

"But it's a cute bird's nest. So you don't want anything?"

"Berries?"

"Berries aren't comfort food."

"They are to me. And anyway, we don't need comfort, we need health. If we're going to be working hard and subjecting ourselves to bucket loads of stress, we need to strengthen ourselves nutritionally."

"Berries." Paige made a mental note. "And more coffee."

"Coffee is bad for you."

"Coffee is my life force. Do *not* go back to sleep." She ripped the cover off her friend. "Get up. We have things to do, places to be, people to please and fortunes to make. If we're going to make a success of this, which we are, we're going to need to work hard. No part-timers."

Eva grunted. "You sound uncannily like Cynthia." But she slid her legs out of bed. "What were you and Jake talking about on the terrace last night? You two looked cozy."

"He was apologizing for being an idiot." Familiar with Eva's ability to find romance in any situation, Paige jogged quickly to the door. "Don't you dare go back to sleep. I'll see you in an hour." Relieved to have escaped the inquisition, she ran down the stairs and knocked on the door of the ground-floor apartment.

At least Frankie wouldn't ask the same question. Frankie didn't see romance even if a couple were tongue wrestling in front of her.

Her friend answered the door in a pair of pajamas. She was holding a small basil plant in her hand and it was obvious from the dark smudges under her eyes that she hadn't slept much, either.

Paige wondered if there had been more texts or phone calls from her mother.

"I'm going for a run. Do you want to join me?"

"Dressed like this? I don't think so."

"We live in Brooklyn. It's acceptable to be different."

"I'm the responsible one in the family, remember? And anyway, I want to finish my model."

Paige glanced over her shoulder and saw the half-built LEGO model on the table. "Is that the Empire State Building?"

"Yeah. Matt gave it to me for Christmas. I was waiting for a stressful moment to build it."

"I guess yesterday qualified." Paige looked at the detail, marveling at Frankie's dexterity. "Was it the job or your mom that made you open it?"

"Both." Frankie rubbed her fingers over her forehead. "Look—you don't have to worry. I'm dealing with some stuff and—it doesn't matter. Building the model works for me. I'll meet you when you're back. I need to tend to my *Ocimum basilicum.*"

"Your—? Oh, you mean your basil plant. You could just call it a basil plant. On the other hand that would be a waste of your fancy training." She smoothed down her ponytail. "Right, well I'll leave you and your *Ocimum basilicum* in peace and I'll see you for a breakfast meeting in the Urban Genie offices at seven-thirty."

Frankie blinked. "We have offices?"

"Your kitchen is our office until we can afford something more official. Ours is a little bigger but your doors open onto the garden and it's lovely in the summer. And your kitchen table isn't covered in Eva's cookery experiments. Don't prepare anything. Eva is in charge of catering."

"As long as she doesn't expect me to drink a kale and spinach smoothie. It's not often I agree with Jake, but on that we are in total accord."

Wishing Jake's name wouldn't keep coming up in conversation, Paige jogged down the steps to the street.

It was her favorite time of year, when spring nudged the edges of summer and the cherry blossoms and magnolia burst into bloom. They filled the air with scent and color as if the city was celebrating its release from the deep layers of snow that had buried its charms over the long winter months.

In the winter and the height of summer she took spin classes indoors, but right now there was no better way to enjoy the weather and her neighborhood than running.

She loved the wide streets and the symmetry of the historic brownstones shaded by cherry trees. It was quintessential laid-back Brooklyn. Some people chose to live here because they couldn't afford Manhattan. She lived here because she loved it—the smells, the vibe, the rhythm of the neighborhood. Although it was early, the streets were already alive with activity, and she watched people going about their lives as she ran to the park, feeling the sun warm her neck, breathing in spring air scented with blossom and baking.

The panic of the previous day had eased, along with those unsettling feelings that being with Jake had unleashed.

Today would be all about planning. She'd already had ideas and her light had been on most of the night as she'd made notes.

Like Jake, she loved technology. It satisfied her need for organization and allowed her to track projects and maximize efficiency. Maybe she didn't understand the detail in the way he did, but that didn't mean she didn't enjoy using the results of other people's creativity.

She tried telling herself that the reason she hadn't slept much the night before was all down to nerves, excitement and the use of her mobile devices late into the night. Everyone knew that using screens at night was bad, didn't they?

Her sleepless night had nothing to do with Jake Romano.

Except—

She ran into the park and picked up her pace.

Being evasive with romantic Eva was one thing, but what was the point in lying to herself? Better to admit that she was in trouble. At least that way she would be on her guard. And although she hadn't wanted to be flattered, his attention had felt nice. He'd boosted her confidence when it had reached the point of collapse. He'd pushed her when she'd wanted to hide and play it safe.

She was accustomed to Jake saying the wrong things. There were days when she was convinced he chose his words with the intention of annoying her, but last night he'd said all the right things. He'd made her feel as if she could do this. He'd given her assurance when she'd needed it most. He'd made her feel—he'd made her feel—

Crap.

She stopped running and bent over to catch her breath, frustrated that he could still make her feel this way.

She'd been seventeen when she'd first laid eyes on him. Because her condition had required specialist care beyond the capabilities of her local hospital, she'd had surgery in a hospital in New York, which meant Matt had been able to visit her.

The first time he'd brought his friend Jake with him, she'd thought she was hallucinating.

It was lucky she hadn't been rigged up to a heart monitor at the time or she was pretty sure she would have had every doctor in the building running to help with the emergency.

From that moment, everything changed. It was as if someone had flicked a switch and changed her life from black and white to color.

People commented on how brave she was, and how well she coped with the boredom of being in hospital.

What they didn't know was that she'd spent almost every hour thinking about Jake.

Eyes closed or open, he was always in her head.

She'd lived for his visits, even though she was rarely alone with him. When her dad's commitments to his law practice in Portland, Maine had prevented him from being by her bedside, her mother had been there, and if neither of them could make it, then Matt was there. Their cumulative anxiety levels had filtered through to her.

Jake was different.

He'd entertained her with outrageous stories, and on the nights when Matt had been studying for exams, it had been Jake who had stayed late, keeping her company.

Paige had fallen in love.

First love.

Everyone said you got over it and they were right.

For her, humiliation had proved to be a magical cure.

Unfortunately sexual attraction hadn't proved so easily destructible.

Most days it was easy to ignore because Jake was as irritating as he was attractive. But last night—

Last night had been an aberration. A response to the fact she'd lost her job.

Pushing him out of her mind, she took a shortcut that led through the trees back to the street.

Early-morning sun was the best, she thought. Bright and mood lifting, and after the long bitter chill of winter it was blissful to be outdoors.

She passed people she knew and exchanged a smile and a few words.

New York was a city of neighborhoods, and the neighborhood where they lived felt like a village. Wide, leafy streets were lined with historic brownstones and row houses, bustling cafés, family-owned stores brimming with fresh produce, flower and craft shops. Families had lived in the area for generations.

In the evenings the air was filled with the sounds of children playing and crickets chirping, the smooth notes of someone practicing the saxophone against an accompaniment of honking horns and the occasional shriek of a siren.

She loved the fact that within minutes of walking out of her door she could take a spin class, buy a slice of cheesecake, have a haircut or join a yoga session in the park. She could buy everything from fried chicken to organic smoothies.

Within two blocks of their brownstone there was a thriving independent bookstore, an art gallery and Petit Pain, the bakery that doubled as a coffee shop. And, of course, there was Romano's, the local Italian restaurant owned by Jake's mother. In the summer their tables spilled into the street, a web of vines shading the eating area from the bright evening sun.

Frankie believed they made the best pizza anywhere in New York City, and given that she'd eaten pizza on almost every street at one point or another, no one argued with her.

This early the tables were empty but already the scent of garlic and oregano wafted through the air.

The door to the kitchen was open and Paige ducked through it. As expected, Maria Romano was already at work making pasta.

"Buongiorno." That was one of the few words of Italian Paige admitted to knowing. The others were her secret, part of a time when she'd deluded herself into thinking something might happen between her and Jake.

"Paige!"

Instantly she was embraced by flour and affection. "Am I disturbing you?"

"Never. How are you?"

Paige took a deep breath. She'd fallen in love with Maria Romano from the first moment Jake and Matt had introduced her. It had been during her first week in college, when being in New York had felt like landing on an alien planet.

"I didn't get the promotion. I lost my job."

Maria released her. "Jake told me. He called by last night. I have been worried about you. Sit down. Have you eaten?"

"I'm having breakfast with Frankie and Eva. We have things to talk about. But coffee would be good." It didn't surprise her that Jake had called by. He was fiercely protective of Maria, who had taken him in when he was six and later adopted him. It was Jake who had bought the restaurant and provided his mother, her brother and several cousins with employment and accommodation.

Five minutes later Paige was sitting with a cup of perfect espresso in front of her telling Jake's mother everything from her meeting with Cynthia through to an edited version of the conversation on the roof terrace.

She wasn't sure exactly when she'd started to confide in Maria. It had happened gradually after she'd moved in with Matt in her first year of college.

Too busy to cook, he'd taken her to Romano's to make sure she had a decent meal once in a while. Friday evenings in Romano's had become as much of a routine as their Saturday movie nights, and those evenings spent with her friends, against the backdrop of sounds and smells from the restaurant, were often the best part of the week for Paige. She loved the warm family environment, the laughter, the controlled chaos.

Maria was caring, without being smothering. Somehow it was easier to talk to her than it was her own mother, simply because she didn't feel the pressure of someone trying to protect her.

"So you're setting up business on your own." Maria sat down opposite her. "And you're feeling scared and wondering if you've done the right thing."

Paige's stomach rolled. She was glad she'd refused breakfast. "I'm excited."

Maria picked up her own coffee. "You don't have to keep up a brave face with me."

Paige gave up trying. "It's scary. I didn't sleep at all last night. I kept thinking about all the things that could go wrong. Tell me I'm being pathetic."

"Why would I tell you that? You're being honest. Feeling scared is natural. It doesn't mean you've made the wrong decision."

"Are you sure? I'm worried I'm being selfish, that I'm doing this for me. I spent my whole childhood with other people in control of what happened to me, and I want to feel as if I have some of the control now. Even if that means failing. But if I fail, I take my friends down with me."

"Why would you fail?"

"Jake will tell you how many businesses fail."

Maria sipped her coffee. "So it's my boy who has been scaring you?"

Boy?

Paige pushed aside a vision of strong shoulders and hard muscle. "He laid out the facts. The facts were pretty scary."

"Don't let that put you off. If anyone can help and advise you, he can. It's because of him that I have this place. He bought it, then he taught me how to run it and spent time with Carlo showing him how to do the financials." Maria put her cup down. "Talk to Jake. You've been friends a long time. You know he would help you if you were in trouble."

Paige knew she'd have to be desperate before she'd ask Jake for more help, but she couldn't explain why to Maria. "I'm not in trouble. I *am* worried about what happens if this doesn't work out. Eva needs the money badly and so does Frankie." It was the thing that bothered her the most. "What if I let them down? It isn't just about me. I'm asking them to take a risk."

"You're asking them to take a chance. Life is all about taking chances."

"But this was my decision. My dream. I swept them along with me." And it was the thought of what would happen if it didn't work out that had kept her awake for most of the night. "Frankie is brilliant with flowers and gardens and Eva is a fabulous cook, but in the end I'm the one who has to bring in the business. It's all down to me. What if I can't do it? What if I'm being selfish?"

Maria fiddled with her empty cup. "The night before I opened the restaurant I didn't sleep at all. I thought to myself, 'what if no one comes.' It was Jake who told me that my job wasn't to worry about people coming, but to concentrate on doing what I do well. Making great food in great surroundings. And he was right. You know you're good at your job, Paige. Do it well, and people will eventually come to you."

"It feels like a big risk."

"There's always risk in life." Maria reached across the table and took her hand. "When my grandparents came here from Sicily in 1915 they had nothing. They had to pay back the cost of their passage and for years they lived in poverty, but they chose to come because they believed they could have a better life."

"Now I'm feeling guilty for moaning."

"You're not moaning. You're worried. And that's natural, but life doesn't stand still." Maria squeezed her hand. "There is always change. Some people try and avoid it, but it finds them anyway. My grandparents wanted this even though they knew it wouldn't be easy. For years we struggled. I never dreamed I would have my own restaurant with my family. We had nothing and now we have—" she glanced around the restaurant "—everything. Because of my Jake and his ambitions. Do you know how many people laughed at him when he knocked on their doors? So many. But he kept knocking, and now they are the ones knocking on his. So don't ever tell me a dream can't come true."

"But Jake is brilliant with computers. He has a real talent. What do I do? I organize things for people." Paige finished her coffee, questioning the decision she'd made. "A million people can do what I do but hardly anyone does what Jake can do. That's why they knock on his door."

"Plenty of people can cook, but still my restaurant is full every night. You underestimate yourself. You have a way with people, an eye for detail and good organizational skills. And you have passion and determination. You're a hard worker."

Was it enough? Would that be enough?

"Losing my job has knocked my confidence but confidence is exactly what I need if I'm going to persuade people to give business to Urban Genie." Paige stared into her cup. "How do you act confident when you don't feel it?"

"You pretend. You pretend all the time, Paige." Maria's voice was quiet and Paige shifted awkwardly.

"Some of the time. And rarely with you." She was honest with Maria on every topic except one. Maria had no idea how Paige had once felt about her son.

"Carry on doing that and then one day you'll wake up and realize you're not pretending anymore. That it's real."

"I hope you're right." Paige glanced at her phone and stood up. "I should go. I'm meeting Frankie and Eva at seven-thirty. And I'm supposed to pick up fresh berries. Thanks for the coffee and comfort."

"Come in one morning and have your breakfast meeting here. I'll give you granita and brioche. I can't help with your business but I can feed you, Sicilian style. And remember that even if a road is hard and bumpy, it doesn't mean you should stop walking it."

"I should embroider that on a throw pillow." She kissed Maria on the cheek and carried on along the street, picking up berries and fresh plums from the fruit vendor and a bag of freshly ground coffee from her favorite coffee shop.

Eva was already in Frankie's kitchen, her hair piled on top of her head in haphazard waves that would have looked messy on anyone else, but on Eva looked perfect. Her lower lip was trapped between her teeth as she sprinkled cinnamon onto oatmeal. "You bought berries?" She added a golden swirl of maple syrup. "Put them on the table. And if you're taking a shower, don't be long because this is almost ready. Frankie is getting dressed. She had another text." She lowered her voice, but Paige didn't have a chance to ask more because the door opened and Jake appeared, his shoulders almost filling the doorway.

She hadn't expected to see him again so soon.

He lived in fashionable Tribeca, in a converted loft that Eva always joked had a view as far as Florida on a clear day.

He yawned, and Paige saw that under those thick lashes his gray eyes were tired. His jaw was shadowed and it was obvious that whatever he'd done the night before hadn't involved much sleeping.

Tucked under his arm was a black motorcycle helmet. Not for Jake the breath-stealing crush of public transport. When he made the trip over from Manhattan to Brooklyn, he rode his bike.

Looking at him, no one would have guessed he owned a successful global business. Right now he could have strolled into the more dangerous parts of Brooklyn and fitted right in.

"Happy first day at work." Despite the lack of sleep, he looked sleek, male and too handsome for his own good.

She, on the other hand, had sweaty hair and sweaty skin and wasn't wearing a scrap of makeup.

Great.

Why couldn't he have showed up ten minutes later, *after* she'd taken a shower and maybe after she'd applied a slick of lipstick?

Not that it would have made a difference. It didn't matter how many showers she took, or which lipstick she chose, Jake wasn't interested.

And why would he be? There was a waiting list of women wanting to date Jake Romano.

To him she was still that pale, skinny teenager who'd embarrassed herself and him. She'd decided to live in the moment, and she'd picked her moment badly. She'd often wondered what would have happened if she'd made a move on him a few years later.

Would he have seen her as an adult then, old enough to play grown-up games?

"What are you doing here?" It took all her willpower not to smooth her hair.

"I had some business to discuss with my uncle. Thought I'd drop by and wish you all luck."

With none of Paige's reticence, Eva stood on tiptoe and kissed Jake on the cheek. "You're the best, even if you are badly in need of a shave. Did you eat breakfast? Because I can fix you something."

Paige gritted her teeth. Having him around made her jumpy.

"I had breakfast. My kind of breakfast." Jake winked at Eva and she gave him a delighted smile.

"Don't tell me. You had a naked blonde."

"Don't wind her up or she'll be booking the Plaza for your June wedding," Paige said. "He means that he drank nothing but espresso shots. That's his kind of breakfast."

"Did someone say *naked blonde*?" Matt walked in behind Jake, a tie draped around his neck and a stack of papers in his hands. "Don't pick up your phone this morning, Paige. Mom already called four times. She and Dad heard the news about Star Events."

"How? I thought they were in Venice." Their parents, after years of barely leaving home, had finally embarked on a tour of Europe. Matt and Paige had both been receiving regular updates.

"They are. You know Dad. He can't not stay up-to-date with the business news."

"So they called to check up on me?" Her heart sank. "What did you say?"

"That you'd already found yourself another job and were doing fine." He dumped the papers on the table. "Don't spill anything on those, they're important."

"You told them I had another job?"

"Yes, and they asked for the name of the company so that they could check it out."

Paige cringed. "So you caved and told them the truth?"

"Hey, do I look like a wimp?" Matt leaned across and stole some berries from the bowl Eva had placed on the table. "I've been handling them as long as you have. Longer, in fact, although things didn't get complicated until you came along with your dodgy heart and blue lips. Attention seeking, I call it."

"You think I dug a hole in my own heart?"

"Having seen the mess you made with your food when you were two, I wouldn't put it past you. You were probably aiming for a chicken nugget and missed." He always made her laugh.

"So you told them your life was too busy to be able to keep track of mine?"

"No. That would have brought them running home, and then I would have got it in the neck for not taking better care of you." He ate the berries. "I told them you were excited about your new job—which is true—relieved to be away from Sociopathic Cynthia—also true—and then I gave them the highlight reel of my life and encouraged her to tell me about the frescos."

Paige knew her mother would have talked for hours about frescoes.

"Thank you. I *will* tell them, but better to do it when things are up and running. I don't want to worry Mom."

"Agreed. And you don't want her taking the first flight from Italy to come and see if her baby girl is all right."

"I hate to say this, but you're the best brother any girl ever had. Superbro."

"I know. And for that reason alone you can feed me."

"I'll feed you," Eva said. "Sit down, Superbro. You're always welcome at my table, providing you promise never to show up wearing lycra."

"No chance. But I can't sit down. This is a walk-through breakfast."

"A walk-through?"

"Yeah, I walk through and you hand me something. Preferably something with bacon in it." He tied his tie, flicking one end over the other, and Jake watched, incredulous.

"What is the *purpose* of a tie?"

"It fools a certain type of client into thinking I know what I'm talking about. Paige, I've set up a meeting with my lawyer at 4:00 p.m. His offices, downtown. All three of you will need to be there. Don't be late because the amount he charges makes Jake look cheap. After him, we're seeing the accountant." His phone beeped and Matt glanced down and read a text.

Paige reached for her phone. "I could have set those meetings up myself."

"I had to speak to the lawyer anyway. Economy of time and effort." Matt scrolled through his emails. "He'll go through the business with you. You need to get that part right."

"So we have to trek into Manhattan?"

Jake glanced at her. "I can give you a ride on the bike if you like."

"Yes!" Paige didn't hesitate. "I've always wanted to go on your bike!"

"No." Matt glanced up, his expression stony. "You are not taking my sister on the back of that damn machine."

Paige opened her mouth but Jake spoke first, his tone mild.

"That 'damn machine' is a top-of-the-range piece of artistry. Its engine is—"

"Its engine is precisely why my sister isn't going on the back of it."

Jake raised his eyebrows. "I have a spare helmet. I've given women rides before. They're still alive."

"They're not my sister. Are we doing movie night on Saturday?"

Exasperated, Paige glared at him. "Matt—"

"Of course we're doing movie night," Eva interrupted, soothing the choppy atmosphere. "Can we watch something romantic for a change?"

"I was thinking horror." Matt typed a reply to one of his emails. "*Silence of the Lambs*, or maybe some Stephen King—"

"No way!" Eva recoiled. "I *hate* horror. Unless you want to wake up and find me shivering in your bed because I'm too scared to sleep alone, you'd better pick something else. No serial killers. No dead children. Those are my rules. Can we watch *Sleepless in Seattle*?"

"Not unless the reason they're sleepless is because there's a serial killer on the loose." Matt's phone rang. "I need to take this." He strolled away to answer it, leaving Paige simmering.

"What is wrong with him?" She turned to Jake. "I'll take that offer of a ride."

Jake gave a faint smile. "No way. If the two of you are going to fight, that's great. Always invigorating for the rest of us, but don't put me in the middle of it."

Making a mental note to take it up with Matt later, Paige opened her laptop. "The event part of our business is straightforward, but on top of that I've written down everything a corporate concierge should do." While Matt was occupied on his call, she showed Eva. "Anything I've missed?"

Jake glanced over her shoulder. "I don't see sex anywhere on that list."

"You're not funny. I've made a list of companies whose executives are all cash-rich and time-poor."

Eva poured coffee into mugs. "But why would they use *us*?"

"Because we're going to make their employees more productive. And their lives so much easier they're going to wonder how they ever survived without us. I did some research online last night—do you know how many working hours are lost because employees are sorting out their personal lives at work?"

"Mine don't." Jake accepted a cup of coffee from Eva.

"I bet they do. You don't know about it because you're the boss. The moment you walk into the room they minimize the screen."

"You're suggesting I'm not in touch with what's going on in my own company?"

"I'm suggesting that most people are now working such long hours and their work/life balance is so totally skewed that they're forced to sort out personal issues while at work. We can help with that."

"Work/life balance? What the hell is that? I need to go," Matt said as he hung up the phone, straightened his tie and checked his reflection in the gleaming surface of the microwave oven. "I'll see you later." He paused as Frankie walked through the door. She was wearing cargos and a clean T-shirt, her hair a tumbled mass of fiery curls over her shoulders.

Paige saw her brother's eyes linger on Frankie's hair. Then he scanned her face, taking in her taut expression.

"Everything all right?" He spoke quietly and Frankie said something that Paige couldn't hear, but she saw her brother nod and move away without pushing the subject further.

Her brother, Paige knew, had a seriously low opinion of Frankie's mother.

On the few occasions she'd come to see Frankie in the apartment, Matt had made it his business to be there. Frankie would probably rather have endured the humiliation of those moments in private, but knowing how it affected her, her friends tried to be present whenever Gina Cole made one of her impromptu "parent" visits.

Paige was touched that Matt insisted on being there to support Frankie. She'd even occasionally wondered if there was more to the gesture than another example of her brother's protective nature, but that thought hadn't lasted long.

Matt needed, and expected, trust in a relationship.

Frankie trusted no one. She was the first to admit she was so twisted when it came to relationships she could have been used as a corkscrew.

"Are you sure you won't stay, Matt?" Eva gestured to the table. "I declare this breakfast meeting in session. Anyone still in this kitchen in two minutes will be eating my oatmeal."

Matt and Jake bumped into each other in their attempt to make a quick exit.

"Why arc men so averse to healthy eating?" Offended, Eva spooned creamy oatmeal into bowls and added almonds and berries.

"Probably because diet cola tastes better." Frankie sat down and picked up a spoon. "If I eat this, will you stop nagging me?"

"Maybe."

Paige pushed her laptop across to Frankie. "Take a look at my list."

Frankie dug her spoon into her bowl and read. "Damn, we're good. And *you're* good, putting all this together so fast. Are you sure we can do all this?"

"If we can't, then we know someone who can. I've already started a spreadsheet for suppliers, venues, etc. We have a lot of contacts and several people have been in touch, wanting to work with us. Turns out Star Events had irritated more than a few people."

"Wasn't there a noncompete clause in your contract?"

"Only if I resigned. I didn't. Matt already checked that for me. I've gone through all our competitors and looked at their biggest events over the past year. I've added those names to another list." She leaned across and opened another file.

"You're all about lists." Frankie glanced at it. "And that's a long list."

"I started with all the companies that have given Star Events business, and then listed their competitors and companies linked with them. So far I have seventy names. Clear your diaries because we're going to be busy." She raised her coffee mug. "To us."

Frankie lifted her mug. "Urban Genie. Your wish is our command."

Eva lifted hers, the contents sloshing over the table. "May the wishes overflow."

"Like your coffee mug," Frankie said, and reached for a cloth.

Later that day in his offices in Tribeca, Jake emerged from one client meeting and was preparing for another when Matt strolled into his office.

"I need to talk to you."

"I'm busy."

"It's about Paige."

He didn't want to think about Paige.

He was careful never to touch her, but last night he had.

He could still feel the slight shake of her hand under his and smell the light summery perfume she always wore. Her perfume always messed with his senses. It made him want to strip her naked, throw her down in the nearest field of wildflowers and do very bad things.

"I won't take her on the bike if it bothers you so much, but you should let her make that decision on her own. You're overprotective."

Matt sprawled in the nearest chair. "This isn't about the bike. It's about the business. The business you told her to set up. What the hell were you thinking?"

"I was thinking she needed more control over her life. You saw her—she was feeling powerless and scared. I reminded her that she could take back some of the power, that's all."

"You made her angry."

"Yeah, I made her angry. Better angry than crying."

"She wasn't crying. I have never seen my sister cry, not even when she was going through all that trauma when she was ill. Not once."

Jake, who had trained himself to spot female tears at a thousand paces, wondered how Matt could be so clueless. "She was on the verge of losing it. And if she had, she would have been mortified. She was already feeling bad. She didn't need to feel worse. What she needed was to be galvanized into action, and there is no better motivator than anger. You should be thanking me."

"You made her angry on purpose?" Matt ran his hand over his jaw and swore softly. "I didn't see that. How come you know so much about women?"

"Extensive experience along with an extraordinary gift for driving women crazy." His phone rang and he silenced it with a stab of his finger.

Matt eyed the number on Jake's screen. "Brad Hetherington? You really are moving in illustrious circles. You need oxygen up there?"

"No, I need shovels to dig my way out of the bullshit."

"You're not taking his call?"

"I would, but you're sitting in my office. And sometimes it pays to be a bit elusive. I have something he wants. Make him wait and he'll pay more."

Matt shook his head. "How does it feel to have everyone queuing up at your door?"

"It feels busy." Jake leaned back in his chair, looking at the man he regarded as a brother. "So did you just come here to punch me for making your sister angry or was there something else?"

"Something else. I want you to help her with her new business."

Jake stilled. Caution seeped into every bone of his body. "Why would I do that?"

"Because you were the one who pushed her into it. You owe it to her not to let her fail."

"What makes you think she'll fail?"

"The fact that she equates asking for help with weakness. We both know that running a business is a steep learning curve. The more you ask, the faster you learn. My sister has turned independence into an art form. She is never going to ask. So you have to offer."

No way.

Jake tapped the desk with his fingers. Nudging her in the right direction was one thing; getting personally involved was another. "She won't want my help. You heard her last night."

And he knew it wasn't simply a need to be independent that would prevent Paige from asking him for help.

Neither of them mentioned it but the past simmered in the background, coloring every interaction.

She guarded herself around him and that suited him just fine.

"I don't know anything about running a concierge service or events management."

"You should. You attend enough events."

"To network, get drunk or get laid. Sometimes all three. I

don't plan them." It was like standing on the edge of quick-sand knowing that if you stepped in the wrong place you were going to be sucked in too deep to escape. "You have as much business experience as I do. You help her."

"She thinks I'm overprotective, and she's right. I try not to be, but I get it wrong. Every damn time. Remember when she was learning to drive?" He saw Jake wince and nodded. "Yeah, that time. I'm too worried about her to be objective." Matt stood up and walked to the window. "Great view," he said absently.

"I'm usually too busy to look at it."

His friend didn't take the hint. "To me she's still that little girl with a heart problem. I can still see her in the hospital, blue lips, struggling to breathe."

"If you're going for emotional blackmail, don't. It's not going to work."

Except the words conjured up images Jake had worked hard to forget, along with a ton of other stuff he never wanted to look at again.

"It's not emotional blackmail—it's the truth. I want to cover her in bubble wrap and fix everything. I always have. Right from day one."

"That's because your parents gave you the responsibility." Jake stood up and joined his friend by the window. "They trusted you to keep an eye out for her. That's a hell of a burden."

And he'd always thought it was a tough deal for his friend.

Matt frowned. "It isn't a burden."

"Maybe it's time to let Paige live her life and make her own mistakes. Instead of trying to catch her before she falls, you could wait until she does and then pick her up."

"I don't want her to be hurt. I don't want her to fail at this."

"You're too afraid of failure. I guess that comes from having overachieving parents. Failure is part of life, Matt. Success teaches you nothing, but failure teaches you resilience. It teaches you to pick yourself up and try again."

Matt dragged his hand through his hair. "You used to be as protective as I was. Hell, you once spent an entire night sitting by Paige's hospital bed when I couldn't make it. Or maybe you don't remember."

He remembered every moment. "I realized that protecting her doesn't do her any favors. She doesn't want to be protected."

But he did protect her, didn't he?

He protected her from himself.

He knew he was capable of hurting her. He'd done it before.

Neither of them mentioned it, but he was well aware of the pain his rejection had caused. He knew it had changed her. Gone was the openness he'd found so refreshing. With him she was always slightly guarded and he made it easy for her to be that way by ensuring their relationship always skirted on the edge of antagonistic.

Matt turned away from the window. "Maybe she doesn't want to be protected, but I want you to help her. I'm asking you as a friend."

And their friendship was the reason he didn't want to do it.

"Why can't you do it?"

"Apart from the fact she automatically ignores anything I say to her, there's the fact I'm a landscape architect. I can design her a breathtaking roof terrace, complete with dramatic water feature and a swing seat, but I'm no expert on digital marketing and I don't have the ear of every top executive in the city. You do. You could open doors."

"Which she would then slam in my face."

"You have the ear of Brad Hetherington." Matt waved his hand toward Jake's phone. "That guy virtually owns Wall Street. His business alone would make Urban Genie successful."

Jake thought about the rumors floating around. "Trust me—Paige doesn't need Brad Hetherington in her life."

"Personally, no. But professionally? The guy has deep pockets. And so do any one of the many other companies you work with. She doesn't even need to know you're helping. Pick up the phone and make a few calls. Half of Manhattan owes you favors."

"I'm always transparent in my business dealings." But he hadn't been transparent in his relationship with Paige, had he?

She thought he had no feelings for her.

She thought that, to him, she was nothing more than his friend's little sister.

"I'll do you a deal." It was the only way to get Matt out of his office. "If she comes to me and asks for help, I'll give it."

Matt swore under his breath. "You know she won't come to you for help."

Jake gave what he hoped passed as a sympathetic shrug.

He was counting on it.

Five

Reach for the stars, and if they're too far away, wear higher heels.

—Paige

Paige sat, slumped at her favorite corner table at Romano's, with Eva and Frankie, trying to formulate Plan C, since Plan A and B had crashed. It had been two weeks and they were nowhere.

The comforting smell of garlic and herbs wafted from the kitchen and through the open window she could see her brother talking on the phone to a client.

It was Friday night and dinner had been his suggestion, his treat, but his phone hadn't stopped ringing from the moment he'd sat down.

Her phone, on the other hand, had been depressingly silent.

No one had taken her call, and no one had called back in response to the messages she'd left. This wasn't what she'd imagined when she'd dreamed about starting her own business.

She promised herself that one day she was going to be successful enough to buy her brother a million dinners. Her phone would ring so often she'd have to hire someone to answer it. She hoped that day wasn't too far in the distance.

"You've been rushing around all week." Maria put heaped bowls of pasta in front of them, topped with her signature red sauce. "You need food. *Buon apetito*."

"Soon we won't be able to afford to eat," Paige said gloomily. "We'll be sniffing around the trash like stray cats."

"Claws was a stray cat." Frankie picked up her fork. "She eats like a queen most days."

Maria patted her shoulder. "You can eat here every day. We love having you."

Carlo, who happened to be passing, nodded agreement. "With you three girls in the window, business booms."

Everyone's business seemed to be booming but hers.

Paige glanced around the crowded restaurant. There wasn't an empty seat in the place.

Normally just being in Romano's lifted her mood. She loved the intricate metalwork of the tables and the photographs of Sicily on the wall. She knew each one in detail. There was the familiar snowcapped peak of Mount Etna, the pretty town of Taormina with its twisting medieval streets, a fishing boat bobbing on a sparkling blue sea.

Laughter and conversation echoed around the room.

Everyone was having a good time.

Everyone, that was, except the team from Urban Genie.

Paige was in charge of company morale and so far she was failing.

"It's early days." She made a superhuman effort to be positive. "There are plenty more businesses out there."

Frankie glanced at her. "You've made one hundred and four calls and the only business we've been given is to pick up someone's dry cleaning and arrange a cake for a woman's ninetieth birthday."

"Her name was Mitzy and she was adorable." Eva twisted pasta around her fork, her appetite apparently unaffected by the pressures of their new venture. "Do you know she flew American military aircraft in the war?"

"No." Paige frowned, distracted. "How would I know that? And how do *you* know that?"

"Because I spoke with her when I delivered the cake and we bonded. She showed me some amazing photographs, and then one of her grandsons turned up to visit and she asked me to stay for tea."

Frankie paused with her fork halfway to her mouth. "You stayed for tea?"

"Of course. It would have been rude to say no, and anyway she was interesting and he was pretty cute, in a slightly uptight banker sort of way. Mitzy is worried he's single, but she's even more worried about his brother. He's a well-known writer. He lost his wife in an accident a few years ago around the holidays and since then he's become virtually a recluse." Eva's eyes filled. "Isn't that awful? I keep imagining him all alone in his big empty apartment. Money doesn't matter, does it? It's love that matters. It's the only thing that's important in the end."

"Unless you don't have a job." Paige handed her a napkin. "And then money becomes pretty important. But I agree, it is awful. Can't be easy to get over something like that."

"He hasn't. Mitzy is worried he never will and she's tried everything to get him out there again. Poor man. I want to pick him up and hug him."

"You don't know him," Frankie pointed out, "so technically you'd be assaulting a stranger. It's a sad story, I agree, but I don't understand how you can cry over a stranger."

"I don't understand how you can be so hard-hearted." Eva blinked back the tears. "And after a few hours together, Mitzy didn't feel like a stranger."

Frankie dropped her fork. "A few *hours*? Delivering that cake was supposed to take no more than forty minutes. How long were you there?"

"I didn't really check the time." Eva looked vague. "It was probably closer to four hours by the time we'd had tea and I'd taken her dog for a walk."

"Four hours?" Paige blinked. "You could have charged her for that time, Ev."

"It wouldn't have seemed right after she made me such a delicious tea. It's not as if it made me late for another job. We don't *have* any other jobs. And she was interesting." Eva paused. "She reminded me of Grandma."

Hearing the wobble in her voice, Paige gave her hand a squeeze. "It's fine, Ev. It's not as if we're exactly busy doing other things."

"It's not the time that bothers me," Frankie said, "it's the fact that these people were strangers. They could have been knife-wielding psychopaths. Do you have no sense of self-preservation or caution?" Frankie shook her head and Eva looked at her patiently.

"In my experience most people are pretty nice."

"Then your experience is limited." Frankie retrieved her fork and stabbed it into her pasta. "I hope your faith in human nature is never shaken."

"So do I, because that would be truly horrible." Eva took a sip of her drink. "By the way, Mitzy's grandson—the one I met today, not the one who never leaves his apartment—is CEO of a private bank on Wall Street so I gave him our card."

Paige stared at her. "Seriously?"

Frankie reached for more garlic bread. "She tells us this *after* she's given us Mitzy's life history." She took a bite and glanced at Eva. "You didn't maybe think that would be the information that would interest us most?"

"Everything about humans interests me. I don't know if I ever told you that the woman in the room next to my grandma was—"

"Ev—" Paige interrupted her "—you were telling us about Mitzy's grandson. The rich one who owns a bank. You gave him our card, and—?"

"And nothing. He took it and put it in his wallet."

"Did he say he might call? Can you call him? Follow up?"

"No. I didn't ask for his number and I don't know the name of the company. Don't look at me like that." Eva's rounded cheeks were tinted pink. "I hate asking for business. I am not a salesperson. What if they say yes because they feel pressured? Or worse, what if they say no? That would be so awkward for both of us."

"I've had one hundred and four 'awkwards' over the past two weeks," Paige said wearily. "I'm an expert. Did you find out anything about him?"

"He's allergic to strawberries and he was the first person in his family to go to college. He's very successful. Mitzy is so proud of him. And he wished us luck."

"Luck." Paige felt a rush of despair. Was she the only one who was worried about their fledgling business?

Maybe these things *did* take time but they didn't have time.

"I had no idea it would be this hard. The internet is full of tales of success, people who started businesses while at college, got crowdfunding and sold their company for billions of dollars. I can't even persuade people to pick up the phone and talk to me."

"I've already told you, you should talk to my Jake." Maria put more garlic bread in the center of the table. "Ask him to make some introductions. He knows everyone worth knowing in Manhattan. Paige, eat something. You will fade to nothing, girl."

Maria walked away to serve a customer and Paige stared at her plate.

She was not going to reach out to Jake.

She was never, ever going to make herself vulnerable around him again.

"I still have a few people to call and I'm making a new list tomorrow. I'm going to widen the net."

"Maria has a point. Jake could reel you in a big fish with one cast of his rod." Frankie looked at her strangely. "Why not ask? You're not afraid to call any of those strangers on your list. Why not Jake, who you've known forever?"

"Because—" She groped for an excuse that would sound believable. "Because this is our company."

"So? People network and make recommendations all the time. It's how business is done. What's the difference?"

"Is this to do with what happened when you were a teenager?" Eva's eyes narrowed. "Because if it's the whole 'he saw me naked' thing that's getting in the way—"

"It isn't!"

"I was going to say, then you should forget it. Jake has seen plenty of women naked since then."

"Is that supposed to make her feel better?" Frankie looked at Eva with exasperation. "She doesn't want to hear that, Ev."

"Why not? It's not as if she's in love with him." Eva paused and looked at Paige. "Are you?"

"No," she croaked. "Definitely not."

"Right. It's an embarrassing incident in your past, nothing more. You should forget it."

"She's trying to," Frankie muttered, and Paige took a deep breath.

"It has nothing to do with that. He's probably forgotten it ever happened."

But she knew he hadn't forgotten.

He was wary around her. Careful. As if he saw her as a potential threat.

Which was mortifying.

As a result she was also careful. She hadn't touched him since that night.

But the other night *he'd* touched *her*, and for a moment she'd thought—

She stared down at her hand, still able to feel the warm strength of his fingers closing over hers.

Then she shook her head impatiently. Those thoughts were *exactly* the reason she kept her distance.

It had been comfort. Nothing more.

"I'm not asking Jake. There are plenty more calls I can make. Something will turn up."

Unfortunately the "something" was Jake himself.

The door to the restaurant opened and Paige automatically glanced toward it, as if something in her was programmed to sense his presence the moment he walked into a room. Tonight he was wearing a button-down shirt with jeans, but he turned as many heads as he did when he was wearing a suit.

And he turned hers. She had time to register the lift of her heart and the lightness of her mood before his gaze met hers.

She could tell from the faint narrowing of his eyes that he hadn't been expecting to see her there, and for a moment she was eighteen again, offering him everything and seeing the shock on his face.

In her dreams she'd imagined him being overcome by lust. Instead, he'd been kind and the kindness had simply added to the humiliation of his rejection.

Kindness had to be the cruelest response of all to wild teenage love. It was a soft, gentle emotion. A direct contrast to her extreme, out-of-control feelings.

His gaze held hers, his focus on her alone, and she felt her heart beat a little faster. She felt as if she were floating. Flying higher and higher. This was the first time she'd seen him since that night on the terrace when they'd spoken alone. He'd touched her hand. He'd—

Jake opened the door a little wider and a woman walked past him into the restaurant.

Her blond hair fell to her waist and she was so slender she looked as if a gust of wind would blow her over.

The floating, flying feeling died. Paige's mood plummeted, like a paraglider losing a thermal.

She felt an uncomfortable twist of pain. The same thing happened every time she saw Jake with a woman.

"I was enjoying my pasta but suddenly I feel horribly fat." Eva pushed her plate away. "What happened to Trudi? I liked Trudi. At least she had a body."

"Trudi was a few months ago." Trudi. Tracey. Tina. They all merged, but what it meant was that Jake Romano was taken.

By every woman in Manhattan, or so it seemed.

Paige hated it. She hated noticing. Most of all she hated that she still cared.

She needed to get a life.

She needed to get a man.

Maria was back at their table, this time serving them house

salads. "That woman with Jake looks as if she needs a good meal." Clucking her disapproval, she put the plates in front of them. "He brings a different girl in here every month. He needs to change his ways or he'll never meet the right woman."

Paige picked up her fork.

She was pretty sure she knew why Jake didn't want a real relationship and it had nothing to do with meeting the right woman.

It had to do with his mother. His birth mother.

He'd talked about it once, when he'd spent all night sitting by her hospital bed. Something about the sterile darkness had made him open up.

It was a conversation she'd never forgotten.

She put her fork down, appetite gone, watching as he strolled across the restaurant toward them. He lifted a hand in greeting to his uncle, who was heading for the kitchen, and paused to kiss Maria. He said something in Italian that Paige didn't catch but she saw Maria's expression soften.

Frankie gave her a sympathetic look. "Hard to be irritated with a guy who is so fiercely protective of his mother. Here—" She topped up Paige's glass. "Drink some more wine."

Paige took a sip. Frankie was right. With other people Jake was impatient and direct to the point of brutal. With his mother he was infinitely patient.

His date was hovering, and he turned and beckoned her over.

"It's our lucky night. They're joining us." Frankie topped up her own glass. "Oh well, look on the bright side."

"There's a bright side?"

"Yes. That girl hasn't eaten for a decade. There is no chance she will steal our food."

Jake paused by the table, the woman's hand in his. "Company meeting? How's it going?"

Paige kept her eyes on her plate.

Was he holding the woman's hand because he wanted to send her a message?

Frankie picked up her glass. "Well, since you ask—"

"It's going well," Paige interrupted quickly. She didn't want Jake knowing the truth. She didn't want him feeling sorry for her. She'd had enough of being the object of pity. "We're struggling to cope with the volume of business."

"Yes, we'll be expanding and taking on new staff any day now." Ever loyal, Eva took Paige's lie and galloped into the sunset with it. "We're thinking about opening offices in Los Angeles and San Francisco."

Jake's eyes gleamed. "And you'll be flying there by Magic Carpet Airways?"

He knew, Paige thought miserably. He knew it was bullshit.

The man was sharper than the business end of a kitchen knife. Nothing escaped him.

"Maybe." Eva grinned, unabashed. "Aren't you going to introduce us to your new friend?"

The blonde tossed her hair back. "I'm Bambi."

Bambi?

"Good to meet you er—Bambi." Eva gestured to the table. "Are you joining us?"

Paige felt her stomach lurch. Meeting Jake's date in passing was one thing, but watching Jake laughing with her over dinner was something else entirely.

Please don't join us.

"I can't." Bambi gave them an apologetic look. "I have a shoot tomorrow and just breathing in the fumes of that garlic bread will make me bloat. I really have to watch what I eat. I so envy you all not having to care about your size."

It took all Paige's willpower not to glance down and check she hadn't turned into a whale. "You're a model?"

"You're right," Eva interrupted. "We are lucky because this garlic bread is the best thing I've ever tasted. You're sure you wouldn't like to try it?" She pushed the plate under Bambi's nose and gave an evil smile. "It's truly delicious. Yummy scrummy. Romano's garlic bread is the stuff of legends around here, as is the pizza."

"I'm a raw vegan." Bambi backed away, as if afraid that the mere mention of the word *pizza* might be enough to make her gain weight. "I haven't eaten carbs in forever, and if I took one bite of that pizza I'd eat the whole thing like I was starving. It was good meeting you guys. Jake? Are you ready?"

"Yeah." He was still looking at Paige. "I'm glad everything is going well, but if you need help, call me."

"Thanks." Over her dead body. Her pizza-loving, sex-starved body.

With a last look at Paige, Jake followed Bambi to the door.

Frankie leaned out of her seat and studied the other woman's butt curiously. "Ready for what, do you think? She can't have energy for much. And someone needs to tell her that *like* isn't a conjunction."

Eva leaned out, too. "I've seen bigger toothpicks. You're much prettier, Paige."

"We're not in competition."

Except that it felt as if they were.

Why did she compare herself with every woman Jake dated? Why did she do that?

Frankie finished her salad. "Raw vegan. Where does pizza fit in that?"

"It doesn't." Eva shuddered. "I'm all for healthy eating, but not denial. It's a medically proven fact that when you can't have something, you crave it all the more."

Paige pushed her salad around the bowl. Was that why she'd never been able to cure herself of her attraction to Jake?

Denied him, she just wanted him more.

If she'd been allowed to binge, maybe she would have been cured a long time ago.

"I can't imagine Jake enjoying a night out with an organic vegan." Miserable, she speared a salad leaf. "Jake is the twenty-first-century equivalent of Tyrannosaurus rex. He can't get through the week without devouring at least one big fat juicy steak. There have been times when I've wondered why Maria doesn't just serve him up a live cow with a knife and fork."

Frankie turned back to her food. "I will never in a million years understand men. What does he see in her?"

"If she turned sideways he wouldn't see anything at all." Eva pushed the garlic bread toward her. "Cheer up. She'll be gone by next week and he'll have another one on his arm. Disposa-girl."

"I haven't been on a date in nine months. I'm a failure," Paige muttered. "A big fat, failure."

"But you have amazing taste in friends," Eva said cheerfully. "Now shut up and eat something or we'll force-feed you and it won't be pretty."

Just at that moment Paige's phone, which had been depressingly silent for the past two weeks, rang. All three of them stared at it, and then at each other.

"This is it. This could be it." Paige sprang from her seat and took the call outside, passing Matt, who was on his way back into the restaurant with Jake, who appeared to have ditched the blonde toothpick.

"Urban Genie. How may we help?"

Five minutes later Paige bounced back into the restaurant, her spirits restored to a reasonable altitude. "We are on our way!"

This was why people ran their own businesses, she thought. Because when it went right, you knew it was down to you.

The buzz and excitement was incredible.

Even the fact that Jake had joined them at the table couldn't spoil her evening.

Matt had finally put his phone down and was tucking into a bowl heaped high with pasta, as was Jake. "On your way where?"

"Downtown Manhattan. A group of lawyers want us to arrange a bachelor party for one of their colleagues who is over on a business trip from Europe. Our first piece of business. Hopefully it will lead to more." She understood the importance of word-of-mouth recommendation. She was fine with that. It wasn't the same thing as asking for favors.

Matt ground pepper over his food. "Is it a company you've worked with before?"

"No, which is great! I sent follow-up emails to some of the people who wouldn't take my calls—this lead must have come from that." She wondered what had happened to Bambi, but asking Jake would show that she cared and she had no intention of showing him that she cared.

"So you don't even know if it's legit?"

Paige, who'd been expecting him to be pleased, felt a flicker of frustration. "You want me to do a police check on everyone I work for?"

"No." Matt stuck his fork into his food. "But I want you to be careful."

"I can look out for myself. I'm emailing venue suggestions and once we've agreed on that, we'll arrange catering and all the extras. We're in business." She waited for him to say something encouraging, but he carried on eating in silence and she looked at him in exasperation. "We have to start somewhere. Jake? What do you think?" At least he wouldn't protect her.

Jake reached for his wine. "This time, I agree with your brother."

"You're both ridiculously cautious. If we do a good job here, hopefully they'll recommend us to others." And right now she was willing to take any business she could if it meant not asking Jake for help. "Does it make you feel strong and macho to fix things for me, is that what this is? Is this about your ego?"

Jake laughed. "Honey, my ego is bulletproof. You couldn't take it down with a rocket launcher."

"If I had one right now, I might be tempted to try. And I've told you before not to call me honey."

"I'll try and remember that, honey."

"Enough, both of you." Matt was trying not to smile. "Jake is looking out for you, that's all, as any good friend would."

"I don't want him to. I don't need him to."

"How about a compromise. You're going to need extra help. Jake and I could disguise ourselves as butlers."

"Bow tie and bare flesh," Jake drawled. "Shame it's not a bachelorette party."

Paige's irritation rose. "You want to hover over us like bodyguards? No, thank you!"

Her brother put his fork down and reached for his beer. "At least promise me you won't go alone. All three of you together at all times."

"It's a job." She wondered what she had to do to stop Matt being so overprotective. "Everything is going to go like a dream, and then I can say I told you so, and you and Jake can crawl at my feet on your hands and knees and apologize for seeing catastrophe on every street corner."

Jake's gaze locked on hers. "Let's hope that's the way it goes."

Six

When you make a mistake, don't be afraid to eat humble pie. It's calorie-free.

—Eva

Jake stared at the screen.

It had been a while since he'd done this. A while since he'd looked.

He could close the laptop. He could—

With a soft curse, his fingers flew over the keys as he searched for the information he wanted.

For someone with his skills, it was easily accessed.

He read, checking for anything new, and saw that she had a new job. Promotion. Everything else was the same.

She was still living in a Tudor revival in upstate New York. Still happily married with two kids and a dog.

Life was good.

With a soft curse, he closed the page.

What the hell was he doing?

But he knew the answer to that one. Maria had given him

the "isn't it time you settled down" look. Whenever she did that, he felt the need to remind himself of the reasons why he couldn't.

The door to his office opened and he looked up with a frown, irritated by the disturbance. "What?"

Dani looked at him searchingly, but said nothing. "There's someone to see you."

"I don't have any meetings today."

"Her name is Paige." Dani leaned against his door. "It's weird, boss. She was standing outside for at least ten minutes deciding whether to come in or not. She walked away twice, then came back again. We were watching from the window laying bets as to whether she would pluck up the courage or not. Maybe you have a stalker. Want me to send her away?"

They obviously thought she was one of his ex-girlfriends, come to give him a hard time.

"Don't send her away."

"Do you know why she's here?"

No, but he could guess. He didn't know what bothered him most, the fact Paige had finally had to come to him for help or the fact that it was clearly killing her to do so.

Jake stood up and flipped his laptop shut. He was glad now that he'd looked. Every piece of information on that screen reminded him to be cautious in his relationships. "Send her in."

He didn't need to wonder why Paige had walked away twice. He knew. She hated asking for help. Especially his help.

What he didn't understand was what had finally driven her to his door.

He'd assumed things were going well for Urban Genie. He and Matt had shared some beers a few nights ago and Matt hadn't mentioned anything.

While he waited, he paced over to the glass window and

stared across the city, through concrete canyons that stretched from Canal Street to Lower Manhattan. Once an urban wasteland of industrial warehouses, it had been transformed into one of the country's most expensive zip codes, a thriving neighborhood filled with affluent creative and financial talent. That was the reason he'd chosen to live and work here. That, and the fact that it was a heartbeat from the city's financial district.

"Jake?" Her voice came from the doorway. Husky. Feminine. It was like being stroked with a fur glove.

He braced himself. All he had to do was treat her like his best friend's little sister. *Little sister.* He repeated it in his head like a mantra.

Except that he knew damn well that she wasn't little. He'd been right there, up close and personal, when she'd grown up.

One minute she'd been wearing cartoon T-shirts, her hospital room populated by cheery balloons and oversize stuffed toys, the next she was experimenting with makeup. Out with the kids' stuff, in with slinky Victoria's Secret.

The night she'd revealed not only Victoria's Secrets but most of her own was welded into his brain and yet somehow, despite having her naked body offered to him virtually on a plate, he'd managed to do the right thing.

And he'd done it in a way that ensured neither of them had to go through that again.

He turned and almost swallowed his tongue. She was wearing a tailored black suit that nipped in at her narrow waist and skimmed her hips. Her heels were high and her hair—the color of rich, dark chocolate—fell straight and gleaming over her perfect white shirt. She looked efficient and corporate. And all woman.

He was aware of her in a way he never was with any other woman. Her faint floral scent flavored the air but it wasn't just that. It was *her*. Something about her seeped through to his brain and senses.

He wanted to touch her.

He wanted to strip off those clothes and taste her.

He was in trouble. *He was in big trouble.*

"Paige?"

Underneath her flawless makeup, her face was pale and she looked exhausted, as if she hadn't slept properly for nights.

He wanted to haul her into his arms and fix everything, an impulse that made him step back.

He wasn't going to screw with his best friend's sister.

When he had a fling, which he did far less frequently than people thought, he picked strong women with spines of steel and hearts of stone.

An ex-girlfriend had once told him caustically that dating him was like driving off-road in very rough terrain.

Paige looked as if she'd break at the first pothole. If there was one heart he was never going to damage, it was hers. It had already sustained more than enough damage at the hands of Mother Nature and a bunch of doctors. At least that was what he told himself.

"How are things at Urban Genie? Busy?" He saw her cheeks turn from pale cream to strawberry blush. "How was your bachelor party? Any business leads?"

"Not exactly." She fiddled with the edges of her jacket. "That didn't work out."

"No?" He wished she hadn't chosen to wear that cheerful coral lipstick.

Paige's addiction to lipstick was a source of amusement to most people. To him it was one more thing that tested his will-power. It drew attention to her mouth, which made it tough on him because that was one part of her he tried never to look at.

He'd kissed plenty of women in his time and not one of those kisses had stayed with him.

He'd never kissed Paige, and he thought about it constantly.

"It's not important." She dismissed his question with the smile he'd seen her use a million times with her parents and her brother.

"What happened?"

She eyed him. "It was everything you said it would be, so unless you're longing to say 'I told you so,' now would be a good time to move on. You don't need details. Let's just say it didn't work out."

He watched as she curled her fingers into her palms. "What happened, Paige?"

"Nothing."

He knew her well enough to know that "nothing" was a whole lot of "something." "I want to hear about 'nothing.'"

"You'll freak out and overreact. Then you'll tell Matt and he'll freak out and overreact. If I wanted Matt to know I would be sitting in front of him now, not you."

"I promise not to overreact."

"They wanted a few too many extras. Extras that weren't included in our list. That's your cue to say 'I told you so.' Laugh and get it over with."

He'd never felt less like laughing.

Anger stirred inside him. "They made a move on you?"

She gave him a warning look. "You promised you wouldn't overreact."

"I lied." He spoke through his teeth. "And I want details."

"They thought we were the entertainment, but we handled it. That's all you need to know."

His vision darkened. "Give me their names."

"Don't be ridiculous. What are you, Batman? Are you going to beat them up on a dark night? I told you, we handled it."

"But what if you hadn't been able to?" The thought of what could have happened sent rivulets of ice down his spine. "You never should have put yourself in that position."

"What position? We were doing a job. Trying to start our business. You want me to take female-only clients? Sit at home all day in case something bad happens?" Her tone told him that she was close to the edge and he took a deep breath. He'd pushed all her hot buttons and he tried hard not to do that.

"Now you're the one who is overreacting. I'm not trying to protect you. All I'm saying is—"

"That you want to wade in there and take over. Defend me. That's being overprotective."

He rubbed his fingers over his forehead. No wonder Matt always got it wrong. It was like walking on eggshells in heavy boots. "Is that so wrong?"

"Yes." Her eyes were fierce. "Don't do that, Jake. Don't look at me as if you're ready to lock the door from the outside and never let me out. You're the one person who doesn't do that."

He forced himself to relax. "You called Security?"

"No need. We had Frankie." The corner of her mouth flickered into a faint smile. "The human weapon."

"Frankie?"

"They'd already been drinking when we arrived and we knew right from the moment we walked through the door there was going to be trouble. We probably should have left then and cut our losses but we were so desperate for business we all agreed we'd keep going and hope it worked out."

A film of sweat chilled his brow. "Paige—" he spoke through his teeth "—fast forward to the part where Frankie turned into a superhero."

"Eva was doing her usual thing where she speaks without thinking. She was aiming for good customer service and asked what would make their evening special."

Jake swore under his breath. "Someone needs to talk to her."

"Frankie already did. Anyway, predictably one of the guys said 'you and me, horizontal, baby.' He stuck his hand under her skirt. The next moment Frankie had thrown him and was standing with her stiletto jabbed in his abs." She started to laugh. "I don't know why I'm laughing. They certainly won't be recommending us."

"I don't know why you're laughing, either." Jake gripped the corner of his desk. "If Frankie wasn't a black belt with a bad attitude—"

"We would have handled it a different way, and Frankie has a perfect attitude. She's the total opposite of Eva. Eva trusts everyone. Frankie trusts no one. Eva thinks the world is full of sunshine. Frankie sees black storm clouds everywhere. But the best thing is that she's so slight, everyone misjudges her. There are no hints that she can knock you unconscious with one kick so she always catches people off guard."

Jake started to breathe again. "From now on you deal with companies, not individuals. Go through formal channels."

"Companies haven't exactly been queuing outside our door. You have no idea how many calls I've made." The laughter had gone and now she looked tired and dejected, as if all the spirit had been sucked out of her. "That's why I'm here. This is me, crawling to you for help. Savor the moment."

He'd never savored anything less. "It isn't a weakness to ask for help, Paige. It's sound business practice."

"Couch it anyway you like, but it comes down to the fact I couldn't do it by myself."

"That's crap." He stood up and walked around his desk. "I know you hate being smothered and protected—"

"Yes, I do. And you don't usually do it. You're a pain in the butt—" she sent him a look "—but even when you're being a pain in the butt and goading me, part of me likes the fact you don't hold back."

She had no idea what he was holding back.

"The skill of building a business is to recognize what you lack and employ people who can fill that gap. And that requires frank, honest self-appraisal."

"I can't afford to employ anyone right now. We have no business."

"What do you want from me? Why are you here?"

"Because Frankie threatened to kick my butt if I didn't talk to you," she said, "and she's too good at that to ignore the threat. But mostly I'm here because I feel responsible. Eva and Frankie did this for me. They could have looked for jobs, but I persuaded them this was a good idea. And now we have no business and we're making no money and I can't sleep and— it's horrible. I don't know how you do it."

Jake resisted the impulse to hug her. "You need to stop thinking about it and focus on building the business. If a door closes, open the next one."

She nodded. "That's the theory, but a lot of doors are closing."

"Matt doesn't know any of this?"

"No. I can't deal with him right now. We'd argue about it and I'm not giving up my dream because of a bunch of oversexed lawyers." She rubbed her fingers over her forehead. "What can I do, Jake? Tell me what to do. I need help."

"Apart from the lawyers—" and he had his own plans for

them "—who have you called? Last time I saw you in the restaurant you told me it was going well."

"I lied. It's not going well. I have called everyone. Everyone we ever worked with at Star Events, everyone we wanted to work with, and everyone we hadn't even got around to thinking about working with. I have pounded the streets and apart from the lawyers, the only business we've got so far is to deliver one person's dry cleaning and make a birthday cake for a ninety-year-old who is, by the way, Eva's new best friend. Which is lovely, but doesn't create any business. I had no idea it would be so hard."

"It's always tough at the beginning." Jake gave her the advice he would have given to any other person asking for his thoughts on a start-up. "You face countless rejections. Everyone does. It's part of the process."

"There's tough and there's 'not happening.' Right now this isn't happening and I'm spending hours a day on it."

"You've got to look past the highs and lows."

"I'm still waiting for the highs. Even a molehill would be welcome." Her crooked smile tugged at him and he resisted the urge to reach out and comfort her.

"The highs will come."

"What if they don't? At what point do I give up and look for a job? I don't have time to do both. If I stand any hope of making this work I have to give it my all, and if it were only about me I'd carry on until the bitter end, but it isn't just me." She bent to rub her ankle and a glint of silver caught the light as something slid forward from the neck of her shirt. "I'm worried about Frankie and Eva. I'm responsible for them, and I wasn't prepared for how that would feel. I'm lying awake at night panicking about it."

He stared at the necklace. It had been hidden under her shirt, invisible.

A million memories came flooding back.

She caught his eye and quickly tucked it away.

"I didn't know you still had that." His voice was as rough as sandpaper and she blushed awkwardly.

"You gave it to me the night before my operation. For courage. Remember?"

He remembered. He remembered plastic cups brimming with really bad coffee, tired-looking doctors in white coats, too busy saving lives to stop and talk. He remembered echoing corridors and anxious relatives. And Paige. White-faced and brave, keeping everything inside. Except for that one time when she'd lowered her guard and opened her heart.

That one time he'd crushed it.

"I assumed you'd lost it years ago."

"No. I kept it safe. It reminds me to be strong when life is tough. And right now life is definitely tough. I'm scared for the future, not for me because I have my parents and Matt, even though I would hate to have to turn to them, but for Eva and Frankie. They put their faith in me. I can't let them down."

The necklace was no longer visible but it didn't make a difference because now he knew it was there.

It felt strangely intimate, seeing something he'd given her in close contact with that creamy skin.

His throat closed. He dragged his gaze from the neck of her shirt and forced himself to concentrate on what she was saying. "You didn't force this on them. It was their decision."

"But they wouldn't have done it if I hadn't driven it. This was down to me and—" She rubbed her fingers over her forehead. "You've run your own business for ages. How are you not stressed out every minute of the day?"

"I'm not employing people I've known since I was ten years old."

"Six," she said absently. "We were six. Eva fell over in the classroom and Frankie picked her up, which has pretty much been the pattern ever since. But it isn't one-sided. Eva softens Frankie. She makes her laugh and relax. We're a good team, but somehow that makes it harder, not easier."

"I can see how working with your closest friends would add an emotional dimension, but you have to ignore that side of it. Don't let emotion color your judgment."

"How? How do you switch that off? How do you stop your feelings getting in the way?"

"You bury them."

"Eva and Frankie were there for me right through the bad times. I don't want to let them down. I'm scared of messing this up."

And that, he knew, was the only reason she was here.

Because of her friends.

Nothing else would have brought her to his door.

"Stop thinking about it. Just do it. Take a deep breath and jump."

"I'll fall."

"You'll fly, Paige. Don't think about your business, think about the job. Stop thinking about all the things that could go wrong, and focus on what needs to be done. Do the job. Do what you're good at. Once you've done a few jobs, others will follow."

"But how do we get those first jobs? If you have any advice I will gladly take it." She swallowed hard. "I'm starting to think we need a miracle."

"Word of mouth is the most powerful form of recommendation."

She nodded. "We need a big event that will impress people, but no one is going to recommend us until they've hired us, and no one will hire us until someone has recommended us. And I've been thinking about that—" She bit her lip. "What if Chase Adams is telling people not to hire us?"

"He isn't."

"How do you know?"

"Chase Adams has been out of town and out of contact for a few weeks. His office said he's on vacation." He frowned. "Which is strange, now I think about it."

"Why is that strange?"

"I've known Chase for ten years. He's never taken a vacation. At least, not the sort where you don't answer your phone."

"Great. So Matilda was fired, we all lost our jobs and he's on vacation! I hope he's having a really great time." Anger barely masked the misery and Jake made a decision.

"When he finally reappears, I'll handle him. In the meantime, I've been thinking of running a corporate event." He hadn't, but it would do him no harm to hold one. "Showcase some of our work. Invite current clients and a few people I'd like to have as clients but who currently haven't seen the light."

"It sounds like a good idea. I hope it goes well."

"It will, because Urban Genie will be running it. Actions speak louder than words. You'll do a great job and by the end of the evening you'll have more work than you'll be able to handle at your kitchen table."

"You want *us* to run it?" There was a shine in her eyes. "That's…too big a favor."

"It's not a favor," he said smoothly. "When I run an event I want the best, and I know that's Urban Genie, even if other people don't know it yet. Talk to your team and come back to me with a detailed proposal. Stun me. I want your best, most creative ideas." Because that was what would guarantee her more business for the future.

She stirred. "How many guests?"

"I want it exclusive." He narrowed his eyes, thinking of how it would work best for Paige. "Senior staff only." She needed to meet people who could make decisions and sign off on the budget. "Small and select. One hundred maximum. Any venue suggestions?"

The uncertainty left her and she was all professional. "Rooftop. Glitzy. Manhattan at its starlit, magical best. Do you have any dates in mind?"

"I want it in the next month." It was an almost impossible challenge at such short notice. He waited for her to tell him it couldn't be done, that an event of that nature took months of planning, but she didn't. In fact he could have sworn there was a glimmer of a smile on her face.

"Downtown?"

"I leave that decision to you."

"There's the Loft & Garden at the Rockefeller Center. They have a beautiful English garden with a reflecting pool." She was thinking aloud, her eyes unfocused.

"Don't they have a list of preferred vendors?"

"Yes. I'll need to talk to them. At this short notice, our options will be limited."

"You don't think you can do it?"

"We can do it. But we might need to be creative. And persuasive." Energized, she whipped a tablet out of her bag and he watched, curiosity getting the better of him, as he saw her access a list.

"Which app are you using?"

"I'm not. I couldn't find one that did what I needed so I use a spreadsheet that I customized."

"That's not very time efficient."

"It works for me."

"I'll design you something better. Something tailored to your needs."

She looked up and smiled. "Let me organize your event first. When that's a success maybe I'll be able to afford to commission you to build me an app." She typed quickly. "I'll make some calls. See what's available and get back to you. I'll send you a shortlist and you can choose. You'll want to make some sort of corporate presentation?"

"No. Too formal."

"Maybe an informal version? Giant screens, with a show reel of highlights? And maybe stations with tablets and laptops where people can access some of the technology and ask questions."

"I like that idea."

"You'll need a professional lighting company."

It fascinated him to see her like this. Animated. Confident. Sexy. Unfortunately it did nothing to support his attempt to see her as Matt's little sister. "The venue can't switch the lights on?"

"It's not about lighting the space. Lighting is more than making sure people don't trip over—it's about making your event memorable. I presume you want memorable?"

What he wanted was her, naked in a darkened room.

Screw lighting.

And he knew it would be memorable.

"You're the expert."

"Frankie will manage that side of things. She has often used lighting companies to enhance her floral designs." She glanced down. "Catering? Any specific requests?"

"I'm going to leave it all to you, or rather Eva."

"You don't want input?"

"Unlike you, I don't insist on doing everything myself," he drawled. "I delegate, and this time I'm delegating to you. I don't micromanage." Especially not in this case. He wanted to have as little contact with Paige as possible.

For both their sakes.

"What's your budget?"

"Tell me what I need to spend to make sure this is the party everyone is talking about for months."

Her eyes widened. "Seriously?"

"Yes." It would give her scope to run an event that would stand out and guarantee her other business. "Come back to me with a venue and a date and I'll have my staff put together a guest list."

"I know you don't want to give me a brief, but is there anything you hate? Apart from ties. I know you hate ties." Her gaze lingered at the open neck of his shirt, and then lifted to his. "What else do you hate?"

"New York when the snow melts, warm beer, people who lie, being crushed on the subway with a million other people—"

"I meant in the way of food or decor." She smiled. "You haven't been crushed on the subway for years."

"I try and eliminate the things I hate from my life." He stretched his legs out in front of him. "You know me, Paige, and I trust you to make all the right choices. I'm putting the whole thing in your hands."

"Thank you. We'll make sure you don't regret this."

"I know I won't." He watched as Paige tucked her tablet back into her bag. "Are you still working from Frankie's kitchen table? How is that working out?"

"It's been all right. Mostly because we don't have any work."

"And now you do. You're going to be busy. We have vacant office space next to my mobile development team. It's yours if you want it."

"Seriously?"

He didn't blame her for being surprised. He was, too. He wondered if he'd inhaled something and blown his brain. Inviting Paige to work out of his offices? Right under his nose?

"If you're based here, it will be easier to update me on the progress of our event. It's a temporary solution until you're on your feet or until we need the space." Which gave him an exit clause. He might have to expand his company just to give himself a reason to reverse his decision. "Come back to me when you have a plan."

"We'll put it together." She stood up and he walked her to the glass door that separated his office from the rest of the team. "Thank you." She touched his arm gently. "This is good of you and I'm grateful."

"Don't thank me."

His actions might be good, but his thoughts were all bad.

Seven

When putting your best foot forward, don't forget to wear gel inserts.

—Paige

Paige focused on her laptop, putting the final touches to her presentation.

She wanted everything to be perfect. There wasn't going to be a single question she couldn't answer.

"This view is truly spectacular." Eva gazed, mouth open, and Frankie grunted, her head buried deep in a box she was unpacking.

"We have three weeks to put together this event. You don't have time to look at the view."

"The view is energizing. It's *exciting*, Frankie. All over the city deals are being made, people are falling in love."

"People are not falling in love, Eva. This is New York. All over the city people are shoving each other out of the way while they sprint to the next bit of their life."

"You're wrong. Magic happens in this city. It's full of hope and possibilities." Eva leaned her head against the glass window, her expression dreamy. "I think I'm going to love working in a fancy office with the world at my feet. Now I know why Jake works such long hours. Why would you ever want to leave this office?"

Paige didn't look up.

Jake had given them a chance. It was her job to make sure they didn't blow it.

She'd worked nonstop for three days and most of last night before putting together a plan. At four o'clock in the morning she'd fallen asleep with her laptop open on the bed and had been woken at six-thirty by a sleepy Eva with a mug of strong coffee and a blueberry muffin she'd risen early to bake.

Knowing how Eva struggled with early starts, Paige had been touched.

And now the meeting was only minutes away.

Frankie looked at her. "I can't believe you've done it. When you told us that he wanted an event within a month I didn't know who was crazier—him for suggesting it or you for agreeing."

"I wanted to prove we could do it."

"Well, you proved it. He's going to be impressed."

"I meant to myself. I needed to prove it to myself." If they could handle this, they could handle anything. "And we have a long way to go. This is just the start."

"But it's a good start. I hope Jake recognizes your superpowers at negotiating."

"Our job is to make it all look smooth and easy, not challenging. Your wish is our command, remember?"

"I have a feeling this event could be 'your wish is our nervous breakdown,'" Eva said. "You're sure this is just professional pride? You're sure there's nothing more personal going on?"

"No." Paige took a deep breath. "What would be going on?"

"I don't know, but the two of you shoot off so many sparks when you're together it's like Fourth of July fireworks. On a dark night I bet they can see you from New Jersey."

"It's true there are times when it feels as if we're permanently in conflict." And she hated it. She missed the easy, close relationship she'd had with him as a teenager.

"Conflict?" Eva looked at her steadily. "I would have described it as chemistry, but I was never much good at the sciences." She stood up. "We're going to impress him. After today, Urban Genie will officially have taken the first step to success."

Chemistry?

Of course it wasn't chemistry. He took pleasure in goading her, poking at her flesh until she snapped at him.

"Hi." Dani stood in the doorway. "Jake's finishing up a call, and he asked you to come to his office in fifteen minutes."

Paige felt her stomach drop but her smile stayed steady. "Thanks."

Dani paused. "Have you worked with Jake before? Because there are a few things that will make your meeting go smoother."

Eva looked anxious. "Like what?"

"Keep it brief. Jake hates wasting time. He doesn't do small talk and don't ever lie to him. If he asks you something and you don't know the answer, say you don't know. Don't bullshit. Don't ask me how, but his bullshit detector is infallible, and if you tell him a lie once he will never believe you again."

Frankie stood up. "Anything else?"

"Yes. Don't try and impress him. He hates it. He's impressed by good work, not by people trying to impress him. He sees through it."

"I've known Jake for years," Eva muttered, "and suddenly my knees are wobbly and my stomach is filled with wriggly snakes."

"Yeah, he has that effect on people. And that brings me to my last piece of advice—" Dani gave a crooked smile. "Don't fall for him."

Paige had heard enough. "Thanks, Dani. We'll be ready in fifteen minutes." As Dani left the room Eva bit her nails.

"This is Jake, right?" She straightened her pink shirt and applied a quick slick of gloss to her lips. "I mean, we've drunk beer with him on the roof terrace and eaten Maria's spaghetti with red sauce with him a thousand times."

"Don't think about it." But that was easier said than done. To distract herself, Paige scrolled through her notes. "Treat him as we would any other client. It's professional."

Except that the personal was there, simmering beneath the surface.

She'd sensed so many swirling undercurrents during that first meeting that she'd been tempted to ask for a life belt.

And it would have been easier to keep it entirely professional if he hadn't seen the necklace.

She should have stopped wearing it years ago instead of giving it a place next to her heart.

She hated the fact she wasn't able to consign it to the back of a drawer along with other pieces of jewelry she rarely wore.

And now he knew. Her secret, a secret no more.

She couldn't have felt more uncomfortable if someone had put a photo of her naked on an electronic billboard in Times Square.

Exactly fifteen minutes later, Paige looked at Eva and Frankie. "Ready?" She felt ridiculously nervous as Jake waved them into his glass-walled office.

Jake was on the phone, feet on the desk. "Yeah, well you don't pay me to agree with you or say what you want to hear." He glanced toward them and gestured at the meeting area in the corner of the room. "You pay me to tell you the truth and that's what I've done. What happens next is up to you." He ended the call and swung his feet off the desk.

Paige hovered, unsure whether to sit or stand. Her legs felt weak and rubbery. Being enclosed in a small space with Jake did that to her. Her world shifted, as if it had been hit by an outside force more powerful than both of them.

And this was a different Jake. He was all coiled strength and restless impatience, his hair ruffled and his jaw dark with five o'clock shadow. Dani had mentioned that the dress code was informal, but Jake looked as if he hadn't been to bed.

She knew he often worked into the night.

Since starting Urban Genie, she did, too.

He prowled around his office like a panther stalking his territory, so self-assured and confident that she felt her own nerves step up a notch.

How had she ever found the courage to tell him she loved him?

Maybe he'd been more approachable back then.

Jake looked at Eva. "Have you settled in?"

"We've made ourselves at home," Eva said cheerfully. "Thank you for letting us use your beautiful offices. I hope you're not expecting us to ever leave."

His gaze warmed. "I intend to bill you. Do you have everything you need?"

"A few clients would be nice." Frankie dumped a file on the table. "But we're hoping to address that. I guess we have you to thank for the chance."

"Don't." Finally he glanced at Paige. "Dani will join us.

That way, if I'm out of the office and you have questions, she can act as liaison."

Sliding into the nearest chair, Paige opened her laptop. "I've put together a presentation that shows our plan for the event."

Dani walked into the room and sat down next to Jake.

"Sorry, boss." She was breathless and smiling. "I was way-laid. Brad again. The man doesn't give up. You going to talk to him anytime soon?"

"Maybe." Jake nodded to Paige. "Go on. Talk me through it."

"We have a shortlist of three venues. This is our recommendation." She hit a key and brought up the image. "It has fabulous views of the Chrysler Building. Comfortably accommodates the numbers you specified. Fifty percent of the space is covered so if the weather isn't kind, the event isn't ruined. Inside or outside, it's magical. I've organized events here in the past and their team is imaginative, reliable and efficient."

Dani leaned across to look and gave a slow whistle. "Wow. Glitzy. What do I have to do to get an invite?"

"You're one of the team. You'll have an invite." Jake studied the photograph. "Didn't Matt design that roof terrace?"

"It was one of his first projects. It's one of the hottest venues in Manhattan right now. The only reason it's available is because they had a cancellation."

"And Paige is a killer negotiator," Eva said. "But she won't tell you that herself."

Jake sat back in his chair. "What's your vision for the event?"

Paige relaxed a little. That part was easy. "Your business is about communicating, about finding new, innovative ways to display data so that the end user experience is good. We're going to reflect that in our design." She showed him more images. "You want to make it easy for people to mingle and mix.

The acoustics are good. And as I mentioned, fifty percent of the space is under cover, which will mean we can use whatever technology you want without risking weather problems."

Dani nodded. "Cool. Because water and hard drives don't mix."

"We deal with all on-site management and logistics. Eva is in charge of food and beverage planning." She looked at Eva, who proceeded to talk through her plans.

"For this project I'm working with a company called Delicious Eats. They're based in SoHo and they pitched for a piece of business with Star Events, but Cynthia didn't want to give business to a company she didn't know. For her, sitting in on pitches was a formality. A tick box exercise before giving the business to her friends. I think they're perfect for your event."

Jake came back at her with questions and Paige felt a rush of pride as she watched Eva handle each one of his concerns without faltering.

Jake seemed impressed, too. "So food is covered. I'll leave the detail to you, Eva. What else?"

Paige stepped in again. "Frankie will deal with decor and flowers. It's a rooftop event so lighting is important. I mentioned that when we first met."

Frankie pushed her glasses up her nose. "We work with a company who are experts at lighting outdoor events. I also have a team of florists and floral designers. They're freelance, but I've worked with them all before and their work is the best there is. The roof terrace is already stylish and well lit. We'll add to that and create touches that will make sure this is the party people are talking about for the next six months."

Paige knew presenting was Frankie's least favorite thing, but she did a good job, outlining all the key points she thought Jake needed to know.

And then it was her turn. "We'll deal with any audio-visual needs and transportation. I'll also need to know if any of your guests will need accommodation."

"They won't. I'm feeding them and giving them champagne in one of the most exclusive rooftop venues in Manhattan," he drawled. "If they can't find their own way, then that's their problem. Anything else?"

"Client gifts?"

"Yes. But Dani can deal with that."

She was used to dealing with clients who fussed over every tiny detail, and then changed their minds. "There's nothing you want to change? No requests?"

"No. When I hire people to do a job I like to let them get on with it. I do need to see the venue though, because that will help me decide on how to best display the technology." He glanced at his phone. "I have meetings today and a project I need to work on tonight. Does tomorrow at nine work for you?"

"Nine in the evening?"

"It's a nighttime event. I need to see the roof terrace in the dark."

Paige flushed, feeling foolish. "Of course. I'll just need to check with the venue that they don't have a private event."

"They do. And the reason I know that is because I'm invited. I wasn't planning on going because it's black tie and posing, but maybe we'll show our faces for a short time."

"We? You're taking Dani?"

"No." He stood up. "I'm taking you."

"Me?" The blood pulsed in her ears. "Why me?"

"Because you're the one running the event," he said gently. "If there are issues, I want to discuss it with the man at the top. That's you."

"But I'm not invited."

"The invitation said 'plus one.' You're my plus one." He turned to Dani. "Call and accept, and arrange for a car to pick up Paige at home and take her straight to the venue. I have a meeting in Boston tomorrow, so I'll meet you there, Paige." His phone rang and he answered it as he walked out of his office with Dani following close behind.

Paige waited until the door closed, and then let out a long breath. "That felt scary." She couldn't remember ever being so nervous in a meeting before. But maybe that was because no meeting had ever seemed as important as this one, and not just because it was Urban Genie's first real piece of business, but because it was Jake. She'd wanted him to be impressed and she was confident that he was. "Great job, team."

Eva was smiling. "He *loved* your ideas. Now we have to hope he loves the venue. Lucky you, a date going to a romantic rooftop glitzy party with the sexiest bachelor in New York City. Jake wearing a tux and Manhattan wearing lights. Who knows what might happen."

Frankie stuffed her papers into her bag. "You are such a romantic. What does it take to cure you?"

"Being a romantic isn't an illness, and if it was I wouldn't want to be cured."

"It's not a date." Paige closed her laptop. "And I know what will happen. We'll visit the venue, he'll make some comments, probably sarcastic ones, I'll take notes, then we'll leave."

That was it.

It wouldn't even be awkward because there would be so many people there.

"Cinderella thought she was just going to a ball and look what happened to her."

"She lost a shoe, that's what happened to her, which is what happens when you're stupid enough not to carry flats on a night out." Frankie stood up, too. "Better take a spare pair in your bag, in case."

"I always do. And gel inserts and plasters for blisters." Paige walked toward the door, thinking about all the work they still had to do. "Do you have everything you need, Frankie?"

"Yes. I have a meeting with the lighting company later and I need to call Buds and Blooms. I'm working on the color palette and tomorrow I'll check out the flower market. Hello, early start. Still, at least I won't be partying late into the night like you."

"I'm not partying. I'm working. I'll probably be there for less than an hour, and then I'll be back home in my pajamas."

"Or you might be in Jake's bed, naked." Eva waggled her eyebrows suggestively and Frankie rolled her eyes.

"He's a client. You can't have sex with a client. Company rules."

"We own the company. We make the rules. If we want to eat cupcakes for breakfast, we can. If we want to drink champagne in business meetings, we can do that, too."

"Except then we'd be fat and broke." Frankie opened the door. "Paige sets the company rules. And the dress code, while flexible, does not including wearing your underwear around your ankles."

Eight

Confidence is like makeup. It changes your appearance
and no one needs to know what's underneath.

—Paige

Jake changed into his tux in the back of the car on his way
from the airport without interrupting his phone conversation.

"You need to look at the flow and think about the end user."
He buttoned the shirt and looped the bow tie around his neck,
intending to tie it at the last minute. He hated ties so much he
only owned two. This one, and a Tom Ford bought for him by
a date who had wanted to gentrify him.

The roads were gridlocked, which meant that by the time
his driver pulled up outside the building he was already late.

He strode into the foyer, past security and saw Paige pacing
by the bank of elevators, her thin, spiky heels tapping a rhythm
on the polished marble floor. Dressed in a simple black evening
dress, she looked classy, stylish and efficient. Ready to work.

And then he took a closer look at the shoes.

They were the same hot red as her lipstick and those heels were as high as a Manhattan skyscraper.

Shit.

She looked sexy.

One of the security guards was clearly thinking the same thing and Jake stepped in front of him, blocking his view and ruining his fun. He briefly considered ruining other things for the guy, too. Like his ability to walk in a straight line and keep his teeth to old age.

"Paige?"

She turned. "You're here!" The warmth and spontaneity of her greeting knocked him off balance. He rarely saw her unguarded and by lowering her own defenses, she sneaked under his. For a moment he couldn't remember why he was holding back. The car was just outside. He could power her into the backseat, strip her naked of everything except those hot red shoes and taste every inch of her.

Why not?

And then she smiled at him, that lovely open friendly smile that was all Paige.

And he remembered why not.

A fling with Paige would never be simple.

No matter how hot, intense and satisfying it might be at the time, ultimately it would end, as all his flings did. He'd learned at an early age that love was fleeting and unpredictable. It was something that could be taken away as easily as it was given. His preferred way of dealing with that was to keep himself emotionally detached. Which was one reason why Paige would always be off-limits.

She was a risk he wasn't prepared to take.

And then there was the promise he'd made to her brother...

"I'm late. Bad traffic." He cooled his tone. "I apologize."

"For the traffic? Even you can't control that, I imagine. And it doesn't matter." Her smile dimmed a little. "You're the client. You're allowed to be late. Are you ready?"

Client. That's right, he was her client.

He relaxed slightly.

All he needed to do was put her firmly in the box labeled Business. And forget about the hot red shoes.

"Jake?"

"Mmm?" He realized she'd asked him a question. "What?"

"I asked if you were ready."

"Ready for what?" Ready to find a dark corner in this building, undress her and screw her until neither of them could walk in a straight line?

Hell, yes. He'd been ready for that for a long time.

"I presume we need to go upstairs? The party?" She said it slowly, as if he were a tourist with a language problem. "You seem a little distracted."

Distracted was one way of describing it. Turned on would have been more accurate.

"Party. Yes. Let's go." He strode past her, keeping her out of his line of sight. It would have done them both a favor if he'd taken the stairs but he wasn't about to run up fifty floors wearing a tux, so instead he chose the express elevator.

The doors slid open and Paige walked in, giving him a perfect view of her back.

Jake admired the straight column of her spine and the line of her shoulder blades.

He wanted to ease those narrow straps over her shoulders and embark on an exploration of all the parts of her body hidden by the dress.

He wanted to drive her to the back of the elevator, close the doors and make the most of every one of those fifty floors.

It was only when her gaze met his that he realized that the elevator walls were mirrored.

Emotion flickered briefly in her eyes. There was confusion and a hint of something else that she tried to hide. He pretended he hadn't seen.

She was silent, her chest rising and falling unsteadily as if breathing was a conscious effort.

"Jake?" Her voice held a question he had no intention of answering.

He stepped into the elevator and the doors slid closed.

The heat was stifling, the space smaller than he had imagined. Or maybe it was being with Paige that made the space seem small. Torture, he discovered, was being alone in an elevator with a woman you wanted and couldn't have.

He lifted his finger to loosen his top button and discovered it was already undone.

There was nothing else he could do to cool himself down.

He was probably supposed to be making conversation, but his tongue had twisted itself into a knot.

"I like your dress." It was the least imaginative compliment he'd ever paid a woman but it was the best he could do. "Linguini."

"Excuse me?"

"The straps. They're wider than spaghetti. Linguini."

She looked amused. "Given that you grew up around linguini, I'm not arguing with you. Aren't you going to finish dressing?"

For a moment he wondered if she'd been picturing him naked, too, and then he realized she meant his bow tie.

He was about to tie it, but she got there first.

"I can do it. I'm good at this. My dad taught me." She

stepped closer to him. Her fingers tangled with his as she took the tie, and her eyes were fixed on the task as she concentrated.

Even though she was wearing those thin spiky heels, he was still more than a head taller than her. When he looked down he had a perfect view of the thick sweep of her eyelashes, the soft curve of her lips and the slope of her bare shoulders. She held her breath as she concentrated and he closed his eyes, disorientated by lust.

She was dressing him, not undressing him. It shouldn't feel this intimate.

There was the scent again, summer meadows and wild-flowers, and this time there was no escape. His mind picked up the scent and ran with it, providing him with disturbingly vivid pictures. He pictured her in the shower, water flowing over that perfect body, sliding into all the parts he wasn't allowed to touch. He imagined droplets of water and opalescent bubbles of soap clinging to that creamy skin.

Trying to shake off the images, he opened his eyes and fixed his gaze on the illuminated buttons, willing the elevator to rise quickly, trying to ignore the gentle brush of Paige's fingers against his throat. Never before had he considered having sex with a woman in an elevator. He was a man who thought that if something was worth doing it was worth doing well and sex in a moving capsule would be like eating fast food while walking to work.

Why had he suggested visiting the venue?

He could have seen it perfectly well from the picture.

He could have—

"There—" she stepped back, releasing him from his erotic thoughts. "That's better."

Not for him.

He pressed his shoulders back against the mirrored wall,

putting as much space between them as possible. If there had been an emergency exit, he would have taken it.

"How was your day?"

"Busy." She checked her lipstick in the mirror. "Frankie was talking to one of your designers and she has come up with an idea for a floral design in binary code. It's original and very cool."

"Binary code." He glanced at the illuminated buttons—35, 40, 45—*hurry up.* "That sounds innovative." He didn't care if the flowers sang and danced, he just wanted to get out of this damn elevator.

The doors slid open, releasing him from his torment and he forced himself to let her walk out first.

When her back was turned he ran his hand over his forehead and straightened his jacket.

Security staff stood aside to let them pass and they were greeted by their host.

Alysson Peters was CEO of a successful tech start-up. Jake had been an early, and generous, investor and it was that generosity that earned him an enthusiastic greeting.

"I didn't think you were coming!" Alysson embraced him. "This is great."

"I wouldn't have missed it." Jake kissed her on both cheeks, ignoring Paige's raised eyebrows. "Where's the bar, Aly?"

"Of course that *would* be your first question. You're a Bad Boy, Jake Romano. Which is why I love you, of course." Amused, she slapped him gently on the arm. "Everyone will want to be introduced to you, but as you're at the top of the food chain you can afford to ignore anyone that doesn't interest you. And anyway, I see you brought company." She smiled at Paige. "Aren't you going to introduce me to your date?"

"Paige Walker." Paige stepped forward and shook hands.

"Paige is CEO of a new start-up, Urban Genie, an event and concierge company." Jake dropped it in casually, his eyes scanning the room. "If you ever want a fabulous event and flawless execution, you should give her a call. If she's able to fit you into her schedule, it will be your lucky day. She's the best there is."

"Is that right? In that case—" Alysson held out her hand. "Do you have a card?"

Paige handed one over and Alysson glanced at it and slipped it into her purse.

"I'll be in touch. Have fun!" She walked away to greet more guests.

"Thank you for the introduction—" Paige sounded breathless "—but it might have worked better if you hadn't all but told her we were too busy to fit her into our schedule. Now she won't call."

"She'll call. First rule of human nature—people always want what they can't have. If you're in demand, everyone will want you." He lifted two glasses of champagne from the tray of a passing waiter and handed her one.

She took it, but only because he gave her no choice. "I'm working."

"Tonight you're working for me, and I order you to drink champagne."

With a faint smile she raised her glass. "What are we drinking to?"

To the ability of alcohol to numb the senses.

"To your exciting future. Soon you'll be too busy to drink."

"I hope so. Do you want me to show you around and talk you through my vision for the event?"

"Yes." He steered her into the center of the room. The more public, the better as far as he was concerned. The wall of glass separating the dance floor and bar area from the roof terrace had been opened up and the crowd spilled out onto the roof-top garden, drinking in the breathtaking views of starlit Man-hattan. The city dazzled and charmed, seduced the eye and bewitched the brain.

"You need to see this view." She walked to a section of the terrace with no crowds, leaving him no choice but to follow.

"I've lived in New York my whole life. I'm familiar with the view."

"But each time you look, it's different. This place is so New York. It's vibrant, exciting, the views are spectacular—" She lifted her face to the sky and closed her eyes.

"I thought Eva was the dreamer, not you."

"Everyone is capable of dreaming." She opened her eyes and smiled at him. "Aren't you?"

Right now his dreams were all X-rated.

He glanced over his shoulder.

The center of the terrace was dominated by an elaborate water feature, the bubbling water muffling the sounds of traf-fic from the streets below.

He wondered whether he was the first to contemplate strip-ping off and dipping in the temptingly cool water.

"It's a great place." He kept his eyes away from Paige and scanned the crowd. "Do you know why so many women wear black to an event like this?"

"Because black is classic. Timeless."

"No." Jake lifted the glass to his lips and drank. "They wear black because it's safe. They know they won't stand out. They're afraid to take a risk."

"Maybe. But Jake—" she sounded amused "—I'm wear-ing black."

He knew what she was wearing. If someone had handed

him a pencil he could have drawn every detail of the dress. *And the woman.*

"That's different. You're working. You're not allowed to up-stage the guests." He leaned on the railing, staring out across the city.

Paige looked out at the view, too. "My dream was to be here, in New York City, living this life, looking at this view, being part of it." Memories misted her eyes. "When I was at home, I was addicted to any TV series that had New York as a back-drop. I imagined how it would feel to stand at the top of the Empire State Building, to row across the lake in Central Park or walk across the Brooklyn Bridge. There are days when I still can't believe I'm actually here. I step out of the door, run past the magnolia trees and the street vendors, catch a glimpse of the Manhattan skyline and think, 'Wow, I *live* here.' I am a small-town girl living in this amazing city and I feel like the luckiest person in the world." She broke off and gave an em-barrassed laugh. "That probably sounds crazy, but there were so many times I never thought this could ever happen. That it would only ever be a dream."

There had been times when none of them had thought it could happen.

She'd been at death's door at least twice in her teens, when there had been complications following heart surgery.

He didn't mention it. A shared past provided a foundation for intimacy. He didn't want to tighten the loose threads that bound them together, didn't want to do anything that would draw them closer.

He'd tried to forget it, just as he was trying to forget that she was standing next to him in her little black dress. One small movement and he could have buried his face in her hair, and from there he could reach her mouth in seconds.

"You don't miss home?" He kept his eyes forward and his hands on the rail. "Puffin Island?"

"No. Not that I don't love Puffin Island, I do, but it's so *small*. Not only the place, but the pace. Everything is so slow there, which is what some people love about it, of course, but not me. Growing up, I felt as if life was going on somewhere else, across a stretch of water. I felt as if I was on the outside of a big party, looking in, excluded. I always felt as if I was missing something. That probably sounds stupid."

"Not to me." He knew all about being on the outside, looking in.

Same feeling. Different stretch of water.

"But you were born in Brooklyn. You're a genuine New Yorker."

"Yes." All through his early years when he'd felt rootless and insecure, like a rescue dog that no one had wanted to rescue, the city had been the one constant in his life. The place he'd slept had changed, the people who had taken him in had changed, but New York had stayed the same.

It was home.

Paige gazed at the Chrysler Building, its famous steel-and-glass rooftop illuminated against the midnight-blue sky like a jeweled wizard's hat. "Name another city where you can see anything as beautiful as that? It's pure fairy-tale."

He didn't disagree. "William Van Alen, the architect, secretly constructed the spire in the ventilation shaft and raised it in ninety minutes. Made it higher than 40 Wall Street, which was being constructed at the same time. Can you imagine thinking you're building the tallest building in the world, and then looking up and seeing that?" As someone with a brutally competitive nature, Jake appreciated the motivation behind the action. "They must have been so mad. The added height made it the tallest building until they constructed the Empire State Building."

She smiled. "It's magical. My favorite building in New York."

He knew people who came to New York just to say they'd done it. People who stayed awhile, then left because they needed space, a yard, an apartment where they didn't have to use the oven for storage, or slog down ten floors to do the laundry. No honking of horns, no sirens, no venting of steam, cleaner air, a slower pace—there were a million reasons to leave.

Jake only saw the reasons to stay, and Paige was the same.

He raised his glass to her. "To you, city girl."

"To you, city boy." She tapped her glass against his and drank. "Do you think New York is a man or a woman?"

The question made him smile. "It's a woman. So many different moods, the way she plays with people's emotions—has to be a woman, don't you think?" he teased.

"I don't know." She tilted her head, her expression thoughtful. "It could be a man. An elusive billionaire, showy about his wealth, secretive about his dark side. You think you know him, but he's always capable of surprising you."

"It's definitely a woman. So many different looks. A whole closet of different things to wear."

The crowd had increased and music drifted from the dance floor and floated into the night.

Ahead of them lay the Empire State Building and, beyond that, the bright lights of Broadway. The lights dazzled and danced, a city permanently awake.

Paige touched his arm. "Do you want to dance?"

He turned his head and looked into her eyes.

He wanted to do something with her, but it wasn't dancing.

Dancing would mean holding her, and holding her would mean body contact and he wasn't going there. "I don't dance."

Her smile dimmed. "Right. Of course." She finished her drink and put her glass down. "It's so pretty out here for a moment I forgot this was all about business. So let's do this. See the venue properly. I'll walk you through my ideas, and then you can do whatever it is you have planned for the rest of the night." She walked away, elegant, dignified and all woman.

But not his woman.

Never his woman.

Jake stared after her, his gaze traveling from her ankles to her hips and lingering there.

He'd look around the venue, make all the right noises, and then go home and dance with a bottle of whiskey.

What had she been *thinking*?

She'd asked him to dance, as if this was a *date*.

What was the matter with her? Where was her brain?

For a moment, under the glittering starlit sky and lights of Manhattan, she'd forgotten to keep her distance. She'd stopped thinking of Jake as a client and started thinking of him as a man.

She made an impatient sound. Who in their right mind would ever forget that Jake Romano was a man? He was testosterone in a tux. She'd been aware of every single sexy part of him from the moment he'd strode into the foyer of the building. He didn't blend into his surroundings like so many other people at this event—he owned them. Talking to him, sharing a conversation that for once hadn't felt like unarmed combat, had tipped her over from professional to personal.

And she'd made it awkward for him and embarrassed herself.

Again.

All she could do now was get through the rest of the evening as fast as possible.

Trying to pretend it had never happened, she adopted her most professional expression and showed him the rest of the venue, introducing him to the conference manager and walking him through Urban Genie's plan for his event.

He listened carefully, asked a few questions, added a few ideas of his own, all of them good.

By the time they'd finished talking, there was a crowd of people hovering close by hoping to grab a slice of his attention.

It was always the same. Some, she knew from experience, would have tech ideas they wanted to discuss with him. Some would simply be looking for business advice, some would be hoping for investment. Some of the women would be hoping for something more personal, too, and Paige didn't want to be around to see if he delivered on that.

"You're in demand, so I'll leave you now and see you at the office tomorrow." She managed what she hoped was a professional smile and walked to the bank of elevators.

Her feet were telling her that her choice of shoes sucked and she was longing to change into her flats. There was some footwear that even gel inserts couldn't rescue.

She'd chosen them based on the height of the heel. Intimidated enough by Jake's presence, she'd thought the extra height might give her confidence.

All it had given her was blisters.

Her feet, at least, were happy he'd refused to dance.

The moment she walked through the door she was going to take a long bath. With a glass of wine and a good book maybe. Or perhaps some brain-pounding music. Something to fill her head and distract her from thoughts of Jake.

Paige lifted her hand to press the button but a strong male hand reached past her and pressed it first.

She'd been so lost in her own thoughts she hadn't heard him come up behind her, but she'd know that hand anywhere.

"What are you doing?"

"I'm leaving, too." He hadn't touched her, but his voice alone was enough to send sizzles of awareness across her skin.

It was brutally unfair that she felt this way about a man who wasn't interested in her.

"You had a crowd of people wanting your attention."

"I'm with you."

If only. "This wasn't a date, Jake." She was pleased with how casual she sounded. "It was business. And anyway, since when did the presence of one woman prevent you from pursuing another?"

"I've never cheated on a woman." His voice was quiet and disturbingly close to her ear. "And I always make sure a woman gets home safely."

Her stupid heart, the one bit of her that never behaved as the textbooks said it should, skipped a beat. "You're taking women home now? Careful, that sounds almost like commitment."

"Their homes, not mine." There was a smile in his voice. "And it's good manners, rather than commitment."

She wished the elevator would hurry up. "Have you ever given your address to a woman?"

"Never, although they do occasionally show up at the office."

"Given that you virtually live there, they probably think that's the best place to catch you."

"My team make good bodyguards." The elevator finally arrived and he held the door while she walked past him. "My driver is waiting downstairs. He'll give you a ride home."

Her feet were yelling at her to accept without argument. Her independent streak made her shake her head. "I can take the train."

Jake stepped into the elevator. "Yeah, but you're not going to." He leaned against the mirrored wall and removed his bow tie with a few flicks of his fingers. "I know you like to be independent. I understand the reason and it's an admirable quality, but once in a while it would be good if you said yes to something without arguing."

There was a soft purr as the doors slid shut, enclosing them. "I say yes all the time."

There was a skeptical gleam in his eyes. "Give me an example of something you'd say yes to."

Right now she would have said yes to sex. Where he was concerned, she would have said yes to virtually anything. She'd promised herself she was always going to seize the moment, and right now she wanted to seize him. But she'd made a fool of herself once, and no way was she ever doing it again. "I say yes to Eva's cooking, to drinks on our roof terrace, to movie night even though Matt never lets us watch romantic movies. I say yes to a run in the Botanical Gardens, to a bagel fresh from the cart. Want me to go on?"

He was impossibly handsome, so gorgeous it fried her brain to look at him. Even now, half-undressed, he looked better than any other man dressed to impress up on that roof terrace.

His bow tie hung around his neck with casual disregard for its future appearance. His shirt was open at the neck, revealing a hint of dark chest hair. His jaw, clean shaved first thing in the morning, was dark with shadow.

He shouldn't have looked this good, but if she'd ever seen a sexier man, she couldn't remember it.

He watched her with that disturbingly intimate gaze that

made her wonder if he could read her mind. She was an expert at hiding her feelings. She'd learned to protect others every bit as much as they protected her, but somehow with Jake she had to work harder.

He saw things. He paid attention.

She was about to make a flippant comment when the elevator gave a jolt. Thrown off balance by her uncomfortably high heels she was flung against him, smacking into the hard wall of his chest. For a moment all she was aware of was the solid bulk of his biceps under her fingers and the warmth of his breath on her face. Desire uncurled inside her, a slow warmth that immediately flared to burning heat.

His mouth was right there, *right there*—if she turned her head—

His hand slid around her waist to steady her and he frowned at the control panel. "Did you press something?"

"No." Her teeth were gritted. It had been years since she'd been this close to him, and yet it felt as natural as if their bodies had been glued together for a decade. "I didn't touch anything. It stopped by itself."

"Must have been my electric personality."

She pulled away from him, irritated by the depth of her attraction. Why couldn't she feel this way about a man who was interested in her? There was no justice. "Perhaps you'd like to use your electric personality to get us out of here, then. Press the button." As the sharp edge of her desire faded, she felt a lurch of fear. She wasn't good with enclosed spaces. Never had been.

It would be fine, she told herself. Probably something simple.

The button for the ground floor was already illuminated but he pressed it again.

There was a clicking sound.

Nothing happened.

Paige felt her palms grow clammy. Her chest tightened. Elevators were fine as a means of getting from one place to another, providing they were moving, but being trapped in a tight airless space? She'd always hated it. As far as she was concerned being in an MRI scanner felt like being buried alive.

"Maybe the venue have trapped us here until we've paid for our event." She tried to lighten the atmosphere but it grew heavier, as if the walls were coming in to squeeze her.

"Maybe." His gaze skimmed the control panel. Then he reached into his pocket and she saw a brief flash of metal.

"Is that a screwdriver? You carry a screwdriver around with you? Why?"

"This isn't the first time I've had to get myself out of a tight spot. Hold my jacket." He shrugged out of it and threw it to her, then rolled back his sleeves.

"What was your last tight spot? Was she married?"

He smiled as he worked. "I never touch married women. Too complicated. Put your hand out—"

"Why?"

"Paige—" his voice was patient "—this is another one of those occasions when you say yes and do it. You don't ask a million questions and you don't argue with me."

She put her hand out and hoped he didn't notice it was shaking.

He dropped a couple of screws into her palm. "Now I can take a closer look."

"Look at what? What are you doing?" Whatever it was, she hoped it worked. "You're intending to dismantle it and reprogram it? You're going to hack into the FBI and tell them to come get us?" She wished they would. She wished anyone would. The walls seemed to close in a little more. Closing the screws in her fist, she wrapped her arms around herself and tried to breathe steadily.

Her heart rate had picked up and she felt panic swoop down on her.

Beads of sweat cooled her forehead. Was it her imagination or was the capsule shrinking?

Jake straightened. "Can you—" He broke off as he saw her face. "What's wrong?"

"Nothing." She clenched her teeth to keep them from chattering. "Just get us out of here."

"I'm working on it." He slid the screwdriver into his pocket. "Why do you always pretend to be all right when you're not? Why not admit you're scared?"

"I'm not scared. But I'd rather not spend an entire evening in an elevator."

"It's not going to plummet to the ground if that's what's worrying you, so don't panic."

"I'm not worried and I'm certainly not panicking." Two lies in less than ten words. That was probably a record. Paige concentrated on her breathing, the same way she'd done countless times as a child.

Pretend you're fine. Pretend you're fine.

The panic grew.

"Do something, Jake."

He turned back to the control panel so she couldn't see what he was doing, but she heard him give a soft curse and slam his palm against the metal. "Doing my best, but unfortunately on this rare occasion my best isn't good enough." He leaned on the emergency button and moments later a disembodied voice echoed around the enclosed space asking what the problem was.

"We're stuck in the elevator and a rapid extraction would be appreciated." Jake named the building and the street and glanced at Paige quickly.

Still focused on her breathing, she gave him a look of disbelief. *Rapid extraction?* She mouthed the words and he shrugged and glanced up at the roof of the elevator.

"I thought it sounded better than 'get us the hell out of here.'" He moved closer to the intercom. "What's your name?"

"Channing."

"And where are you, Channing?"

"Houston, Texas, sir."

Paige's mouth dropped. "Houston—? How can someone a four-hour flight away be operating our elevator?"

Jake lifted a hand to silence her. "And how's the weather down there right now, Channing? I bet you're sweltering in a whole lot of heat and humidity."

"Yes, sir."

"So are we as it happens. And I'm with a lady who is starting to find this whole experience a little uncomfortable, so I'm going to need you to do whatever it is you do when there's an emergency and get us out of here as fast as possible. And by that I mean preferably within the next couple of minutes." Humor was neatly layered over steely authority.

"I'll notify the maintenance team and the fire department. You stay right there, sir." There was a pause. "And ma'am."

As if they had any number of alternative options.

Paige leaned against the wall. Her chest ached and her heart was pounding.

"Hand me the screws—" Jake held out his hand and she stared at him blankly, trying to focus through the panic.

It was fine. Everything was going to be fine. Someone would get them out soon.

Jake reached out and uncurled her tightly clenched fist.

He stared down at the ridges and indentations made by the screws and glanced at her face. "Paige?"

"I'm fine." She said it like a mantra. "Totally fine. Don't worry about me."

Jake pocketed the screws and pulled her into his arms. "You don't like enclosed spaces," he murmured. "How could I have forgotten that? It's fine, honey. I'm here. I'm going to get you out of here soon, I promise."

His words and the sure confidence of his tone should have been enough to quell the rising panic, but it wasn't.

"How?" She gave up all pretense of being all right. "That man's in Houston. We're here."

Her breath was coming in snatches. Her chest felt tight and heavy.

"The maintenance guys are right here in the city." He smoothed his hand over her hair. "Relax, baby."

"Did you seriously just call me 'baby'?" She pressed her palm to her chest, trying to soothe the tightness. "Normally I'd punch you for that."

"Normally I wouldn't call you 'baby.'" He eased her closer, molding her into his warmth and strength. "I'm not your brother and I'm not your parents. You don't have to do the happy act with me. I can cope with the truth."

She was held snugly against him, the hard muscle of his thighs supporting her shaking limbs.

"My heart…" She hated herself for being so weak. "I'm— It's—"

"It's not your heart, Paige." He lifted his hand and stroked her face gently with his fingers. "It's not your heart, sweetheart."

She tried to breathe. "But—" She inhaled male warmth and strength and closed her eyes. "It's—I'm—"

"Your heart is just fine." His voice was sure and strong. "Paige, look at me—"

She couldn't.

She stared at his chest, her breathing shallow and rapid, and then felt his fingers slide under her chin as he lifted her face to his. His touch was comfort and sin all at the same time.

"You're panicking because you hate tight spaces. I should have remembered that. I need you to breathe slowly. That's it." With one hand he continued stroking her face, and with the other he held her close, so close her body blended with his. She could feel the warmth of his skin through the thin fabric of his shirt and the warmth of his hand soothing her spine. She should have felt secure and safe, but nothing, not even being held by Jake, could dispel the panic. It rose like floodwaters, seeping through her, out of control.

Her lungs felt tight. There was a crushing sensation in her chest and she curled her fist into the front of Jake's shirt, her knuckles white.

She wanted to tell him that she couldn't breathe but she couldn't find the air to talk.

Through the swirling mists of panic she heard him curse softly, and then felt his hand move from her back.

She was about to cling to him and beg him not to let her go, when she realized he wasn't letting her go. He was pulling her closer. He slid his hand into her hair with a slow, deliberate movement and stroked her cheek with his thumb.

"Look at me, Paige. Look at me, honey—" His voice was firm, his eyes hooded and silver gray as he held her terrified gaze. His face was familiar and yet unfamiliar, those hard masculine lines stamped with a determination she didn't recognize. Or maybe panic had distorted her vision as well as all her other faculties.

She was holding her breath, her mouth a mere whisper away from his, and then his head lowered and he took her mouth in a slow, hard, deliberate kiss.

She gave a start of shock but he held her firm, her body locked against his.

What was he doing?

She didn't have the breath for kissing.

She didn't—

Desire ignited, engulfing fear, and she moaned against his lips, breathed him in and tasted the essence of him as he kissed her slowly and thoroughly. Holding her head still, he explored her mouth with long, leisurely kisses that changed the source of her shivering from fear to arousal. Her mouth opened under his in complicit surrender. She'd often wondered how it would feel to be kissed by Jake, and now she knew. It was like drinking champagne too fast, like riding a roller coaster with your eyes closed, like diving from a high board into deep water. She swayed, dizzy, but he held her captive, anchoring her against the power of his body with strong hands. And just when she thought she'd felt everything there was to feel, the kiss changed from slow and seeking to rough and raw, from gentle seduction to pure primal sex. She'd never experienced anything like the erotic intimacy of being kissed by Jake. It was wild. Thrilling. And it awoke something inside her that had been dormant her whole life.

Excitement exploded in a starburst, shocking her with its intensity. It was like suddenly discovering a whole new part of herself. A part of her more alive than any other.

The jacket slithered from her fingers to the floor.

She rose on her toes to bring herself closer to him and in

doing so felt the effect she was having on him, felt the hard thickness of him through the fabric of her dress.

Shoots of delicious pleasure spread through her, the anticipation and promise of still more to come almost unbearably exciting. She held herself still, waiting on the edge of something, and then his hands were there, on the thin, flimsy fabric of her dress, finding access points, sliding the roughness of his thumb over the straining peak of her nipple until her vision blurred. Logic told her there had to be a ceiling to the excitement, but if there was she had yet to reach it.

He urged her back until she was sandwiched between the hard, unyielding glass of the elevator and the hard, unyielding power of his body. He murmured something against her ear, a deliciously explicit suggestion of what he wanted to do to her and exactly how he intended to do it, and she closed her hand over his shoulder, digging her fingers into the pumped-up swell of male muscle. She might have taken a moment to savor the feel of those muscles, but then he was kissing her again and she'd wanted him to kiss her for so long she wasn't going to waste a single second of it. Then she felt him jerk her dress up to her waist and felt the warm slide of his palm on her bare thigh.

So close, so close...

His tongue was in her mouth, his kiss hot, searching and so insanely skilled she felt sorry for all the women in the world who had never been kissed by Jake. She felt that kiss shimmer through her body, connecting to someplace deep inside her. And she kissed him back, consumed by desire, her fingers locked in the silky spikes of his hair, dragging his head to hers, terrified in case he changed his mind, in case he stopped. She'd dreamed about this so many times and it had been frustrating because she'd never been able to totally imagine what it would be like. There was an elusive quality to Jake, a hardness, a hint of sexual experience that she knew would make being with him different from her few other encounters. And it was different. She inhaled him and he inhaled her, his mouth devouring hers as if she were the last thing he was ever going to taste before his life ended. The kiss was tinged with hints of desperation, colored by their personal history, made intimate by their knowledge of each other. It was the most intense, shockingly personal connection of her life. She'd imagined his mouth on hers, his hands on her body, so many times, but not even the most erotic of her daydreams had ever come close to the reality.

She never wanted it to end.

And it showed no signs of ending. He kissed her as if he couldn't stop himself. His palm held her breast, and then slid down and curved over her thigh and he lifted her leg until she had no choice but to wrap it around his back. Her shoe fell to the floor with a soft clatter. Still he kissed her, but now his hand slid lower, between her parted thighs, to the access he himself had created. She felt the brush of his hand against her bare thigh, the touch of his fingers against sensitive, quivering flesh.

Her body was already close to exploding.

Somewhere in the distance there was a metallic, grinding noise and then the sound of voices came from somewhere above her head. Jake pulled away from her with a rough sound and straightened her clothes in a single movement.

The fact that he could move at all proved he was more together than she was.

Paige stood, disorientated, trying to regain her balance, and then heard the voices again, closer this time.

"Are you all right?"

No she wasn't all right.

Except—

She frowned as she realized what she was feeling was no longer panic.

"Yeah, we're good." Jake's voice was as raw as his kisses had been seconds earlier. His gaze was fixed on hers and his hand, that same hand that had almost driven her wild, smoothed her hair gently. "How's it looking up there? Any chance of getting us out of here?"

"Working on it right now."

A moment ago Paige had been desperate to escape, but now she would happily have died right here in this small confined space, provided Jake was with her. Her lips tingled, her skin ached and throbbed. Everything felt unfinished, as if he'd taken her apart, unraveled her, but forgotten to put her back together. She felt like one of Frankie's half-built models.

Jake bent to retrieve her shoe and his jacket and she stared at his profile, at those perfect angular lines and masculine bone structure, wondering what he was thinking, searching for signs that she wasn't the only one feeling this way.

Whatever happened next, there was no more pretending that he didn't feel anything for her.

There was a clatter and a scrap of metal against metal, and then two maintenance men were peering down at them.

"You guys were quick." Jake slid his jacket back on and looked up at them. Calm. In control. "Did you bring a ladder?" His voice sounded steady. Normal. Nothing like the voice that had, only moments earlier, woven her insides into a mesh of insane desire as he'd made her aware of his intentions.

Somehow she slid her foot back into her shoe and Jake urged her toward the ladder. "Can you climb?" There was a rough edge to his tone and she felt the warmth of his hand on her back.

"Yes." She climbed, conscious that he was beneath her, probably with a perfect view up her skirt where his hand had been only minutes earlier.

What happened after that blurred. She remembered laughing with the maintenance men, making some quip, assuring a few waiting guests that she was fine, and then somehow plucking up the courage to follow Jake into a different elevator, this time with a crowd of people, and travel down to the foyer.

Jake made polite conversation with someone eager for his opinion on a new piece of computer software.

He didn't look at her.

She didn't look at him.

Outside the building his driver was waiting, and he opened the door for Paige to step inside the warmth of the car.

Now what?

Would he kiss her in the car or would he take her home?

Her heart was pounding with anticipation, but instead of following, he leaned inside. "Gavin will drop you home. Get some sleep."

That was it? That was all he was going to say? "You're not coming?"

"I'll walk." His tone was neutral. "It's a nice evening. The fresh air will do me good."

In other words he didn't want to get in the car with her.

They'd virtually set fire to the elevator shaft and he wasn't even going to mention it?

That was it?

She sat, bemused, trying to make sense of it. Through a cloud of questions she heard the door of the car slam shut and heard him exchange a few words with the driver.

"Take her home, Gavin… Yeah, right to the door and wait until she's inside. I want to know she's okay."

Paige stared straight ahead. She wasn't okay.

She was *not* okay!

What had just happened?

Had she imagined the kiss in the elevator? Had she imagined that raw passion?

She touched her fingers to her mouth. Her lips still tingled and the sensitive skin on her cheeks was a little sore from the rough scrape of his jaw.

No, she hadn't imagined any of it.

Was he really trying to pretend nothing had happened?

Jake kissed a lot of women—she knew that.

But he didn't kiss her.

He never, ever kissed her.

So what happened next?

Nine

If you can't stand the heat, remove a layer of clothing.

—Eva

"So was it romantic?" Eva was dancing around the apartment in her pajamas, headphones covering her ears and her hair wrapped in foil when Paige arrived home twenty minutes later.

"It wasn't a date—it was a venue visit." Paige dropped her keys on the table, her head still reeling. She studied her friend in disbelief. "You look like something from another planet. What happened to your hair?"

"Mmm?" Eva swayed her hips and her head to a rhythm only she could hear and Paige tugged off one of the earphones.

"Until you learn to lip-read you have to take these off when you're having a conversation."

Eva slid them down to her neck. "I'm pampering myself. Coconut oil hair mask. It's a miracle and magic all-in-one package. You should try it. Leaves your hair feeling like silk. In my case, rumpled silk."

"It will take more than a miracle and magic to sort out my

problems." Tired and confused, Paige slid off her shoes, made her way to the bathroom, pulled her dress over her head and stepped into the shower.

By the time she emerged, Eva had made tea and was curled up on Paige's bed.

"Tell me about the problems."

Paige flicked on the light by the bed.

How had it happened? Who had started it? She couldn't even remember. One minute she'd been panicking, the next they'd been kissing like maniacs.

She felt a flash of horror.

It was so unprofessional.

"This event—" Her voice was urgent. "It has to be the best thing we've ever done."

"Of course. It will be brilliant. You've never organized any-thing that *hasn't* been brilliant. What happened? Sit down and talk to me." Eva patted the bed, her eyes kind. "Jake didn't like the venue?"

"I—" She realized she didn't know. "I didn't ask him."

"But that *was* why you went tonight, wasn't it? To show him the venue. Was everything all right?"

"Yes. It was great. Beautiful." *Romantic.* Oh crap, it had been romantic. With the whole city spread before them, spar-kling like a tray of diamonds at Tiffany's.

"Good." Eva curled her fingers around her mug. "So did whoever kissed you kiss you at the beginning of the night or the end?"

"What makes you think someone kissed me?"

"The stubble graze on your cheek is a little clue, as well as the fact that there is no trace of lipstick anywhere on your face and the only time I ever see you without lipstick is when you're asleep." Eva put down her mug of tea. "I'm the first to admit that numbers challenge me, but I'm fluent in body language and the language of love and you're showing all the signs of someone who has been thoroughly, deliciously kissed by a man who knew exactly what he was doing. Tell me everything."

What was there to say? "It's late—we should get some sleep."

"We both know you're not going to sleep after that kiss, and I won't sleep until you tell me everything I want to know, so you might as well satisfy my curiosity. And anyway, this coconut smelly thing has to stay on my hair for ten more minutes or it won't work and I'm not spending all that money for nothing." She nudged Paige with her shoulder and picked up her mug again. "Go on. Who was it? Are you seeing the guy again? And how did you manage to ditch Jake?"

She could lie, but Eva knew her too well.

"It *was* Jake."

Eva choked on her tea. "You kissed Jake? *Our* Jake?"

"He kissed me. We kissed each other. I don't know. It was— confusing. The elevator broke down. We were trapped."

"Trapped?" Instantly understanding, Eva reached for her hand. "You hate being enclosed. That must have been awful for you."

"It was. Until Jake kissed me."

"That is *so* romantic."

"It wasn't. I—" Paige frowned. "I don't know what it was, Ev. It was—it was—"

"*It was what?* It was gentle? Brotherly? Comforting? He kissed you as though—?"

"—as though I'd died and he was trying to bring me back to life."

Eva stared at her. "Holy crap. That's the kind of kiss I dream about. The-world-is-ending-so-let's-just-kiss-all-the-way-through-it kind of kiss. Didn't I tell you that kissing Jake should be on everyone's bucket list? I can always tell when a man is going to be a good kisser and I bet Jake is an expert."

Paige thought back. "I don't know why."

"Well, he's had loads of practice of course, but I think some men are born with great kissing DNA and have natural talent. I bet Jake is one of those. He's the sort who pays attention."

"I meant I don't know why he kissed me."

"Oh." Eva blinked. "Presumably because he wanted to. What happened next? I need to know the ending. Don't keep me hanging on—I'm terrible with cliff-hangers."

"There is no ending."

"There has to be an ending. He looked deep into your eyes and said, 'This isn't over, Paige'?"

"No. He said, 'Gavin will drop you home. Get some sleep.'"

Eva looked taken aback. "That's it? He was silent for the whole trip home? He didn't smolder at you, reach for your hand or say 'We'll talk about this tomorrow,' in that deep, sexy voice that makes you want to leap on him and strip him naked right down to the bone marrow?"

"I was on my own in the car. He walked home." And that was the part that confused her most.

The bedroom door opened and Frankie walked in. "I heard you come home. Wanted to check everything went smoothly."

"Jake kissed her. You missed the details." Eva wiped a drop of coconut mask from her cheek. "I'm confused about why he walked home by himself."

"That makes two of us." Paige flopped back against the pillows. "I have no idea what's going on. I kept waiting for him to say something and he didn't. We virtually set fire to the building and he didn't mention it."

Frankie looked confused. "You set fire to the building?"

"With the kiss. And of course he didn't mention it. He's a guy." Eva shifted on the bed and the scent of coconut wafted around the room. "Work. Sex. Beer. Sport. Big noisy engines. Anything that moves fast. That's their world. Emotions are this murky, dangerous thing hovering in the background like bad weather they hope will pass them by."

Frankie joined them on the bed. "That is generalizing, not to mention sexist."

"It's the truth. You always tease me, but I understand men better than you think." Eva put down her empty mug. "If they can't drill a hole in it, have sex with it, get drunk on it, kick it around a field, or watch it on a massive screen, they're mostly not interested. That's the way the male brain is programmed."

Paige blinked. "Matt isn't like that."

"Of course he is! And he's cleverer than most because he found a job that uses power tools. I mean, he could delegate but I've often seen him rigged up, drilling holes in concrete or sawing through tree trunks to make garden seats. He owns a tool belt. Does he have to do it? No, but blasting apart masonry and chopping down trees is one of the fun parts of the job, so he's not going to delegate that bit. Come on, wake up." Eva looked at her in exasperation. "I know he's your brother but he has a man cave, Paige, complete with cinema screen, Xbox, weights I can't even lift off the ground and a fridge full of beer. He has poker nights. Poker nights are an excuse for men to have conversations they wouldn't have in front of women. I rest my case."

Paige tried to adapt to this new image of her brother. "Sorry, what was your case?"

Frankie laughed. "Don't train to be a lawyer, Ev. By the

time you reached the end of your argument the jury would have forgotten the beginning."

"I was saying that what Paige did with Jake didn't fit neatly into any of those categories. I understand why he was confused."

"He didn't look confused. He looked—" She thought back to it. "He looked normal." And she hadn't wanted him to be. "I was the one who was confused. Still am. So what happens now? I might see him in the office. I *will* see him in the office. Do I mention it? Do I not mention it?"

"Who started it? Who made the first move? Him or you?"

"I don't know. One minute we were trapped and I was stressed, and then he held me for a moment and it just happened."

"So it was him. He made the first move. Wow. I wish I could have seen that. Sounds like that movie with Cary Grant and—anyway, never mind. That's good, because he won't be able to say you were the one who put the moves on him. So what should you do? Mmm—give me a minute while I think."

Frankie made an impatient sound. "Just ask him!"

"Ask him?"

"Yes! Walk into his office and say, why the hell did you kiss me? It's called communication!"

Paige stared at her.

"Frankie might be right." Eva slid off the bed. "I need to wash this thing out of my hair or tomorrow when you wake me up you'll find a gnarled coconut in the bed. Go to sleep and have really dirty dreams."

"I think the term you're looking for is *sweet dreams*."

"No. Those are boring. Dirty ones are much better. And don't waste all night thinking about it or you'll look tired tomorrow, and you don't want to give Jake the satisfaction of knowing he gave you a sleepless night."

"Does that advice come straight from the Eva school of dating?"

"Maybe, but it's all theory, of course. I haven't had a practical session in a long time, but I'm working on that. In fact I have a date tomorrow."

"You do?" Grateful for the distraction, Paige tried to push Jake to the back of her mind. "Who? Not that guy who hit on you in the street the other day?"

"No." Eva blushed. "Someone else. He's NYPD."

"You're dating a *cop*? How did you meet him?"

"Well, I managed to lock myself out of the apartment a few days ago. He happened to be passing and spotted me trying to climb in through Frankie's window. He stopped to help me. Actually, I think he stopped to arrest me, but once he realized I was clueless about breaking and entering, he helped me. We swapped numbers and today he called."

"Is he hot?"

"I don't know. He wears a uniform," Eva said simply. "Every man looks hot in uniform."

"We should make a plan."

Growing up, they'd always made a plan when one of them had a date. Because Paige was often in hospital, it was something they did to pass the time when Eva and Frankie were keeping her company. They'd bring in dresses, make-up and plan the whole date.

"My plan is to get some sleep." Frankie stood up, too. "First thing tomorrow, go and ask Jake why he put his tongue down your throat."

Paige gave a weak smile. "I might word it differently."

"Fine." Frankie shrugged. "But don't word it so differently he doesn't understand the question."

In his office, Jake was sprawled at his desk, trying to wrap his brain around a creative content issue. He looked at the problem again, played with a few ideas on his screen and came to the conclusion that his team had done a good job. There were a few refinements he might have added, but those could be inserted in the next phase when they rolled it out.

All he had to do now was talk the client through it and get their buy in.

This was the part of the job he loved. The sparring.

He took a bottle of water from the fridge beneath his desk and drank. It had been a complicated brief. At the moment, their solution was a little too complex for the client to grasp, but he'd fix that. One of his skills was to translate technology into something a six-year-old could understand. And most CEOs, in his experience, had a lot in common with six-year-olds. When this was launched, their business would increase. Again. There would be more enquiries, more business, an increased flow of money. The thought of it soothed him. As long as the money was flowing unimpeded, a river in full flood and not a dried-up riverbed, he was happy.

He had three computer screens on his desk, all of them switched on. His eyes were on the middle one when he sensed movement out of the corner of his eye.

Paige stood in the doorway. Her blue eyes were fixed on his, and an electric tension snapped the atmosphere tight.

He'd planned on doing them both a favor and avoiding her for a while. He'd banked on her doing the same with him. He figured that if they both worked hard enough at it, they could go at least a couple of days without laying eyes on each other. Maybe even a week.

Apparently not.

He would have told himself she was here about a professional query if he hadn't seen the spark in her eyes.

He knew a woman on a mission when he saw one, and Paige was a woman on a mission.

"Hey." He kept his greeting casual, hoping he was wrong and she was going to ask him something work related. "How are you doing? No aftereffects from being trapped in the elevator?"

"Not from the elevator, no."

Shit.

"Good. In that case——" He shifted in his chair, wishing he had an ejector seat. He would happily have taken an impromptu flight over the Hudson to avoid this situation. "I'm a little busy right now so if you could close the door and——"

She closed it with herself on the inside.

Heat spread across the back of his neck.

He was doomed.

"I'm busy right now, and——"

"Then I'll make it quick. I want to talk about what happened."

He hedged. "Talk about what exactly?"

"The kiss." She walked toward his desk, and something in the sway of her hips made his mouth dry.

He could remember the taste of her, the soft lick of her tongue against his, the rapid beat of her pulse under his fingers.

"You were scared. I was trying to distract you."

"Which part was supposed to distract me? The part when you had your tongue in my mouth or the part when you had your hand up my skirt?"

Her words took him straight back there.

If she'd been anyone else, he would have hauled her straight back to his apartment and screwed her until neither of them had the energy to leave the bed.

But instead, here he was, trying to do the decent thing and she was making him feel bad about it.

The injustice of it made him irritable.

He pushed back from the desk. "You were hyperventilating."

"You kissed me to stop me overbreathing?"

It sounded ridiculous even to him. "You were scared and I comforted you. That's what it was about. Don't make something of it, Paige."

"Don't *make something* of it?" She paced to the desk on those crazily long legs that had been wrapped around his waist the night before.

Restless, he shifted his gaze from her legs to her mouth. That didn't help, because her mouth was soft and glossy and he knew exactly how it tasted. The truth was there wasn't a single part of her that didn't tempt him. He tried staring at his computer screen. "Yeah, you know—don't spin things."

"Things?"

He ground his teeth. "Fairy tales. That's Eva's domain."

"And what are you in this fairy tale, Jake? Prince Charming? Because I don't remember being asleep. The big bad wolf? *All the better to eat you with?*"

"It was a kiss, dammit." He stood up, irritable, cornered. Dragging his fingers through his hair, he looked at her. "What do you want me to say? I kissed you."

"I know you kissed me. I was there. What I don't know is why. And don't tell me you were trying to stop me hyperventilating."

Why had he kissed her?

Because for a few seconds he'd let his guard drop. "You were upset."

"You don't kiss women when they're upset. You hug them. You pat them. You say 'there, there.'"

"It started that way." *Why the hell couldn't she let it alone?*

"But it didn't end that way."

"No, it didn't." The memory of how it had ended had kept him awake for most of the night. He'd paced the considerable length of his loft apartment several times. He'd taken two cold showers. "Do you always analyze everything?"

"No, not everything. But I'm analyzing this."

"You need to let it go."

"You think we can ignore it?"

"Yeah, that's what I think."

"Tell me you're not interested and I won't mention it again." She dropped the words into a pulsing, thickened silence.

She had him trapped, squirming like a fish on a hook.

"I'm not interested. Look, we were two people trapped in an elevator—you were stressed, I comforted you and it turned into more than I planned. I'd had a glass of champagne, you were there all cute and vulnerable, your mouth was all red and kissable. But it was just a kiss. It happens." He hoped she'd leave it at that, but of course she didn't.

"It wasn't just a kiss. It was—" she'd lost a little of her confidence, seemed puzzled "—more. It was more, Jake. I felt it. It was different."

"No it wasn't. I kiss like that all the time." He stripped the emotion out of his voice. "That kiss felt the same as all the others." He shot the arrow straight through her heart.

The hurt pulsed from her and right at that moment he truly hated himself.

Why the hell had he taken the elevator with her?

"So you're saying you kissed me because I was there. Because I happened to have a mouth, and I was wearing red lipstick." Her voice was monotone. "That's all it was?"

"Yes."

She stared at him for a moment and then picked one of the smiles from her collection. She had several that he knew of. There was the "I'm fine" smile. The "I'm not in pain" smile and the "I don't care" smile.

This was a combination of all three. Matt would have called it her Brave Face.

"Right—well, I appreciate your honesty." She straightened her shoulders. "Sorry to disturb you. If you have any questions about the venue, let me know. Otherwise Urban Genie will carry on with the planning."

"I don't have questions." Except for wondering why he'd agreed to this. "Do your thing."

As long as she did her thing well away from him, they might even survive this.

Ten

Men are like lipstick; you have to try a few before you find the perfect one.

—Paige

"So how's business?" Jake was sprawled on the sofa in Matt's man cave killing zombies on the Xbox while they waited for the rest of their friends to arrive for a game of pool. "Busy?"

"Yeah. Did you drink all the beer from my fridge? I could have sworn it was full last week."

"It was. Then we had poker night. You're forgetting."

"I'm not forgetting. I lost more than beer that night." Matt gave a grunt and stood up. "If you empty the damn fridge, you should fill it up, especially as you walked away with half my money last time."

It was an easy exchange. One they'd had a hundred times before.

"I seem to recall emptying your fridge was a joint project, and as I filled it up in the first place you can't complain. And

I'm empty-handed this time because I came on the bike. I can go to the restaurant if you like and raid supplies."

"You'd steal from your own mother? You have no conscience."

Given that his conscience was the only thing holding Jake back from screwing Paige, the accusation made him irritable. "Do you want beer or not?"

"Well, aren't you in a sunny mood?" Matt studied him. "Do you want to talk about it? Or would you rather have a tantrum by yourself?"

"By myself works fine." Jake destroyed more zombies.

"So you're not going to tell me what's wrong?"

"Nothing's wrong. And since when did you encourage me to talk about my problems? That's Eva's role."

Matt looked at him steadily. "Right, I get it. You don't want to talk about it. And don't worry about the beer. We have enough for tonight. I told Paige I'd drive the van to pick up some scaffolding for your event tomorrow, so I can pick some more up then."

"Scaffolding?"

"They're building a centerpiece—they haven't told you?" Matt frowned. "Paige has found a set designer. Don't you have meetings about this stuff?"

Not if he could help it. "We had a meeting at the beginning. I told her what I wanted. They're coming up with a plan that fits. I glance at the emails occasionally."

"You didn't give them a budget?"

"Open-ended."

Matt winced. "You gave Eva an open-ended budget? She'll open an account at Bloomingdale's and strip the place bare. I thought you were a businessman."

"I gave Paige the budget. I want to make a splash. It will

be worth the investment, I'm sure." And he'd wanted to give Paige full rein to wow Manhattan's finest. That much he could do for her.

"You're telling me you don't know the details?"

"Why buy a dog and bark yourself?"

"Are you calling my sister a dog?"

"No." Jake got violent with the zombies. "I'm telling you I know how to delegate. I don't care what's in the food, as long as my guests are fed and happy. It doesn't matter to me if the mushrooms are chanterelle or oyster, which is what I told Eva when she tried to discuss details with me. She's the food expert. I'm leaving it to her."

"And Paige is overseeing the whole thing. She's working twenty-hour days for you, so you'd better say something encouraging."

Jake kept his eyes on the screen and killed a few more zombies. Since the conversation in his office, he'd stayed out of her way.

"How is she doing?"

"Why are you asking me? I thought she was sharing your office?"

"She is, but she's working and I'm working and we're not working on the same thing." Jake destroyed everything on the screen in a violent bloodbath.

Matt raised his eyebrows. "Is something wrong?"

"Nothing is wrong. Why would you think anything is wrong?"

"Because you're tense and you've killed a hell of a lot of zombies."

"That's the point of the game. To kill zombies." Jake dropped the controller, hating the fact that he felt guilty. What did he have to feel guilty about? He was doing this for her. Putting himself through the hell of sexual frustration for her. "So last time you saw Paige, she didn't seem upset?"

"Upset?" Matt's eyes narrowed. "Why would she be upset? Has something happened?"

Yeah, he'd virtually stripped her naked and feasted on her mouth as if she were his next meal. "It was a friendly enquiry, that's all." He felt his neck grow hot. "She's been working hard."

"I thought you hadn't seen her."

"That's how I know she's working hard. I haven't." Apart from in the elevator when he'd seen, and tasted, far too much of her.

"You haven't put your head around the office door once to check on her?" Matt sounded more amused than annoyed, but the whole situation was as uncomfortable as walking on gravel in bare feet. Jake shifted.

"I've been busy. I have my own business to run." And if he'd put his head around the door to check on her he might have come away with a black eye. He wouldn't have blamed her for punching him. Guilt scraped over his conscience like sandpaper. "What more do you want from me? I've invited everyone important in my contacts. The rest is up to her."

"Hey, you've been good to her, Jake." Matt's tone was warm. "You've been a good friend."

There was a cold, knotted feeling in his gut.

He'd been the worst friend.

"I should have checked on her, I suppose, but I haven't been in the office much." He'd found a thousand reasons not to be there. He'd flown to LA to talk to a client instead of making them fly to him. He'd driven to DC to discuss a security issue with a high-level contact there and taken his time returning.

He hadn't seen Paige in over a week.

It annoyed him that he couldn't stop thinking about her, and it annoyed him that he hadn't been able to keep his hands off her in the elevator.

He couldn't stop replaying that damn kiss in his mind.

Matt put his hand on Jake's shoulder. "Don't feel bad about it. I appreciate what you're doing for her, I really do. I owe you."

Jake felt guilt shoot through him. This was his friend. He'd never deceived his friend before. It didn't feel good. "You don't owe me, but if you really want to pay me back you can let me win tonight."

Matt grinned. "You couldn't beat me even if I was wasted."

"Is that a challenge?" Right now drinking everything in sight seemed like a good way to go. "Let's try it."

"That was the worst, most embarrassing date of my life. Thank goodness for the emergency phone call."

Frankie was on her knees, tending the roof garden. "I'm not going to say I told you so."

"Good." Eva slipped off her shoes and dropped onto one of the cushions. "Because right now I'm feeling evil and I'd probably deadhead you alongside your roses."

Paige lit the candles. It was the first time they'd been up on the roof garden all week. They'd been working long hours and there had been plenty of days when they'd gone straight from the office to bed and then back again.

Still, at least working hard had dulled the acute pain she'd felt after her encounter with Jake. She was too exhausted to feel anything.

She flopped on the cushions next to Eva. "Tell us about your date."

"I don't want to talk about it." Eva shuddered. "It was bad enough experiencing it once, without reliving it."

Frankie carefully added another layer of soil to the planter. "Are you going to tell us where he took you?" She paused as Matt emerged onto the roof with Jake behind him.

Eva and Frankie both sent anxious looks in her direction.

She'd told them about the conversation that had followed that kiss. They knew she hadn't seen Jake since that day. He'd been avoiding her, and the thought of it sent a flush of embarrassment across her skin.

Why was he here now? And with Matt? Was he afraid he might have to fight her off?

Frankie rose to her feet, protective as a bodyguard. "I thought it was poker night?"

"Pool night, but two of the guys didn't show. Pressures of the corporate world. We thought we'd come up here and drink our beer with a view. Unless we're disturbing you."

Yes, Paige thought desperately, *you are*. She was tired and looking forward to an evening chilling with her friends. She didn't need Jake intruding on that. Being near him was anything but relaxing. For the second time in her life she'd humiliated herself around him. No amount of wafting plants, scented candles or chilled white wine was going to help with that.

Matt put his beer down on the bluestone patio. "Are we interrupting an off-site meeting of Urban Genie?"

"No. We were catching up on all the juicy intimate details of Eva's love life." Paige hoped that would be sufficient to have them running for the stairs.

Instead, Matt sat down. Given it was technically his roof terrace, Paige couldn't argue his right to do that.

"You have a love life, Ev? Update us."

"That won't take long. It was short. And not at all sweet. I never want it mentioned again. It was my lowest dating moment." Eva slumped in the seat. "Tell me I'm not the only one to have ever had an embarrassing date. Paige? Make me feel better. Tell me your most embarrassing incident with a guy ever."

They were piling up. And all of them involved Jake.

He was standing in the shadows at the edge of the roof garden, and although his expression was sheathed by the darkness she knew he was watching her.

She'd spent years wishing he'd kiss her, and now that he had, she wished he hadn't because every intense, erotic detail was imprinted on her brain.

"Tell us about the date, Ev." Fortunately Matt took the heat off Paige for a moment.

"He took me to a fight club. I *hate* all forms of violence." Eva curled her legs under her, indignant. "What sort of person thinks that is a dream date?"

Paige stole a glance at Jake, and then looked away again.

Part of her was annoyed. Why had he kissed her? If he'd wanted to distract her he could have used other methods. Knowing how she'd once felt about him, he should definitely have used one of those methods instead of doing something so, so—*personal.*

Where did their relationship go from here? How did you rewind the clock from intimacy to mere acquaintance? Somehow she had to forget the feel of his mouth on hers, the skilled stroke of his hand on her thigh and the brutal explosion of heat.

If that was how all his kisses felt it was a wonder half the women in New York hadn't gone up in flames.

"Dream date?" Matt sounded amused by the question. "Hey Jake, what's your idea of a dream date?"

"A night of incredible, amazing sex, preferably with Swedish triplets who are only in town for a night."

Paige tightened her grip on her glass and Eva quickly changed the subject.

"If you were going on a date with *me*, Matt, where would you take me? And please don't say a fight club."

"I would never take you on a date, Ev."

Eva bristled. "Why not?"

"Because I've known you since you were four years old."

"Are you saying I'm not cute?"

"You're cute." Matt's hand locked around a bottle of beer. "But it would be like dating my sister."

"What about Frankie?"

There was a brief hesitation and then Matt lifted the bottle to his lips. "Same."

Something in his tone made Paige think it wasn't the same at all, but she didn't say anything.

Matt's love life was his business and she had enough problems with her own.

Taken aback, Eva glanced at Jake. "Would you ever date one of us, Jake?"

"Of course he wouldn't," Matt said easily. "For a start he knows you almost as well as I do and it would be weird, and then there's the fact he knows I'd beat him to a pulp if he put a hand on any of you."

Paige stopped breathing.

Through the darkness her eyes met Jake's, and she knew he was thinking of that moment in the elevator when he'd put both hands on her. And his mouth.

"If none of us are dating and Jake can drag himself away from his Swedish triplets, we should take a picnic up to Central Park one weekend, all of us." Matt carried on talking, oblivious to the tension. "Eva could make something delicious, we can walk, maybe take a couple of boats out, listen to the jazz—"

Frankie gave him a quick smile. "Sounds good."

"I can't make it." Jake's tone was short and Matt frowned.

"I didn't fix a time so how the hell do you know you can't make it?"

"I have a lot on right now."

Paige felt a rush of misery.

She knew exactly why Jake couldn't make it, and it made her feel horrible and a touch exasperated.

He was the one who had kissed *her*, not the other way around.

He'd created this situation.

A lifetime of uncomfortable encounters stretched ahead of her.

She needed to meet someone else. She need to bring a hot guy up to this roof terrace and laugh and joke with him so that Jake could see she was happy.

She needed to stop thinking about Jake.

She needed to stop thinking about that kiss.

The conversation drifted around her, driven mostly by Frankie and Matt.

"How was your day, Matt? Weren't you meeting a new client?"

"I produced a concept design package for a guy on the Upper East Side who has more money than taste."

Frankie wiped the soil from her fingers. "So are you going to work with him?"

"I haven't decided. I'm meeting him again tomorrow. We're visiting a couple of sites together. I need to hang out with him for a while and decide if he's going to be too much trouble."

Paige wondered how it felt to be able to turn down business. "When do you get to the point where you feel able to say no? I can't imagine that time ever coming."

"It will come. One day you'll look at your schedule and realize you're juggling, that you can't do it all. Then someone will ask you to do something that doesn't feel quite right and you'll realize that your reputation matters and that you want what you do to stand for something. You'll choose not to take jobs that clash with that."

Frankie stared at him. "You turn projects down?"

"Sometimes. You get a sense for when a client is never going to be satisfied. If I'm going to spend more time undoing than doing, I'm not interested."

Paige's phone rang and she reached for her bag, but by the time she found her phone the caller had hung up.

"No number." She checked her missed calls. "I wonder who—"

Eva's phone started to ring and she grabbed it. "Hello?" There was a pause. "Matilda? It's you? We've been calling you and calling you! Why didn't you—" She broke off and her mouth dropped open. "You're *kidding*!"

"What?" Paige sat down next to Eva, concerned. "What's happened? Where has she been? Tell her we can give her a job. We'll work something out." She was torn between relief that Matilda had finally called and guilt at not having been able to stop Cynthia firing her friend.

"Wait—shh, I can't hear—" Eva turned away slightly and Frankie rolled her eyes.

"There are days when I could strangle her. You?"

Paige wanted to know about Matilda. *Is she okay?* She mouthed the words, but Eva shook her head and covered her other ear so that she could listen.

"We heard Chase Adams insisted you were fired." She paused. "He *did what*? Wow. What sort of guy does that?"

"A guy who is a dumbass," Frankie muttered. "Why does she ask such obvious questions?"

Jake raised his eyebrows. "He's an astute businessman, not a dumbass."

"He fired Matilda. That makes him a dumbass."

"Shh—" Eva waved her hand to silence them. "Say that again, Matilda, from the moment you dropped your phone in the bath—"

Paige gave a half smile. That sounded so like Matilda.

Frankie looked baffled. "Who takes a phone into the bath? And she wonders why she has so many accidents—"

Paige was watching Eva. She said nothing, simply listened, and then huge fat tears welled up in her eyes.

"Matilda—" her voice was choked "—I—I don't know what to say." Tears spilled down her cheeks and Paige felt sick.

It was obviously worse, much worse, than she'd feared.

She held out her hand. "Let me talk to her. Give me the phone, Ev." She was determined to make it right. She'd give Matilda a job even if it meant living off instant soup for the rest of her life. *"Ev!"*

"Wait!" Eva held on to the phone, scrubbing her face with her free hand as she listened. "Great. Yeah, that's right. We set up our own business. Urban Genie. We were going to offer you a job—I know! Incredible. We'll see you then. It's going to feel weird. Will you still speak to us?"

Frankie growled again. "It's going to feel weird when I rip that phone out of her hand. And why wouldn't Matilda speak to us? It was Cynthia who fired her, not us."

Eva hung up. "Well! Can you believe that? Amazing."

"I'm counting to three," Frankie said pleasantly. "And then you're dead. You only get one warning."

"Why did you hang up?" Paige was frustrated. "Why didn't you tell her we'd give her a job?"

"Because she doesn't need a job." Eva looked dazed. "She's doing fine."

"She's found another job? How? What?"

"Her book is being published."

Paige felt her spirits lift. "That's great news! I'm so happy for her. But I can't imagine that's going to make her enough to live off, at least not for a while. She's still going to need—"

"She doesn't need anything." Eva wiped her eyes again. "You always laugh at me, but this is proof that happy endings can happen in real life as well as in books and movies."

"So she has a publishing deal—that's great, but—"

"That's not all." Eva sniffed. "It's the most romantic thing I ever heard. After she spilled the champagne, Cynthia told her to go home, remember? Which was why we couldn't find her. So she got into the elevator and guess who was in there with her? Chase Adams. But she didn't know who he was—"

"Only Matilda wouldn't recognize Chase Adams."

"I haven't finished."

"Then finish, before we all die of old age."

"This is a real-life fairy tale. I'm not rushing it. She didn't know who he was, but they had this amazing chemistry going so she went home with him."

"She went home with a guy she met in the elevator?" Frankie gaped. "Holy crap, she's as bad as you are. Please tell me that at some point she found out who he was, and then she punched him?"

"They fell in love." Eva's eyes filled again. "Sorry, but I'm so happy. It proves that when it's right, it's right. You don't need years together to know."

"What? Wait a minute." Paige was confused. "You're telling us she met Chase Adams, fell in love and—"

"—and now they're going to live happily ever after."

Frankie was incredulous. "Does she know he demanded Cynthia fire her?"

"That isn't what happened." The smile left Eva's face. "He didn't care about the spilled champagne. He didn't say or do anything—until Matilda told him Cynthia had fired her. Then he pulled his business because he was so mad with Star Events for firing Matilda."

Stunned into silence, Paige absorbed the truth. "So you're saying Cynthia lied? Again?"

Matt exchanged glances with Jake. "We did tell you it didn't sound like the sort of thing Chase would do."

"But—why would Cynthia lie?" But she didn't need to hear the answer to that. She already knew it. "Because she didn't want to take responsibility for her decision. Because she's a coward."

"So Chase is, in fact, indirectly responsible for the fact that we lost our jobs." Frankie gave a short laugh. "There is a certain symmetry in that. We should probably be mad."

"We should be grateful." Paige stood up. "It's because we lost our jobs that we now have Urban Genie. And I'm so relieved about Matilda. Where has she been all this time?"

"Holed up in Chase's beach house in The Hamptons having lots of beach sex and writing her next book. Because she dropped her phone she lost all her contacts, and of course when she called Star Events to speak to us they wouldn't pass on personal details. Chase bought her a massive diamond from Tiffany's. And we'll see them soon enough because the two of them are coming to Jake's event."

Paige glanced at Jake. "You didn't mention it."

"Chase Adams was on the list. I didn't know he'd accepted and I knew nothing about this Matilda person."

Matt put down his beer. "You must be excited, Paige. This is your first big event."

Excited? She was dreading it. All she could think about was the fact that Jake would be there and everything felt awkward.

"Of course she's excited. We're all excited!" Filling the silence, Eva bounced to her feet. "It will be lovely to see Matilda again."

That much was true. Aware that they were all looking at her, Paige nodded. "It will."

She needed to move on and forget what had happened.

She needed to think of Jake as a client. Nothing more.

She'd be professional, friendly and efficient.

And she'd avoid elevators at all costs.

Eleven

When life sends you lemons, ask for a return address.

—Eva

Paige walked around the rooftop terrace in Lower Manhattan, checking every small detail.

It was hard to believe that weeks of work were about to come to fruition.

The rooftop echoed with hammering and shouts as the crew Frankie had hired put the final touches to the display and tested the lights. They'd been there until late the night before and were back again at dawn. Frankie, dressed in jeans with her red hair pulled into a careless ponytail, stood like a fierce warrior, directing proceedings. She'd set up a staging area where they could untie the bundles of flowers and prepare them.

Paige had to admit that what they'd designed together was impressive.

On the other side of the terrace Eva flitted backward and forward as she coordinated final details between the venue and Delicious Eats.

The elevators had been transformed into futuristic pods, ready to transport the guests into a new cyber age. From there they were directed through two cleverly lit "tunnels" onto the roof terrace, where the world opened up to them, symbolizing cyber technology.

There wasn't a single possibility Paige hadn't considered. She had two contingency plans for every element of the evening and she was convinced that there was nothing that could go wrong that she couldn't handle.

Jake said that you couldn't control things, but she could control this.

And she didn't only have Plan A; she had Plan B and C.

There was a storm forecast, but all the signs were that it would arrive after the event had ended. If it came early, then she was prepared for that, too. They would close the glass doors and bring everyone inside.

"I am never making a round canapé again," Eva moaned, coming over to join Paige. "I will be seeing ones and noughts in my sleep."

"It looks incredible. So clever, Ev."

Frankie joined them, her eyes tired. "I have climbed that scaffolding so many times in the last two days my pecs are going to be bulging."

"It's all brilliant. All we need now is guests." Paige reached out and wiped off a dirty mark from Frankie's face. "And maybe we need to change because right now the staff of Urban Genie are looking a bit, too, er, urban. We need to make it look effortless. As if we did all this while filing our nails."

Nerves fluttered and danced in Paige's stomach as all three of them escaped to the private room that had been reserved for their use.

Eva and Paige wore the same short black skirt teamed with

heels, but Frankie, who hated skirts, had opted for tailored black pants. Each had a different-colored shirt with Urban Genie picked out in silver on the front pocket.

Paige's was black, Eva's was midnight blue and Frankie's was a deep forest green, the color in her outfit complementing the fierce blaze of her hair.

Paige looked at her friends and her eyes filled.

"I'm so proud of you. Of *us*. Can you believe we're doing this together? It's *our* business. You've worked so hard. We're going to make this company the biggest success. Thank you for taking the risk and saying yes."

Frankie flushed. "We said yes because we trust you. I don't know anyone as driven and focused as you are. Or as determined. If anyone could find a way to make this work it would be you."

"You trust me because I'm your friend."

"You're more than a friend. You, Eva and Matt—even Jake. You're family. The family I would have loved to have."

It was an unusually emotional speech for Frankie, and Eva reached for her hand and then Paige's.

"It's going to be incredible. Let's knock them dead."

"I hope that's a figure of speech," Frankie said, "because we don't want to be sued for manslaughter on our first event." But she gave Eva's hand a squeeze before walking to the door.

Paige wondered if she was the only one whose knees were shaking.

She wasn't sure if she was more nervous for Urban Genie or because Jake would be there.

She so badly wanted everything to be perfect.

The moment they stepped out of the door they were swept up in last-minute preparations for the event. The trickle of early arrivers became a steady stream and soon the terrace was filled with laughter, conversation and oohs and aahs as heads were tilted upward toward the eye-catching lighting and floral designs. Lips moved in conversation and hands were busy with food.

The interactive areas where people could try out the technology proved very popular, with small crowds waiting for a turn.

Paige checked and double-checked everything.

She'd forgotten how much she loved this part of the job. The moment where it all came together, all the work, the discussions, the angst in the past. Now it was about checking tiny touches and detail. She loved the circulating— looking for smiles, conversations, spotting problems before they happened.

She loved the buzz and the responsibility.

And this time the responsibility was all hers.

It was a surprisingly good feeling.

She spotted when a female guest suffered a broken heel, and replaced the shoes with a pair they had in their "emergency" supplies. Plain black, mid heel. A perfect substitute. When a male guest had a red wine accident on his partner, she dealt with it promptly. In her store behind the scenes she had Band-Aids, spare bow ties, white shirts in different sizes and her phone, which had every contact she'd ever need to solve any problem. She could call cabs, doctors and dry cleaners if necessary, but so far everything was running smoothly.

The weather was still good and a light summer breeze cooled the terrace after a day of hot sunshine. In the distance a few storm clouds were gathered, but they were far enough away that Paige didn't need to worry yet.

The dance floor was a blur of color. Silver, red and blue shimmered alongside tuxedos and gleaming white shirts.

She was aware of Jake in the center of it all, talking to each of the guests as they arrived.

He didn't need to move, she thought. They all came to him.

But he did move; he circulated and networked, and every so often he brought someone across to Paige. His introductions were always amusing and complimentary.

It was fairly clear that after tonight, Urban Genie was going to be busy. She'd been asked to pitch for everything from product launches to birthdays, bar mitzvahs and baby showers.

"Urban Genie." A tall man with a severe expression studied the lettering on her chest and nodded. "Jake tells me you're the most sought-after events company in Manhattan. Do you have a business card?"

Paige handed it over.

"Paige," Eva whispered in her ear, "take a look over there. By the fountain. It's Matilda. She looks *amazing.*"

Paige looked and saw Matilda, tall and leggy, holding the hand of a tall, broad-shouldered man.

"He loves her." Paige's heart lurched. "You can tell by the way he looks at her."

Eva sighed. "I want that one day. I won't accept anything less."

"Then you'd better prepare to be single," Frankie said, waving at Matilda and melting into the crowd.

Eva stared after her in exasperation. "What is *wrong* with her? She can't see a happy ending even when her nose is pressed against it."

Paige thought about Frankie's mother. "I guess if you've never seen it up close, it's hard to believe in it."

"Well, she's seeing it now. Oh no! I see a food crisis. I'll catch up with Matilda later." Eva bounced away and Paige walked across the terrace to greet Matilda.

She thought about how much their lives had changed since the last time they'd met.

Chase Adams was cool and a little intimidating initially, but relaxed as Matilda introduced them.

"Matilda speaks highly of you." He shook hands with Paige. "She loved working with you."

Paige felt color flood her cheeks. "Thank you."

"It's so good to see you." Matilda hugged her tightly, knocking her champagne glass into the fountain in the process.

Chase rescued it without comment. "I gather I'm responsible for the fact that you lost your jobs." He set the glass down out of range of Matilda. "I won't apologize for pulling my business because the way they treated Matilda was unacceptable, but I am sorry you were collateral damage." His gaze was direct and Paige shook her head, appreciating his honesty.

"You did us a favor. It's because of you that we're doing this. And you're right about what happened to Matilda. It was unacceptable." The thought of it mortified her even though she hadn't had the ability to change what had happened. "I tried to find her that night and—"

"I know." He smiled, and the smile made him infinitely more approachable. "She's told me all about it. And about Urban Genie. How's it going? The market is pretty tough."

She decided honesty deserved honesty. "It's been a slow start, but we're hoping that after tonight things will pick up."

Matilda tugged at his hand. "Chase—"

He turned to her, instantly attentive. "Sweetheart—?"

"Will you do something for me?"

"You know I will." His voice was soft. Intimate. "Name it."

"Will you tell all your friends to use Urban Genie? Paige is brilliant."

Paige wondered how a man like Chase would react to

being told how to run his business, but if anything he seemed amused.

"Of course. I was going to do that anyway." He turned back to Paige, his gaze sharp and assessing. "Can you handle the business if it comes your way?"

"Yes." She didn't hesitate. "We're building up a list of preferred vendors and suppliers. We can handle anything."

"Good. In that case I can guarantee you're going to be busy."

Matilda hugged him impulsively. "You're the best."

Chase kissed the top of her head. "More champagne?"

"I had a full glass a moment ago. I have no idea what happened to it—" Matilda looked around, confused, and Chase laughed.

"It landed in the fountain. It's fine. Jake Romano can afford to lose a little champagne. And talking of Jake, I should introduce you to him. Good meeting you." He nodded to Paige. "If you need anything at all, call me."

He and Matilda strolled away, and moments later Eva and Frankie joined Paige.

"Well?" Frankie's tone was sharp. "Is he good enough for her?"

Paige stared after them, feeling a tug of envy. "Yes."

"That," Eva said dreamily, "is what love looks like. Frankie, how can that not melt that stone in your chest you call your heart?"

"I'm not in a melting mood. He'd better not mess her around, that's all."

Eva gave her an exasperated look. "He's not going to mess her around. Did you see the way he looked at her? And the way he calmly rescued her glass of champagne. He *adores* her. He fired Star Events because of the way they treated her.

What more does the guy have to do to convince you? I love him to bits already."

"You love everyone to bits." But Frankie's voice was softer than usual. "Yeah, okay, I admit they were cute. And I liked the fact he seemed to find her clumsiness adorable."

"And for once she was wearing heels because he's even taller than her. I'm so excited she's back in New York. It means we'll see more of her." Eva danced off across the terrace and Frankie stared after her in disbelief.

"She thinks life is a fairy tale."

"No, she doesn't." Paige watched as Eva circulated, serving food and beaming smiles in equal measure. "She knows how to make the most of the moment. She believes in love. She knows bad things happen. She was devastated when her grandmother died, but she got out of bed every day and went to work. And even when she's feeling low she still tries to find the positive in every day. It's true that she's a dreamer, but she's also fiercely loyal and her loyalty is real. When Eva loves, she loves forever. I guess that makes us lucky."

Frankie stirred. "I guess it does. Friend-love I believe in."

"Me, too. Friends are the best thing. Thank you." Impulsively Paige hugged Frankie. "Thank you for doing this with me, for taking the risk. I know how big a risk it was for you. I love you."

"Hey—enough." Frankie's voice was gruff but she hugged Paige back before stepping away. "Don't you get all emotional, too. It's enough coping with Eva. People are leaving. I'll go and do farewell duty. *Goodbye* is my favorite word after a long night."

Paige stood for a moment, thinking how unpredictable life was.

Who would have thought that getting fired would have been the best thing that could have happened to Matilda?

Who would have thought that her, Eva and Frankie losing their jobs would have turned out so well?

Urban Genie existed only because life had laid a twist in her path.

Change had been forced on her, but it had proved to be a good thing.

Instead of fighting it, she should embrace it.

What had Jake said?

Sometimes you have to let life happen.

Maybe she should try and do that a bit more.

She needed to find time to date other men and hope that one day she found someone that made her look the way Matilda did when she smiled at Chase.

And maybe one day she'd look back and realize that *not* being with Jake was the best thing that could have happened because if she'd been with Jake she wouldn't have met—

Who?

Would she ever meet someone who made her feel the way Jake did?

She stood, leaning on the railing, gazing at the city she loved.

The lights of Manhattan sparkled like a thousand stars against a midnight sky, and now, finally, as the last of the guests made their way to the elevators she allowed herself a moment to enjoy it.

"Time to relax and celebrate I think." Jake's voice came from behind her and she turned to find him holding two glasses of champagne. He handed her one. "To Urban Genie."

"I don't drink while I'm working." And while Jake was present, this was definitely still work.

She knew better than to lower her guard a second time.

"The guests have gone. You're no longer working. Your job is done."

"I'm not off duty until the clear-up has finished." And then tomorrow was the follow-up, the post mortem. Discussions on what they could have done differently. They'd unpick every part of the event and put it back together again. By the time they finished they'd have found every weak spot and strengthened it.

"I don't think one glass of champagne is going to impair your ability to supervise that. Congratulations." He tapped his glass against hers. "Spectacular. Any new business leads?"

"Plenty. First up is a baby shower next week. Not much time to prepare, but it's a good event."

He winced. "A baby shower is good?"

"Yes, partly because the woman throwing it for her pregnant colleague is CEO of a fashion importer. But all business is good."

"Chase Adams is impressed. By tomorrow, word will get around that Urban Genie is the best event concierge company in Manhattan. Prepare to be busy."

"I'm prepared."

His praise warmed her. Her heart lifted.

He stood next to her and the brush of his sleeve against her bare arm made her shiver.

His gaze collided briefly with hers, and she thought she saw a blaze of heat, but then he looked away and she did, too, her face burning.

She was doing it again. Imagining things.

And it had to stop.

It had to stop right now.

No more embarrassing herself. No more embarrassing *him*.

She turned her head to look at him but he was staring straight forward, his handsome face blank of expression.

"Thank you," she said.

"For what?"

"For asking us to do this. For giving us free rein and no budget constraints. For trusting us. For inviting influential people and decision makers. For making Urban Genie happen." She realized how much she owed him. "I hate accepting help—"

"I know, but that isn't what happened here. You did it yourself, Paige."

"But I wouldn't have been able to do it without you. I'm grateful. If you hadn't suggested it, pushed me that night on the terrace, I wouldn't have done it." She breathed. Now was as good a time as any to say everything that needed to be said. And if she said it aloud, maybe it would help both of them. "There's something else—" She saw him tense and felt a flash of guilt that he felt the need to be defensive around her. Definitely time to clear the air. "I owe you an apology."

"For what?"

"For misreading the situation the other night. For making things awkward between us. I was—" She hesitated, trying to find the right words. "I guess you could say I was doing an Eva. I was looking for things that weren't there. I was close to panic and you were trying to distract me. I understand that now. I don't want you feeling that you have to avoid me, or be careful around me. I—"

"Don't. Don't apologize." He gripped the railing and she noticed his knuckles were white.

"I wanted to clear it up, that's all. It was a kiss. Didn't mean anything. Two people trapped in an elevator, one of whom was feeling vulnerable." *Shut up right now, Paige.* "I know I'm not your type. I know you don't have those feelings. I'm like your little sister. I get that, so—"

"Oh for—*seriously*?" He interrupted her with a low growl and finally turned to face her. "After what happened the other night you really think I see you as a little sister? You think I could kiss you that way if I felt like that about you?"

She stared at him, her heart drumming a rhythm against her chest. "I thought—you said—I thought you saw me that way."

"Yeah, well, I tried." He gave a humorless laugh and drained his champagne in one mouthful. "God knows, I tried. I've done everything short of asking Matt for a baby photo of you and sticking that to my wall. Nothing works. And do you know why? Because I do have feelings, you're not little and you're not my fucking sister."

Shock struck her like a bolt of lightning.

They were the only two people left on the terrace. Just them and the twinkling lights of Manhattan. The buildings rose around them, dark shapes enveloping them in intimate shadows and the shimmer of light.

The storm clouds were gathering, creating ominous shapes in the dark sky.

The sudden lick of wind held the promise of rain.

Paige was oblivious. The sky could have come crashing down and she wouldn't have noticed.

Her mouth was so dry she could hardly form the words. "But if you feel that way—if—you do have feelings, why do you keep saying—" She stumbled, confused. "Why haven't you ever done anything about it?"

"Why do you think?" There was a cynical, bitter edge to Jake's tone that didn't fit the nature of the conversation. None of the pieces fit. She couldn't think. Everything about her had ceased to function.

"Because of Matt?"

"Partly. He'd kick my butt and I wouldn't blame him." He stared down at his hands, as if they were something that didn't belong to him. As if he was worried about what they might do.

"Because you're not interested in relationships—or complications as you call them."

"Exactly."

"But sex doesn't have to be a relationship. It can just be sex. You said so yourself."

"Not with you." His tone was harsh and she took a step back, shocked. They'd often argued, baited each other, but she'd never heard that edge of steel in his voice before.

"Why? What's different about me?"

"I'm not going to screw you and walk away, Paige. That's not going to happen."

"Because of our friendship? Because you're worried it would be awkward?"

"Yeah, that too."

"Too? What else?" She stared at him, bemused.

He was silent.

"Jake? What else?"

He swore under his breath. "Because I care about you. I don't want to hurt you. There's already been enough damage to your heart. You don't need more."

The first raindrops started to fall.

Paige was oblivious.

Her head spun with questions. Where? What? Why? *How much?* "So you—wait—" She struggled to make sense of it. "You're saying that you've been protecting me? No. That can't be true. You're the only one who *doesn't* protect me. When everyone else is wrapping me in cotton wool, you handle me like you're throwing the first pitch at the game." He didn't protect her. He didn't. Not Jake.

She waited for him to agree with her, to confirm that he didn't protect her.

He was silent.

There was a throbbing in her head. She lifted her fingers to her forehead and rubbed. The storm was closing in—she could feel it, and not just in the sky above her.

"I know you don't protect me." She tried to focus, tried to examine the information and shook her head. "Just the other night, when we found out we'd lost our jobs, Matt was sympathetic, but you were brutal. I was ready to cry, but you made me so *angry* and—" She stared at him, understanding. She felt the color drain from her face. "You did it on purpose. You made me angry on purpose."

"You get more done when you're angry," he said flatly. "And you needed to get things done."

No denial.

He'd goaded her. Galvanized her into action.

"You challenge every idea I have." She felt dizzy. "We fight. All the time. If I say something is black, you say it's white."

He stood in silence, not bothering to deny it, and she shook her head in disbelief.

"You make me angry. You do that on purpose because if I'm angry with you then I'm not—" *She'd been blind.* She breathed, adjusting to this new picture of their relationship. The first boom of thunder split the air but she ignored it. "How long? How long, Jake?"

"How long, what?" He yanked at his bow tie with impatient fingers. His gaze shifted from hers. He looked like a man who wanted to be anywhere but with her.

"How long have you cared? How long have you been protecting me?" She stumbled over the word, and the thought.

He ran his hand over his jaw. "Since I walked through the door of that damn hospital room and saw you sitting on the bed in your Snoopy T-shirt, with that enormous smile on your face. You were so brave. The most frightened brave person I'd ever seen. And you tried so hard not to let anyone see it. I have always protected you, Paige. Except for the other night when I let my guard down."

But he'd been protecting her then, too. He'd been taking care of her when she was so terrified she hadn't known what to do.

"So you thought I was brave, but not strong. Not strong enough to cope alone without protection. I don't understand. I thought you weren't interested—that you didn't want this, and now I discover—" It was a struggle to process it. "So this whole time you *did* care about me. You do."

Rain was falling steadily now, landing in droplets on his jacket and her hair.

"Paige—"

"The kiss the other night—"

"Was a mistake."

"But it was real. It wasn't anything to do with my shoes or the color of my lipstick. All these days, months, years I've been telling myself you didn't feel anything. All the time I've been confused because my instincts were so wrong and I couldn't understand why, but now I do. They weren't wrong. I wasn't wrong."

"Maybe you weren't."

"So why let me think that?"

"Because it was easier."

"Easier than what? Telling me the truth? News flash, and, by the way, I thought you knew this—I don't want to be protected. I want to live my life. You're the one who's always tell-ing me to take more risks."

"Yeah, well, that proves you shouldn't listen to anything I tell you. We should go inside before you catch pneumonia." He eased away from the railings and she caught his arm.

"I'll go inside when I decide to go inside." The rain was soaking her skin. "What happens now?"

"Nothing. I know you don't want to be protected, but that's tough, Paige, because that's what I'm doing. I'm not what you're looking for, and I never have been. We don't want the same thing. There's a car waiting downstairs to take you and the other two home. Make sure you use it." Without giving her a chance to respond, Jake strode away from her toward the bank of elevators and left her standing there, alone in the glit-tering cityscape, watching the entire shape of her life change. Another twist. Another turn. The unexpected.

Twelve

Life is too short to wait for a man to make the first move.

—Paige

Jake ripped off his jacket and flung it across the bed.

How had he got himself pulled into that conversation? *How?* He'd dropped his guard for a moment, that was all, and Paige had sneaked under it with her baby blues and disarming honesty.

Beyond his windows, lightning split the night sky but all he could think of was Paige apologizing for "misreading" a situation she'd read perfectly.

He should have shut her right down. Instead, he'd dished out some honesty himself. Way too much honesty.

There was a hammering at his door, and he swore under his breath, knowing it meant only one thing.

He dragged it open, ready with his excuses.

Paige stood there, her dark hair wet from the rain and her eyelashes gleaming with raindrops.

Jake stared at her as if she were a drug he shouldn't touch, torn between slamming the door between them and hauling her inside. Before he could make his choice she stalked past him into the apartment.

Shit.

His brain and reflexes functioning in slow motion, he closed the door and turned to look at her.

He didn't know what it was about her that sent his senses into overdrive, but he knew he needed to get her out of his apartment.

Failing that, he had to get himself out of his apartment.

Being in the same space wasn't a good thing.

Especially when she was all fired up and hot. And one glance at the tilt of her chin and the stormy blue eyes told him she was steaming mad.

In this mood, she was dangerous and quite capable of doing things she'd regret later.

She was still wearing heels and the Urban Genie shirt, which told him she'd come straight from the venue.

He should have triple-bolted the door and set a thousand alarms. "How did you get past the doorman?"

"I smiled at him."

He could have fired the guy, except that he had some appreciation of the power of Paige's smile.

He noticed she wasn't smiling now.

"It's a filthy night. You should be at home."

"There are things I need to say."

He was pretty sure it was going to be nothing he wanted to hear. "Paige, it's late and—"

"Since when did that bother you? You're not a sleeper. Neither am I."

Right now he was willing to be anything to get her out of his apartment. "You're wet."

"Then I'm better off in your apartment out of the rain." She flung her handbag down on the nearest chair and slid off her heels. "Do you know what drives me crazy?"

He opened his mouth to answer, and then realized she wasn't expecting a response.

This was a monologue and he was expected to listen so he closed his mouth and decided to wait out the storm. The one inside his apartment, not outside. He watched warily as she paced over to the wall of glass that gave him a view over Downtown Manhattan.

"Being protected." She turned. "Being protected drives me crazy. I thought you knew that."

Her wet clothes clung to every taut line of her body and he wondered how her bare feet could be so much sexier than those thin spiky heels.

Behind her, through the glass, he could see lightning shoot across the sky, bathing the city in a strange luminous glow.

It mirrored Paige's temper and the electric atmosphere in the apartment.

"I've spent my whole life being protected. At school during sports the teachers were always asking me how I was feeling, if I was breathless, if I was doing okay—" She paced again, her feet soundless on his wooden floor. "They had meetings about me, and if there was a new teacher, they were briefed. This is Paige—she has a heart condition. You have to watch her. Be careful. Don't let her overdo it. If there's a problem, call this number. It was all rules and protocols and watching, always watching, when all I wanted was to be normal. I wanted to do all the things the other kids did. I wanted to get into trouble and mess up, but I couldn't. My parents were worried about me all the time, and I spent so much time protecting them, pretending I was fine. And then there were the weeks in hospital, when everyone else was getting a prom dress and I was getting a scar on my chest. I didn't feel like a person. I was a medical condition. And the worst thing was having no control over any of it."

Jake watched her in silence.

It twisted him up inside to think of her scared. He wanted to smother her in bubble wrap, as her family did.

"Now I'm an adult, and my parents still worry about me." She eyed him. "I choose to protect them as much as I can because I know that no matter how old I am I'll always be their little girl. I call and I tell them I'm fine. I hide things that would worry them because they've had enough worry for a lifetime and now they deserve to enjoy time together without me being the dampener on their happiness. I don't need them to protect me. I want to live my life." The way she was looking at him told him that last statement was aimed at him.

"Paige—"

"You were the one who told me to embrace risk. You don't get to decide what risks I embrace, Jake. I do. I decide."

"You shouldn't be here."

"Why not? Because I might get hurt? Being hurt is part of being alive. It isn't possible to live a full life and not be hurt at some point. You have to live bravely. You taught me that. It was that night you walked into my room pretending to be a doctor, carrying that gift for me. Or maybe you've forgotten."

"I haven't forgotten." He hadn't forgotten a single thing.

"You made me feel normal. You were the first person who didn't treat me like I might break at any moment. You made me laugh. You made me feel good. You were all I could think about, which was a refreshing change after a lifetime of thinking only about hospitals, doctors and my stupid heart. You made me feel like a person again." She made a sound between a laugh and a sob. "You made me see the importance of living life today, not keeping myself safe for tomorrow. I decided I didn't want to protect myself like china that is brought out once a year on special occasions."

Jake kept silent and watched while she paced and spilled it all out, her emotions flowing like floodwater.

"I decided right then to live life bravely. I knew I loved you, and I was sure you loved me, too. Why else would you have spent all that time in my hospital room talking, listening, bringing me gifts and making me laugh? After I was discharged I spent a few nights in Matt's apartment because the hospital wanted me close for a while in case there were problems. You visited me there—do you remember?"

"Yes." There were a thousand things he could have said, but that was the only word that came.

"My first act of courage, my first leap into my new life, was to tell you how I felt. I told you I loved you and I was so sure of myself I was naked when I did it. I offered myself and you rejected me—" Her voice cracked and he ran his hand over his forehead, torn between going to her and keeping his distance.

"Paige, please—"

"You weren't cruel—you were kind, but somehow that made it a thousand times worse. If humiliation could kill, I would have died that day. I couldn't believe I'd got it so wrong. I couldn't believe I could have made such a mistake and embarrassed both of us. And after that our relationship changed, of course. We lost something. Something special. And I wished so many times that I hadn't taken that risk because I lost more than my dignity and my dreams, I lost my friend." Her gaze locked on his and the sheen in her eyes tortured him as much as her words.

"I didn't—"

"We started arguing, something we'd never done. There were days when it seemed to me that you were trying to drive me crazy, and I didn't understand it. Maybe it would have been easier if you hadn't been my brother's closest friend because then you would have been out of my life, but you were always there, a constant reminder of what happens when you take a risk in love and get it wrong. The only good thing was that at least you didn't protect me. Or so I thought. You say I'm the bravest person you know, but then you insist on protecting me." She paused, her breathing shallow. "I want to ask you a question, and I need you to be honest. Back then in the hospital when we spent night after night talking—you did feel something, didn't you? I've spent years thinking it was my stupid teenage brain spinning things, but you did have feelings. I wasn't wrong."

"I don't see the point of—"

"Tell me!"

He'd thought the evening couldn't get worse but he was watching it get a whole lot worse.

"You should leave now, Paige. You shouldn't be here. We shouldn't be having this conversation."

"I decide where I go and what I say, and we should have had this conversation a long time ago. We would have if you hadn't been protecting me. Because that's what you were doing, wasn't it?"

"You were a teenager."

"But I'm not a teenager now. We've wasted a lot of time, Jake." She walked toward him, purpose in her eyes and her fingers on the buttons of her shirt.

Oh holy shit.

"So what is this? Fuck-a-friend day?" He was trying to shock her into backing off but she didn't miss a stride.

"Maybe it is."

"It's not a good idea."

"It's a perfect idea. I stopped taking risks with my heart that day you rejected me, Jake. I didn't even realize it until recently, but I've guarded myself ever since. I've had a few relationships, but I've never given my whole self. After what happened with you, I've protected myself."

"That's probably a good thing." He licked his lips, unsettled by how badly he did not want to think of Paige with another man.

"It isn't a good thing. I don't want to get to the end of my life and say 'at least I was careful.' That's not how I want to live. You were the one who taught me that."

"Maybe you should stop listening to me."

"I reached the same conclusion. Which is why I'm here now."

"And now you've said what you came to say, you can leave."

"Are you protecting me or yourself now?" She closed the distance between them. "I thought you were a risk taker?"

Not with her. Never with her.

He never made a move on a woman without assessing every single possible outcome. One former lover had observed snappily that he had the mentality of a bodyguard—he checked the exits before he went into the room. He was his own bodyguard. And all his instincts were screaming that this was a mistake.

"You don't want this, Paige."

"Don't tell me what I want. I know what I want and I think I know what you want. The only question is whether you're man enough to admit it." She was standing close to him and she lifted her hand to his jaw, her fingers exploring. "Are you?"

"No. I'm not man enough." He growled the words through a surge of lust. "I don't want you."

"No?" She smiled and covered him with the flat of her hand, slowly tracing the shape of his thickened, straining erection. "Are you sure?"

He couldn't speak. He clenched his jaw tight as his senses and his body responded to the intimate touch of her hand.

She stood on tiptoe, her mouth a breath away from his. "You didn't kiss me in the elevator to distract me. You kissed me because you couldn't keep your hands off me. Because your control snapped. Finally."

Pleasure shot through him in burning streaks of light. He was burning up with desire.

"Maybe I do want you." The admission was dragged from somewhere deep inside him. "But I'm not doing anything about it, Paige."

Her smile widened. "Then I'll do it. Feel free to join in whenever you like."

All he wanted to do was to keep her happy and safe, and he knew that if she tangled with him, that wasn't going to happen.

He'd broken plenty of hearts in his time, but the one heart he'd never touched was hers.

A relationship with him, any sort of relationship, wasn't compatible with a healthy lifestyle.

Falling into the sexy gleam of her eyes, he groped for reasons, excuses, anything that might make her think twice.

"Matt—"

"I love my brother, but who I have sex with is none of his business. It isn't anyone's business but mine. And maybe yours." She slid her fingers between the buttons of his shirt and pulled him closer. Her lips nibbled at his, her breath warm and sweet as she teased his mouth with her tongue.

Still, he held it all back, hauled it inside, even though it strained every part of him to do so.

"I don't want to hurt you."

"Maybe I'll hurt you. But then again, there's always the possibility that neither of us will get hurt. It's just sex, Jake. One night. I can handle that if you can. Stop thinking."

He felt her move closer, felt the curve of her breasts brush against his chest. "I can't have sex with my best friend's little sister."

"How do you know if you've never tried?"

Once they crossed that line they could never go back.

He knew that whatever happened, nothing would be the same. There would be twists and turns and complications, and not just between the two of them. There was their wider friendship group to consider, but none of it seemed to matter anymore.

He could no longer remember why he was holding back.

Slowly, he lowered his head, his gaze locked on hers.

Time was suspended, the intense, fierce chemistry dancing around them like flames.

He was brutally aroused, so hard it was difficult to focus on anything.

"I don't think I can wait around while you wrestle with your conscience." She rose on her toes and kissed him. The touch of her mouth sent a shock wave of pleasure through him and exploded the final layers of his self-control. He pulled her in, his senses saturated by desire and raw lust. Her damp clothes clung to her body, molding to the dips and curves. He closed his hands over the adherent fabric of her skirt, easing it upward until it was high on her thighs, until damp fabric revealed damp skin, until he was so aroused that he was tempted to skip the part where he undressed her and take her right there against the nearest wall.

But this was Paige.

Paige.

She'd been off-limits for so long it was ingrained in him to be careful. His hands were anchored by the contradictions swirling in his head. He wanted to take her instantly, and he wanted to take his time. He wanted to feast, and he wanted to savor. To rip off her clothes, to unpeel them slowly. The only thing that was clear to him was that he wanted all of her. *All of her.*

He felt her hands on his shirt, dealing with each button with the same deft fluency as she stripped him to the waist. She pushed the shirt away from his shoulders and trailed her hands over his shoulder.

He closed his eyes, absorbing the brush of her hands over his skin.

"You're strong." She whispered the words, and he opened his mouth to contradict her because he knew that if he'd been strong he wouldn't be doing this, but then her fingers moved lower and he caught his breath.

"Paige—"

"Unless you're going to tell me you want me, don't speak."

He felt the soft, slow slide of her lips across his jaw and down his neck. She began a slow descent, each seductive brush of her lips sending lightning bolts of pleasure through his body. She was in no hurry, lingering and tasting before she moved lower. And lower.

He ached with need, so lost in the sensations she spun that it took him a moment to realize she'd opened his zipper.

He tried to speak, to tell her that she couldn't do that, but she drew him into the delicious warmth of her mouth and the groan that emerged from his throat blocked the words. His ability to think left him next, his brain wiped by the lavish, clever strokes of her tongue. It was the most erotic, intimate experience of his life, and it was only when he realized he was so close it was all going to be over in moments that he finally managed to pull away.

He lifted Paige to her feet, taking back control in a single resolute move that made her gasp.

"You're not going to change your mind, are you?"

"Does this feel as if I'm changing my mind?" He curved his arm around her and pulled her hard against him, leaving no room for doubt. Her eyes were huge, shining luminous blue under the soft, shadowy lights of his apartment.

"Jake—" The urgency of her tone was all he needed to hear.

With his free hand he cupped her cheek, feeling the softness of her skin against his palm and the silk of her hair teasing the tips of his fingers. "Patience."

"I'm not patient. I don't want to wait."

"It will be worth waiting for. Trust me." He felt her quiver of anticipation and lowered his head to take her mouth. All the reasons not to touch her had melted away, and he kept his mouth on hers as he slid his hands into her hair, his fingers stroking through soft silk and droplets of rain. His thoughts dimmed, the world receded, his senses steeped in texture and scent. Smooth dark chocolate and silk, tropical flowers and summer rain.

She was trembling against him, her fingers stroking into his hair as her kiss blended perfectly with his. There was no awkwardness. No fumbling. It was as if someone had carefully choreographed each move. He gathered her closer and felt her hands slide down to his shoulders, felt her fingers press hard as if she was afraid that if she didn't hold on he might disappear.

Easing away slightly she took his hand and placed it on her breast, and he felt the lush fullness and the thrust of her nipple through the thin fabric of her shirt.

He held her gaze as he undressed her, stripping off the damp layers until there was nothing between them but cool air and the delicious shiver of expectation.

There was a faint streak of color on her cheeks.

Self-conscious, she lifted her hand to her chest. "Does my scar bother you? You're staring."

"That's because I've stopped myself looking for so long I have a lot of time to make up." He lowered his forehead to hers. "You're beautiful, *tesoro.*"

"You spoke Italian. You never do that."

"I'm doing it now." He kissed her. Gently, on the shoulder blade, then lower to the straining peak of her breast. As he circled it with his tongue, he heard her moan and felt her fingers slide into his hair again. He drew her into his mouth, teased her with slow, lazy flicks of his tongue savoring the smooth texture of her skin. His head was spinning with a desire so intense it unbalanced him. But it wasn't enough. None of it was enough. He wanted more. He wanted all of it. All of her.

She gave a faint moan and then there was no more holding back.

Their mouths collided, fierce, hungry with need.

He scooped her up and carried her to the bedroom, leaving their clothes littered across his apartment. He lowered her gently onto the bed and came down on top of her, feeling her arch into him.

Paige.

Her eyes darkened and she wrapped her arms around his neck, her eyes clouded with anticipation. "Now. Please."

"Soon." He kissed his way down her body, lingering, tasting, breathing her in until she was writhing under his hands and mouth. Pleasure slid through him, thick and throbbing, but he held it back, made himself wait as he explored every part of her. He pushed her legs apart, traced the inside of her thigh with his tongue, taking his time.

Impatiently she shifted her hips but he kept her pinned with his hands as he toyed with her, learned what drove her wild, what drew a gasp and what made her moan. He absorbed every quiver and cry, every squirm and sob, drawing out the delicate threads of her response.

Finally, when she was begging him, when he couldn't deny himself any longer, he shifted over her again and reached for a condom from the nightstand.

She took it from him, fumbling in her haste, and he covered her hand with his and took over.

Her cheeks were a soft flame, her hair a dark, tumbled mass on his pillow where she'd shifted impatiently.

"Look at me." He paused on the edge of that final intimacy, not because he was uncertain but because he wanted to take his time. He'd been waiting too long for this to rush it.

He entered her gently, but still he heard her breath catch and felt the sharp dig of her fingers in his biceps.

He made himself pause, forced himself to stay still and wait while her body grew accustomed to him. It was the hardest thing he'd ever had to do, but he reminded himself that this was Paige. *Paige.* He lowered his head to kiss her again, felt her relax and shift against him and surged deeper, entering her by slow degrees, coaxing her to take more of him until finally they were so deeply joined that every movement her body made was transmitted to his.

He stayed still for a moment, breathing in the soft scent of her and the feel of her hands stroking her skin.

The heat was incredible, the connection intimate and deeply personal. In that moment there were no boundaries between them, and he knew she sensed it, too, because she stroked her hand over his head and whispered his name against his mouth, her gaze locked on his.

In her eyes he saw desire, and he saw trust.

She trusted him.

"Am I hurting you?"

"No!" She brushed a kiss over his mouth. "It's just that you're—well, you know—"

"I'll take it slowly." And he did, even though it was almost killing him to do so. Enveloped by the smooth slickness of her, he started to move, gently at first, his slow rhythm creating a delicious friction that brought an agonized groan to the back of her throat.

He locked his fingers into hers and drew her hands above her head, holding them there as he kissed her deeply.

Her thighs widened and she wrapped her legs around his back, lifting her hips to urge him deeper. He released his hold on her hands and immediately felt her touch on his body, first his shoulders, then his back, then lower as she urged him on. Through the mists of desire he heard her say his name, over and over again, and that part of him that kept him safe, that protected him from feelings he didn't want to experience, suddenly unraveled. The feel of her, the taste of her, the scent of her ripped apart every layer he'd put between himself and the world. Exposed and vulnerable he thrust deep and felt the first flutters of her body ripple down his shaft. Her orgasm closed around him, triggering his own release. As he swallowed her cries with his mouth he knew that no matter what price he had to pay for this, it would be worth it.

Thirteen

Love is like chocolate. It seems like a great idea at the
time but you often regret it later.

—Frankie

"I think you might have killed me. If I'd known it was going
to be that good I would have thrown ethics and willpower out
of the window a long time ago." Jake's eyes were closed and
Paige was relieved he'd spoken first because she really didn't
know what to say after what had just happened.

How had she thought it would be just sex?

It was so much more than that. The closeness between them
had returned, and not just because of the new physical intimacy. Intimacy wasn't sex, she realized. It was knowing someone. And Jake knew her.

He opened his eyes and turned his head to look at her, no
doubt wondering about her silence.

She was probably supposed to make some light comment
in return. "We should have done it years ago. I blame you for
the fact that we didn't." It was the best she could manage, but

it seemed to be acceptable because he gave that lopsided smile that turned her legs to jelly every time.

"Sleep with the teenage virgin sister of my best friend? Honey, there's risk, and then there's suicide."

"I lost my virginity when I was—"

"I don't want to know. I might have to kill the guy." He closed his eyes again. "If I'd slept with you then I wouldn't have lived to do it now and think what we would have both missed."

She shifted slightly so that she could look at the view. The whole of Manhattan was spread before them.

Despite the years they'd known each other, she hardly ever visited his apartment. The first time had been with Matt, and her memory of that visit was of hovering by the door while he and Jake had discussed plans for converting the outdoor area.

Originally a textile warehouse, the space had been transformed into several vast, light-drenched lofts. Jake's was on the top floor, with views across downtown and the Brooklyn Bridge. It was as beautiful at night as it was breathtaking in the day.

Tonight, it felt close to perfect.

Or maybe she was seeing things differently. Lying here in the safe circle of Jake's arms, the world felt like a softer, gentler place.

"We wasted a lot of time. I might have to kill you anyway."

"As long as you do it slowly and pick a method that involves sex, that's fine by me. Do anything. Have your evil way. Chain me up. Torture me, but if you could use your incredible mouth as your lethal weapon, that would be great." He slid his hand behind her neck and pulled her head close to his. "My new favorite hobby might be kissing off your lipstick."

His mouth was so close to hers they were breathing the same air, and that suited her fine.

"Lipstick is my addiction."

"Kissing it off could become mine." He barely moved, but his mouth took hers in a slow deliberate kiss that sent waves of desire shimmering across her skin.

She'd dreamed of this for so long she'd assumed she'd inflated it way beyond reality, and yet in the end it turned out that her imagination had produced a sparse, insipid version of the real thing.

Dreams were made of this, spun from hope.

She always said that she wanted to live in the moment, and if she could have picked one moment it would have been this one.

Eventually, when he'd turned her insides to an unstable version of the original, he rolled onto his back, taking her with him.

She snuggled close. "The view from your apartment is amazing. You could sell tickets. I don't know how you ever persuade women to leave."

"Easy. I don't bring them here."

Surprised, she shifted to look at him. "Never?" She savored the perfect lines of his profile, admiring the slant of his cheekbones and the straight blade of his nose.

"You're the first woman I've brought here."

The rush of euphoric pleasure made her giddy. "You didn't bring me here. I showed up on your doorstep and forced my way in." She slid her arm over him, feeling the roughness of chest hair brush against the sensitive skin of her inner arm. "Why don't you bring them?"

"Because I'm like you—I like to be the one in control. I like to be able to walk away when it suits me."

"Are you saying I'm controlling?" In a swift, smooth movement she straddled him, and he gave a smile and closed his hands over her hips, steadying her.

"I have no problem with you being controlling when this is how it looks."

It looked good from where she was, too. "So what happens? You usually stay at their place?"

"I don't know. I can't concentrate on anything while you're in this position."

She leaned forward, so that the tips of her breasts brushed against his chest. "How about now?" She murmured the words against his lips. "Can you concentrate now?"

"My mind is blank." He locked his hand on the back of her neck and kept her mouth against his. "Are you going to stop talking now?"

"That depends on whether you answer my question."

He sighed and released her. "Sometimes we go on a date and then I take them home. I don't sleep with every woman I meet, Paige."

"I assumed—"

"Yeah, well, you assumed wrong." His voice was husky. "Dates don't have to end in sex."

"According to you they do."

"You don't want to believe everything I say."

"If it's not true, why say it?"

"Because it winds Eva up and that's always fun." He smiled, and the smile was pure Jake. That smile, she thought to herself, was the reason he'd had an endless stream of women queuing up for his attention. He'd never even had to turn his head to find someone. They'd been right there, under his nose.

"You're bad."

"Yeah. Want me to show you how bad I can be?" He rolled her onto her back in an easy movement that left her gasping and flattened by his weight.

"Do you think they can see us from Brooklyn?"

"Well, not *us* specifically, but this building, yes. I grew up over there." His mouth brushed over her jaw and down her neck. "I used to spend most of my time gazing over here and dreaming."

"Was that when you lived with Maria?"

"No. Before that."

She stroked her hand over the taut muscles of his back. "You used to talk to me about it, all those years ago when I was in the hospital. Do you remember?"

"Yes." He paused. "I don't know why. I never used to talk to anyone else. Not even Matt."

She felt a rush of warmth and pulled him closer. "It was the setting. Beeping machines and stark hospital corridors create the sort of intimate atmosphere that makes a person want to spill all their secrets."

He gave a soft laugh. "That must have been it."

"You were the only person I could be honest with. Everyone else put on this huge act in front of me and I put on a huge act in front of them. It was exhausting. But you—" She stroked her fingers gently down his back again. "You listened. You sat on the edge of my bed and you listened. I don't think I would have got through it without you." She felt his arms tighten.

"Yeah, you would. You're tough as nails."

"Are you saying I'm hard?"

"Not all of you. Some parts of you are soft." He eased away from her, a smile tugging at his mouth. "The important parts."

She closed her eyes as she felt the slow stroke of his knowing fingers on her thigh. "You're a bad boy, Jake Romano."

"I know. That's why I stayed away from you." His mouth took hers as his hand worked magic that had her trembling and moaning his name. It was as if he'd stolen the blueprints to her body and memorized every tiny detail. Access points, sensory pathways—he knew every connection and used his knowledge without hesitation or concession.

She was exposed, vulnerable, and he took full advantage, exploring every part of her with an almost-ruthless patience until her excitement levels were so stratospherically high that she half expected his high-tech apartment to sound some sort of warning alarm.

He held her right on the edge of orgasm, until the only way he could still the writhing of her hips was to hold her down, until she was feverish and desperate. He waited until her entire focus was one thing and one thing only. Him. Only then did he shift her underneath him, trapping her with his weight. Now there was no time for breathless anticipation. No time to ask herself if she was going to be able to handle him. There was no slow, gentle option, no time for her to worry that she might not be able to accommodate the thickness of him. Instead he thrust deeply, timing it perfectly.

He filled her, driving into her in a perfect rhythm until he brought pleasure crashing down on both of them in brutal waves. She cried out, her orgasm so intense and so prolonged that for a moment the world around her disappeared. She was aware of him and him alone, of the hard heat of his body, the uneven rasp of his breathing and the shudders of his own release.

Afterward she lay still and shocked, unable to comprehend that she was capable of a response like that.

Jake pulled her against him in a possessive gesture, wrapping her in warmth. "Sleep."

"I'm too awake to sleep. And how can anyone sleep with a view like this in front of them?"

"Sleepless in Manhattan." There was a smile in his voice. "There's plenty about this city that tempts you to stay awake."

Him.

He was the reason she wanted to stay awake. She didn't want to miss a single moment of being with him. She didn't want morning to come, but soon it would and she knew she had to leave before that happened.

Jake didn't invite women back here, let alone invite them to stay over.

She didn't want him to regret what they'd done.

Forcing herself to move, she eased out of his arms and slid out of bed.

Jake shifted onto his elbow, the muscles of his arms bunching as he watched her with that dark, sleepy gaze. "Where are you going?"

It was no wonder he didn't bring women back here, she thought, because what woman in her right mind would want to leave when there was a man like him in the bed?

"Home." Providing she could walk in a straight line on her jelly legs. She felt like a tightrope walker, conscious of every step as she walked through the open doors of the bedroom into the living room and swiftly gathered up her clothes. They were spread across his wooden floor like stepping stones, a treasure trail marking the adventure that had led from the front door to the bed. "Thanks for a great evening, Jake."

"Wait—shit—stop! You're leaving? It's virtually the middle of the night." He slid out of bed and followed her, padding through the apartment with the lithe grace of a jungle cat. "You can't leave now. Come back to bed. That's an order."

He had the body of a Greek god, all honed muscle and virile, tensile strength. How was she supposed to concentrate when he walked around naked?

She pulled on her skirt and then her shirt before she could change her mind. "Put some clothes on, Jake. Over there in

Brooklyn some woman is probably watching you through her telescope."

"Telescope?" His eyes gleamed with wicked humor. "You think it needs magnifying?"

"I—" She remembered how careful he'd been with her, how he'd given her time to adjust and heat infused her cheeks. "Go back to bed."

He grinned and stayed right where he was. "You're cute when you blush."

"You're not cute." The way he was looking at her made her stumble over her shoes and her words. She'd known him for years, but this was a different Jake. A sleepy, sexy, dangerous Jake. "You're infuriating."

"Admit it, the sex was incredible."

She jammed her feet into her shoes and stumbled. "It was slightly above average."

"Honey, I turn you on so badly you can hardly walk."

"That's bullshit. I can walk just fine."

He rubbed his hand across his jaw, not bothering to hide the smile. "You'd find it easier if you put your feet in the right shoes."

She glared at him and kicked her shoes off. "No one is going to need a telescope to see your ego, that's for sure."

"Tell me why you're leaving, Cinderella."

Her heart bumped hard against her chest. "Because those are the rules."

"There are no rules for what you and I just did. It was one night—we both know that." And Paige needed to leave now, before she started to question that decision. And before he had second thoughts about what they'd done.

And before her friends in Brooklyn woke and asked her lots

of awkward questions, although knowing them they already knew exactly where she'd spent the night.

And then there was Matt. *Oh God, Matt.*

How could she have forgotten about her brother?

"We can't tell Matt." Her tone was urgent. "He can't know about tonight."

The smile faded from Jake's face, and she knew he hadn't thought of that, either.

"He's my closest friend. I won't lie to my friend."

"I'm your friend, too, and I'm not asking you to lie. I'm saying we don't need to tell him."

Jake was silent for a moment and she sensed his internal battle. It was visible in the tightening of his mouth and the taut lines of his shoulders, and she stood, drenched in guilt, knowing that she'd made things difficult.

"This is all my fault," she sighed.

"Yeah, because you had to force me. Did you notice that?" He took her face in his hands and kissed her gently. "Why don't you want to tell him, honey?"

He'd used endearments before, but never with his voice so rich with affection.

"You know why. Because he's overprotective. Because he'd read too much into it. Make something of it. And anyway, what is there to tell him? It was one night of sex." Until she said the words aloud she hadn't realized how badly she wanted him to contradict her.

It seemed inconceivable to her that something that felt so life changing and perfect could be extinguished so quickly, but she knew Jake. And because she knew Jake, she wasn't surprised when he nodded.

"All right. We'll do it your way."

She had no right to feel this crushing disappointment.

She knew the way he lived his life, and she, better than anyone, understood the reasons.

His mother had walked out and left him.

It was something she found hard to imagine. She thought about her own mother, the laughter they shared, the love. She counted on her parents 100 percent. Yes, there were times when they drove her insane because they were so protective, but she also knew how lucky she was. Never, not once, had she ever doubted that they would be there for her.

True, Jake had Maria, but she hadn't been able to undo the damage that had already been done.

And Paige had walked into this knowing that and knowing the rules.

Jake dragged his thumb slowly over her lower lip, and then bent to kiss her. "Wait there."

He was back moments later, wearing jeans and a shirt.

She looked at him in surprise. "Where are you going?"

"I'm taking you home."

"I don't need you to take me home. There are no expectations, Jake. No responsibilities or commitments. I walk out of that door and we both go back to doing what we were doing, with whoever we want to do it with."

His brows drew together in a frown. "What's that supposed to mean?"

"It was one night. I told you I could handle it and I can. We go back to our lives. Neither of us needs to feel awkward. You can date people and I can date people. No problem."

His frown deepened. "You're dating someone? You're seeing someone?" His tone was several degrees cooler, and she was surprised by the change in him until she realized he was probably thinking that she'd cheated on some guy.

"No! I'm not seeing anyone right now. You think I would have done what we did if I was? I was talking hypothetically."

"Oh. Right." The frown cleared. The warmth returned to his eyes and his voice. "Put your shoes on. I'm taking you home. And don't argue."

"I won't argue, providing you take me on the bike."

He shot her a look. "Paige—"

"We both know that if you were making a trip to Brooklyn at this time, you'd take the bike."

His smile was back, that slanting, seductive smile that always left her defenseless. "That's how we bad boys like to get around at night, but that doesn't mean—"

"I want to go on the bike. I always have." She picked up her bag. "And because you don't protect me, I know you're going to say yes. Do you have a spare helmet?"

He laughed, disappeared again and returned carrying soft leathers and a pair of boots.

"You need to wear these. If you want to ride on my bike, you'll wear what I tell you to wear. No negotiation."

"These won't fit me."

"They'll fit and before you ask searching questions I can tell you they belonged to a niece of Maria's who was visiting from Sicily. I showed her around."

She dressed and they walked to the elevator together.

He took her hand. "Do you want to take the stairs?"

"No. I came up in it. I can go down in it. Does it often break?"

"Never." He nudged her inside. "And if it does I'll distract you with sex until it's fixed."

"I almost want it to break."

He hit the button on the wall and pulled her against him, kissing her so thoroughly that she couldn't work out whether the lurch in her stomach was due to the elevator or the skill of his mouth on hers.

When the doors opened, he released her reluctantly and led her through to the underground garage.

She was aware of every movement he made, from the long, lazy stride to the fluid way he mounted the bike.

She settled herself behind him, her view mostly obliterated by the broad planes of his shoulders and back.

The engine fired to life with a throaty growl and Paige decided there was something erotic about a motorcycle. Or maybe it was the fact that Jake was the one riding it. The raw power of the man in front of her would have made any mode of transport attractive.

She slid her arms around him and sucked in a breath as the bike roared into the night, the engine vibrating with power.

He steered skillfully through the backstreets, down to Lower Manhattan.

Her legs were pressed against the hard muscle of his, her arms locked around hard male strength.

She inhaled it all, the man, the cool night air and the smells of New York City.

All around them the streets were beginning to come to life. There were lights on in bakeries and plumes of steam rose from vents in the surrounding buildings, clouding the air.

They wound their way to the Brooklyn Bridge, connecting Lower Manhattan to Brooklyn.

Paige turned her head and looked back at the skyline glittering and twinkling like a film set.

Surely nothing compared to the magic of the Brooklyn Bridge at night?

How many lovers had walked across this bridge? How many proposals and promises had been made on this incredible feat of engineering high above the fast-flowing waters of the East River?

She felt the cool air rush past her face, watching as a new day dawned, as fingers of light fractured the dark sky.

It was a perfect moment.

She had no idea what happened next and right now she didn't care.

She had this moment and she was going to make the most of it. Knowing that it was fleeting simply made it all the more precious.

She gave a whoop of delight and felt Jake's answering laugh.

The bike swooped through the streets of Brooklyn, past silent parks and along darkened streets and finally drew up outside the brownstone Paige shared with her friends and her brother.

Home.

Like Cinderella after the ball.

She slid off the bike and stood on the sidewalk, breathing in the smell of summer, her stomach twisted into knots. She dragged the helmet off her head, laughter bubbling up like champagne from a freshly opened bottle.

"That was truly amazing."

"We'll make a bad girl of you yet." He took the helmet from her, his fingers lingering on hers, and she swallowed, because this was it and she had no idea how to end an evening like the one they'd shared.

Goodbye didn't feel right.

"I'll give you the jacket when I see you."

He gave a brief nod. "Thank you for tonight."

For a moment she thought he was thanking her for sex, then realized he was talking about the event.

It seemed like a lifetime ago.

The adrenaline and the thrill of it was still there somewhere, but right now it had been surpassed by the excitement of being with Jake.

"I'm glad it worked well. Eva, Frankie and I will have a meeting tomorrow and we'll send you through a report."

It was hard to act and sound professional when her body ached from the deep, intimate invasion of his.

His gaze met hers and she knew he was thinking the same thing.

It seemed impossible that this was it.

She wanted him to say something. Something personal. But he didn't.

Fighting disappointment, she was about to turn away when he slid his hand behind her head and drew her mouth to his.

His kiss was fire and heat, a brief afterburn of what they'd shared earlier, and it shocked her because, had her friends or her brother chosen that moment to look out of the window, there would have been no secret to keep.

Slowly, he lifted his mouth from hers. And smiled.

That smile connected with every single part of her, melting her bones to liquid.

She kept her hand on his arm, dizzy, steadying herself. "Why did you do that?"

"Because I wanted to." He ran his fingers across her cheek in a lingering stroke. "Paige Walker, I predict that from tomorrow your phone will be ringing nonstop. You're going to be busy."

"I hope so."

Forcing herself to move, she took the steps to the front door.

As she opened it she heard the throaty rumble of the engine as Jake roared away and she stood for a moment on the steps, watching and listening as the sound faded into the distance.

Happiness, she thought, felt like this. Exactly like this.

Fourteen

If there's one thing better in life than a true friend, it's two true friends.

—Eva

"This is a celebration breakfast." Eva put bowls and spoons in the centre of the table. "It went well! Everyone thought so. And at least six people asked for my card."

"Me, too." Frankie closed the book she was reading and put it down on the table. "Pass the yogurt, Ev. And while you're in the fridge, pass me a diet cola. I'm so tired I'm thinking of drowning myself in it."

Eva dived into the fridge and emerged with berries and yogurt. She ignored the cans of drink lined up in rows, saying, "You don't really want that. I refuse to poison my best friend. One day I'm going to detox your fridge."

Eva and Paige were in Frankie's kitchen because Eva had been cooking since dawn and their own kitchen was covered in the results of her various culinary experiments.

Sunlight poured through the windows and pots of herbs

clustered around the open door to the small garden. Every surface in Frankie's small apartment was covered in plants she was propagating. They crowded the windowsills in rows and sat on the counters alongside notepads covered in Frankie's neat handwriting.

"If even half of those people call, we're going to be busy." Frankie stood up and helped herself to a soda, ignoring Eva's disapproving look. "And I love my fridge. My kitchen, my vice, my decision. You drink coffee. There's no difference."

"Coffee is a natural substance."

Ignoring her, Frankie opened the can and sat down again. "I still haven't recovered from the shock of seeing Matilda with Chase Adams."

"They were perfect together. Cinderella and her Prince." Dreamy, Eva reached for the food and knocked Frankie's book off the table.

Frankie bent to retrieve it. "You never give up, do you?"

"No. Love is out there somewhere. For all of us. Even you, and—holy *crap*—" Eva snatched the book from Frankie, gazing at the photograph on the back. "This guy is smoking hot. Look at those *eyes*. Who is he? He's a perfect romance hero. I think I'm in love." She turned the book over and dropped it. "Ugh. Is that blood?"

With a sigh, Frankie picked it up again. "No. It's tomato ketchup. The guy had an accident in the kitchen."

"Sarcasm is very unattractive. I don't know how you can read this stuff."

"It's called horror, and I love it. Lucas Blade knows exactly how to sneak into your mind and keep you awake at night—"

"I wouldn't mind him keeping me awake at night, and I'm not talking about his book. Wait a minute—Lucas Blade?"

Eva frowned and took the book from her. "That's the author? The guy on the back?"

"Yes. And if you drop my book a third time I'll eviscerate you."

"It's him." Eva handed the book back triumphantly. "It's Mitzy's grandson! Remember I told you about him? The reclusive author. Lucas Blade."

It was Frankie's turn to stare. "You know Lucas Blade? Eva! He's *huge*."

"I told you he was well-known. I'm sure Mitzy could arrange an introduction if you're interested."

Frankie's expression blanked. "No thanks. I admire his work, that's all. Spend your day dreaming for yourself by all means, but don't waste time dreaming for me." She glanced at Paige. "So what time did you finally come home? We waited for you until two, and then gave up."

"We were hoping you'd met someone to take your mind off Jake. Did you see that incredibly sexy British businessman with the wire-rimmed glasses?" Eva was wearing a shirt in a vivid shade of green teamed with a jeweled turquoise scarf. "There's something about men in glasses. I want to rip them off and get up close so they can see me. Seriously, it makes me dangerous."

"When are you not dangerous?" Frankie rubbed sleep out of her eyes. "Do you have to wear such bright colors so early in the morning? It's blinding."

"If my clothes are cheerful, I'm cheerful."

"You're always cheerful, even when it's too early to be cheerful. If the world was ending, you'd still be cheerful. I'm going to dress you in black." Frankie yawned. "Feed us, woman. It's what you do best."

"I am feeding you. Paige needs calories after the amount

I'm betting she used up last night and this morning. And this is delicious. Try it. I included coconut." Eva tipped homemade granola into bowls and gave Paige a knowing look. "So?"

"So, what? I love coconut. You know I do." Paige, who'd had less than four hours sleep, should have felt like death but instead felt dizzy and energized. Her head was swirling with memories of the event, and Jake. Jake.

"I'm not asking what you think of the food, I'm asking about the man who kept you out until dawn, put that smile on your face and gave you stubble scrape on your neck."

"What?" Paige lifted her hand to her neck. "Where?"

"You'd better wear a scarf today or you'll be getting knowing looks." Eva pushed the bowls toward them, along with berries and yogurt. "Eat. I'll sit here and die of envy while you tell us everything. I want to know how many calories you used up."

"I have no idea how many calories."

Eva dug her spoon into her granola. "If you tell me the position, I can tell you the calories. Of course if you licked melted chocolate and whipped cream off each other's bodies, that complicates the math. Tell me quickly, before Matt joins us."

Paige paused with her spoon halfway to her mouth. "Why would Matt join us?"

"Because I invited him. It's a celebration breakfast."

Crap.

"Ev, I wish you'd—"

There was a tap on the door and Matt walked in.

Paige froze. It didn't help telling herself she had no reason to feel guilty.

She felt guilty.

Eva deftly removed her scarf and looped it around Paige's neck.

"This color looks good on you. Keep it on for a while.

Hi, Matt." Her voice was casual. "You're looking exception-ally handsome today. Khakis and a button-down shirt. You're dressed to impress, which means you're leaving your chain saw at home and you're off to a meeting."

Paige fiddled with the scarf.

She was an adult with a perfect right to a sex life. So why was she afraid to tell her brother the truth?

There was a long list of reasons, but top of that list was the fact that it was unlikely to ever happen again.

"You're perky for someone who was on her feet all night." Matt scanned the table. "I was invited to a celebration break-fast, but I don't see bacon. Everyone knows a celebration breakfast has to include bacon."

Eva shuddered. "We have homemade granola and berries."

"That's what I was afraid of. What does a guy have to do to get red meat around here?"

"Hang out with someone who isn't vegetarian," Eva said tartly, and Matt grinned and helped himself to granola.

"Apart from your weird dietary habits, you're cute. You'll be even cuter if you have strong coffee. So how did it go?"

"We're the talk of the town." Eva stood up and poured cof-fee into a mug. "Frankie will make you bacon if you really want it."

"Don't worry. I'll choke this down." Matt picked up a spoon and dug it into the granola. "So it went well?"

"It surpassed all expectations," Eva said. "I predict the phone is going to ring and ring."

"Good." Matt reached for his coffee. "Jake's not here yet, then?"

Paige stared at him. "Why would Jake be here?"

"Because I invited him. You said it was a celebration break-fast and he was the one who gave you the business."

Paige choked on her food and Eva poured her a glass of water.

"Are you all right? Was it the coconut?"

"I'm fine."

Matt had invited Jake? There was no way he'd accept.

Not after what they'd done the night before.

It would be too awkward. It would be—

"Anyone home?" Jake's voice came from the doorway. "I was invited to a celebration breakfast, but I don't smell bacon so I'm wondering if this is the right place."

Paige knocked a plate onto the floor and it rolled and spun to a halt at Jake's feet.

"Well, that's a novel way of giving me a plate." Calm, he stooped to retrieve it, smiling at her briefly before strolling to the empty chair at the end of the table.

Paige looked at him, and then looked away again.

How could he be so *normal*?

Frankie pushed an empty mug toward him. "Coffee? Given that you're the hero of the hour, you deserve hero treatment."

"I heard Urban Genie was the hero of the hour." He reached for a chunk of freshly baked bread. "This smells incredible. Did you make this, Ev?"

"It's sourdough."

"My favorite. And it goes perfectly with crisp bacon."

"No chance of that around here." Matt glanced at him. "I called you last night to see how the event went. You weren't answering your phone. Presumably you were with a woman."

Paige wanted to slide under the table.

This wasn't just complicated—it was a nightmare.

How had she thought this would be easy to handle?

What was Jake going to say? Obviously he wasn't going to admit he was with a woman, so—

"I was with a woman." Jake smiled at Frankie as she poured coffee into his mug.

"Just the one?" Matt sounded amused. "She must have been special."

"Yeah, she was special."

"Hot?"

Holy crap.

"Do we need the details?" Paige was so hot she thought she was going to burn through the chair.

"She was hot. She was incredible." Jake gave Paige a wicked smile. "Are you all right? Only you have a lot of color this morning. I hope you're not coming down with something."

She was going to kill him. "I'm fine."

Matt frowned at her. "Jake's right. You have a lot of color. You're not getting a temperature?"

"No! I'm great. Never better. A little tired, that's all."

"Yeah, you were late last night. I popped down to see you to find out how it went but neither of you answered. Eva was singing in the bath. That's probably why you didn't hear me."

"That's probably why." Paige felt weak.

"Any business from it?"

"Not yet, but give us time." She felt hard pressure on her leg and realized it was Jake. He rubbed his calf against hers in a slow, sinuous movement that took her mind straight back to the intimacies of the night before.

Desire rushed through her and her heartbeat was so loud she wondered why they couldn't all hear it.

What was he doing?

Matt put his coffee down. "So, tonight is movie night. I have a few friends coming over. You're welcome to join us."

Frankie looked interested. "What's the movie? Kisses and romance or shoot 'em up?"

"There's a body count." Matt drained his coffee. "Blood and guts might be involved."

Frankie didn't hesitate. "I'm there. Front row seat."

Eva shuddered. "I'm not there. One day I'm going to tie you all up and torture you with romance night. Can't we have a chick flick marathon?"

"Not on my watch." Matt smiled. "You coming, Jake?"

There was a long pause, and then Jake stirred.

"Not tonight. I have plans."

Matt reached for more bread. "I'm guessing those plans are female."

"They are."

Paige felt a sudden stab of misery. It was one thing to know that last night had been a one-off and that he was going to date other people. Another thing entirely to hear the details. If he was seeing a woman, she didn't want to hear about it.

Matt looked interested. "Same woman as last night?"

"That's right." Jake's voice was steady. "Same woman."

Same woman?

Paige gripped her spoon. Her gaze flickered to his but he was eating, completely relaxed, as if he hadn't just dropped a bombshell into the middle of the kitchen table.

She stared into her bowl of granola, reexamining the words, checking she hadn't made a mistake.

He wanted to see her again.

Happiness rushed through her, and with it a thousand questions.

Why? When had he decided it wasn't going to be just one night?

Matt finished his breakfast and stood up. "I have to go. I have a meeting on the other side of town." He paused at the doorway, his eyes on Paige. "Take it easy today," he said quietly. "You had a very late night."

"I can cope with a late night, Matt."

"I know. But I still think you should take it easy." He studied her for a moment. "And I agree with Ev, that scarf looks great."

Jake drained his coffee and stood up, too. "I'll walk with you. I need to be in early today. Thanks for the food, Ev." He stooped to kiss Eva casually on the cheek and then strolled out of the room after Matt.

Eva slumped in her chair. "Now I'm going to have to give you my new scarf. And I might need a whole new nervous system while we're at it. I'm not built for drama."

"Are you kidding me?" Frankie stood up and started to clear the plates. "You invented drama. You could marry drama, have its babies—which, by the way, would be called Crisis and Panic—and live happily ever after."

"She had a hickey on her neck! Someone had to save the day. I thought I was impressive."

Frankie shook her head. "You hid the hickey on her neck, but you didn't do anything about the fact her face was the color of a tomato."

Paige stood up and loosened the scarf from her neck. "Thank you for this."

"Keep it. It's yours. The color really did look good on you until your face turned puce. And anyway, I can't have it back now. I'll always associate that scarf with stress and anxiety." Eva pushed her back into the chair. "You're not moving until you've told us all about sex with Jake."

Paige froze. "What makes you think it was Jake?"

"Your face when Matt walked into the room and then your face again when Jake walked into the room. Then there was all that delicious innuendo from bad, bad Jake—and I need to probably tell him that if he's going to have under-the-table foot sex, he needs to not sit next to me while he does it. Also, I heard the motorbike," Eva confessed. "So being inquisitive by nature—"

Frankie stacked plates on the counter. "By which she means incurably nosy."

"Inquisitive," Eva said firmly. "I rushed into the living room and peered out of the window through a crack in the blinds. I saw him kiss you. Great kiss by the way. Loved the way he hauled your mouth to his. Masterful and romantic at the same time. Very, *very* hot."

"You saw that?"

"It was my lucky night. If I can't watch romantic movies or have sex in my own life, I have to live through you vicariously. It's your duty to allow me to peek. What are friends for? It was your lucky night, too, from the look of it. Jake is obviously as good at kissing as he is at other things."

Paige slid down in her chair. "Is it weird?"

"You and Jake? You tell us, but from where I was standing it looked hot, not weird."

"I meant, weird because he's part of our group. Friends and sex don't mix, do they?"

"They can." Eva shrugged. "There are loads of instances where friends become lovers. *When Harry Met Sally* is one of my favorite movies."

"Life isn't a movie, Eva. But that isn't why it's weird." Frankie reached for Matt's empty mug. "It's weird because the two of you have been swiping at each other for most of your lives. And after that kiss in the elevator you thought he wasn't interested."

Paige put her spoon down. "Turned out he was interested, but he was protecting me."

"From what?"

"Isn't it obvious?" Eva popped a berry into her mouth. "He was protecting her from himself. He doesn't want to hurt Paige. That's *so* romantic."

Paige wondered why Eva had been so quick to spot something she hadn't. "It's not romantic. It's super irritating. I thought he was the one person who *didn't* protect me, and it turns out he's been protecting me all along. I would rather have known."

"No you wouldn't. Because then you would have been angry. You're stubborn about people helping you. Not that I don't understand," Eva said quickly, "but it's true."

"I'm not stubborn." Paige looked at Frankie. "Am I stubborn?"

Frankie put the yogurt back into the fridge. "Yeah, you are. You'd fall on your face rather than take help. Makes you difficult to help sometimes."

"I don't want help!"

"Everyone needs help, Paige! That's what life is all about. Reaching out and supporting the people around you. You can't do it on your own. There is a difference between being overprotected and being helped. If we hadn't forced you to go to Jake, last night wouldn't have happened."

"Maybe it would have been better if it hadn't."

"I was talking about the event," Frankie said slowly, and Paige felt her face heat.

"Oh. Well, we still don't know if that has worked. The phone hasn't rung yet."

"It will. And networking is part of business."

"Great. I'll network as part of business."

"And what about the rest of it? What happens now?" Frankie pushed the fridge door shut. "How does this play out?"

Paige glanced at her. "Are we still talking about Urban Genie?"

"No. We're talking about your sex life." Eva leaned forward. "This wasn't a one-night thing. You heard him—he wants to see you again."

"I know." Thinking about it sent excitement rushing through her. She tried to contain it. "That part I don't understand. He didn't suggest seeing each other again when we were together."

"Well, he's obviously had a change of heart." Frankie picked up a cloth and wiped the table. "Everyone can see the chemistry between you. The only reason Matt didn't shock himself on the electrical impulses traveling around this room was because the last thing he expects is for the two of you to get together. But, Paige, he is going to find out, and when he does he'll be hurt that you didn't tell him. And you'll feel terrible that you hurt him. I don't want either of you to feel terrible."

"What would I say? There's nothing to tell. I can't tell him what's going on because I don't know what's going on!"

Eva glanced between the two of them. "Paige has a point. If she says it's just sex then Matt would beat Jake to a pulp, except that Jake can handle himself, which means it will get very messy. I don't like fighting, and I agree—the situation is complicated."

"This is why I prefer dealing with flowers and plants. They're not complicated." Frankie thumped the cloth back onto the counter. "If the two of you have finished spinning fairy tales, we should go to the office. Whether Jake is there or not, we have work to do. We run our own business now, remember?"

"In a minute." Eva stayed glued to her chair, her eyes on Paige. "We need details."

Frankie rolled her eyes. "I don't want details."

"I do." Eva was emphatic. "I want to know every single detail working backward from the moment he dragged your mouth to his and tried to eat you alive in the street outside. Come on, Paige. The least you can do is earn the scarf you're wearing and make up for the fact I ruptured my larynx singing loudly in the bath so I didn't have to answer the door to Matt and explain why you weren't there."

Fifteen

To make your dream a reality, first you need to wake up.

—Paige

The phone didn't stop ringing.

Within an hour of reaching the office they had six new clients, all of whom wanted events and additional concierge services.

"Goodbye sleep," Eva crowed. "Goodbye sanity."

"Goodbye money worries." Frankie was ever practical. "We're going to need help. There are only three of us and this is a lot of business."

Paige felt giddy. Any concern that she wouldn't be able to focus on work melted away in the excitement of the moment. "Our business. It's *our* business. How cool is that? We decide what we say yes to."

"We say yes to everything," Eva said firmly. "Your wish is not only our command, it's our income."

It gave Paige a massive buzz to see business finally taking off, and being busy stopped her thinking about Jake.

He'd implied that they'd be seeing each other tonight, but how was that going to work?

Was he going to call her?

Or was she expected to call him?

Why did things have to be so complicated?

"We'll outsource. We don't want to increase our overheads at the moment. I do not want to lay people off if things don't work out." She'd learned that from Jake. Watch the numbers. Staff appropriately. "Let's sit down and see what we have."

The phone rang again.

Paige made a grab for it. "This is insane."

"But in a good way. Pretty soon we'll be able to buy out Star Events and fire Cynthia," Frankie said.

Paige answered the phone. The woman who had booked the baby shower last night also wanted regular dog walking and a gift basket for the colleague who was going on maternity leave.

"Tell me a little about her. What does she enjoy?" While she was talking, Paige created a new file, made notes and exchanged a few ideas. "We'll come back to you with a list of suggestions. You can tick the ones you like and we'll do the rest."

She ended the call and forwarded the list to Eva. "This one is for you. Go shop."

"You're paying me to go to Bloomingdale's? I've died and gone to heaven. Have I told you how much I love being in business with you guys?" Eva checked the list. "I might change the brand of scented candle. And the scent. You have to be careful with scent when you're pregnant."

"That's why you're doing this job. Do whatever it takes to make sure this woman recommends us to her friends. Next we need to talk about—" Paige paused as her phone rang at the same time as Frankie's. "Or maybe we won't talk."

She took the call and Frankie did the same, walking out of the office as she discussed colors, petals and blooms with the person on the end of the phone.

"Yes, concierge services are available to our clients," Paige explained to her caller. "Waiting list?" Her eyes met Eva's and she smiled. "You're in luck. We have capacity at the moment. Why don't I come to your offices and we can talk about your needs? I'm sure Urban Genie can help."

By the time she ended the call she had a brief for a corporate training session and the promise of a major product launch in the fall.

"Can you believe this?" Eva's eyes were shining. "We really are in business. All we have to do is not mess it up."

"We're not going to mess it up—" Paige updated her spreadsheet "—but I'm starting to wish I'd had more than four hours of sleep last night." Her phone beeped and she checked her texts.

It was Jake.

My office. Now. Debrief.

Her stomach flipped and she stood up. "We can finish this later. Jake wants a debrief, and then I have a meeting over on Fifth. I need to run." She scooped up her bag just as Frankie walked back into the room. "Well?"

"That was a bride-to-be who was at the event last night and loved the floral designs. She wants something similar for her wedding."

Eva blinked. "She wants scaffolding at her wedding? What's the theme? Prison Break? How is that romantic?"

"She wants a gazebo, you baboon." Frankie was busy making notes. "And she wants to walk on rose petals."

"Did you just call me a baboon? Because if so, I'm reporting you to Human Resources for bullying and abuse. And someone needs to warn the bride that rose petals are slippery. Either that or call the hospital and have an orthopedic surgeon on alert."

The phone rang again and Paige looked at her friends with a mixture of excitement and disbelief. "We need to find a way of consolidating these calls so that we all know what's going on."

"You always know what's going on. You're the detail woman. I'll take this one." Eva reached for the phone, a smile in her voice. "Urban Genie, your wish is our command—" Her smile faded as she listened. "No, not *that* sort of wish. That isn't what we do." She ended the call, her cheeks pink. *"Well!"*

Frankie looked at her expectantly. "Are you going to tell us?"

"No, I'm not! I'm not repeating it." Eva sniffed. "Never tell Jake. We'd get a big, fat 'I told you so.' He warned us 'your wish is our command' would get us into trouble."

Paige loaded her laptop into her bag.

She had a feeling she was already in bigger trouble than any of them could possibly have predicted. Had she really thought sex with Jake would be simple?

Wondering what happened next, she walked toward Jake's office and spied him through the glass.

He was prowling around as he talked, looking insanely gorgeous in snug jeans and a button-down shirt. It wasn't hard to see why Jake Romano had his pick of women.

He turned and caught her looking.

"I'll call you back." Without waiting for a response he ended the call and beckoned Paige into the room. "So we have a choice—" His tone was businesslike and she forced herself to sublimate the indecent thoughts she was having and respond in the same way.

"A choice?"

"I can have sex with you right here—" he rested his hip on the corner of his desk "—or I can take you home and do it there but that will mean a delay. I'm pretty impatient by nature. When I want something, I go after it. I'm not good at delayed gratification."

"I—I thought you wanted a debrief." It took her brain a moment to catch up. "You're giving me a choice about whether we have sex again?"

"No. We're having sex again. I'm giving you a choice of venue."

The sound she made was half gasp, half laugh. "You have a glass-fronted office."

"I know." There was an edge to his tone. "A design decision I'm now regretting. So it will have to be my place. Fifteen minutes?"

A zing of excitement shot through her body. "I have a meeting across town."

"Rearrange it."

"Jake, I can't! This is my business, and thanks to you the phone is finally ringing off the hook."

"I never should have let you organize that event." He dragged his hand over the back of his neck. "Fine, take your meeting. But come to my place straight afterward. Don't go home first."

She couldn't breathe. "But if I'm seeing you, then I want to change, and—"

"Whatever clothes you put on, I'm going to strip them off and whatever makeup you wear I'm going to kiss off so don't waste time."

Her heart was pounding. This was Jake, Jake, talking to her as if she were a woman. He wasn't holding back and he certainly wasn't protecting her.

"I thought—we weren't—" She was torn between elation and confusion. "It was an amazing night, Jake, but I thought we agreed that it was just one night."

"You said that. I didn't."

"I assumed it was what you wanted."

"It isn't what I want. I've driven myself crazy protecting you and keeping my distance. You don't want that, and I don't want that, either."

Her heart was pounding. "So—"

"So that's settled. I'll see you later. As soon as you can make it. Oh, and Paige—" his voice stopped her in the doorway "—there won't be other people."

"Excuse me?"

"You said that we were both free to see other people, but when I'm with a woman, I'm with a woman. She is my starter, my main course and my dessert. There are no side dishes."

The breath left her lungs in a rush. "I didn't know you had a possessive side."

He dug his hands into his pockets and gave a wry shrug. "I guess we don't know everything there is to know about each other. In some things, I don't share well. This is one of them."

"Neither do I." She could have told him that he didn't need to worry about sharing her. Not only would she never dream of being in a relationship that wasn't exclusive, but her love life was more of a calorie-controlled diet than a feast.

"I'll take my meeting," she said huskily, "and then I'll see you at your place."

The following Friday, Jake strolled into Romano's to talk to Maria and saw Paige at their usual table in the corner, talking to Frankie and Eva.

Jake only saw Paige. The late-evening sun sent light dancing across her dark hair and she was laughing with that wide, generous smile that always made him want to smile, too.

He'd been in San Francisco for the past couple of days, and he'd thought of her every minute. His concentration was shot. People had to say things to him twice.

For years he'd kept his hands off her, and he had no idea how.

It was a wonder he hadn't blown out a few mental circuits.

He wanted to haul her into his arms and make up for lost time, despite the fact that they'd spent every spare minute of the past week doing exactly that.

"Hi, Jake." Matt stood up, and Jake realized with a start of shock that he hadn't even noticed his friend.

Paige had filled his field of vision.

He was about to say something when Maria appeared from the kitchen.

"Jake!" Always demonstrative, she walked across to embrace him just as Paige glanced across and noticed him.

Their eyes met and held briefly, and then she turned back to her friends.

The way she smiled at him had changed, he thought, releasing his mother. Everything was colored with new shades of intimacy and knowledge.

Maria gave him a questioning look. "Are you joining your friends or are you expecting another guest? Matt told me you're seeing someone."

He wished now that he hadn't confessed to Matt that he was seeing someone. He also wished that Paige wasn't so stubborn about not telling her brother about the shift in their relationship.

But even while part of him was working out how to persuade her it was the right thing to do, another part of him was wondering how Matt would react.

He'd made Jake promise that he wouldn't lay a finger on his sister.

That had been almost a decade ago, he reasoned. She'd been a vulnerable teenager. This was different.

"No guest. Not tonight." And the person he was "seeing" was right there in front of him.

He strolled across and took the seat next to Paige, surprised by the lift in his mood.

Being with her always did that to him.

They all shuffled across to make more room but still space was tight.

"How was your trip to San Francisco?" The bright, cheery way Eva asked the question told him that she knew what was going on, and it didn't surprise him. The three women were as close as sisters and shared everything from makeup to confidences, so there was little chance that this new development hadn't been noted.

As someone who had never felt the need to hide his relationships, it didn't bother him. The only thing that bothered him was that Matt didn't know.

He was going to address that.

On the other hand, was there any point in telling him about something that was probably going to end soon?

Maria put a heaped plate in front of him. Spaghetti with meatballs.

It brought back memories of his childhood. For a moment he was six years old again, sick to his stomach, and scared. His life had unraveled like a ball of wool in a cat's paw. His world had been blown apart, his future dark and uncertain.

He'd learned a lot of things that night. He'd learned that adults talked in quiet voices when they didn't want children to hear, he'd learned that Maria, their neighbor, was the best cook and the kindest person he'd ever met, and he'd learned that love was the most unreliable emotion there was.

He glanced at his plate and then briefly at Paige.

Her open, honest smile shook the foundations of his confidence.

She'd said that she was tough enough to handle their relationship, but could she?

What if he hurt her?

"How was business?" Matt pushed a beer toward him. Normal. Friendly.

The fact that he was so friendly made Jake feel worse.

It was time to be honest with his friend.

"Business was good." He reached for his fork. "How is Urban Genie?"

"Busy." Frankie had abandoned her pizza and was scribbling notes on a pad next to her plate. "Right now we have more business than we can handle."

"But we are handling it." Paige picked at her food. "We have good contacts, and we weren't the only ones that Cynthia got rid of. I've been on the phone for the best part of two days."

Because he couldn't wait another moment to touch her, he dropped his hand to her leg and discovered that her thigh was bare.

"Someone asked me today if we have a website," Eva said. "I guess we need one. Something that says what we do. What do you think, Jake?"

He couldn't think of anything except Paige and the smooth softness of her skin. He moved his fingers higher.

What was she wearing? Shorts? A skirt that barely skimmed her bottom?

His brain fused.

Matt raised his eyebrows. "No thoughts?"

"Thoughts?" He was incapable of thoughts. He was going crazy. He couldn't form a sentence. "On what?" He glanced down.

Skirt, he thought. It was a skirt. But there wasn't much of it. She had incredible legs.

"A website." Matt gave him a curious look. "What's wrong with you?"

"I've got a lot on my mind." Paige. Naked. Those long legs wrapped around him. Those were the things on his mind. "What's the problem?"

Paige took a sip of her drink. "The problem is that we're having to field all these calls, and some of them are for small tasks. Dry cleaning and things like that. We're getting no work done because we're answering the phone all the time. We need to filter calls from clients."

Frankie twisted spaghetti around her fork. "Maybe we need a receptionist."

Jake forced himself to concentrate. "What you need," he said, "is an app."

"Why do we need an app?"

He could feel Paige looking at him but he kept his eyes on his plate. If he looked at her, he was pretty sure he'd kiss her and hang the consequences. "You're a genie, aren't you?" Hopefully humor would cover up his clumsy approach. "People are going to want to rub your lamp." He dug his fork into his pasta.

"That's not such a stupid idea." Matt reached for his beer. "Could you do that for her?"

Jake swallowed the food in his mouth before it choked him. "Do what for her?"

"Design the app," Matt said patiently. "What is wrong with you?"

"I'm hungry. I can't think when I'm hungry." And he couldn't think with Paige's bare thigh pressed against his. He contemplated making some excuse. Vanishing to the men's room, and then taking a seat on the other side of the table when he returned.

"You want me to take your sister on as a client? You're kidding. I'd rather rub my flesh with an armadillo."

Frankie grinned, but Paige made a little sound of protest. "I'm great to work with."

He kept his eyes on his plate. "You're a control freak, Paige."

"I'm a perfectionist." She hesitated. "Although I admit there are times when I like to be in charge. You're not afraid of strong women, are you, Jake?"

He thought of her, riding him lightly, that wicked smile on her face.

"There's strong and there's controlling. You can't even order food in a restaurant without wanting to go and cook it for yourself."

"I like things the way I like them. What's wrong with that?"

"Nothing. Except that I also like things the way I like them. You and I together would be a fast road to frustration." It would also be a fast road to sexual oblivion. He knew. He'd already taken that road. "I don't want to work with you. I might kill you. But I can give you some tips."

Matt frowned. "Are you seriously refusing to help my baby sister?"

Baby? *Baby?*

Thinking about what they'd done together made heat break out on the back of his neck.

"Yeah. I'm seriously refusing. I let her run my event."

"Which we did brilliantly," Paige said, and he inclined his head.

"Which you did brilliantly. But that was your expertise.

I draw the line on taking you on as a client. It would ruin a beautiful relationship. I don't want to mess that up." Except that he'd already messed it up. Or she had. He could no longer remember who was responsible for what had happened between them. The whole thing was a hot blur of chemistry and steamy moments.

"Nothing will get messed up. I don't want anything complicated," Paige said. "But maybe you can't handle it."

He wondered whether she was talking about the app or their relationship. "The complicated part isn't the technology. I could put that together for you while drunk."

"Then what's wrong?"

Why the hell was she asking? She knew what was wrong.

"I'll talk to one of my team. Get them to work something up."

Matt looked baffled. "Why don't you do it yourself?"

Because things were getting complicated with Paige. It had only been a week, and already he felt unsettled. He never felt unsettled in relationships. His relationships were the one simple part of his life. "I don't mix business and friendship—"

"You're building her an app," Matt said mildly, "not sleeping with her."

Eva knocked her drink over, flooding the table, and Paige shot to her feet, long legs glistening with sticky liquid.

Frankie pushed a napkin in her direction, and Jake slid out of the booth before he could be tempted to lick it off her bare legs.

"I'll build your damn app," he muttered. "And Dani can find someone to help with receptionist duties until you're on your feet."

Paige brushed past him on her way to the restroom, and for a brief moment he felt the heat of her body against his.

Then she was gone, leaving him disorientated.

Holy shit.

He stood for a moment, wondering how he was going to unravel this.

Frankie, ever practical, had finished mopping the table, and Matt sat down again.

Jake saw Paige walk around the back of the restaurant and vanish toward the restrooms.

"I'll get you another drink," he said to Eva, and followed Paige.

He caught her before she could step through to the restroom, closed his hand around her arm and drew her outside into the narrow passageway that ran alongside the restaurant.

He pushed her against the wall, caging her.

"What are you doing? What's wrong with you?" Her eyes widened. "You don't need to build an app if you don't want to. There's no need to—"

"You're driving me crazy." He could smell her hair and the faint scent of her perfume. He wanted to strip off her clothes and kiss his way down her delectable body. Instead, he kissed her lips, hard, demanding and felt her moan against his mouth.

"Jake—"

He jammed his fingers into her hair, holding her head still for his kiss, feeling the bite of her nails in his shoulders as she kissed him back.

Far in the distance he heard the muffled sound of conversation and laughter, the scent of garlic mixing with the humid summer air, but out here there was nothing but the two of them.

He pressed her back against the wall, slid his hands up her bare thighs and felt her strain against him.

"I missed you," he murmured.

"You were gone for two days."

"It was too long." He stroked between her legs and felt her gasp against his mouth. "You want me, too."

"Yes—"

Who knew how far that kiss would have gone, but then there was a clatter from the kitchen, interspersed with colorful Italian swearing.

Paige pulled away, eyes wide.

They stared at each other, gazes locked, and then it occurred to him that if they didn't go back to the table soon, someone would come looking for them.

He moved his hand. Reluctantly he stepped away from her. "We need to get back. What are you doing this weekend?"

"I— Nothing. Working, I guess."

"Spend it with me."

He couldn't believe he'd said it.

He'd never spent an entire weekend with a woman. Two consecutive days.

Paige smiled. "That sounds good. What do you want to do?"

"You need to ask?"

Sixteen

If you think love is the answer, you're probably asking the wrong question.

—Frankie

"Are you joining us this weekend?" Frankie closed down her laptop and stood up. "Eva and I are taking a picnic to Central Park tomorrow."

Paige shook her head. "I need to work."

Frankie gave her a long look. "Does your 'work' have rock-hard biceps, a very sexy smile and run this place?"

Euphoria mixed with anxiety. "Do you think I'm crazy?"

"Honestly? Yeah, I do." Frankie slipped her laptop into her bag. "I'm fond of Jake, but the guy is a notorious player."

"I'm playing, too. I'm having fun."

"Are you? Because that's great, as long as you don't fall in love with him."

Paige felt her whole body tense. "I won't."

"Are you sure? Because this is the fourth weekend in a row

you've spent with him and if you're dreaming of carriages and white dresses, that's not Jake."

"I know that's not Jake. I've known him longer than you have."

"Yeah, the difference is that I haven't been in love with him for most of my life." Frankie stuffed a thick pile of papers into her bag and Paige swallowed.

"I'm not—maybe I was once, but not now and—"

"Good." Frankie pushed her glasses up her nose. "So your only other problem is Matt. Have you told him yet?"

Paige felt a rush of guilt. "No. It was just one night and—"

"And now it's a few nights." Frankie's voice was flat. "You should tell him, Paige. Creeping around in a relationship is a really bad thing. Believe me, I know. I was brought up with creeping. It always, always comes out in the end and when it does it's always hideous."

Paige knew she was thinking of her mother. "This is different. What would I tell him? We're having fun, that's all. We're both unattached. It's probably going to end soon. There's nothing to tell, Frankie."

"You're setting fire to the sheets with his best friend. That's something he should know. What does Jake think?"

It was the one point of disagreement between them.

"He wants to tell him, but I made him promise not to."

"That's tough on him. You're putting him in a difficult position."

Paige sighed. "Frankie—"

"I love you. You're my best friend. But I'm worried about you. This is going to come back and bite you. If Matt finds out, he's going to be hurt and then you'll be hurt, too. I don't want that to happen. I like Jake, but that won't stop me killing him if he hurts you both."

Paige rubbed her fingers over her brow. "I'll think about it. I'll see how it goes this weekend. Before you leave, is there anything new I need to know?"

"Everything is under control. The wedding is organized. They wanted me to recommend a photographer so I called Molly."

"Good choice." They'd all worked with Molly at Star Events and found her to be a talented photographer. "We should ask Molly if she'd like to be one of our preferred suppliers. Anything else?"

"Matt asked me if I could quote for designing a roof garden. Victoria, who normally does that for him, is overloaded." Frankie heaved the bag onto her shoulder. "I'd like to help out, but I understand if you'd rather not overlap business."

"We're partners," Paige said. "You don't have to ask my permission. If you'd like to do it, then do it. And I can't think of anything better than sharing business contacts with my brother."

"You didn't want favors."

"This isn't a favor. He's employing our services. I'll charge him."

Frankie grinned. "You're turning into a ruthless tycoon. I'll say yes then and go over to the space with him and take a brief. It's a big place over on the Upper West Side and they want to throw a party once it's done. A kind of 'roof warming.' I'll make sure Urban Genie gets the chance to pitch for that."

Frankie left the room and Paige settled down to work.

She made it through the afternoon without making any major errors. She put together financial estimates for two events, made appointments to see two new venues and took calls from two people looking for a job. She added them to a list and promised she'd be in touch if, and when, they started recruiting.

Until they were established she didn't feel safe employing people. She didn't want to have to lay people off.

She settled down to work on a pitch for a major marketing event and by the time she looked up again the sky was dark and lights had come on all around the city.

She stood up and stretched, her bones aching from sitting for too long in one place.

"You're working late." Dani stood in the doorway, her hair tumbling around her narrow shoulders. "Jake asked me to talk to you about what you need. Said you wanted someone to answer phones and stuff. Laura can do that for you. She's smart. Been with us a couple of weeks."

"What did she do before?"

"She was at home with kids. Lost a bit of confidence and found it hard to get back into work. Now she's working for us."

"You took her on?"

"Not me. Jake. She was a risky hire, but Jake is never afraid of risk. He saw something in her that others didn't. He's almost always right." Dani eased away from the door frame. "I'll bring Laura to you tomorrow and you can explain what you need. She used to work as a receptionist in one of the big hotels before she had a family. When she gets her confidence back she's going to be great. You going home anytime soon?"

"Yes. Actually no, probably not." Paige blinked, realizing her mind had been miles away. "Not for a while. I have work to do."

The other woman grinned. "I'm starting to understand why Jake gave you office space here. You fit right in."

Paige carried on working until her head throbbed, and then finally switched off her laptop.

It was almost midnight and she appeared to be the last person in the building.

Jake's team frequently worked until the early hours but she knew that at the moment lots of them were in the San Francisco office preparing for a major pitch.

Yawning, she grabbed her purse and walked out of the office she shared with Eva and Frankie.

"Paige."

Jake's voice came from behind her, deep and sure. She felt a rush of excitement closely followed by exhilaration.

Hauling her feelings behind a mask of indifference, she turned. "Hi. I didn't realize you were still here. It's late."

"It's midnight. That means it's the weekend. And we have a date."

"I assumed that started tomorrow."

"It's starting right now. I've been working all week and so have you. Come into my office. I have something to show you."

The look in his eyes made her heart race.

"I've already seen it. Pretty impressive in fact."

He laughed. "That's not the only thing I have that's impressive."

She raised an eyebrow. "Now I'm intrigued." She stepped over the threshold of his office and he closed the door behind her.

"It's been a long week." His eyes were dark, fathomless pools and Paige felt her heart beat faster.

"Yes."

He slid his hand behind her neck and lowered his forehead to hers. "I came looking for you earlier on today and you were on the phone to a client. Otherwise I would have pinned you to the desk and done indecent things to you." His voice was thickened. "What does that say about me?"

"It says you're a risk taker and that you have no respect for office furniture."

"And how about you—" His mouth hovered dangerously close to hers. "Are you a risk taker, too?"

She hooked her finger into the front of his shirt. "I think I might be."

He lowered his head and kissed her, his hands in her hair, his mouth hot and demanding. She melted into him and with a groan he powered her back across the office until her shoulders hit a wall.

He fumbled behind her, opened a door she hadn't even realized was there and pushed her through.

Dimly she registered smooth counters and more doors. "What is this place?"

Without releasing his hold on her he pushed the door closed, trapping them inside. "Storage, dressing room—there's even a bed in here in case I'm working late but I don't often use it."

"A bed?"

"Yeah." He yanked at her dress, and then she gasped as she felt the warm slide of his hand over her skin, seeking. Finding. And then there was only the skilled stroke of his fingers and the rush of desire that spread through her with delicious, syrupy warmth.

"Jake—"

"You're beautiful." He kept his mouth on her, kept his hand on her, sending her higher and higher with every intimate brush of his fingers until she moaned and squirmed against him.

She felt the rigid thickness of him straining against her and fumbled with his zip until she freed him.

Neither of them moved. They stood, locked against the door, lost in their own private world of steamy desire. And then she felt his hand slide to her thigh, urging it upward. She curled her leg around his back, her eyes still fixed on his.

His first thrust brought a cry to her lips, and he crushed her mouth with his, swallowing the sound so that all that was left was sensation. The sensation of him filling her, possessing her, taking everything she had to give until orgasm rushed down on her so fast she had no time to breathe. She heard him curse softly as she tightened around him, felt him thrust deep to counter the seductive ripples of her body, felt the moment when he tipped over the edge.

Then there was only the hot pulse of him, the heat of his mouth and the incredible intimacy that was being with Jake. It felt deeper and more intense than anything she'd ever experienced before.

Maybe it was because she'd known him so long. Wanted him for so long.

Finally he eased away from her and stood for a moment, steadying his breathing, his forehead resting on his arm while with the other arm he held her close.

Her forehead was on his shoulder, and she closed her eyes as she breathed in the scent of him, absorbing every movement and texture. Man and muscle.

"We just had sex in your office."

"Yes. At the time I wondered if this was a waste of office space but now I'm kind of glad I built it."

She felt weak and shaky. "I'm glad, too. I've never had sex up against a door before."

He gave a husky laugh and eased away so that he could look at her. "All part of your education." He lifted his head and stroked his fingers over her face in a gesture that was both possessive and intimate. "Are you all right?"

"I think so. Although I can't believe we just did that." She'd had sex with Jake in his office. Standing up. "Or maybe you do it all the time."

"Never. I'm starting to think sharing office space with you might not have been such a great idea." His voice wasn't quite steady, and he released her and gently smoothed her dress down.

"You said you had something to show me." She tried to sound normal, as if being with him hadn't just rocked her world. "Was that it?"

He stared at her blankly, and then his expression cleared. "No, that wasn't it. I built you an app."

She was touched and more than a little excited. "You did?"

"Yeah, I was going to show it to you but I got distracted. I blame you."

"You could show it to me now."

"Or I could wait until Monday and show it to all three of you." He lowered his head and kissed her again. "The weekend has started. Work can wait."

"I don't want to wait. I want you to show me the app."

"I'll show you over dinner."

"Now? It's late."

"That must be why I'm so hungry." His smile was wickedly sexy. "And this is Manhattan. There is no such thing as late. There's this fantastic Greek place around the corner. Stays open until all hours."

"Does your mother know you eat Greek?"

"My mother doesn't know half the things I do." He took Paige's hand and led her out of the office, winding past empty desks to the elevator.

They descended to the street in a silent glide of simmering chemistry and leashed sexual desire. Her heart gave a little flutter. She didn't think she made a sound, but she must have done because he sent her a searing glance that raised the temperature of the enclosed space by several degrees. She looked away quickly, knowing that if she didn't they'd end up having sex in the elevator.

Somehow they made it to street level, and then she felt the light brush of his hand on her back as they walked two blocks to the restaurant.

Despite the hour, it was crowded. A small, friendly crowd inhabiting an intimate space filled with delicious smells and sounds that transported her straight to the Mediterranean.

Jake waved aside the menus, ordered for both of them and then pulled out his tablet computer. "Get ready to be blown away."

His enthusiasm made her smile. "I'm ready. And, by the way, I can order my own food."

"I know you can, but I eat here all the time and I know what's good. Move closer." He tugged at her chair. "See this? This is your app."

"It's so cute." She smiled. "A genie lamp. Do I rub it?"

"You tap it." He tapped his finger on the screen and she watched, intrigued as he took her through the different features. "It's easy to use, so even nontechnical people will find it easy. Your clients can use it to send requests for concierge services. Laura can filter them and direct them to the appropriate person. It means you don't have to be involved with simple requests. If the dog needs walking or someone needs dry cleaning collected, Laura can allocate it to the best person. Frees you up to deal with the events and more complicated requests."

She asked him a few questions, and then experimented herself. "This is amazing. I love it. Did you program it yourself?"

"Yes."

"But you've been so busy with that pitch in San Francisco and—I didn't think you did much of the hands-on work now. Apart from cyber security. I thought you were all about clients."

"I am."

She handed the tablet back to him. "So why did you program our app?"

"Because it was for you. You needed it." His gaze held hers and she felt warmth spread through her.

"Thank you. We'll pay you, obviously."

"I don't want you to pay me. And I have to do something with my time since I'm sleeping less than usual." He waited while their waitress delivered food to the table, an array of small dishes with warm freshly baked pita bread. "What shall we do this weekend?"

She smiled. "I'm going to keep you awake."

Seventeen

Just because a man doesn't ask for directions, doesn't mean he isn't lost.

—Paige

That Saturday, they walked the High Line, the historic disused railway track that had been transformed into Manhattan's highest public park. A mile and a half long, it meandered through the neighborhoods of West Manhattan, a vibrant, verdant walkway of rambling gardens, wildflowers, grasses and shrubs softening the hard angles of the surrounding buildings.

When they were tired of walking, they bought coffee and settled themselves in a beautiful shady nook directly above West Fifteenth Street. From here they had sweeping views of the Hudson River, the Empire State Building and the Statue of Liberty.

"I love this place." Jake squinted against the sun. "It reminds me that things don't have to stay the same. That they can change, be reborn and regenerated."

Settling her coffee in her lap, Paige stretched out her legs and tilted her face to the sun. "That's your whole job, isn't it? Finding new ways to do things? Refreshing the old?"

"I don't refresh. I innovate."

She closed her eyes and smiled. "Mr. Sensitive."

"No woman has ever called me sensitive before."

"I know all your sensitive parts." Her phone rang and she opened her eyes and dug it out of her bag. "I ought to check who this is—" It was her mother, and she answered it with an apologetic glance toward Jake.

"Mom?" She turned away slightly, smiling as she listened to her mother's excited update on their latest travel adventures around Europe. "That's wonderful. I'm so happy you're having such a great time— Yes, everything is fine here. Work is great. Couldn't be better." She talked to her mother for a little while, and then ended the call. "Sorry about that."

"Don't be." Jake finished his coffee. "You've got a mother who wants to know how you're doing. You get on well together. You're lucky."

She toyed with her coffee. "Did you ever think about trying to contact your mother? Your real mother? When we talked about it that time, years ago, you said you were thinking of it."

"What would be the point? I figured that if she'd wanted to know where I was and what I was doing, she would have stayed in touch. She was the grown-up. I was the kid. She knew exactly where I was living."

She pressed closer to him and he turned his head and smiled.

"Don't look at me like that, with those big sad eyes. It was a long time ago. I can honestly say I rarely think about it now."

That might be true, but the experience had become part of who he was, she knew that. "If you ever want to talk about it—"

"There's nothing to talk about. Maria is my mother and she's been my mother since I was six years old. I don't have room for another mother in my life, particularly not one who made it clear she didn't want me. Anyway, can you imagine having two mothers?" He shuddered. "Two women asking you when you're going to settle down and give them grandchildren. Spare me that." He rose to his feet and reached out his hand. "Let's walk. And then we should probably go home, because tonight I'm cooking you dinner."

She let him pull her to her feet, wishing she could heal all the hurt. She had scars on the outside but Jake's were no less significant just because they weren't visible. "You cook?"

"Hey, I was raised by an Italian woman. Once you've tasted my lasagna you're going to beg for more." He hauled her against him and kissed her. "And that's not the only thing you're going to be begging for."

Back home, Jake opened wine and cooked dinner while she watched. It felt easy and natural to be in his apartment, watching while he wandered barefoot around his spectacular kitchen.

"This was one of the first dishes my mother taught me." He chopped, diced, fried and eventually layered everything into the shallow dish.

"That's impressive." She helped clear up as he cooked. "You look like a professional chef."

"You'd better taste it before you give your opinion. Does your mother cook?"

"Yes. We had a home-cooked meal every day the whole time I was growing up. And because Puffin Island was small, I used to go home for lunch when I was at school."

"What was your favorite meal?"

"That's easy. Lobster bake on the beach." She sipped the glass of wine he'd poured her. "We used to sit with our toes in the sand, watching the sun go down. Bliss."

They talked, swapping stories, learning more about each other, each tiny detail cementing the foundation of their relationship.

When the meal was ready they ate at the table, watching the sun go down over the Hudson.

"Maria taught you well." Paige put her fork down and stared at her empty plate. "Delicious. So tell me how it went in San Francisco? Did they like what you did for them?"

"Yes. Do you want to see?"

"Do you need to ask?"

He smiled and opened his laptop.

She focused on the screen as he showed her the design. Her brother had always told her how smart Jake was, and since sharing his office she'd seen it for herself. She saw how his team deferred to him, how many potential clients he had calling him up. He never had to cold call anyone. They always came to him.

He had more business than he could handle, and that, she thought, was because he was good at what he did. The best.

She needed to make sure Urban Genie gained the same reputation.

For the next half an hour he took her through the design and showed her what it could do.

"Jake, this is incredible." She explored it, fascinated. "It's going to transform their business."

"They think so, too." He closed the laptop. "I'm glad you approve. I keep forgetting I'm dating Geek Girl. It's pretty cool."

"I am not Geek Girl. I am Incredibly Hot Girl who just happens to love technology."

"You're Geek Girl. I don't suppose you could wear glasses while we have sex?"

"Would it make me sexier?"

"Nothing would make you sexier." He pulled her onto his lap and she grinned.

"Careful with the hardware."

"I love your hardware." He slid his hand down her body. "Your software isn't bad, either."

"Is this Geek sex?" She murmured the words against his mouth. "It's like phone sex only—geeky. Is that a USB stick I can feel pressing against me?"

He laughed. "You're the sexiest woman I've ever met."

"You're pretty sexy, too, for a guy who communicates in code. I love that you're so passionate about what you do." She kissed him. "I guess I could borrow Frankie's glasses if you thought it would make the sex hotter."

He scooped her up, carried her to the bed and dropped her in the middle of it. "Do you seriously think the sex between us could get any hotter?"

Not hotter, but it was changing. That frantic, crazy, let's-make-up-for-lost-time sex that had blinded them both in the beginning was now interspersed with something different. Something more intimate. Personal. There was still discovery, but there was also knowledge.

She gave him a suggestive look. "We could try for hotter. What do you think?" She started to unbutton her dress and saw his eyes darken.

"I think you're a tease." He stripped off his shirt and joined her on the bed.

"If I were a tease, I wouldn't follow through, and I have every intention of following through." She slid her hand over his abdomen to the snap of his jeans and heard him suck in a breath. "Still want me to borrow Frankie's glasses?"

"No. Besides, you wouldn't be able to see through them. Is she shortsighted or long?"

Paige hesitated. The reason Frankie wore glasses wasn't something she had any intention of discussing. "I'm not sure," she said finally, and lowered her head. "Fortunately for you, my vision is perfect and I see something that interests me. Come here so that I can take a closer look."

The weekend merged into a lazy blend of laughter, conversation and sex.

On Sunday they ate brunch in a little café near Central Park and walked hand in hand along winding paths, watching in-line skaters, families with strollers and dedicated runners.

They reached the boating lake and Jake paused.

"What?" She looked at him, and then followed his gaze to the lake and started to laugh. "You're kidding."

"I'm not kidding."

"You want me to get in a boat with you?"

"You've done everything else with me." He wondered how she could still blush after all the things they'd done together. "You're so cute."

"I'm not cute." Her eyes challenged him. "I'm sexy. I am the CEO of Urban Genie. You've probably heard of it. We're pretty famous now."

"I've heard the CEO is hot stuff." He pulled her close and felt her gasp as he tipped her off balance. "You are sexy. And you're going to look even sexier when I've capsized the boat and dumped you in the water because then you'll be wet."

"You just want to see me in a wet T-shirt, like the night I showed up at your door after the event last month."

Last month?

Had it really been that long?

He felt a twinge of surprise.

"What?" Her smile faded. "What's wrong?"

"Nothing. I'm good." His voice was croaky. "Just remembering that night you showed up at my door all wet. Makes me tempted to toss you into the water right now just to re-create that look."

"I haven't rowed in years. Matt took Eva, Frankie and I the week after we arrived here for college. We had fun."

And the situation with Matt was something else he had pushed to the back of his mind.

He'd told himself that the fact that this relationship was going to end at any moment was reason enough not to tell his friend, but it hadn't ended.

In fact it was the longest relationship he'd had with a woman.

And the reason for that was obvious. The sex was spectacular. Why would he end something so great? Especially when their relationship was so—he struggled to describe it—*easy.* That was the word. It was easy. Probably because they knew each other so well. Somehow knowing her made the sex even hotter.

It was true they were spending a great deal of time together doing other things, but that was because they couldn't spend all their time having sex. Anyway, she seemed to have fun, and he liked seeing her having fun. She *deserved* to have fun after the tough times she'd had growing up, and it felt pretty good to be the one that was putting a smile on her face.

Relaxing slightly, he took her hand. "Let's take a boat out."

They did, and after much laughter and splashing on the lake, an incident with the oars that almost got them banned and several near misses with a family of ducks, they lay on their backs in Sheep's Meadow, watching the clouds.

"We should have dinner this week. Tuesday? Damn, I can't." He frowned. "I have to fly to Chicago. How about Wednesday?"

"I have an event."

"Thursday? No that doesn't work for me." He felt a rush of frustration. "How about Friday?"

"It's the night you meet Matt. You've canceled the last three weeks. If you cancel again he'll ask questions. And anyway, I have an evening event on Friday, too."

"I'm starting to wish you weren't so successful." He realized that between his work schedule and hers, he wouldn't be seeing her. "I'll see Matt on Friday evening, and you and I can meet later on. You can come over after your event."

"I don't know what time I'll finish. And you don't know what time you'll be home."

"I'll give you a key."

What the hell was he saying?

When had he ever invited a woman home with him before, let alone given her a key?

But this wasn't any woman.

This was Paige.

He'd known her forever.

She didn't treat it as if it was a big deal.

And she wasn't looking at him as if he'd shown her the end of the rainbow. She was nodding as if it was a practical solution.

"All right. I guess that would work. I'll probably get there before you."

He relaxed. It was just a key for goodness' sake. He could get it back anytime. All he had to do was ask. No big deal.

Eighteen

Life going right is what happens just before it goes wrong.
—Frankie

"So it is serious?" Eva asked, putting the finishing touches to a tower of cupcakes that formed the centerpiece for a girls-only thirtieth birthday party they were arranging. They'd booked the terrace of an exclusive boutique hotel in Chelsea. "You've spent every spare moment with him the last month and when the two of you are together the chemistry is powerful enough to provide energy for the whole of New York City."

"I— No, it's not serious. And let's face it, there haven't been that many spare moments since we started this company." Paige kept her head down, checking off everything on her list. This was their fifth event, and so far each one had gone smoothly. She didn't want this one to be any different. "Jake and I are having fun, that's all."

"Jake doesn't make a habit of 'having fun' with the same woman more than a few times. You two have been sneaking off and setting off smoke alarms all around the city."

"Not all around the city. And we were friends before we were lovers, so it's different." And she'd discovered that the edges were blurred. They laughed in bed and conversations frequently ended in sex. How did you separate the two things? She didn't know.

It was because they were friends that he'd given her his key. He'd wanted her to let herself in to his apartment.

Eva added a delicate dusting of sugar to the cupcakes. "Being in love is different. How does it feel, Paige?"

"I have no idea. Why are you asking me? It's not as if he— He's not—I mean, we're not— I'm—" Paige stared at her friend, her stomach churning. "Oh."

"Oh?" Frankie raised an eyebrow. "What does that mean?"

"I know what it means." Eva added the final cupcake and stood back. "So now I'll ask you again. How does it feel, Paige?"

"Scary." Almost too scary to think about. She'd felt this way about him before and he'd rejected her. Hurt her. What had she been thinking? Had she really thought that this time she'd be immune? That she could keep this up until they both—until they both what? "It feels terrifying. Like I'm about to jump from a plane with no parachute."

Like the biggest risk of all.

"Are you going to tell him?"

"No!" Never in a million years would she have the courage to put herself out there again.

"You should." Frankie was blunt. "You should tell him."

"I told him once before. It didn't turn out well."

"That was different. It was years ago. You were virtually underage."

"I was not underage! And it went badly wrong. This time I'm keeping my feelings to myself." She'd promised him, hadn't she? She'd promised him she could handle this. That she was fine with this. It wasn't fair on him to suddenly change her mind about that. "I have to—I have to think about how to handle this. I have to think about the options."

"And the obvious option isn't to tell him straight?" Frankie looked at her with exasperation. "And you wonder why I avoid love? This is why! It's like one of those cryptic crosswords. No one actually says what they really feel."

"If I tell him how I feel, I'll lose him. It's too much of a risk."

"But you're always saying you want to take risks. That you want to live."

"I do, but—" Paige thought about the consequences if she was wrong. She thought about how much it had hurt the last time. "This is different." She could carry on with the affair. Carry on having sex and having fun. She didn't need to put a name to it.

The door opened and she glanced up.

"We can talk about this later. Let's keep it professional, gang. Our client is here."

"And it looks as if our client has already had a drink or ten," Frankie muttered. "Better water down the champagne. And put the paramedics on standby, because if she falls in those heels there is going to be damage."

Paige walked across the room to meet her client, her smile warm and sincere.

"Happy Birthday, Crystal."

"I'm not sure how happy I am." The woman teetered on impossibly high heels. "Thirty. Can you believe that? I was trying to keep it quiet at work, but they opened champagne for me. I may have drunk too much too fast. And there was no food."

"We have food." Paige gestured discreetly to Eva and took

Crystal to one of the tables that had been laid for dinner. "You should eat something before your friends arrive."

"I don't even know why I'm celebrating, frankly. And if you tell me I look twenty I'll know you're lying, so don't."

"You don't look twenty. You look a whole lot better than twenty." Paige narrowed her eyes. "I don't know about you, but at twenty I was gawky and I didn't know who I was or what I wanted, and even if I had known I wouldn't have had the courage to go after it. At thirty, you're confident about who you are. And Crystal, you look incredible."

Crystal blinked. "I do?"

"You know you do. You chose the dress. I bet you stood in front of the mirror and thought *this is it*." Paige's smile was genuine. "It's perfect. You look perfect."

Crystal glanced down at herself. "I *did* fall in love with the dress. It was my consolation for being thirty and not having achieved any of the things I wanted to achieve."

"What did you want to achieve?"

"Oh, you know, all the usual things—" Crystal gave a wistful shrug. "I wanted to change the world and make a difference. Instead I'm a tiny cog in a wheel."

"You don't always have to change the whole world," Paige murmured, "just a small part of it, and sometimes those changes are small but it doesn't make them less important. Without the cog, the wheel wouldn't move."

Crystal gave her a long look. "That's nice. I like it."

"Tonight is about having fun with your friends. That's what a thirtieth birthday should be about. Fun. You've left your angsty twenties behind. You don't have the responsibility of the forties. Thirties is all about you."

"All about me. I like the sound of that." She sighed. "Sometimes I look back and wonder if maybe I made the wrong decisions. Played it safe when I should have taken a risk." She waved her hand in apology. "Listening to my sob story isn't part of your job. Sorry. I never should have drank that champagne. Drink always makes me talk too much. Or maybe it's just that you're a good listener."

"My job is to make sure you have the best time tonight." She hesitated. "What risks would you have taken?"

"Mostly with my love life." Crystal looked down at her hands, bare of rings. "I was too careful. My parents divorced when I was twelve and it really affected the way I approached men, dating and my own security. I wanted guarantees and assurances. I never took a step unless I knew I was on solid ground. I was so afraid of falling. I'm aware of it, but somehow that doesn't make a difference. I didn't know how to be any different."

Paige stared at her, mouth dry. She understood that feeling so well, only in her case her need for security and control had stemmed from a childhood of being ill, where others made the decisions for her. She needed control so badly she was afraid to let go and take risks.

Eva stepped forward and put a plate of canapés in front of Crystal. "Eat these. They're delicious. And if you want my opinion, I think sometimes you just have to take that leap," she said firmly, "and trust that it will be all right. Trust yourself."

Paige glanced at her friend.

Was Eva talking to her or the client?

Crystal reached for a canapé. "Like leaping from a plane with no parachute, you mean?"

Paige stirred. "I think the parachute is inside you." She thought about what Jake had said that night on the roof terrace. "Your skills. Who you are. You have to trust that whatever happens, you'll cope. I think sometimes we're so busy clinging onto the present that we don't lift our heads to see what might be out there. We think safe is what we know, but sometimes the unknown turns out to be the better option."

When Paige lost her job, she'd felt as if she'd lost her security, and yet here she was in a better, happier place. With Urban Genie the ultimate risk was hers, but the rewards were also hers. Not financial, although she was hoping those would come, but in terms of control. She no longer had to work with other people's bad decisions. She made the decisions.

And yet she knew in her heart she wouldn't have started Urban Genie at this point in her life unless she'd been forced into it by circumstances.

She hated it when other people protected her, but hadn't she been doing exactly the same to herself?

She'd lived her life in a safe way. Made choices that were safe. In her work. In her love life.

And safe choices had their basis in fear.

"It's natural to want to protect yourself when you've been hurt before," Crystal said. "There's a lot to lose. But part of me wonders if there's more to lose by not being courageous enough to take the risk. There *was* a man, a couple of years ago—" She gave a shrug. "I blew it. I protected myself so carefully he assumed I wasn't interested. There isn't a single day when I don't wake up and wish I'd played it differently. And now it's too late. I can't believe I'm telling you this. Tell me to shut up. And don't give me any more champagne or I'll be sobbing into the canapés."

"Are you sure it's too late?" Paige's heart was pounding as if it was trying to give her a wake-up call. "It's never too late to tell him how you feel."

"In this case it is. He met someone else. Someone who wasn't cautious like me. They've been married a year and have a baby on the way. I wish I'd done things differently, but I didn't. I was scared. And now I'm paying the price. But hey—thirty is a whole new start, right? It's too late for that relationship, but I could still meet someone. It's not too late for that."

"It's never too late to live life bravely," Paige said.

At least, she hoped it wasn't.

Because that was what she intended to do.

And maybe she'd be hurt, but at least she wouldn't be hitting a milestone birthday wishing she'd taken a risk on something that mattered.

"I feel better." Crystal reached for more food. "You should sell your services as a motivational speaker."

Paige handed her a glass of water, thinking that it was time she took her own advice. "Enjoy your party and instead of looking back, look forward. The view is shiny and bright right in front of you. If you need sunglasses, let me know."

Crystal drank the water. "I need you three in my life all the time. Urban Genie has done a wonderful job, and the concierge service for clients is genius." Her eyes widened as she noticed the cupcakes. "Oh! That's incredible." She turned as she heard laughter. "They're here. My friends."

They piled out of the elevator, armed with gifts, balloons and beaming smiles. A group of women all with one aim in mind—to give their friend the best birthday ever.

Crystal met them with hugs and laughter, and Paige gave them a moment to squeal and admire and catch up before going over to offer champagne.

"Friends," Eva murmured as Paige headed over to join her and Frankie. "Everything is all right with the world if you have friends. I hope you're both going to bring me prettily wrapped gifts when I'm thirty."

"We're going to pour margaritas down your throat until you

can no longer remember how old you are." Frankie watched as the women oohed and ahhed over the cakes. "They're pleased. Those women have great taste. Great job, Ev."

"Yes. Great job." Paige paused. "Can you believe she lost the man she loved?"

"Yes, I can," Frankie said flatly. "Like I said, love is a cryptic crossword."

Paige took a deep breath. "I don't want it to be cryptic. I'm going to tell Jake how I feel. I'm going to tell him I love him."

Eva exchanged glances with Frankie. "How do you think he'll react?"

"I don't know." She thought about the time they'd spent together. About the times they'd laughed and the hours they'd spent talking.

Urban Genie wouldn't exist if it hadn't been for Jake.

He was the one who had pushed her to take the step and follow her dream.

He knew her better than anyone.

"I think he loves me, too, but if he doesn't, then I'll handle it." She'd handled it before, hadn't she? Not very deftly, perhaps, but she'd got on with her life. "I don't want to look back and wish I'd told him. That would be the worst thing of all."

If she was going to live life bravely, she needed to start right away.

Jake prowled around the pool table in Matt's den, staking out his shot.

"Anytime in the next century would be good." Matt snapped the top off a beer and handed it to Chase. "I hear you bought a new boat?"

"I did, and she's a beauty."

"Is she going to sit in the dock while you admire her or are you going to get her wet?"

"I'm going to sail her." Chase lifted the beer to his lips. "I've had what you might call a realignment of my priorities."

Matt lifted an eyebrow. "Did Matilda have something to do with that realignment?"

"She might have."

"More evidence that women are dangerous creatures." Jake took the shot and pocketed the ball. "One minute you're having fun. The next, life as you know it is over." Which was why one of his skills was in ending relationships. He'd learned how to pick the perfect time, before emotions were involved. That was why he always kept his relationships short.

Except with Paige.

He frowned.

There was no way he could describe his relationship with Paige as short.

But they'd been friends for a long time, which complicated the math.

And she was different. She understood him. She understood that he didn't do hearts and happy endings.

"I happen to prefer my new life to my old one," Chase said mildly. "Matilda is more fun than a sixteen-hour working day."

"You should bring her over one night." Matt prepared for his turn. "The girls have talked about her a lot. They were worried."

"She talked about them, too." Chase drank. "She thinks Paige has what it takes to make a big success of this."

"She does. She's incredible." Jake saw Matt glance at him and shrugged. "What? Your sister can juggle more balls than an acrobat and her attention to detail is astonishing. She stresses out a bit, that's all. Keeps her phone by the bed and makes notes in the middle of the night."

Matt gave him a curious look. "How do you know she keeps her phone by the bed?"

"She told me." Jake covered his mistake smoothly. "We share an office, remember?"

"You gave her office space, but I didn't realize you spent enough time together to be familiar with each other's work patterns."

"She occasionally runs things past me."

"In that case you need to tell her to chill a little. Urban Genie isn't going to fold if she takes a night off. She's working too hard. I hardly ever see her and she's missed movie night three weeks in a row. Come to think of it, so have you."

"I've been busy."

Chase finished his beer. "After what happened, I'd like to see her make a big success of this. And not just because Star Events deserves to have some serious competition. Does she need backing? Because I'd be prepared to—"

"Don't even suggest it." Matt potted the ball. "My sister takes independence to a whole new level. If she hasn't done it by herself, she thinks it doesn't count."

"Matilda was horrified when she discovered they'd all lost their jobs. Whose idea was it to set up on her own?"

"Jake's. At the time I didn't agree. I thought it was too soon." Matt flicked him a glance. "But you were right."

Jake reached for another beer. "I'm always right."

"Not always, but this time you were. I've never seen her happier. She bounces into the house and she's smiling from dawn to dusk."

Jake shifted uncomfortably. He was pretty confident he

knew why Paige was smiling, and Urban Genie was only part of it. "I'm glad she's happy."

"You've given her a lot of time. Been patient." Matt's expression was serious. "I haven't thanked you enough for everything you've done for her. You've given her a lot of time and attention."

Knowing just how much time and attention he'd given her made Jake sweat. Guilt rubbed over his skin like sandpaper.

"Forget it."

It was time to be honest with Matt. He wished they'd just told him after that first night, as he'd wanted to. What was he going to say now?

I'm having sex with your sister.

That one would earn him a black eye before he'd finished the sentence.

Guilt mingled with irritation.

Hell, she was happy, wasn't she? Surely Matt should be pleased about that.

He'd tell him the truth. It wasn't as if that much time had passed. They'd only been seeing each other a few weeks.

"So how about you, Jake?" Chase stood up and put his beer down, ready for his turn. "Which woman is occupying your time right now?"

"That's a good question." Matt's gaze was speculative. "He's been very quiet about his love life lately. Whoever it is, she's taking up more of his attention than usual."

Jake stirred uneasily. "I don't have a love life. I have a sex life."

"You've been seeing the same woman for a while."

"Doesn't mean I'm in love. Just means the sex is great." So whatever he had with Paige had lasted longer than any of his other relationships. So what? Why the hell would he walk away from great sex? Jake stepped up for his turn and kept his eyes fixed on the ball while he tried to rationalize his actions. Paige understood him.

She understood that they were having fun.

In fact she was close to his perfect woman. Sexy, good-humored and happy to live in the moment.

Matt strolled around the table. "Whoever she is, she's got your attention. She's obviously hot—that goes without saying. Blonde or brunette? Give us a hint. And why haven't you brought her over to Romano's?"

Because she already spent as much time at Romano's as he did. And each time they went there as a group it became harder to behave as if nothing had changed. He no longer remembered what "normal" was. How he'd behaved before they'd taken intimacy to a whole new level.

The truth was he hadn't thought it would last this long. Normally when he began a relationship he was already planning when he'd end it.

But none of his relationships had felt as good as this one.

Jake took the shot. Missed, and glared at Matt. "Laugh it up, why don't you?"

"Don't worry, I will." Matt grinned. "Your mind is elsewhere, which is lucky for us. Whoever she is, we salute her. For the sake of my bank balance, I hope it never ends. Now pay up, you two."

What happened when their relationship *did* end?

Would he still see her? Of course he would still see her. They were friends.

In fact since he'd stopped trying to keep her at a distance, they were as close as they'd been when she was a teenager. Closer, because the sex had given everything a different dimension.

When they'd had enough of the sex, they'd still be friends.

And since he wasn't near having enough of sex, it wasn't worth dwelling on.

Muttering protests, Chase reached for his jacket. "If I carry on hanging out with you I'm going to need to go back to working eighteen-hour days. Talking of which—" he threw a bundle of notes at Matt "—I need some rooftop landscaping for a building in Tribeca. Big project. Are you interested?"

"That depends. Are you expecting me to take my fee out of that lump of cash you just handed me?"

"No."

"In that case, yes, I'm interested."

"Good." Chase flung his jacket back over the chair. "Because I want your company to do the work. Are you busy this weekend? You're welcome to join Matilda and me at the beach."

"A weekend sailing in the Hamptons. Now that's tempting." Matt slid the money into his pocket. "Jake?"

"Not me. I'm busy." He kept his head down, careful not to reveal that it was Matt's sister who would be keeping him busy.

Right now she was probably waiting at his apartment.

He'd given her his key.

Not that the gesture had meant anything. It was convenience, that was all.

Nineteen

Life is an unpredictable mix of sunshine and showers.
Always carry an umbrella.

—Paige

Paige greeted the doorman in Jake's apartment building and
headed for the elevator, her arms loaded with so many bags
she could barely see where she was going.

She felt the weight of the key in her pocket. Not just the
metal, but its significance. The knowledge that Jake had given
it to her made her light-headed.

She was pretty sure he had never given his key to a woman
before.

That had to mean something, didn't it?

It was evidence that he trusted her, that she was important
to him.

Just how important was something she intended to find
out. Maybe he hadn't expressed deeper feelings, but their relationship had changed; she knew it had. And she knew not

just because of the confidences they'd shared, but because of the way they were together.

What made their relationship special was the fact that they knew each other so well. They already knew everything there was to know.

And one thing she knew about Jake was that he loved Italian food, which was why her bags were filled with plump, ripe tomatoes, fresh basil and a bottle of good olive oil.

She'd hung around Romano's enough for Maria to have taught her a thing or two and she was ready to show off her skills. He wasn't the only one who could make a delicious meal.

Balancing the bags, she stepped out of the elevator, opened the door to Jake's apartment and let herself into the spacious loft. It was a thoroughly masculine space, where soft leather and polished wood were wrapped by floor-to-ceiling glass offering views spectacular enough to make the most jaded New Yorker stop and gasp.

She knew how hard Jake had worked to get here and she admired everything he'd achieved.

Paige paused for a moment, drinking in the silver gleam of the Hudson and the twinkle of lights on the Brooklyn Bridge. Then she dumped the bags on the kitchen counters and started unloading. Jake's love of technology was evident in his living space. Lights, temperature and sound system were all powered from a central control that he could program from anywhere in the world.

It was fortunate she shared his love of technology, she mused, or she wouldn't have had a clue how to turn the lights on, let alone operate the stove and make a tomato-and-basil sauce to go with the fresh pasta she'd picked up at the market.

She slipped a bottle of champagne into the fridge to chill.

Tonight was going to be romantic. Special.

And when the moment felt right, she'd tell him how she felt.

She was chopping garlic and a heap of fresh basil when the door opened and Jake strolled in.

Sunlight gleamed off his dark hair and his eyes glinted silver gray. Even though she saw him regularly, he could still make her catch her breath.

He threw his keys down on the nearest surface, toed off his boots and she knew instantly that something was wrong.

"Bad day?"

He glanced at her, and then at the half-prepared food on the counter. "You're cooking? I thought we were going out to eat?"

"I thought it would be nice to stay in. It's been a long week and we're both tired. Anyway, I owe you a meal. You cooked for me last week." She knew better than to push him. If he wanted to tell her what was wrong, he'd tell her. She was well aware that there were parts of his past he didn't like talking about, and she respected that. "There's champagne chilling, too."

"Are we celebrating something?"

"Another account for Urban Genie and a successful event today." She added the chopped tomatoes to the pan. "Both leads came from the event I ran for you. I can't thank you enough for letting us organize that."

"You were the one who did the work. But if you want to thank me, I can think of a few meaningful ways."

"How was your pool evening with Matt and Chase?"

"I lost."

"You never lose."

"I lost tonight."

Was that what was wrong? "Were you distracted?"

Jake gave her a long look, and then nodded. "I had a few things on my mind. So what was the event today?"

"Thirtieth birthday party." She checked the pan and lowered the heat. "It went well. Eva and Frankie did most of it. I just smoothed and soothed."

And dreamed. And made decisions about her own future.

A future she seriously hoped would have Jake in it.

He opened the champagne and poured. "What form does smoothing and soothing take at a birthday party?"

"Mostly reassuring the victim that she doesn't have wrinkles, that it isn't all downhill from here and that her life is not over."

"At thirty? That's a concern?"

"There were things she wanted to do that she hasn't done. Things she was afraid to do. I don't ever want to feel that way. Listening to her made me so relieved I'd gone ahead with Urban Genie. It's thanks to you."

"You would have done it yourself. All I did was speed up the process." He prowled around the kitchen, restless. "Paige, we need to tell Matt."

"I agree." She took it as a positive sign that he wanted to tell her brother. It meant he wasn't planning on ending it anytime soon. And now she understood why he seemed on edge. Matt was his closest friend, and it wasn't going to be an easy conversation. "When do you want to tell him? Sunday? Eva is cooking. We're both invited."

"Probably not something to be done in public. I'll talk to him privately. That way when he decks me, no innocent bystanders will be harmed."

"Why would he deck you?"

"Because I'm doing this." He hauled her hard against him, holding her thigh to thigh. He brought his mouth down on hers in a lingering kiss that robbed her legs of strength. It didn't matter how he kissed her, whether it was slow and smoldering or rough and ravenous, the sensation went straight from her head to her toes, taking in all the parts of her body along the way. It unbalanced her and made her head spin. Tonight there was a desperation in him she hadn't felt before. She fumbled with the buttons of his shirt, exposing hard muscle and the strong contours of his body.

"Are we in a hurry?"

"Yeah, we really are." His mouth brushed across her jaw and down her neck.

She closed her eyes. "Any particular reason?"

"I want you. Is that a good enough reason? Sex with you is—it's—" He sank his hands into her hair and took her mouth with his. "Do we have to talk about it?"

"No—" her legs were weak "—but I'm going to burn the food and then you'll think I'm a terrible cook."

"I won't think that, but if it bothers you, turn the heat off."

She did just that, and then felt his hands on her, stripping her clothes off so fast she wondered if they were going to make it out of the kitchen.

"If you distract me, dinner will be delayed."

"I don't care." He scooped her up and carried her through to the bedroom as if she weighed nothing.

"I can walk."

"I know, but that would spoil my fun, and I didn't get a workout in today."

"I'm not sure I appreciate the implication that I'm heavy enough to be someone's workout."

He dropped her gently in the center of the bed and came down on top of her, pinning her to the bed with his weight.

I love you.

The words were in her head but she couldn't quite say them. Not yet.

"So you let Matt win?"

"No. He won on his own." He unbuttoned her shirt with impatient hands.

Paige barely heard him. He was kissing his way across her shoulder and down to her breast, and her skin was alive with sensation. He removed her bra with ridiculous ease and then traced the shape of her with his hands.

She moaned. "Jake—"

"You're so beautiful." He lowered his head and closed his mouth over the tip of one breast, tasting and teasing until she found it impossible to stay still.

"I forgot to ask—" He raised his head, his eyes glinting in the fading light. "Did a guy from an investment trust call you? Because I gave him your card."

It was impossible to focus with the weight of him pressing down on her and his hand moving over her body.

"You expect me to talk about work when you have your hand where you currently have your hand?"

"You mean here?" His hand stroked higher, lingering in the dark shadows of her thighs. "Or maybe here?" His fingers slid over her with intimate skill, touching her in a way only he knew how to do.

She was breathless. "Can we talk about work later?"

"Sure. Or we can stop talking altogether." He brought his mouth down on hers, kissing her with raw possession and devastating skill.

He drew her arms above her head, laced his fingers between hers and held her trapped. He lowered his head fractionally, teasing with his mouth and with his gaze. "I've got you where I want you. No escape."

"I don't want to escape." She stared into his eyes and what she saw there made her heart race. She knew, with utter confidence, that he loved her. It was in his eyes. In his touch. In all the small things, like the way he listened and paid attention. All the million tiny ways he tried to make her life easier.

He cared.

He slid his hand under her hips, lifting her against him as he thrust into her and she moaned, deep in her throat, all her thoughts blending together in an incoherent mess.

She couldn't concentrate when they made love. Could think of nothing but the heavy thickness of him and the delicious pleasure he conjured with each thrust. He left no part of her untouched or unexplored. With knowing fingers and consummate skill he unwrapped, discovered, experimented, took liberties no man had ever taken before and she urged him on because this was Jake, her Jake, and she couldn't remember a single day of her adult life when she hadn't been in love with him.

Unbalanced, shaken, she unlocked her fingers from his and rested her hands on his shoulders, dragging her fingers lightly over the hard swell of muscle. She often forgot how strong he was because with her he was always so gentle.

He paused, his eyes holding hers. "Are you all right?" His voice was rough and sexy, his breathing as unsteady as hers.

"I'm always all right when I'm with you."

He lowered his mouth to hers again, kissing her with explicit intent as he shifted position and brought another gasp to her lips. He drove into her and she moaned, shifted and stirred with each movement of his body and each slide of his clever hands. He touched, teased, swamped her senses with sensation until her only focus was pleasure.

He drove her higher and higher until her world exploded. It was raw and real, the connection between them so deeply personal that her feelings refused to be contained. It was as if something had been unlocked. Released.

"I love you." She'd worried about when to say it, but in the end the words spilled from her unplanned. She wrapped her arms around his neck. "I love you so much."

"Yeah." He smiled, eyes closed. "Glad it was good for you, too."

It was a typical Jake response.

"I'm not talking about the sex. I'm talking about the way I feel about you."

"Honey, some women see God, others see love, but either way it amounts to the same thing. Sex that good can make anyone emotional."

She frowned.

Did he really not understand the reason it was so good between them?

Reining in her frustration, she raised herself up on her elbow. "I love you, and loving you has nothing to do with the fact that you know all the moves in bed. Yes, the sex was good, Jake, but that's not what I'm talking about. I love the way we are together."

His eyes opened. His smile disappeared. "Paige—"

"I love you." She spoke quickly, unable to hold her feelings in any longer. "I love everything about you. I love your mind, your laugh and the way you listen. I love the way you employ people no one else would touch. I love that you're so passionate about things. I love how loyal and protective you are to your friends. To Maria. My brother. And most of all I love the way you are with me. I even love that you protect me, even though it drives me insane." It was only as the torrent of words and feelings slowed that she realized he hadn't said anything. He lay ominously still, his gaze fixed on her.

And she felt the first shoots of doubt spring to life inside her.

The longer the silence stretched, the bigger the doubt grew.

She'd freaked him out.

She shouldn't have said anything. It was too soon. She should have let things ride a little longer and waited for him to come to the conclusion himself instead of bashing him over the head with it. But how long was long enough? When you were as sure as she was, what was the point in waiting? Life could be unpredictable, she knew that. You needed to seize the moment.

But by seizing the moment had she ruined everything? "Jake? Say something."

He stirred. "Something? We both know what you want me to say, Paige. That's how this game works, isn't it? You tell me you love me, and either I don't say it back and therefore we break up, or I say it back and we stumble along together until one of us decides that in fact we *don't* love the other anymore, and then we break up. Either way, we break up. Generally I prefer that to happen sooner rather than later. It's cleaner for everyone concerned."

"Cleaner?"

"Yeah. The deeper the roots, the harder it is to dig them up."

"Roots are a good thing. They keep you secure."

"There's nothing secure about love." He pushed the covers back and sprang from the bed like a tiger who had just discovered that someone hadn't locked the cage. "Love is the most unpredictable thing out there. It's just a word, Paige, and words are easily spoken."

"It's not just a word. It's a word that comes with a whole lot of feelings. Important feelings." She paused and breathed deeply. "You haven't had a great day—I get that. It must have been difficult with Matt, so we'll tell him Sunday and we'll just talk about this another time."

"There's nothing more to talk about. And there's nothing to tell Matt." He snatched at his jeans, pulling them on. "I don't know what you were expecting from me, but whatever it is I can't deliver."

Frustration gave way to the first seeds of panic.

"I wasn't expecting anything." A small part of her knew that wasn't quite true. She had been expecting something. She'd hoped. And she'd been so sure that he felt the same way. They'd spent time together. He'd given her a key. She made a last attempt to force him to take another look at his feelings. "What we have is special. We've had fun the last few weeks."

"We have, which is why I don't understand why you did what you just did. Why ruin everything?"

She took a deep breath. "Maybe because I don't think love ruins a relationship. Nor do I consider love to be the worst thing that can happen to a person." Her heart broke for him. And it broke for herself. "Love is a gift, Jake. The most important, valuable gift of all. You can't buy it, you can't produce it on demand, and you can't switch it on and off. It has to be given freely, and that's what makes it so precious. That's what I'm offering you."

"You're wrong. It can be switched on and off. And 'I love you' is the easiest thing in the world to say." He stared at her, his face an expressionless mask. "I don't want what you're offering, Paige. And you should leave now."

He might as well have slapped her.

"I— *What?*" She gaped at him. "I tell you I love you and you tell me you want me to leave?"

"I don't want you to love me. I'm sorry you think that you do."

"I don't 'think' it. I know I love you."

He swore under his breath. "This is exactly why I didn't get involved with you before now."

"What? Wait!"

"I should have ended it sooner. We shouldn't have carried on seeing each other for so long." He said it with the emotion of someone informing her that her library ticket had expired.

This was about his mother.

She knew this was about his mother.

"Jake, my feelings for you aren't new. I've been in love with you for most of my life." She kept her voice calm. "Or that's how it feels."

"Then you lied to me, because you told me this wouldn't happen."

"I didn't lie. I just—" She breathed, trying not to let her emotions escalate. "I just underestimated how deeply I was already involved."

"I know. You're like Eva. You believe in love and happily ever after. You want that."

"Yes, I do. I won't pretend otherwise, and I won't apologize for wanting it."

And so did he; she knew he did.

But he was afraid to trust it.

"I don't want it, and I won't pretend, either." His tone was blunt. Resolute. "I thought you knew. I thought I'd made that clear. When we started this, we agreed it was just sex."

"I know. But things changed. I thought you felt it, too." She tried to reason with him. "This time we've spent together—it hasn't been just about sex. We've had fun. We've laughed. We've talked."

"We spent some time together. We weren't looking for the end of the rainbow. You said you were cool with this." His voice was low. Tight. "You said you could handle a relationship that was just physical. Now you're telling me you can't."

"I'm not telling you that. I'm telling you I love you, that's all." She took a deep breath and took the plunge. At this point, what did she have to lose? "And I think you love me, too." Except that right now she didn't see love. She saw blind panic.

There was a protracted silence, so tense she could have sliced through it with a blade.

"You're wrong. I don't." His features were set. Immovable. Serious.

It was hard to recognize him as the laughing, sexy guy she'd spent the past few weeks with.

He'd gone from warm and relaxed to cold and unapproachable. And she knew it was a defense mechanism.

"Are you sure? Because I'm sensing this isn't about us, Jake. It's about your mother."

"Maria is my mother."

She closed her eyes. "Jake—"

"You need to leave, Paige."

"I can't imagine what it must have done to you when she didn't come home that night. You told me how it felt and I've never forgotten that conversation. My heart breaks, thinking about how lost and confused you must have been and how you must have wondered and worried."

"It was a long time ago."

"Time heals some things but it doesn't erase. It was a long time ago, but it's still with you. It has to be. You carry something like that forever. Oh, you adjust and learn to live alongside it, but it scars and occasionally that scar aches and reminds you that you need to be careful. Is that what's happening, Jake? Are you being careful?" She slid off the bed and walked across the room to him, relieved that at least he didn't back away from her.

She closed her fingers gently over his arm.

His biceps were hard and tense. His entire body rigid as he held himself still.

"There's nothing more to talk about, Paige. I didn't want you to fall in love with me. That wasn't part of the deal. I did everything I could to stop this happening."

It was as if she hadn't spoken.

As if he'd ignored every word.

"I fell in love with you years ago, so whatever you think you could have done to stop it, you were too late." Her voice was choked. "I loved you from the moment you walked into the hospital with Matt on that first night. I've loved you ever since."

"I'm sorry to hear that."

"And I think you love me, too."

"I don't." His gaze lifted to hers, his eyes cold. Blank. "I'm sorry to hurt you, but I don't."

It was like trying to chisel a hole in a wall with a hairpin.

Her eyes filled, and she grabbed his arm in a final attempt to penetrate that cold layer that insulated him from emotion. "Jake—"

"You need to leave now. You're only hurting yourself by staying."

"Sending me away is hurting me. Rejecting my love is hurting me."

"And I'm sorry for it." He stared down at her fingers on his arm as if steeling himself to do something he found impossibly difficult. Then he clenched his jaw and gently unpeeled her fingers from his arm. "It's probably best if we don't see each other for a while. You can carry on using the office. I'll fly to LA for a few weeks."

"I don't want you to fly to LA. I don't want to not see you. What are you afraid of, Jake? What are you so afraid of? I love you."

There was a long, pulsing silence, and then he lifted his gaze to hers. "She said that. She said that to me every day. She used those exact words the morning she left and never came home again. *I love you, Jake. It's you and me against the world.* I believed her, so I sat on the steps, waiting for her, as I waited for her every night, except that this time she didn't come. She

left a note with our neighbor, Maria, asking her to take me
until the authorities could find me a home. She left nothing
for me. No note. No explanation. Nothing."

Paige felt the hot sting of tears. "Oh God. Oh, Jake—"

"She had no way of knowing that Maria would take me in.
I could have ended up anywhere and she would never have
known because she didn't check. Not once. That's how much
'I love you' meant to her. And far from being the two of us
against the world, it turned out that we were tackling the world
separately, which seems like a pretty daunting prospect when
you're only six years old. I learned a lot of things from my
birth mother, but the most important lesson was not to trust
those words. 'I love you' means nothing, Paige. They're empty
words spoken by millions of people every day. Millions of people who still break up, get divorced and never see each other
again." He looked tired, his handsome face pale and drawn,
and she felt as if someone had placed a heavy brick in her chest.

What should she say?

What could she say?

"Maybe those words are easily said," she said quietly. "But
I've only ever said them to one man, and that's you. And if
you really believe my love means nothing, then you're not the
man, and the friend, I know you are."

His gaze lifted to hers and he looked at her for a long moment.

Then he turned away. "Put the key on the table when you
leave. We never should have started this. I'm sorry we did."

The pain was indescribable.

"I'm not sorry. I'll never be sorry. Yes, it was a risk, but
you were the one who taught me to take risks. You were the
one that taught me to go after the things I wanted in life. It's
because of you I moved to New York. It's because of you I set

up Urban Genie. You taught me to take risks, but you're too afraid to do the same yourself."

"I take risks all the time."

"But not in relationships. Not with your heart. You never risk your heart." She stared at him for a long moment, holding back the tide of misery. "I love you. And those aren't just words, Jake. They're a description of how I feel with all of me, from my eyelashes to my toes. I love you. I'll always love you, and I want us to be together, but most of all I want you to let yourself be loved. I want you to trust that feeling, and not keep running from it or pushing it away. Love can last, Jake. There are examples of that all around you. And even if this really is the end, I'll never regret a single moment of these last few weeks."

She felt as if her chest was splitting in two.

Forcing herself to stay calm, she walked toward the bathroom.

How had they gone from incredible sex to this?

How had it happened?

Why?

But she knew why. She'd put a label on the feelings they shared. She'd made it impossible for Jake to ignore them. She'd told him how she felt, and while part of her didn't regret that, another part did. If she hadn't spoken they'd still be in bed together. If she hadn't spoken, if she'd taken a few more weeks—

Choking on tears, Paige stepped into the shower and turned the flow to maximum. Her tears blended with the water, the shower muffling the sound.

If she was hurt, then it was her own stupid fault. Or maybe it was his stupid fault. Or his mother's stupid fault. She didn't know whose fault it was. She only knew that it hurt. It hurt so badly that by the time she stepped out of the shower she had no tears left.

She felt drained. Numb.

Numb was good. Numb would get her through the next hour. She'd pick up her clothes, gather up the few things she'd left in his apartment, take the subway home, and then unload on her friends.

Friends were what she needed right now. They'd surround her with a loving blanket of support in the way that only people who knew you inside and out could.

Eva would remind her that there were plenty more fish in the sea, and Frankie would say very little, taking it as yet more evidence that men couldn't be trusted.

They'd cry and laugh together. Probably open a bottle of wine and eat chocolate.

Either way, she'd get through it with the help of her friends.

All she had to do was get herself home.

And that was when she realized her clothes were in the kitchen.

Taking a deep breath, she opened the door to the bathroom and was relieved to see no sign of Jake.

His absence was still more evidence that she'd frightened him to death.

It would take two minutes to dress, and then she'd be out of here. He could have his apartment back. He could have his life back.

She was gathering her clothes from the floor of the kitchen when she heard Jake's voice.

"I wasn't expecting you. It's not a great time—"

Paige stood still. He was still in the apartment. And he had visitors? Who would call on him this late?

Given his comment that this wasn't a great time, presumably his visitor was a woman. And just like that the misery was back.

She'd do him a favor and make it clear that she wouldn't be hanging around.

As for the fact he had a woman wrapped in a towel in his apartment—well, she'd let him explain that part.

Gathering her clothes in front of her, she stepped through to the living area and froze.

She'd expected a woman, but it wasn't a woman who stood there.

It was Matt.

And she was standing in Jake's apartment dressed in nothing but damp skin and a wet towel with her thong dangling from her fingers.

Twenty

Don't hide a skeleton in your closet unless you're sure no
one is going to borrow your clothes.

—Eva

Matt's gaze raked over her from head to foot, taking in her
flushed cheeks and the fact that she was naked under the towel.

"What's going on?" His voice was low and deadly, his handsome face unsmiling. "Jake?"

Wishing she could slide through a gap in the floor, Paige
stepped forward. She'd thought life couldn't get any worse.

She hadn't worked out the right way to tell Matt, but she
certainly hadn't wanted him to find out this way.

The last thing she wanted was to hurt her brother. And
right now she barely recognized him. He was always calm and
measured. Strong. The type of man who solved problems with
thought and carefully chosen words, not anger.

"Matt—"

"I'm talking to Jake." His voice was ice-cold and she

flinched. He never brushed her away. He was never anything other than kind and protective.

"Matt, I can—"

"You're having sex with my sister?" All his attention was fixed on Jake. "You have the whole of Manhattan at your feet, but you choose to amuse yourself with my *sister*? How long has this been going on?"

"Awhile."

Matt's face turned white. "You drank beer with me, shot a few games of pool, and you forgot to mention you were screwing my sister?"

"I didn't forget." Jake's tone was flat. He didn't flinch or stammer. He made no excuses. Nor did he mention the times he'd tried to persuade her to let him tell Matt.

"Who else knows? Frankie? Eva?" He took one look at Paige's face and pain crossed his own. "You told them. They know. Everybody knows except me."

Knowing that she'd hurt her brother was the worst thing about this whole situation. "They guessed, but—"

Matt wasn't listening. All his attention was on Jake. "You took advantage—"

"He did *not* take advantage. I'm not some vulnerable teenager." Paige stepped in front of Matt, forcing him to look at her. "I didn't think you'd want details, but since you're jumping to conclusions that have no basis in fact, I'll supply the facts. Jake stayed away from me. All these years, he stayed away from me. I was the one who came to him. I showed up at his door. Gave him no choice."

Matt made a disgusted sound. "I'll bet he fought you off."

"He didn't fight, but he was worried about all the things you're worried about. That I'm vulnerable, that he'd hurt me—" she swallowed "—and I told him all the things I'm always telling you. That I'm an adult. I don't need to be protected."

"I know you." Matt gave her a long look. "You want love and happy endings. Jake doesn't do that. He dates a different woman every week. He can't offer you the type of relationship you want and deserve."

She didn't point out that what they'd had together had already lasted more than a week. "This is my business, Matt."

"He will hurt you." Matt's voice was raw. "He will screw you, and then leave you just like he does with all women because he doesn't want attachment. He's done it before. The difference is that I didn't care about it before, because it wasn't my sister he was banging. He will break your heart, Paige."

How could she argue with that when her chest already felt as if it had split in two?

Across the room, Jake's eyes met hers. "Get dressed, Paige. This is for Matt and I to sort out."

That comment lit the fuse on her temper. "I don't see how our relationship is something for you to sort out with my brother. In case you've forgotten, I'm naked under this towel, Jake, and I took my clothes off all by myself."

Jake dragged his hand over the back of his neck and her brother gave a low growl.

"Ask him how he sees your future." Matt's tone was thick. "Ask him how long he thinks you'll be together."

She already knew the answer to that.

"We're not together. Not anymore. It's over." She managed to say it calmly, grateful that she'd cried herself dry in the shower. "I was about to leave when you showed up."

"Leaving?" Matt's gaze shifted to the pile of clothes in her arms, and then returned to her face, paying attention for the first time. "Your eyes are red. Have you been crying? Damn it, he made you cry?"

She saw her brother clench his hands into fists and spoke quickly. "It wasn't his fault."

Matt made a derisive sound. "Don't tell me—you told him you loved him and he ended it. That's normal Romano operating procedure."

"My business, Matt."

"If he's upset you, it's my business."

"No, it isn't. If I'm upset, then that's my problem and I'll deal with it."

"And you *are* upset." His gaze was steady, his mouth grim. "You're in love with him."

"Yes! I'm in love with him. I'm not denying that."

"And he doesn't love you back. That's why you're crying." Matt's face was white, and he turned to Jake with a low growl of anger. "You made a promise to me. All those years ago, you promised you wouldn't touch my sister. Or maybe you've forgotten."

Paige frowned.

What was he talking about?

"Wait a minute—"

"I haven't forgotten." Jake's tone was flat. "I've never forgotten."

Paige shook her head, trying to clear the clouds of misery so that she could think straight. "What promise? I don't understand."

The two men were nose to nose, as if they'd forgotten her presence.

Matt jabbed his finger into Jake's chest. "She was in love with you. We both knew that, and you promised you wouldn't do anything about it."

Paige glanced between the two of them, the words slowly sinking in.

All the pieces finally falling into place.

"Oh, my God." She faced Jake; her voice was barely a whisper. "The two of you talked about me? You made a promise to him?"

"Paige—"

She turned to her brother. "*You* were the reason Jake turned me down that night?"

"What night?" It was Matt's turn to look confused, and Jake cursed under his breath.

"That isn't—he doesn't—shit—"

Matt's eyes darkened. "So she *did* tell you she loved you?"

"Yes, but—wait a minute. Both of you." Jake ran his hand over his jaw and took a deep breath. "Paige, it's true I promised your brother I wouldn't touch you, but it was my decision. I knew you wanted something I wouldn't have been able to offer."

"How did you know what I wanted? Did you ask me? *Did either of you bother to ask me?* I was eighteen! I wasn't ready to settle down and get married, you arrogant—" The insult was jammed on the end of her tongue. "It was first love, that's all. It happens to teenagers all the time. It's part of life. Part of growing up. Hearts get broken. People survive and move on. I did, except that what that episode taught me was not how to recover from a broken heart, but how I couldn't trust my own instincts. I thought you cared and because of that I offered you everything."

Matt frowned. "What do you mean, 'everything'?"

Paige ignored him, her eyes on Jake. "I stripped myself bare. Humiliated myself. And I've protected myself ever since because I was so afraid of getting it wrong again. You told yourself you were protecting me, but what you were really saying was that you didn't think I was capable of making a decision about my own future."

Jake shifted. "That isn't—"

"You didn't think I should be allowed to decide what was best for me. Maybe I would have settled for sex. Did that occur to you?" She'd gone from feeling miserable, to guilty, to furious.

"You were vulnerable." Matt intervened. "You were going through hell."

"And Jake made it better. And you—" She looked at her brother, truly angry now. "You of all people should have understood how it was for me. You saw how it was. You saw how everyone had a say in my future except me. The doctors, our parents—I thought at least I could choose who I fell in love with, but apparently not."

The first flickers of doubt crossed Matt's eyes. "Paige—"

"No." She stepped back, her legs shaking. "I can't talk to you right now. I can't talk to either of you. I'm leaving, and the two of you can talk about it together, because that's what you're best at. Decide what you like, but leave me out of it."

"You can't leave like this—"

"I can. I'm not fragile, Matt. I can hurt without breaking. I love you, and I love that you care about me, but I don't need you to protect me. You want to know why I didn't tell you about Jake before now? This is *exactly* why. Because I knew you'd interfere with something that is none of your business."

"I'm your brother. As long as I'm breathing, I'll always protect you."

"You're not protecting me. You're making my decisions for me. And it ends now."

"I don't know who to kill first. Jake or my brother." Paige lay on Frankie's bed, drained from crying. "I'm so *angry*. I have terrible taste in men."

"But great taste in friends." Eva shoved a pile of tissues into her hand and Frankie leaned closer.

"Are you sure this is angry? Because it looks more like sad from where I'm sitting. Not that I claim any expertise in the emotional range of *Homo sapiens*."

"*Homo sapiens?* Seriously?" Eva pushed more tissues at Paige. "This is not the moment to be spewing Latin from your encyclopedia of plants."

"It's binominal nomenclature, genus followed by species, and *Homo sapiens* is not a plant. Tell me you know that."

Paige sat up. "Keep talking. I need the distraction and you're cheering me up."

"Yeah? You don't look cheered up." Frankie looked at her dubiously. "Are you regretting it?"

"No." Paige blew her nose hard. "It was the best month of my life. Not only was the sex incredible—"

Frankie turned fiery red. "Too much information."

Eva nudged her out of the way and sat down next to Paige. "Not nearly *enough* information."

"I was saying, not only was the sex incredible, but we had fun. We laughed. We talked. We were close. Apart from you two, I've never been able to talk to anyone the way I do with Jake." Frustration rushed through her. "If he walked in now, I'd kill him."

"Wait—what?" Frankie looked confused. "I thought you loved him."

"I do. That's why I want to kill him. For throwing it away. For refusing to see what's there."

"What did he say when you walked out? He didn't try and stop you?"

"He said he'd take me on his motorbike, and while he was arguing that one with Matt, I left."

Eva curled her legs underneath her and handed Paige the box of tissues. "So there was no finale, as such."

"The finale is probably still going on." Paige gave the box back to her. "I don't want these. I'm all cried out. And you'd better ring your NYPD boyfriend. I suspect there might be two corpses somewhere in a loft in Tribeca."

"He isn't my NYPD boyfriend. And I think you're right that Jake loves you. But he's scared."

Frankie frowned at her. "You can sprinkle perfume on manure, but it's still manure."

"What's that supposed to mean?"

"It means," Frankie said patiently, "that this whole thing stinks, and you trying to make it smell better won't change the fact it stinks. It's a saying. Like one of yours. You can add it to your blog if you like."

"No thanks." Eva recoiled. "Not only is it not optimistic, none of my sayings would ever contain the word *manure*. It's a food-and-lifestyle blog."

Frankie carried on, undaunted. "And whether Jake loves Paige or not, if he's too much of a wimp to act on those feelings, then Paige is better off without him."

Paige wished she believed that.

Was she better off without him?

Maybe she'd think so, one day.

Right now she couldn't imagine how she was going to get through the next minute. The next hour.

"I'm angry and I feel *horrible*, but most of all I miss him and it has only been a few hours." Sadness seeped through her. "Maybe this was a mistake. It hurts."

"You were honest about your emotions, and that is never a mistake," Eva said. "If he doesn't want to spend the rest of his life with you, then he's batshit crazy. I know you're hurting now, but that will fade, and at least you won't be sitting in your armchair when you're ninety wondering what might have happened if you'd turned up at his apartment and stripped off all your clothes. Sometimes we just have to go for it. If we left the big decisions to men, the world would stop turning. Think of all the amazing women who didn't leave things to men—Boudicca, Marie Curie, Lady Gaga—"

Frankie gaped at her. "*That's* your list of amazing women?"

"Just off the top of my head."

"Your head is a weird thing."

Paige reached for a glass of water, wishing it was something stronger. "What bothers me most is the fact that in the end he was protecting me, too. All those years."

Frankie straightened the pillow. "I agree—that sucks."

Eva hesitated. "Actually I don't think that sucks. I think it's adorable."

"Adorable?" Paige rubbed her aching forehead. "How is it adorable to find out that people have been making decisions for you? Decisions you weren't part of and that you didn't even know were taking place?"

"That part isn't adorable, but the sentiment behind it is. They *love* you, Paige." Eva reached out and squeezed her leg. "Maybe they didn't exactly show it in the right way, but they meant well. Where does it ever say that people who love you get it right? They don't. We all mess up. We're human. Or *Homo sapiens*, as Frankie would say. And sometimes *Homo sapiens* have the common sense of an *Ocimum basilicum*." She looked at Frankie triumphantly. "Are you impressed?"

"I'm speechless."

"What's the Latin word for *stupid*?"

"*Plumbeus.*"

"So Jake is *Homo plumbeus*."

Paige knew they were trying to make her smile. "From now on I'm making all my own decisions, and they're going to have to get used to it."

"Well said. You are *Homo decisivus*." Ignoring Frankie's wince, Eva slid off the bed. "And you can start right now. Popcorn or ice cream? Not that I'm trying to influence you, but I have double chocolate chip, which I may have doctored with a few extra sprinkles of sugary goodness."

Paige stood up and checked her reflection in Frankie's mirror. Her eyes were red and mascara lay in dark streaks. "Ice cream. No bowl. Just give me the tub and a spoon."

"Are you sure?" Eva caught Frankie's eye and cleared her throat. "Of *course* you're sure. You know what you want. Ice cream with spoon coming right up. And if you said you wanted it delivered on a truck, that would be fine, too. I will never question a single decision you make. Frankie?"

"Same. Large tub. Large spoon."

"You didn't just lose the love of your life."

"No but I'm soaking up Paige's stress. I'm eating vicariously."

Eva disappeared upstairs to their kitchen and reappeared a few minutes later with ice cream.

They were sitting on Frankie's bed, spoons in tubs, when Matt walked in.

Frankie choked, slid off the bed and grabbed her glasses from the nightstand. "What are you doing here? I rent this apartment from you, but that doesn't mean you can walk in when you like." Her voice was colder than the ice cream. "Right now you are not welcome here. This is a man-free zone."

Matt didn't budge. "I need to speak to Paige. Can you give us a minute?"

"No." Eva stood up, too. For once she wasn't smiling. "Why do you need to speak to her? Have you made some more decisions about her life that she needs to know about?"

Matt winced. "I deserved that. I came to check my sister is all right, but given that you're eating ice cream on the bed, I'm guessing she's not, so I'm not going away, and you're going to have to live with that."

Paige felt nothing but exhaustion. "Did you deck him?"

"No. We talked." He walked over to the chair in the corner of Frankie's bedroom, cleared off the stack of gardening magazines and sat down. "You have every right to be mad with me, but there are a few things I need to say."

Frankie folded her arms. "As long as you know that if you make her cry again, I'll be the one decking you."

"I'm not going to make her cry." Matt leaned forward, his forearms resting on his thighs. It was a moment before he spoke. "Right from the moment you were born, Mom and Dad were always telling me 'take care of your little sister. Watch out for Paige. Keep an eye on her, Matt'—I'm not sure at what point watching over you turned into making decisions for you. I've never even questioned it, until tonight."

Emotion threatened to swamp her. "Don't, Matt—"

Frankie stirred. "You said you wouldn't upset her—"

Matt ignored her, his eyes on Paige. "I'm sorry I made decisions for you. I'm sorry I'm such an overprotective jerk you feel you can't tell me things. Most of all I'm sorry you're hurt. Will you forgive me?"

His heartfelt apology touched her more deeply than anything he'd said to her before.

She slid off the bed and felt Frankie snatch the ice cream from her a second before her brother stood up and pulled her in for a hug.

"I'm sorry, too. I'm sorry I didn't tell you."

"Don't apologize." Matt stroked her hair. "There is no obligation on you to tell me anything. It's your life. You share the bits you want to share. Make whatever decisions you like, do whatever you like, choose whoever you like. I won't try and make your decisions for you, but I'll always be here for you. No matter what."

Eva gave a quiet sob, and Matt glanced at her over the top of Paige's head.

"Why are you crying? Did I say the wrong thing?"

"No." Frankie fiddled with her glasses. "You said the *right* thing, you idiot. Eva cries at everything—you should know that by now. She makes a marshmallow look robust."

Paige pulled away and Matt looked down at her. "Am I forgiven?"

"Maybe." She gave a crooked smile. "If I told you I was about to ride naked over the Brooklyn Bridge on the back of a motorbike, what would you say?"

Matt opened his mouth and closed it again. "I'd say go for it. And then I'd get ready for a phone call from the NYPD."

Paige took her ice cream back from Frankie. "So if you didn't kill Jake, what did you do?"

"I told him he was an idiot." Matt sounded tired and she felt a twinge of guilt.

"For not telling you the truth?"

"No. For not wanting what you were offering."

She felt a rush of love for her brother, closely followed by guilt. "He wanted to tell you, right from the start. I was the one who begged him not to. I put him in an impossible position." And that still worried her. "I don't want to damage your friendship."

"Friendship isn't something you switch on and off when

things get tough. Are things different? Yeah, I guess they are. But we're figuring it out. We're all figuring it out."

Matt was right, this wasn't just about her.

Paige made a decision. "I'll talk to him. Make sure he knows he doesn't have to avoid us. I still want to have our evenings at Romano's and movie nights up on the roof terrace."

"Are you sure? If seeing him is going to hurt you—" Matt eyed her and cleared his throat. "Of course. If that's what you want."

"It is."

Matt glanced at his watch. "I have to go. I have an early meeting tomorrow and you should get some sleep." He hesitated. "Movie night tomorrow? We can make it chick flick night if you like. A romance marathon. Whatever. Your choice. We can order in pizza. Eva can have a night off from cooking."

The *last* thing she felt like doing was watching romantic movies. It was ironic that Matt, who had never suggested it before, would suggest it now.

Men.

On the other hand, was there anything that could make her feel worse than she already did? Probably not, and part of her was touched that her brother had suggested it when she suspected he'd hate every moment.

"Sure." She pinned a smile on her face. "Why not."

Frankie put her ice cream down. "You're seriously offering to host a romantic movie marathon for two emotional women and one emotionally stunted woman? You really *do* have a guilty conscience."

Eva looked interested. "Define *marathon*."

"Three movies. You can each pick one. And I get full possession of the bottle of tequila."

They were all working so hard to distract her and cheer her up that Paige didn't have the heart to tell them not to bother.

"Three movies. Great." Her voice was so cheery she wondered if she'd overdone it. "Our choice?"

"Yeah. But no animation." Matt dug his keys out of his pocket. "And I need to know the titles up front so I can judge the quantity of alcohol necessary for my survival."

Eva was quietly listing them on her fingers. "I'm not sure I can pick three."

"You're only allowed to pick one," Paige reminded her. "One each."

"*While You Were Sleeping*," Eva said, and Frankie looked horrified.

"That's a Christmas movie. This is summer."

"It's romantic. And optimistic. Sandra Bullock is adorable and the bit where the guy gives her the ring at the end is the Best Proposal Ever."

"It's the Most Unbelievable Proposal Ever."

"Not true."

"The guy is in a coma!"

"That's the brother. You need to pay attention. What's your pick?"

"*The Silence of the Lambs.*"

"That's a horror movie."

"I know, but Hannibal Lecter is really into Jodi Foster."

"He's a serial killer! He wants to eat her! We're not watching that one. Paige?"

Paige realized she hadn't even heard what they were saying. Something about the best proposal. In her book any proposal would have worked. "Er—Best Proposal Ever has to be Richard Gere climbing up the fire escape with flowers in his teeth."

Eva sniffed. "Now *that* is unrealistic."

"It's all unrealistic." Frankie put her spoon down. "Expecting happy ever after is unrealistic."

Paige was inclined to agree. No, she wasn't going to do that. She wasn't going to pretend that Jake's fear of relationships extended to all men. She knew it didn't. "Pick a movie, Frankie. No horror."

"*Crazy Stupid Love*," Frankie muttered. "Because at least the title is honest. And I get to see Ryan Gosling naked from the waist up. That's always a bonus."

Paige rummaged in her brain for something. Anything. *"When Harry Met Sally."*

"And you've picked that one because Billy Crystal makes you laugh, right?" Frankie pushed her hair away from her face and gave her a fierce look. "Not because he's a commitment phobic guy who sees the light in the end?"

"I picked it because the dialogue makes me smile." And because she really didn't care what the hell she watched. "Those two have chemistry."

"Good. As long as you know real life isn't like a movie, and Jake isn't going to show up here on a white charger waving his sword."

"I know that." And she felt as if a heavy weight was crushing her chest. A few weeks ago Paige would have pinned on her Brave Face but now she didn't bother. She missed him. She wasn't sure how she was going to get through the next few hours, let alone the days and weeks ahead.

Matt was looking at her. "We're going to distract you. In time, you'll get over him."

"Maybe you could just knock me unconscious and wake me up when that time comes. Alternatively you could knock Jake unconscious and hope when he wakes up he sees sense."

"I thought you didn't want me to hit him?"

"I don't." Paige sighed. "Ignore me. I'm a sorry mess."

"The most comfortable place to be a sorry mess is up on the roof terrace watching movies and drinking tequila." Matt walked to the door. "Call me if you need me. Not that I'd give you advice or anything, but I could listen."

He closed the door and Frankie stared after him.

"Considering he's a man, your brother isn't awful."

Jake had a sleepless night.

He couldn't remember a time when he'd felt this bad.

Or maybe he could.

He'd been six years old, waiting for his mother to come home. The sun had set, the sky was inky dark and still there was no sign of her, and he'd known, deep in his gut, that she'd gone for good. He'd sat there, wondering what he'd done. What he'd said, feeling a bone-deep emptiness and an aching sense of loss.

He felt the same way now.

As the first bright shards of sunlight shone through the windows of his apartment, he gave up on sleep and got up, thinking about the last thing Matt had said before he'd left the night before.

My sister offered you the best thing money can't buy. Maybe you ought to think about that before you turn it down.

Sweat beaded on the back of his neck.

Maybe for some people love was the best thing, but he knew it could also be the worst.

Love was a lottery.

Sometimes it worked. Sometimes it didn't.

In his experience, the odds weren't good. And the more it mattered, the more it hurt.

And Paige mattered.

He paced, trying to work out how to get rid of the ache in his chest, and in the end he did what he always did when life got rough. He rode his bike to Brooklyn to see Maria.

She was the one person who would understand what he was feeling.

She'd give him sympathy, and right now he needed it, because Paige had made him feel like a jerk and Matt had made him feel like a jerk.

Maria definitely wouldn't make him feel like a jerk.

And she'd make him breakfast.

Despite the fact that it was still early, the restaurant was already busy, the morning crowd lingering over their coffee at tables dappled by warm sunlight.

Jake walked straight around the back and found his mother in the kitchen, chopping tomatoes.

It felt familiar and comforting. The smells of roasted garlic and fresh oregano took him straight back to his childhood.

Maria took one look at his face and put the knife down. Without saying a word, she made him a strong coffee and ushered him to the nearest table.

"What's wrong?"

It was a measure of how well she knew him that she could tell instantly that something was wrong.

"Why does something have to be wrong? I'm hungry. I decided I needed to start my day with granita and brioche. And coffee, of course."

"You travel across the Brooklyn Bridge for granita and brioche when you have more fancy restaurants where you are than stray cats, there's something wrong. I assume it's a woman." Her voice was as soothing as warm honey, and he knew he'd been right to come.

He gave up the pretense. "It's a woman."

She nodded, waiting. "And?"

"It's Paige. I've been seeing Paige."

There was a smile, but no surprise. "I've hoped for that for a long time. When I saw the two of you together the other night, I wondered. I sensed things had changed. I'm happy for you. You're perfect together."

It wasn't the reaction he'd expected. "We've been seeing each other awhile. We were having fun."

"Of course you were. You always do. She cares about you." She sat across from him, watching patiently as he drank the coffee and tried to decide how much to tell her.

"She said she loves me." Remembering made his heart race. "But those words mean nothing."

His mother looked at him steadily. "To a woman like Paige, those words mean everything. She isn't the sort to give her love lightly. She's a strong woman and she has the biggest heart. Whatever the problem is, you'll sort this out."

He noticed she said *you*, not *the two of you*, which meant she didn't think the fault lay with Paige.

"It's too late. I ended it."

"You'd been seeing each other for a while, you were enjoying each other's company—so you ended it?"

"I can't give her what she wants. I can't be what she needs. And I don't want what she's offering."

Maria looked at him steadily. "If I've understood you correctly, she's offering you unconditional love, a lifetime of loyalty, friendship, support, encouragement, humor and, I presume, great sex. Why would you not want that, Jake?"

He opened his mouth to reply, but nothing sensible came to mind so he closed it again.

She made him feel like a jerk.

That was three times in fewer than twelve hours, and he felt a rush of something that could have been frustration or desperation.

"I thought you'd understand."

"I understand that you're scared of love. That you don't trust the emotion. But just because we're scared of something and we don't trust it doesn't mean we don't feel it. You love her, Jake."

His palms felt clammy. "I'm not sure that—"

"It was a statement, not a question. You've always loved her. I've known it from the first moment you brought her here. The first moment I saw you together. You sat at what was to become your usual table, all five of you, and you watched over her like a bodyguard. I remember being pleased that Matt didn't need to spend so much time worrying about his sister, because he was able to share the load with you."

"We argued all the time."

"Jake—" Maria was patient "—we both know why that was."

Jake was beginning to wish he'd stopped at some random restaurant for breakfast and not come home. Tension pricked across the back of his neck. "I was fond of her back then, that's true, but—"

"You protected her. And you carried on protecting her. That's what we do when we love someone."

"Unless you're my mother." The words fell out of his mouth without encouragement, and he cursed softly. "Forget I said that. I meant my biological mother. You're my real mother. You know I think of you that way. I always have."

"I know. And you don't have to explain or excuse anything with me, Jake. She was your biological mother." She reached out and took his hand. "And your mother didn't leave because she didn't love you. She left because she didn't think she could give you what you needed. *He's smart, Maria*, she used to say to me. *He needs more than I can give him.* And I told her that what a child really needed was love, but she didn't see it that way. All she saw was all the things she wouldn't be able to give you. The things she couldn't buy and the education she couldn't afford. She thought she was doing what was best for you." She paused. "In the same way you think you're doing what's best for Paige."

"It's not the same thing."

"Isn't it? Does Paige want your protection? Has she asked for it?"

"She hates it." He inhaled deeply. "She needs permanence, and we both know that in love there is no permanence. Love is a risk."

"And why do people choose to take a risk?" Maria squeezed his hand. "Paige took the risk because she loves you. Because she believes that what you share is worth that risk. She put her heart on the line and laid out her feelings, even though she must have known there was a good chance you'd stomp all over them."

Jake winced, because he'd done exactly that.

She'd laid her feelings out and he'd stomped.

Maria let go of his hands. "She made her choice, and now you have to make yours. You have to decide whether you love her enough to take the risk. Are you willing to do whatever it takes? Is she worth it, or would you rather go through life without her?"

"Without her? Who said anything about being without her?" Jake stood up abruptly, wishing he'd found a quiet corner to lick his wounds in private instead of coming to see Maria. "I won't be without her. We'll still be friends. We'll still see each other. She's Matt's sister, for God's sake."

"Yes, you'll still be friends. Until she meets someone. How will you feel when she eventually meets a man who doesn't have your fear of love? Because that's what's going to happen, Jake. A woman like Paige—she'll meet someone else. And knowing the sort of woman she is, loyal and loving, it won't be the sort of relationship that's flimsy and easily broken like the ones you prefer to have."

The thought of Paige with another man made him want to drive his fist through the wall. "What is this? Attack Jake day?"

Maria's expression softened, but she didn't back down. "I think it's probably 'try and persuade Jake to see sense day.' How will you feel when Paige stops crying over you and finds someone else?"

He didn't want to think of her crying over him. And he didn't want to think about walking into the restaurant and seeing her with some guy next to her. Holding her hand. Making her laugh. Snuggling up to her at night.

Sweat cooled the back of his neck.

"If you think you're protecting Paige by staying away from her, then you're deluding yourself. She doesn't want to be protected, Jake—she never did. She wants to live her life, every minute of it. She'll take the laughs and she'll take the blows, because she knows that's what living is all about. Ups and downs. Laughter and tears. You need to decide if you want to be part of that life or not. And you need to make that decision. Your mother made hers. Now you need to make yours, but most of all you need to stop connecting those two things."

"I came here thinking you'd give me a hug, feed me and make it all better."

"I'll give you a hug and I'll feed you, but the only person who can make it better is you. In the end we make our own choices." Maria sighed. "Do you think I like seeing you suffer like this? It kills me. But you're my son, and when a mother sees her son doing something stupid, she says so. It's a duty. Now go and talk to Paige."

"She probably won't talk to me."

"She doesn't need to talk. She's already said everything she wants to say. Now she needs to hear you doing some talking. And you'd better make sure you use the right words."

Twenty-One

Happy endings aren't only for fairy tales.

—Eva

One of the many good things about running your own business, Paige reflected, was that you could work whenever you wanted to, including the middle of the night and on Saturdays.

Work anesthetized the pain in her heart.

Eva was upstairs in their apartment testing a recipe and updating her blog, and Paige and Frankie had chosen to work on Frankie's kitchen table rather than go to the office.

Her phone rang.

Because she knew it wasn't a client, Paige ignored it.

Frankie glanced across and saw the number. "It's Jake. Again. Fifth time. Want me to tell him where to go?"

"No." Her fingers shook on the keypad. "Let it go to voice mail."

"Are you sure? The guy obviously has something to tell you."

"He can tell it to my voice mail. I'll speak to him when I feel ready." And that would be when she was sure she could do it without making a fool of herself. She tapped her tablet screen and brought up her to-do list. "Did you get that request about surprise flowers for a wedding anniversary?"

"I did. Came through the app, which, by the way, is genius. It's handled and they're going to be the happiest couple in Manhattan."

The app *was* genius, but she didn't want to think about the app, because thinking about the app made her think about Jake and she was trying not to do that. "One of our clients put in a request for their roof garden to be maintained."

"I'm going over there Monday to talk to them, and I'm taking Poppy, who I've worked with a million times."

"Poppy? British Poppy with the cute accent and the smile like a lightbulb?"

"That's her. She needs the work and she's good."

"Why does she need the work?"

"Because she wants to stay in New York. I guess she wants to keep a large ocean between her and the rat boyfriend who slept with her friend."

"Enough said. The work is hers." Paige went back to her list and Frankie hesitated.

"Did you get any sleep last night?"

"Not a lot. I spent the night rehearsing what I'll say to Jake next time I see him. I need to order a new lipstick to give me confidence."

"I might be able to help with that." Frankie thrust a package at her and Paige took it,.

"You bought me lipstick?"

"It always seems to cheer you up." Frankie played it down. "I don't get it myself, but hey—whatever works for you. Eva and I went through your makeup drawer to try and find a color you didn't have. Most people have a bag, by the way. You and Eva are the only people I know who need an entire drawer."

Touched, Paige opened the bag. "When did you buy this?"

"I was banging on the door of Saks the moment they opened."

"You hate Saks."

"Yeah, but I love you." Frankie's tone was rough, and Paige felt warmth rush through her.

"You're the best," she murmured. "I have the best friends." She examined the lipstick. "I love it. It's perfect. And now I feel almost ready to talk to Jake."

She'd rehearsed the meeting in her mind and knew exactly how she was going to behave when she saw him. He'd be expecting tears. There wouldn't be tears. He'd be expecting her to be bruised and wounded. She'd be strong. All wounds would be kept firmly on the inside, held together from bleeding with lashings of willpower and female fortitude.

Her priority was to make sure that this hiccup didn't interfere with their friendship.

That was the most important thing now. More important than her own feelings. Those would heal in time. And if they didn't heal, she'd learn to live with a little more damage to her heart. Another scar, only this one wouldn't be visible.

The next time her phone rang it was a client and she took that call and gave it all her attention. And the same for the next one.

She'd get through this, a call at a time. A minute at a time. A day at a time.

And the next call that came thrilled all of them.

Eva rushed into the apartment, her phone in her hand. "Matilda is getting married—she wants us to organize it!"

"She wants us to organize it?" Paige closed the document she was working on. "We've never done a wedding."

"It's no different to any other event." Frankie reached for her can of drink. "Food, drink, guests, music, flowers and a big mess to clear up at the end. At least this time it's for a friend. Of course we can do it. Unless you'd find it difficult?"

"Of course not. Why would I find it difficult?"

"Because she's getting married and that means romantic mush and Jake will probably be there—"

"And I'll be too busy to notice the guests. Say yes. Of course we'll do it."

Eva went back to the call, congratulated Matilda on behalf of all of them and discussed some top-of-the-line ideas.

"Hamptons? Beach wedding?" Eva's expression was dreamy. "It will be perfect."

It was work, Paige told herself, subduing a stab of envy. Work. Another job, which would get her through another day.

After they finished work, she took a shower, pulled on a bright sundress that she hoped would compensate for her mood, used her new lipstick and joined her friends and her brother on the roof terrace.

The sun was setting over Manhattan, sending streaks of gold across towers of shimmering glass and steel.

Matt had the screen ready.

And tequila.

Paige studied the bottles. "Is that what it takes for a man to get through six hours of pure female emotion?"

"That's what it takes to get a man through twenty minutes of emotion. There's more downstairs." He dropped ice into glasses and poured. "What are we drinking to?"

"It's romance night." Frankie took the glass from him. "To fairy tales, happy endings and all that shit."

Eva rolled her eyes. "It's not an accident that you're single."

"You're right—it isn't an accident. I work really hard at it."

Wondering why she'd agreed to romance night, Paige reached for a glass. "Tonight we're drinking to friendship. The best thing of all."

It was her friends who would get her through, as they had every other rough patch in her life.

She heard footsteps on the stairs and saw her brother's expression change.

He lowered his glass carefully. "Jake—" his tone was level "—we weren't expecting you."

"Saturday night is movie night." Jake strolled out onto the terrace. His dark hair gleamed and his eyes looked tired. "Am I still welcome?"

Paige felt a rush of panic.

She wasn't ready to do this yet. She needed more time to prepare.

She could feel them all looking at her, waiting to take their cue from her and realized that this was how it was going to be from now on.

It was up to her to make sure it wasn't awkward.

"Of course you're welcome." She produced a smile so wide her face almost cracked. "It's good to see you. We weren't sure you'd be able to make it, but we're glad you did. Sit down. There's pizza—"

Claws stalked onto the terrace. Without sparing a glance for any of them, she picked the largest, most comfortable cushion and stretched out.

Jake ignored the pizza. "Before we start movie night, I need to talk to you, Paige. I tried calling, but you weren't picking up."

"Work has been incredibly busy."

"That's good to know, but it doesn't change the fact I need to talk to you."

"I think we've said everything that needs to be said, Jake. That's all behind us now. History. Forgotten." Paige waved a hand. "Sit down. We've lined up a trio of romantic movies, so I don't expect you'll be staying long."

She was banking on it.

"You may have said everything you wanted to say, but I haven't. And it isn't history, Paige. It's not forgotten. I've thought of nothing else since the moment you left last night, and I'm sure you're the same."

"I'm not the same. We need to get started or it will be dawn before we've finished all three movies. If you still want to talk at the end, we'll talk. Matt? Press Play." There was desperation in her voice, and she felt a rush of relief when Matt did as she asked.

She estimated that Jake would last five minutes. Ten at the most. Would he see something of himself in *When Harry Met Sally*? Maybe. And if that didn't send him running, then *While You Were Sleeping* definitely would.

Either way, by the end of movie night he'd be gone. She was sure of it. And next time they saw each other, she'd be more together.

She sat down on the nearest cushion and fixed her eyes on the screen.

They watched *Crazy Stupid Love*, and Paige didn't hear a single word.

All she could think about was Jake sitting close to her, waiting.

Waiting for what?

To give her more reasons why he couldn't ever love her?

She didn't want to hear any more reasons.

She wanted the movies to last forever, even if they were making her feel miserably depressed.

Matt opened the tequila. "That's what girls want? Seriously?" He eyed the screen. "I strip to the waist when I'm working if it's a hot day and there's no one around. No one pays any attention. Maybe I need to reenact *Dirty Dancing*."

"If you stripped to the waist I can guarantee that someone, somewhere, would have been paying attention. And this is Ryan Gosling." Eva gestured to the screen. "He could strip to the waist and reenact anything. Or nothing. We'd all still be drooling and think this was the best movie ever."

Paige knew they were trying to defuse the tension between her and Jake, but she didn't have the energy to join in. For once she didn't care what Ryan Gosling was doing.

All she could think about was Jake.

They were halfway through *When Harry Met Sally* when he stood up.

And took off his shirt.

Matt choked on his tequila and Frankie adjusted her glasses. "Eat your heart out, Ryan."

Paige's mouth dried. His body was ripped, but she already knew that of course because she'd had her hands all over it. "What are you doing?"

"I'm doing whatever it takes to get your attention, and right now it seems that this is what it takes. In those movies you love so much, a guy usually rips off his shirt in the final scene and makes a total fool of himself in public."

Eva whistled and reached for popcorn. "Great abs. Did you think of auditioning for *Magic Mike*?"

Paige didn't say anything. She was focused on Jake. And he was focused on her.

Only on her.

His eyes were steel gray, his gaze intense. "There are things I need to say to you."

Frankie stood up quickly, dragging a reluctant Eva to her feet and knocking a couple of cushions to the floor in the process. "We're out of here."

"Why?" He stopped them. "Whatever I say, Paige will tell you, so you might as well hear it firsthand."

"Sounds good to me." Eva sat down again, but Frankie looked horrified.

"If it's private—"

"There is no such thing as 'private' between the three of you. And I don't have a problem with that. I think it's great that the three of you have that close bond." Jake shook his head as Matt stood up. "You might as well stay, too. That way, you can decide if you need to beat me to a pulp or not."

"This is romantic movie night," Paige said. "No one beats anyone to a pulp on romantic movie night. And we still have one more movie to go." She didn't want to do this. She wasn't ready for this conversation.

"Is it *Sleepless in Manhattan*? Do you have that one?"

Paige swallowed. "I think you mean *Sleepless in Seattle*."

"No, I don't. *Sleepless in Manhattan* is a different story." His gaze held hers. "Do you want to know how that one ends?"

"I—"

"The guy is an idiot, pretty much like the guys in all these movies you love. He's slow to work out what he really wants and it takes him a while and he needs a little help from his friends to sort out his priorities." His tone was commanding and he held out his hand to Paige. "Stand up."

"What? I don't think—"

"I said, stand up."

Eva shivered. "I know it's not politically correct to say so, but I love a strong man."

"If you don't keep quiet I'll wring your neck," Frankie muttered. "Then you'll know strong."

Paige was trapped by the look in Jake's eyes. Her heart was pounding. "You want me to run and jump into your arms like they just did on the screen? Because if you lose your balance I'll tumble down three floors and land on my butt in Brooklyn. It won't be pretty."

"Just this once, could you actually do as you're told? Is it too much to ask?" He leaned forward and tugged her to her feet. "The first time I saw you, you were sitting in that damn hospital bed trying to hide how scared you were. I decided then you were the bravest person I'd ever met."

Her heart was hammering. She tried to pull her hand away from his, but his fingers had closed tightly around hers.

"I was scared, so obviously not so brave."

And she was scared now.

Scared of what he might say. And, more importantly, scared of what he might not say.

"Oh, you were brave. Everyone around you was panicking, and you were pretending you were fine. That it was a walk in the park. I thought you were incredible. I kept telling myself that you were a kid, but I knew you weren't. We laughed, talked, joked. I brought food into the hospital—"

"Cookies. I remember."

"We dropped crumbs in your bed. I talked to you in a way I'd never talked to anyone in my life before. Do you know that you are the only person I have ever talked to about my biological mother?" He took a deep breath. "That night you told me you loved me—I was terrified. I had feelings for you, too, but I'd made a promise to Matt and I knew he was right. I would have hurt you."

"Jake—"

"So I turned you down, and I did it in a way that I hoped would kill those feelings of yours. And after that I tried to make sure you didn't have those feelings again."

Matt frowned. "That's why you were always arguing with her?"

Jake was still looking at Paige. "Twice in your life you've told me that you love me, and each time I've handled it badly."

"You were honest."

"I wasn't honest. I wasn't honest with myself, and I wasn't honest with you. But I'm being honest now. I love you."

Her breath caught in her throat.

How long had she dreamed of hearing him say those words to her?

"Jake—"

"You already know I do, but maybe you don't know how much. I still need to show you that, and I will. I've been a coward and an idiot, but that ends now."

She heard someone make a sound. It could have been Eva. It could have been Frankie. It could have been her.

She didn't know, because Jake was still looking at her, and she'd waited to see that look in his eyes for so long she didn't want to miss a moment of it.

"You love me?"

"I've always loved you, but love for me was the scariest thing that could happen to a person. Love, and you can lose. I didn't want to lose. I've taken plenty of risks in my life, but I've never taken a risk with my heart. I told myself that I was protecting you, but mostly I was protecting myself. I told myself love was one risk that wasn't worth the pain. But when you walked out last night I discovered the pain was there anyway, because I'd lost you. And I discovered that loving you, and being with you is more important than anything. I didn't think I was ever going to find a woman worth taking that risk for. I was wrong."

She'd promised herself that whatever he said to her when they finally met up, she'd smile her way through it and make it back to her room before crying.

But she hadn't expected him to say what he'd just said.

"You're sure you love me?"

"Very sure." He gave a lopsided smile. "*Truly, Madly, Deeply* until I'm Sleepless in Manhattan."

Emotion filled her. "I've told you, that's not a movie."

"It should be. It's a great title. I bought you something." He reached into his back pocket and pulled out a small bag. "I hope you like it. It's a shame you weren't watching *Breakfast at Tiffany's*."

She recognized the distinctive packaging and her heart started to beat a little faster.

She didn't dare hope—

She'd done that once before and—

She peeped cautiously into the bag and something glittered at the bottom.

"A ring?" Hand shaking, she pulled it out. Why had he left it loose?

"Last time I gave you jewelry in a box you thought it might be a ring and it wasn't. I saw the disappointment on your face. This time I didn't want you to be in any doubt about what it was. The box is in my apartment if you want it. Marry me—" his voice was husky "—and I promise to keep you in lipstick for the rest of your life."

She shifted her gaze from the gleaming diamond to his face. "*Marry* you?"

"Yes. I love you. You're the only woman I want. The only woman I'll ever want. And I'd take any risk to be with you."

The silence around her was broken only by the distant sound of traffic.

Frankie was silent.

Matt didn't move.

Even Eva had nothing to say.

Paige swallowed. "Jake—"

"It's only ever been you, Paige. And I know I'm going to need more than words to convince you, so I designed something to help you make up your mind." He reached into his other pocket and pulled out his phone. "I made an app for you. It's called Should Paige Marry Jake. It's pretty self-explanatory so you, being Geek Girl, probably won't have any issues with it but I can walk you through it if you like."

"Are you calling me Geek Girl?" But happiness bubbled up inside her. "You've designed a proposal app?"

"No, but now you mention it, it's an interesting idea because trust me, proposing is a terrifying thing. One knee, both knees, no knees? Shirt on, shirt off. The options are limitless."

"Definitely shirt off," Eva breathed, and Paige gave a weak laugh.

"I don't care if you're on your knees or naked—the only thing I care about is that you love me." Emotion overwhelmed her. How did a person go from such misery to such happiness and survive it? "You're asking me to marry you? Are you sure?"

"Yes, and I want you to be sure, too, so before you answer me you'd better check the app. You said you wanted to make your own choices, so I designed something to help you. This choice is important. You don't want to make the wrong decision."

Frankie stood up and leaned over her shoulder, fascinated. "That's pretty cool. Answer the questions, Paige."

"You can swipe for yes or no." Jake showed her. "What's your favorite drink in the morning. Coffee. Mine, too. See? We're perfectly matched."

"Wait a minute—" She swiped one answer, then changed her mind and tried a different answer. And frowned. "Doesn't matter what answer I give, it's still telling me we're perfectly matched."

Jake gave a sheepish smile. "I wasn't taking any chances."

"You fixed it?" Her eyes gleamed. "I thought you were a risk taker."

"There are some things I'm not prepared to risk, and you're one of them."

She knew she'd never forget the look in his eyes right at that moment.

It was all she needed to see.

"I don't need this to help me make my choice." She slid the phone back into his pocket and he pulled her closer, his expression serious.

"Before you give me your answer, I should warn you that I'm never going to stop protecting you. I love you and care about you, and protecting you is part of that." He smoothed her hair back from her face with a gentle hand. "I do promise not to make your choices for you. Whatever you decide, I'll respect that choice."

Her vision was misty and she blinked several times to clear it.

She slid the ring onto her finger and looked up at him, knowing that everything she was feeling was in her eyes. "I love you, too. You know I always have. You're all I've ever wanted. And I'll marry you whether the app says I should or not. And you can protect me, as long as you don't mind that I'll be protecting you right back."

Jake lowered his head and kissed her.

"Romantic movie night—live," Matt murmured and Paige pulled away, smiling.

"You promised me a night of happy-ever-afters. It exceeded expectations."

"It's not over yet." Jake pulled her down on the cushions. "We still have one movie to watch, don't we?"

"While You Were Sleeping." Paige curled up against him and the ring on her finger twinkled in the moonlight and the reflected light from Manhattan. "Think you're man enough to handle it?"

"Of course." Jake pulled her close and glanced at Matt. "Pass the tequila."

* * * * *

Thank You

I recently discovered that I have written seventy-five books for Harlequin. I lost count long ago, and I only found out the number when they gave me a lovely Tiffany key ring in recognition.

I've been so lucky in my career and you'd probably think my first and biggest thanks would go to my publisher—and they are AWESOME—but in fact it goes to my readers.

If readers didn't buy the books, I wouldn't be able to make writing my career. I could still write, of course, but then it would be my hobby, which wouldn't be nearly as much fun— and I'd have to get a "proper job," which definitely wouldn't be as much fun! Many writers are introverts, but I'm an extrovert, and I love the interaction I have with readers. I have the best Facebook community on the planet and if I'm having a hard day I hang out there for a little while and your comments and encouragement always lift my spirits. So I want to say the biggest thank-you to anyone who has bought one of my books, recommended me to friends, chatted to me on social media— you can find me on Facebook, Twitter, Instagram, Pinterest and

Goodreads—all links on my website. I love hearing about your life, exchanging thoughts on books and reading your emails. I'm touched that some of you feel able to share details of the challenging parts of your life and humbled to know that my books have helped in some small way. I know that when life has been difficult for me, the things that help me are family, friends, my writing and reading.

Thank you for making room for me on your bookshelf or your ereader.

*Love has never been a priority for garden designer
Frankie—after the fallout from her mother's endless affairs,
she steers well clear of any emotional entanglements.
But her friend Matt isn't so easily put off! He's the only
man she trusts, but can Matt persuade Frankie
to trust him with her heart?*

*Read on for a sneak peek at the second book in
Sarah Morgan's brilliant new trilogy—brimming with
the excitement and glamour of New York!*

SUNSET IN CENTRAL PARK

"When did you last go on a date?"

"*Me?* Oh…" She hesitated, knowing that her answer wasn't going to paint a picture of her as the epitome of urban sophistication. "Well—I don't know—I've been busy—I don't date that much." What was the point in lying when he already knew she wasn't a party animal? Her shoulders slumped. "When I date I almost always regret it, so I'm just as happy spending the evening thinking about plants."

He removed his sunglasses slowly. "Why do you regret it?"

His eyes were the most incredible blue—warm, interested… and focused on *her*.

She felt as if her insides were slowly melting. "I'm not good at it."

"It's a date. The only requirement is to spend time with someone. How can you not be 'good' at it?"

The fact that he'd even asked her that question revealed the massive gulf in their life experience and expectations, as well as how little he knew about her dating history. And how little he seemed to understand her hang-ups despite the whole glasses incident. And why would he? Matt was confident and self-assured. Dating was unlikely to be something that made him consider therapy.

"It's pressure," she tried to explain. "Will you like them and will they like you? Do you have to be more this or less that? Dating a stranger is pretty fake, isn't it? People project an image. You see what they want you to see and they often hide who they really are. It's like going out with a mask on. I don't have the energy for it."

It was an understatement. She found it monumentally stressful—which was why she'd cut it out of her life.

"How about going out and being yourself? Does that ever happen?"

"That doesn't usually work."

"How can being yourself not work?"

She was acutely conscious of the people working around them and wondered how the conversation had blended so seamlessly from talk of buds and blooms to her own phobias. And it wasn't just the conversation that unsettled her. It was the way he focused on her with that lazy, sexy gaze—as if she was the only person on the roof. In New York City. *In the world.*

She'd always felt safe with Matt, but suddenly she didn't feel safe. She was trying to stay safely in her comfort zone and he seemed determined to nudge her out of it. Which wasn't like him.

She was filled with a whole bunch of feelings she didn't recognise and had no idea what to do with. Her body hummed with awareness and breathless anticipation—although what she was anticipating, she had no idea.

"I don't expect you to understand. When you're with a woman it's probably very simple."

She was about to change the subject when he lifted his hand and pushed her hair back from her face. She felt the rough pads of his fingertips brush gently against her skin and started to tremble.

"When I'm with a woman," he said softly, "I want her to be herself. If someone isn't interested in who you really are, or in showing you who they really are, you're probably wasting your time dating them."

He let his hand drop but the trembling didn't stop. It was as if he'd hit a trigger point—switched something on inside her. She saw his face through a blur of sunlight and the feverish patterns created by her own brain.

When I'm with a woman...

All she could think was, *Lucky woman. Lucky, lucky woman.*

The atmosphere was electric, and she felt a strange rush of awareness brush across her skin. Her heart was pounding so hard she expected his entire crew to pick up the rhythm.

"Are you seeing someone at the moment?"

Why, oh, why had she asked him that question? She didn't want to know. She truly didn't want to know. She rubbed her hands over her arms, wondering how she could have goose-bumps when it was so hot.

"I'm not seeing anyone."

"There's no one who interests you?"

"There is someone who interests me a great deal."

"Oh." Frankie felt as if she'd been kicked in the stomach. "Well, that's...exciting."

Not in a million years would she have expected his announcement to bother her as much as it did. Misery descended like a thick winter mist, smothering her good mood. Excitement was doused like a flame.

She wished she hadn't asked, but at the same time she was

glad she had—because at least it would stop her thinking dreamy thoughts and having anxious moments worrying that their relationship might be changing.

That comment about her having beautiful eyes had been just that—a comment.

For some men dating was virtually a hobby, but Matt was different. Matt, she knew, wasn't the sort of man to sleep his way through the female population just because he could. Nor was he the sort of man who needed a woman on his arm to inflate his ego. If he was interested in someone then she must be special.

Her ribs ached with the acid burn of jealousy.

She saw a brief vision of the future…of evenings spent on the roof terrace with Matt and his girlfriend entwined together on one of the low cushions.

"I'm happy for you." She said the words even though she didn't mean them. "That's great."

What sort of woman had caught his attention? She'd be beautiful—obviously. Smart. That went without saying. And sexually confident. Someone who would definitely know how to flirt when the situation called for it.

Not the sort of woman who wore glasses when she didn't need them.

"It's not great. It's complicated."

Frankie had no idea what to say to that. She felt horribly inadequate. She was the *last* person to give anyone advice on relationships.

"Relationships are always complicated. That's why I don't bother. I have no idea what a normal, healthy relationship looks like. It's nothing *I've* ever seen. And there I go again—being the raincloud on someone's patch of sunshine. Ignore me. If you want advice, talk to Eva. When it comes to love, she has all the answers. And she believes in it, which helps."

"I don't want to talk to Eva."

Was he saying that he wanted to talk to *her*?

She was trapped between wanting to escape and wanting to be a good friend.

She had absolutely nothing of use to say on the subject of love, but that didn't mean she couldn't listen. This was *Matt*. Matt who had given her a lovely home for years.

"I can't give advice, but I can listen if you want to talk."

And if she turned green with envy at least she'd match the plants.

"You'd do that?" There was a hint of humour in his voice. "Even though dating is your least favourite subject?"

"I don't want some woman messing you around. I like you." She felt colour flood her cheeks. She shouldn't have said that. "We're friends. Of *course* I like you. If you want to talk—talk. Tell me about this woman you're interested in. She must be pretty special if you like her."

"She is."

His words added another bruise to the many that were accumulating.

"Why is it complicated? I assume she's not married or still at school?" Seeing him raise an eyebrow, she blushed and shook her head in apology. "Sorry. This is why you shouldn't be talking to me. When it comes to love, my every thought is warped. So what's the problem? Just tell her straight out. Or are you afraid she isn't interested?"

"She's interested."

"Well, of course she is!" Envy made her irritable. "She'd have to be crazy *not* to be interested. You're the whole package, Matt—the three Ss, as Eva calls it."

"The three Ss?"

"Single, sane and s—" She'd been about to say *sexy*, but she suddenly realised how easily that might be misinterpreted. If he knew she found him sexy she'd never be able to look him in the eye again, and that was already hard enough after the whole glasses incident. "Solvent," she muttered. "You're solvent."

"Single, sane and *solvent*?" There was amusement in his tone. "That's all it takes? That doesn't sound like a very high bar."

"In Manhattan, you'd be surprised," Frankie said darkly. "All I'm saying is, if you're interested in someone there shouldn't be a problem. A million women would jump at the thought of having you in their lives."

There was a pause as he scanned the skyline. "The problem is that I don't want a million women—I want her," he said. "And she's scared of relationships. She's not good at trusting, so I'm taking it slowly."

Something in his tone made her glance at him sharply, but he'd slid the sunglasses back onto his nose and she could no longer see his eyes.

Frankie frowned, confused.

Surely he wasn't saying…?

He didn't mean…?

Crap.

A delicious, terrifying excitement ripped through her. She went from envy to euphoria. She was filled with an equal amount of joy and heat. Matt was interested in *her. Her. She* was the woman. The thought made her dizzy with elation. Her palms felt sticky and her heart pounded like the drums in a rock band.

And then it dawned on her that if he knew she was interested, and he was also interested, the next logical step would be to take things to the next level. That would be what he was expecting. That was what normal people did, wasn't it? That was the reason he was telling her how he felt. And if they took things to the next level…

Reality poked its way through the joy, puncturing her elation like a needle pressed against a child's balloon.

Elation gave way to pure panic.

"On second thought, forget it. You want to stay away from— from relationships that are c-complicated." She was stammering, tripping over her words. *Stay away from me.* "Too much trouble. Seriously, Matt, don't go there."

Admiring someone from a safe distance was one thing. When you thought that they weren't interested and that it could never go anywhere it was a safe hobby. But this—this was different. It was like admiring a dangerous tiger in a zoo and suddenly realising that someone had removed the glass between you. There was nothing stopping him coming close.

Up until this moment she'd had no inkling that he was interested in her, but now she knew that he was it changed everything.

It made the impossible possible, and she found the possible terrifying.

"I've never been afraid of complicated, Frankie. I've never been the kind of guy who thinks something worth having has to be easy to get."

"Well, you *should* be afraid." *Breathe, Frankie. In and out. In and out.* "Complicated is bad. If it's complicated, maybe you should rethink. You deserve to find someone special. A nice, dependable, uncomplicated, sweet girl who isn't going to mess you around."

She articulated each word carefully, her tone transmitting the message: *And that's not me.*

"Frankie—"

"And talking of working on a plan—that's what I'm doing now. I'll talk to you tomorrow."

She stepped back from him, tripped over a bag of cement, and virtually sprinted towards the stairs that led from the roof to the top floor of the house.

No *way* was she going to let this go any further. Not just because she believed that all relationships were doomed, but because it would be impossible to get closer to Matt without him discovering all the things about herself she made a point of keeping secret.

Because he knew about the glasses, he thought he knew *her*. What he *didn't* know was that the glasses were just the tip of the iceberg…

Loved this book?

Visit Sarah Morgan's fantastic website
at **www.sarahmorgan.com** for
information about Sarah, her latest books,
news, interviews, offers, competitions,
reading group extras and much more...

...and connect with her online, at:

 @SarahMorgan_

facebook.com/AuthorSarahMorgan

goodreads.com/SarahMorgan_

instagram.com/sarahmorganwrites

pinterest.com/SarahMorgan_

Dark secrets lie just around the corner

Holly Ansell's brother Ben has disappeared. Determined to find out what's happened to him, she visits Ashdown Park where she discovers an old mirror and Ben's research into the house that once stood there. Little does Holly know that Ashdown and the mirror hold so many secrets, scandals and the power of fate…

For fans of Barbara Erskine and Kate Morton comes this unforgettable time slip story about the power one lie can have over history.

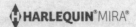

Bringing you the best voices in fiction
🐦 **@Mira_booksUK**

M433_HOS

Loved this book?
Let us know!

Find us on **Twitter @Mira_BooksUK**
where you can share your thoughts, stay up
to date on all the news about our upcoming
releases and even be in with the chance of
winning copies of our wonderful books!

Bringing you the best voices in fiction